PRAISE FOR BARBARA TAYLOR SISSEL

The Last Innocent Hour

"This is a plot worthy of Daphne du Maurier . . . a compelling tale of innocence lost."

—Houston Chronicle

"Sissel's writing is strong and the characters and their motivations clearly drawn."

—Bev Vincent, author of *The Road to the Dark Tower* and *The Stephen King Illustrated Companion*

"A taut psychological suspense thriller, exciting and quite dark with no light in sight adding an almost gothic feel."

—Midwest Book Review

"Sissel's first novel is a worthy achievement . . . along the lines of Iris Johansen. Frightening . . . poignant. Sissel's strength lies in her multi-dimensional characters . . . that make the reader react—with fear, with relief, with anger, with tenderness."

—Book Browser Review

"*The Last Innocent Hour* will ensnare you in a web of family secrets and suspense, powerful crisp writing and characters so real you'll think you've met them."

—Colleen Thompson, bestselling author of *The Salt Maiden* and *Phantom of New Orleans*

The Ninth Step

"Barbara Taylor Sissel crafts a sure-handed, beautiful garden of a novel on ground tilled by Jodi Picoult and Anita Shreve. Firmly confronting issues of human frailty, redemption, and letting go, *The Ninth Step* is a story about what is, but it aches with the stories of what might have been as one man's quest for forgiveness leads him to the impossible task of forgiving himself, and the lives of the people he's wronged are drawn into a shattering spiral of events. Sissel's vibrant voice, rich characters, and deft plotting draw the reader in and keep pages turning to the gripping, unexpected end."
—Joni Rodgers, *New York Times* bestselling author of *Crazy for Trying*, *Sugarland*, and the memoir *Bald in the Land of Big Hair*

Evidence of Life

"The slow pace of Sissel's novel allows readers to savor the language and the well-drawn characters. Exploring love, marriage, deception and trust against the backdrop of a gut-wrenching mystery leaves little time for the hinted-at romance. This quiet story is enjoyable and insightful."
—*RT Book Reviews*, 4 stars

"A chilling mystery with a haunting resolution you won't see coming."
—Sophie Littlefield, bestselling author of *Garden of Stones*

Safe Keeping

"Past secrets contribute to present-day angst in this solid suspense novel, and the even pacing keeps the reader's interest until the captivating conclusion."

—*Publishers Weekly*

"Impressive writing and affecting subject matter."

—Kirkus Reviews

"A gripping read . . . perfect for a book club."

—Library Journal

"A book you need to set aside time for because you will not be able to break away!"

—Suspense Magazine

FAULTLINES

ALSO BY BARBARA TAYLOR SISSEL

FAULTLINES

A NOVEL

BARBARA TAYLOR SISSEL

LAKE UNION
PUBLISHING

Published by Lake Union Publishing, Seattle

www.apub.com

Amazon, the Amazon logo, and Lake Union Publishing are trademarks of Amazon.com, Inc., or its affiliates.

ISBN-13: 9781503938915
ISBN-10: 1503938913

Cover design by Janet Perr

Printed in the United States of America

For Heather and Christy, my borrowed daughters

1

Jordy wasn't dead.

Sandy plucked that single fact from the sea of information she was hearing from the police sergeant, and she clung to it as tightly as she clung to the phone. Behind her, she felt the bed shift when Emmett sat up. She felt his warmth, his sleepy unawareness—his beforeness, and she envied him. "What is it?" he asked, and he was close enough that his breath on her bare shoulder made her shiver.

"Jordy's been in a car accident," she said, and the words floated away from her, separate, foreign sounding.

"What? Is he all right?" Emmett switched on the bedside lamp.

Sandy blinked. "I don't know." She glanced at the clock on her night table. Both hands on its old-fashioned face pointed to the three, while a finer-moving hand ticked off the seconds, oblivious.

The cop—she hadn't caught his name, didn't recognize his voice—was detailing his location, voice rising over the scream of incoming sirens. "I'm . . . *something, something* . . . miles north *something* . . ." *West? East?* Sandy didn't catch it. ". . . of Wyatt on CR 440." He was shouting now.

CR 440 was a county road, but Sandy couldn't place it exactly.

"Is that an ambulance?" Her voice thinned with disbelief.

"We've got two out here," the officer said, not to her but to someone there at the scene. "There's one in the car still, a girl."

Sandy bit her lips, making herself breathe.

Emmett got up and came around in front of her, and mirrored in his gaze, she saw her own denial and the harsher urgency of panic that wanted to come. He wouldn't allow it, and neither would she.

"How bad—how badly is Jordy hurt? Can I talk to him?" Sandy asked the cop.

"No, ma'am. The paramedics are working on him."

"Who else was in the car?" she asked, but she knew before the officer said it that her nephew, Travis, was involved.

"Your son told us Travis is his cousin? We ID'd the girl, too. Michelle Meade. She was in the backseat. Only one with her seat belt on."

Only one with any brains. The cop might as well have said it.

Were they drinking? The question stood up in Sandy's mind, a giant headline, the elephant in the room. "What hospital are they being taken to?" She was on her feet now, grabbing shorts and a T-shirt from her dresser drawer.

"Sandy, what the hell is happening?" Emmett asked.

"Wyatt Regional," the cop yelled. "It's the closest trauma center."

Her mind circled the word *trauma*, keeping a distance from it. It might have been a snake, coiled and ready to strike. But if she kept back far enough, then she'd be . . . *safe.* How she loved the word for the refuge it suggested.

She gave the phone, their landline, to Emmett. "I have to call Jenna."

But when Sandy tried her sister's cell phone, Jenna didn't answer. *Already on her way,* Sandy thought, *and scared out of her mind.* But Troy would be with her. For the first time in a long time, Jenna wasn't alone. Sandy dressed quickly and found her sandals.

"Carter wouldn't tell me how any of them are," Emmett said when Sandy came back into the bedroom.

"Carter?"

"The cop on the phone—his name's Ken Carter. He's new." Emmett pulled on his jeans. "Huck's there, too. Carter said he and Huck were first on the scene."

"Not Len Huckabee," Sandy said, unhappily.

"The very same." Emmett was as grim. He grabbed his keys off the dresser, and Sandy followed him through the dark and silent house.

They both drove trucks. Sandy's was pale green, a vintage 1948 restored Ford F-1 pickup with her logo painted on both front doors: **EJS LANDSCAPE DESIGN**, with a perky daisy painted between the *J* and the *S*. She'd opened her business when Jordy was ten and bought the truck with a portion of her profits when he turned fifteen. He'd spent some time behind the wheel, first learning to drive, then working for her summers and weekends. He and Travis had both worked for her. Now they were twenty, and they teased her about the truck, her attachment to it. It surprised them she didn't park it in the house, tuck it in nights, sing lullabies to it. Ha-ha, she'd say.

Emmett drove a modern-day Ford F-250 pickup, gray with a darker-gray interior. The fenders were scratched, and there was a dent in the tailgate. A thin layer of dust dulled the shine. He was pretty much running the oil-field service company her dad had founded in the 1970s now, but in high school, Emmett had worked in the fields as a roughneck. Sandy's dad had gotten him on with a crew of men twice his age, hard-living, hard-drinking men. Men who lived on the cruder margins. Back then, Emmett had stopped by Sandy's house almost every day after work, and she'd sat with him in the front seat of a different truck, an old Chevy beater he'd named Brownie, while he told her stories. *You won't believe the crazy shit I heard today.* That was how he'd begin. They'd drunk lemonade he spiked with whiskey from the pint of Jack Daniel's he kept in his glove box. She'd run her palm, damp and cool with condensation from her cup, up his forearm, golden haired and brown from the sun, making him sigh with a mix of relief and desire. It had delighted and thrilled her, the power she had over him.

Even then she'd known they would spend their lives together.

Inside Emmett's truck now, Sandy clung to the seat as he backed out of the garage and onto the concrete apron fast enough to make the tires squeal. He looked fixedly into the path of the headlights, minding his direction as they headed down the drive, but Sandy turned to look back, over her shoulder, at Jordy's basketball goal, watching as it got smaller. He'd asked for it for Christmas the year he turned twelve. The plastic, sand-filled base was faded, the net torn. He seldom used it now that he was off at college, the University of Texas, in Austin, but there were days when the windows were open that she would swear she heard the ball smacking the concrete, along with shouts and whoops of laughter, and her heart would fall open, her throat would ache for no reason. It was silly. She faced front.

The truck swung onto the highway, headlights bouncing. They lived on a farm-to-market road, FM 1620, some thirteen miles east of Wyatt and the hospital there. There were no streetlights, and it was pitch-black. *The dark before dawn,* Sandy thought. The rural road rose and fell, dipping blindly among the hills. It rimmed the edges of steep canyons. There were so many roads like this one, so many twisting, rural, go-nowhere roads. The Texas Hill Country where they lived was a lacework of such roads.

Jordy had learned to drive on these roads, mostly in Emmett's truck, with him riding shotgun. Sandy had been too nervous; she'd pushed her foot against her truck's floor, braking for him, slowing him down. He'd been annoyed. *Mom, I'm only going fifty-five.* It was the legal speed limit. She drove at that speed or even sixty or sixty-five and thought nothing of it. But there were times when Sandy thought even the legal speed limit was too fast. She'd hear about an accident and think every road in the county was treacherous, nothing but a way to get injured or die. Carly Maples, a classmate of Travis's and Jordy's, had lost her arm in a wreck when they were high school sophomores. Sandy, Emmett, and Carly's mom, Wendy, had been in the same grade all through school, and while Carly was still in the hospital, Sandy and Jenna had taken meals to Wendy's house. Travis and Jordy had brought Carly her homework; Travis had often stayed to help her with it. He was good like that, and Wendy had appreciated his keeping Carly company, as the girl had been understandably angry and depressed. Wendy had talked sometimes about how difficult Carly was, but Wendy had been grateful to the point of tears that it was only an arm her daughter had lost and not her life. Sandy couldn't imagine it then, the horror of being thrust into a situation where you were thankful your child was only minus a limb.

Now she understood.

Jordy was alive. That was all that mattered.

She jammed her hands against her sides, shivering, wishing she'd worn socks and tennis shoes instead of sandals.

"Are you cold?" Emmett glanced at her, his face a geometry of broken shadows. He turned the AC down, not waiting for her answer.

She flattened her palm on his knee, and he covered it with his own. "Jordy will be so scared."

"We're almost there," Emmett said.

"Do you think he knows we're coming? Will anyone tell him?"

"He doesn't need anyone to tell him, Sandy."

She knew Emmett was right. Jordy would know they were on their way to him. He was their only child. They were always there for him. When he was younger, they'd called themselves the Three Musketeers. She couldn't remember who started it or when the last time was that one of them had said it. But Emmett was the one who'd come up with Jordy's nickname: Choo Choo, for his love of trains. His favorite story as a little boy had been *The Little Engine That Could*, read so often the book was falling apart. He'd printed his name inside it at some point.

She could see it in her mind's eye, the jerky row of letters that spelled Jordan Cline. He'd used an orange crayon.

Wyatt Regional was relatively new, an eighty-four-bed hospital and rural trauma center that wasn't quite ten years old. Sandy's only experience of it had been five years ago, the three days she'd camped out at Jenna's bedside after her sister had had her mastectomy. Folks in Wyatt were proud of the hospital; Sandy had heard good things about it, but pulling into the entrance and following the signs that led around the far right corner of the three-story building toward the emergency room now, she thought how small it was. She thought fleetingly of the huge medical complex that had been near the apartment she and Emmett had shared while attending the University of Houston. By contrast, Wyatt Regional was smaller than the office building in downtown Houston where she'd gone for regular gynecological exams and OB visits when she'd been pregnant with Jordy.

The triage area was chaos, a tangle of tight voices rising and falling from behind curtained cubicles. Sandy felt her knees give; her heart banged the walls of her chest. She heard a sudden shouted command, "Clear!" and went swiftly in that direction but stopped abruptly when the curtain was flung aside and Jenna came into view. Troy had his arm around her. Even so, Sandy could see how badly she was shaking. Badly enough that she'd have fallen without Troy's support.

"Jenna?"

At the sound of her name, Jenna met Sandy's gaze, and the fear in her eyes hardened into something else, something feral, enraged. "You can tell Jordy 'I'm sorry' won't cut it this time."

"What?"

"I can't talk to you right now. They have finally gotten Travis stabilized enough to move him to the helicopter."

"Helicopter?" Sandy repeated.

Several people, three who were obviously paramedics, and two others who were nurses, burst out of the curtained area, rushing a gurney tethered to an assortment of tubes and beeping machinery toward the opposite end of the triage area. Sandy caught a glimpse of the patient on the gurney—Travis? She couldn't see more than his head encased on either side by huge blocks of what looked like foam. The face between them was swollen and blue, unrecognizable. Stunned, she jerked her eyes to Jenna and past her to the now-vacant cubicle.

Blood.

There was so much blood. On the floor, across the face of a metal cabinet. It streaked the clothing that was strewn over the floor. Travis's clothing. Sandy recognized the T-shirt flung into one corner. Jordy had one like it, navy blue, printed in neon green with the slogan: KEEP AUSTIN WEIRD. A pair of jeans, also blood soaked, had a ragged tear up the leg, through the waistband. They'd been cut off him, she realized, and she bit her teeth together, forcing back a dizzying sensation of hysteria.

When she looked around again, Jenna and Troy were gone. A doctor approached. He said his name was Dermott, Kelvin Dermott, and asked for their names. He asked if they were Jordy's parents.

"Yes," Emmett answered. "Where is he? Can we see him?"

"How is he?" *Not like Travis,* Sandy prayed. Not blue faced and swollen beyond recognition, and then she felt ashamed, anguished. She darted her eyes in the direction Jenna had gone.

"We boarded him already," Dr. Dermott said. "We're not equipped to treat critical injuries here. They're going to Mercy Hospital in Austin. They've got an excellent level-one trauma unit there and a great staff, the latest in technology. Trust me, the boys will be in good hands."

"Jordy's going with Travis?" Sandy was confused. She thought maybe he meant Jordy would accompany Travis in a support capacity until the doctor explained there was room inside the life-flight helicopter for two patients.

"Plus the medical personnel to handle the boys' needs," Dermott added.

Sandy felt stupid; she felt battered from the inside by the hammer of her panic.

Emmett asked the hard question. "Is Jordy conscious?"

"In and out. The head CT we did shows some injury to his brain." Wanting to offer reassurance, Dermott patted the air. "It's not so bad as it sounds. The sort of bruising he's sustained usually heals on its own, but it's best to play it safe, I think, and send him to Austin, too."

A sound came, a heavy, rhythmic throbbing. *The helicopter,* Sandy thought.

"You folks know how to get there?"

"We can find it," Emmett said, shortly. "But what the hell happened? Can you tell us?"

"You haven't talked to the police?"

"Yeah, but no one's given us any details."

"It was a car accident, a bad one. A passerby called 911, but I heard he didn't wait."

"Did someone hit them?" Emmett asked, and then as if a switch had flipped, he fired off more questions. "Whose car were they in? Was it a Range Rover?"

The doctor tried to answer, but Emmett wasn't listening. He was explaining that Jordy drove a 1996 Range Rover. "Belonged to Sandy's dad back in the day," he said.

Sandy didn't know how that mattered.

"I don't know about the car they were in," said the doctor, "but your son was driving. Travis was in the passenger seat, and Michelle was in back. She was the only one wearing a seat belt."

When Dermott looked at Sandy, she felt as if she were to blame.

He said, "They were traveling at a high rate of speed, pushing a hundred miles an hour when he lost control. The car skidded sideways through a fence, spun around a few times, and slammed into a tree."

"Jesus Christ," Emmett muttered.

One hundred miles an hour? Sandy's brain seemed stuck on that detail.

"It looked like Travis was ejected through the sunroof. Jordan might have gone through the driver's-side window, or he might have left the vehicle under his own power. In any case, he was found next to Travis. Michelle was still belted in the backseat. But all of this is preliminary."

"What about the air bags?" Emmett asked.

"Only deployed partially, according to what I was told. In addition to abdominal bruising and a dislocated right shoulder, Jordan's got some pretty severe facial and scalp lacerations. They'll monitor his vitals and continue to treat him for shock on the flight over to Mercy, but he was responding to voices and other stimuli. He opened his eyes a few times. One of the EMTs told me Jordan was talking when they got to the accident scene, said he kept telling them he was sorry."

Tell Jordy "I'm sorry" won't cut it this time. Jenna's words surfaced in Sandy's brain. *This time,* she'd said. As opposed to any number of other times, Sandy guessed, beginning with the time Jordy had cut Travis's hair when they were five and then lied that he was responsible. Jenna wouldn't have forgotten; she had the memory of an elephant.

"Huck was trying to talk to your son a while ago." Dr. Dermott divided his glance between Sandy and Emmett, asking if they knew him. "Len Huckabee, the patrol sergeant from Wyatt?"

"Yeah," Emmett said, "we know him."

Dermott went on. "I discouraged him, but once Jordan is conscious, which could be at any time, Huck or some other member of law enforcement is going to want a statement. Just FYI, you know?"

"Are you saying Jordy will be all right?" Sandy's voice seemed faint in her ears, but maybe it was only that her pulse was so loud.

"The next seventy-two hours are critical, but, yeah, overall his outlook is good. All things considered, your son is pretty lucky."

Sandy looked at Emmett, expecting to see his relief, a mirror to her own, but his eyes were hard.

"Why is Huck so interested in talking to Jordy?"

A look of dismay crossed Dr. Dermott's face, and Sandy braced herself as if for a blow.

"I heard when paramedics first arrived at the scene, Michelle was conscious and told them Jordy was the designated driver, the one who was supposed to stay sober. Also, Jordy told them when he came to he was in the driver's seat."

Emmett interrupted. "He was drinking?"

"Blood work's pending, but, yeah. Indications are that all three of them were."

The pained silence was broken by laughter from somewhere down the hall.

"Look, maybe I shouldn't tell you this, but you're going to find out soon enough—" Dr. Dermott spoke quickly as if to cover the sounds of mirth. "Travis is in critical condition, about as critical as it can get. Michelle isn't much better off. There's a good chance neither of them will make it. Your boy, Jordan, if he was driving? He's in a lot of trouble."

2

Lost.

Libby Hennessey was completely turned around. She had felt so sure of herself, she hadn't bothered programming the GPS when she'd driven out of Houston this morning.

"Damn it," she said out loud, then glancing in the rearview mirror, she said it again, loudly, to her reflection. "Damn it."

Libby, you think a lot, but you don't always think about what you're doing.

Beck spoke in her mind. He was a funny guy, her husband. She smiled. He had that talent. After almost thirty-five years of marriage, he could still make her smile. Even when he was nowhere in sight.

The highway she was on dead-ended at CR 440, according to the sign, which was fortunate, because she was pretty sure heading south on 440 would take her back to FM 1620, the road she wanted. The road home. Or it soon would be, once the house was built. The trouble with driving out here in the country was that landmarks weren't as obvious as in the city. But she would learn them in time, she thought, once she was driving the route regularly. She was thinking about how much more peaceful it was driving in the country compared to driving in the city when she crested a hill and saw all the vehicles parked in the grass at its foot. She thought maybe a fruit stand was there, but then she saw the yellow tape, crime-scene tape, looping a section of barbed-wire fencing. A good bit of the fence, including several shattered cedar posts, was lying in the ditch. Some twenty yards away in a field, a crowd of mostly young people was gathered under a spreading live oak canopy. Even from here, Libby could tell they were distraught. A few of the girls were crying.

Accident.

The word took shape in Libby's brain. *A bad one,* she thought. There was no sign of the vehicle or vehicles that must have been involved, but a good-size chunk of bark had been ripped from the oak tree's trunk, leaving a jagged wound. Closer to the road, handwritten cards and bouquets of flowers were strung along the barbed wire, evidence of tragedy, of sorrow and mourning. It made a knot in Libby's stomach. Made her want to get away.

She put her foot down on the accelerator and drove on.

Too fast.

The patrol car came off a secondary ranch road just after she crested the next hill. A moment later, she saw the strobe of its lights. Really? The cop was going to ticket her for doing five over the posted fifty-five-mile-per-hour limit?

They're like the welcome wagon with a badge, the teller at the local bank in Wyatt had warned Libby last week.

And, boy, do they have a gift for you, a woman in line behind her had said.

The three of them had laughed, ha-ha.

Libby pulled onto the narrow shoulder and watched the squad car park behind her in her side-view mirror, brain ticking, thought upon heated thought: she was already late, and now she was going to be even later. She'd never been ticketed. Ever. A fact she bragged about. Not only that, but she couldn't recall ever having met a cop in Houston, but in the bare eight weeks she and Beck had owned property outside Wyatt—property they'd searched two years for—this would be her second encounter with one.

The patrol officer was taking his sweet time. She could see him moving around behind the steering wheel, doing things with his hands, and when he did step outside, he didn't acknowledge her presence. Instead, he seemed to make a show out of adjusting his mirrored sunglasses, letting his fingertips rest on the butt of his gun. It seemed intentional, as if he meant to intimidate her.

What an ass, Libby thought. Lowering her window, she heard the breeze lilting through the grass. She heard the drone of cicadas, the crunch of the cop's booted footsteps, her own pulse in her ears. *Smile,* said a voice in her brain.

"Afternoon," he said.

"I was going too fast," Libby said.

"Yes, ma'am."

When he asked for her driver's license, registration, and proof of insurance, she pulled her license from her wallet and got the insurance card and registration out of her glove box. Other than the owner's manual, they were the only items stowed there. She hadn't had the Lexus long enough to accumulate anything else. She handed them over.

The cop gave the documents a once-over, then shifted his gaze along the length of the Lexus. "Nice car," he said, and there was something faintly damning in his praise.

Some note of ridicule that caused her to squirm slightly in her seat against leather that felt suddenly too rich and buttery soft. No one paid attention if you drove a car like this in Houston, but it was the wrong sort of car out here. She needed a Jeep. No, she thought, what she needed was a truck. Preferably an old truck with fading paint and a few dents. She'd become part of the local color instead of what this law officer likely thought she was: an uppity rich bitch from the city.

He mentioned the city now, inclining his head toward her. "You're from Houston."

"Yes, sir," she said and could have bitten off her tongue. He might be all of forty or forty-five. Nearly young enough that she could be his mother. Would she call her son *sir* if she had a son? Hardly.

He went back to looking at her paperwork. She looked at the front of his tan shirt. The badge indicated he was a patrol sergeant, and above it, his name tag read: L. HUCKABEE.

He handed back Libby's documents. "So where are you going in such a hurry?" He looked at her intently.

His dark hair was shot with silver and cut short, military short, and his eyes were a light shade of brown, almost tawny, and set close together. Any closer, Libby thought, and he would not have been handsome, which he was, but in a way that was almost overpowering. "I'm meeting the contractor who's building my house," she said. "I was late getting out of Houston. There was an accident on the freeway there. Had traffic tied up for miles."

"We had a bad one out here early this morning." The sergeant looked off in the direction Libby had come from. "Three kids out hell-raising, driving drunk, lost control, went head-to-head with a big old live oak. The tree won." Huckabee brought his gaze back; his eyes were hard.

With disgust, Libby thought. Was that what she sensed? But maybe it was only that he was at the end of his shift and exhausted. Or maybe he was sick of his job. Sick of scraping kids up off the concrete. Who could blame him?

He said, "If the driver makes it, he could face charges."

"I haven't been drinking," Libby said.

"If I suspected you had, we'd be having a different conversation." Huckabee's smile was fleeting.

Libby didn't return the gesture.

"Let me give you some advice, ma'am." Huckabee bent his face toward her. "It's as dangerous driving out here as it is back in the big city. Maybe more dangerous. We've posted speed limits for a reason, you understand? Because going faster on these rural roads is hazardous, what with the blind curves and steep hills and drop-offs. Then the lack of regular traffic can lull you into a false sense of security. You get to thinking you're the only vehicle on the road." He lightly tapped the lower edge of her window. "I don't want to have to write up an accident report on you, too, you know what I mean?"

Libby looked into her lap. *I'm not some kid you can intimidate.* The words cut a hot trail across her brain. *Nothing but a badge and an ego.* The thought came and went. She waited for Huckabee to whip out his pad and write her a ticket.

"Tell you what," Huckabee said. "I'm going to let you off with a warning this time, being as how you're new to the area."

Libby looked up, startled. Was he patronizing her now? "Thank you," she said, and wondered why. Had she asked for his favor? She'd almost rather have the ticket.

"You said you were building out here. Whereabouts?"

"The Little B Ranch. Do you know it?"

"Yep. You're going the right way. When you hit 1620 on the other side of Wyatt, take a right. It'll be around eighteen miles farther west on your left."

Libby thanked him.

He tipped his hat. "Not a problem. I know that ranch well. The Scroggins family has been around here a hundred years at least. Folks in town were surprised when Fran decided to sell the land off piecemeal."

"She couldn't find a buyer willing to take on the whole thing. Two hundred forty acres is a lot of land."

"Yeah, it's a shame, though, busting it up."

Libby smiled nicely and said she couldn't agree. "My husband and I might not have found other suitable property out here."

"Well, I don't think Fran's folks left her much of a choice, anyway."

"No." Fran Keller had told Libby her mom and dad were in their nineties. *Can you imagine?* she'd asked. Fran had said she felt old at seventy-one, certainly way too old to make the drive from Austin, where she lived, to the Little B every time a neighbor, or the Wyatt police, or the Madrone County sheriff, called her to report one of her folks had left the stove on or was out wandering the roadside in their pj's.

"I'm curious—how did you hear about the property, that it was for sale, all the way down there in Houston?"

"Ruth Crandall. Maybe you know her. She's a real estate agent in Wyatt."

Huckabee frowned. "You know Ruth?"

"Since college," Libby said. They'd met as freshmen at Southern Methodist University, where they'd shared a suite and everything else— from lipstick to tampons to the heartbreak of that horrible day when Helen, their third suite mate, had died. There was something about sharing grief like that . . . it had bonded Libby and Ruth for life. "Do you know her?" Libby asked the sergeant. "Have you pulled her over for speeding, or did she break some other law?"

Huckabee cracked a smile, but it was brief. "I heard she was handling the sale. You got, what? Fifteen acres? Whereabouts is it, say, in relation to the old farmhouse?"

"We have the adjacent parcel, east of there, where the little gardener's cottage is. My husband is an architect. He designed our house, but we'll live in the cottage until it's built."

"That one-bedroom shack? It's in worse shape than the old farmhouse."

"We've done some work on it," Libby said. "It'll be fine to camp out in."

Whatever, lady. Sergeant Huckabee's expression was full of his doubt.

Libby put the registration and insurance card back in the glove box and tucked her driver's license into her wallet.

The sergeant smiled, and this time it seemed genuine. "I hope the next time we meet, it'll be under better circumstances."

"You can count on it," she said, emphatically.

He turned to go, turned back. "Just so you know, we've had a couple of reports of vandalism at the Little B, nothing too serious. One of the construction workers got his truck door keyed."

"That happened on our property. We're the ones who reported it," Libby said. "A policeman from Wyatt came and checked it out. He thought it was kids."

"Yeah, that'd be my guess."

"I thought stuff like that only happened in the city." Not that she'd ever experienced vandalism, not in all the years she'd lived in Houston, or growing up in Dallas. "People around here are always bragging they never lock anything."

"My advice? Keep your house and car locked up. Crime can happen anywhere, especially in summer. It's hot. Kids get bored. You know."

"Right." Libby didn't have any of her own, but as a former high school guidance counselor, she'd had dealings with plenty.

"Just keep an eye out, okay? You see anything you don't like, give 911 a shout."

Libby said she would; she watched as Huckabee returned to his patrol car, and for a moment, after he settled behind the wheel, their gazes locked in her rearview mirror. She realized he was waiting for her to leave first. *Not out of politeness,* she thought. But because he was the law, the authority in this county, and he wanted her to remember that.

Annoyed, she started her car and drove onto the highway, picking up speed. A couple of miles later, glancing into the rearview mirror again, she saw he was behind her, separated by some two or three car lengths but keeping pace. Was he there deliberately? She checked her speedometer. Fifty-five. Was he baiting her?

They rounded a curve, and the road straightened out. Libby kept an eye on her speed. Huckabee came up behind her so near to her bumper, she could see the collar of his uniform shirt digging into his neck; she could distinguish his facial features, the broad ledge of his brow, the close-set eyes, well-shaped nose and mouth, his square chin. She thought he might be smiling.

Abruptly, the red and blue lights flashed across the top of the cruiser. Libby flinched. Her heart rose, pounding, in her ears. What had she done now? She slowed, heading again for the road's shoulder. But instead of pulling in behind her, the sergeant went around her, engine gunning. The shriek of the siren pierced the air. Watching his taillights disappear, she thought maybe he liked to scare people. Maybe cops in small towns had nothing better to do.

Reaching her own property, she signaled a left turn, and her heart sank when she saw that the gate was open. Augie Bright, her contractor, was already here, then. But of course he would be. Between one delay and another, she was more than an hour late for their meeting.

Still, Libby didn't hurry. The one-lane road that led to the home-site didn't allow for speed. Surfaced in caliche, it unwound along a series of curves, a pale champagne-colored ribbon of rubble, defining a gentle incline. Thickets of native shrubbery pressed close on either side. She let down the windows, and taking a deep breath of the air that was laden with the smell of cedar, she felt her body loosen. There was the sound of the gravel under the tires, the hum of the car's engine, the rush of the warm summer breeze, and her own rising sense of antici-pation. She was bent forward rounding the final curve, and there it was, the view, a vast panorama of undulating hills beneath a depthless vault of sky. It never failed to move her, every time, as if she had never seen it before.

Even the upheaval of construction—the churned ground, the scattered piles of two-by-four stubs, leftover rebar and wire mesh, the smattering of cigarette butts—couldn't dampen her delight, the feeling of satisfaction. This was her land, hers and Beck's, and soon their house would hold its face—the face Beck had poured heart and soul into designing—to this beautiful view. Parking alongside Augie's truck, she got out and walked over to the construction site. When she'd left last Monday, the slab hadn't been more than a pattern on a blueprint. Now a reinforcing network of rebar and posttension cables encased in a wood frame marked the foundation's generous proportions. The footings for the load-bearing walls were in place. Lengths of pipe poked up where plumbing fixtures would later go. The electrical conduit snaking in and out of the backfill led to the kitchen island. It was only a matter of hours now. Augie had said the trucks would arrive tomorrow at first light to start the pour in the cool of morning.

I won't sleep, she thought.

"I was about to give up on you."

Libby turned at the sound of Augie's voice. "Oh, I know. I'm sorry," she said. "First I got lost—again. Then I got stopped for speeding." She made a face. "Don't tell Ruth, okay? She'll never let me hear the end of it."

He laughed and said he'd try and keep his mouth shut.

According to Ruth's aunt Tildy, Augie and Ruth were cousins, but so far removed only Tildy could recite the lineage that linked them. Their real connection was their work, real estate—building it, remodeling it, selling it. Between them they had it covered.

Lifting his broad-brimmed straw hat now, Augie wiped his brow. "Where did you get pulled over?" he wanted to know.

"On 440, not too far from here. I'd just come past the scene of an accident. There were kids all over the place."

Augie clicked his teeth with his tongue. "I heard about it. A couple of local boys and one of their girlfriends lost control and slammed into a tree. No names yet, though."

"The cop who stopped me—I think his name was Huckabee—said they were drinking."

"Ah, yeah, I know him. Len Huckabee, goes by Huck. I heard he was a first responder."

Some note of regard in Augie's voice caught Libby's attention. "He's someone special?"

Augie laughed. "Yeah, you could say—least if you get in a conversation with anyone around here that lasts longer than five minutes, somebody is going to start talking about Huck. He and another guy, John Simmons, are local legends. They took the high school in town to the state football championship back in the day. Both of them got inducted into the Texas Football Hall of Fame. I was in elementary school then, and those two guys were my heroes." Remembered admiration lightened Augie's voice, making him sound much younger.

Libby smiled.

His stare drifted down the back road of a memory she couldn't see. "They played in college, too, on the same team, for Sam Houston State in Huntsville. Both of them on a full-ride scholarship. My dad and I never missed a home game. They were like brothers, those two. Did everything together."

"What happened?" The shadow in Augie's voice prompted Libby to ask.

"They joined the police force in San Antonio, came up through the ranks together. They were both hotshot detectives, got a lot of recognition. But around fourteen years ago, John was killed in a shoot-out with a couple of bank robbers. The crooks acted like they were going to give it up. They laid down their guns and everything, but while Huck had one of them down, the other one somehow got hold of his weapon and shot John in the head. Huck got the guy, but it was too late for John."

It was awful, and Libby said so.

"Yeah," Augie agreed. "It did a number on Huck, for sure. John's wife, Jenna—she's from Wyatt, too—when she moved back here from San Antonio after John died, Huck quit the force there and did the same. The Wyatt police department was happy to have him on the force here." Augie let his gaze drift a moment and then added, "I think he's always felt responsible for her and her son after what happened. He wanted to be close to them, to look after them."

"It's hard on a boy, not having a dad." Libby was thinking of Beck. Before his death, Beck's father, and his mother, too, had been drunk for most of Beck's life. Beck had quit drinking cold turkey when he suspected he might have a problem. His sister, Mia, though, was still drinking. Beck worried that one day booze would kill her the way it had their parents.

Augie was talking about the way Huck had been there for Travis. "Just like a dad," Augie said. "A lot of folks around here thought for sure he and Jenna would end up together. But Jenna's got a different boyfriend now, and Huck got married a few years ago to a little Honduran gal, Coleta. He's crazy about her. She's a real looker—and young, a lot younger—" Augie stopped, grinned sheepishly. "I hear all this stuff from Mandy. You know."

Libby could have said she was learning. Mandy was Augie's wife. She was also a hairstylist at the only beauty salon in Wyatt, called A Cut Above. Libby had yet to meet her, but Augie said she was a talker. He said she could talk the kernels off an ear of corn.

He lifted his hat and resettled it. "Who knows how accurate any of it is when it's a bunch of blue-haired old hens doing the yapping. That's what I tell Mandy."

Libby smiled.

"Ruth knows Coleta," Augie said, grinning again. "Ask her sometime. Stand back, though. Last I heard, she was a little touchy on the subject."

"Really?"

He winked. "We better talk about the slab before I get myself into real trouble."

They talked about the route the trucks would take, and parking logistics. Augie asked about Beck. "Is he coming later?"

"No, unfortunately. Something came up. A meeting," Libby added. "Actually, it's a deposition. I'm a little anxious about it." She was; she couldn't hide it.

Augie waited; for all that he'd repeat his wife's gossip, he wasn't going to pry.

She said, "Beck told you about the balcony that collapsed at the Sea View Terrace in Bay City, didn't he? It happened a few weeks ago."

"Yeah. It's been all in the news, too. Helluva thing. All those folks dying. What was it? Nine?"

"Yes, and several more were injured."

"I heard the architects were getting sued, but Beck didn't work on that project, did he?"

"Not officially. He and his partner, Robert, were called in as consultants. You know how it works. Sometimes with huge projects like the Sea View, the more eyes on it the better."

"Wonder why they're deposing him, if that's all his involvement was."

"Money," Libby answered readily. Beck had talked about settlement figures as high as $15 million, or even more. He'd joked that with that kind of cash on the line, attorneys for both sides would depose a goldfish if they thought it would make their case.

"But the design wasn't the problem." Augie talked as if he was familiar with the tragedy and had given the matter careful thought. "It was the Bituthene membrane, the plastic moisture barrier. That's on the developer or the installer."

"You know how people are, though, when something like this happens."

"Yeah, they want somebody to pay."

"Not just in court, either. At least not in this case. There have been threats."

"You're kidding. Against Beck?"

"Not so far. A couple of the partners, the architects who actually worked on the design, have gotten threatening phone calls and letters accusing them of being murderers, saying they're next. Things like that. We heard some of their employees' cars have been keyed, or they've found dead animals—like raccoons—with their entrails smeared all over."

"Ricky Burrows—one of the guys who works for me?"

Libby nodded; she'd met Ricky.

"His truck was keyed here." Augie pointed at the ground.

"I know. I was here when the cop came to look at the damage." Libby held Augie's gaze.

"You think the incidents are related?"

Libby said she didn't know, that it worried her.

Augie said, "I looked at the balcony-collapse evidence. You can access a lot of it online, the reports of damage, the photos. It's as clear as day—the dry rot was extensive, and it was criminal, all right, but not because of the design."

The squawk of a scrub jay pierced the air, and Libby hunted for it, glimpsing the flash of vivid blue darting through the duller green canopy of the huge cedar tree some thirty yards away on the south side of the homesite. Most of the cedar that had choked the area had been cleared, but they'd left this one. It was a behemoth, wind bent and storm battered, and quite possibly more than one hundred years old. When Libby looked at it, she saw a gentle giant, an ancient druid, leaning on a cane. Beck had humored her wish to protect it from the construction upheaval, driving the stakes into the ground outside the canopy and circling it with a perimeter of orange fencing.

She said, "It's a lawyer's game now, I guess."

Augie hooted. "Yeah, those vultures'll be after the families of the victims like a gang of NFL scouts after a gifted quarterback. It'll take months to sort it out."

Beck had predicted a settlement was years away. He wasn't concerned, either, about his involvement. He referred to it as an inconvenience.

Libby's mind hung on that word: *inconvenience.*

People died. How did it get to be an inconvenience? How did it get to be all about the money?

Augie's cell phone sounded, a series of notes from "Twinkle, Twinkle, Little Star." His daughter had chosen the ringtone and then programmed it into Augie's phone. She was four. Libby had been amazed when Augie told her. He'd flushed with pride.

But now as he spoke, his expression was grave. Libby walked a little away, giving him privacy.

"My God, this is awful."

Libby turned. Augie looked shaken. He kept her gaze.

"That was Mandy. The kids in the wreck this morning? I know them. The boys, anyway. One of them is Travis Simmons."

"The son of the detective who was killed you were telling me about?"

"Yeah, he is such a great kid, too. Talk about a football player. Man, his dad would be so proud of him. And not only for his athleticism but the way he will just go the extra mile for his teammates or anyone. He helped coach a Special Olympics basketball team a couple of summers ago. Last I heard, he's still working with some of the local special-needs kids whenever he's home from college."

"Was he the one who was driving?" Libby asked.

"No. It was the other boy, Jordy Cline. Both he and Trav were Life Flighted to Austin. Wyatt Regional couldn't handle them, their injuries are so severe. Jesus . . . Sorry, it's just—too close to home, you know?"

Libby waved off his apology.

"Mandy heard if Jordy makes it, he'll be arrested. For vehicular assault. Or manslaughter, depending—" Augie stopped again, keeping Libby's gaze. *On whether or not Travis dies.*

He didn't have to say it. The implication hung in the air between them. It made the hair rise on the back of her neck.

. . .

After meeting with Augie, Libby left the homesite and drove to the gardener's cottage, some three miles west. The little house at the end of a dusty, winding trail centered a square of chippy white-picket fencing. It was shingled in cedar and sat close to the ground, reminding Libby of a little brown hen settled on her nest. No one had tended the house or the land around it regularly, though, not in years. Native grasses had almost taken over the perennial borders that hugged the cottage's latticed foundation. Fran had said her great-grandmother Beatrice Scroggins, whom the Little B was named for, had planted the gardens more than one hundred years ago. But, amazingly, some of the long-ago plantings still existed. Thick clumps of bearded iris and silvery lamb's ears were visible on either side of the front porch steps. In the side yard, an arbor made from cedar logs was wrapped in the thick-trunked grasp of a thorny old rose climber. Devil's trumpet grew along the fence as vigorously as the native sumac and kidneywood.

Libby had fallen in love with the cottage the moment she saw it. It seemed enchanted to her despite the signs of ruin. Going over it, Beck had pronounced it basically sound. Like the bones of the garden.

The structure, the framework, remained—a beautiful relic waiting to be unearthed. She didn't mind the work that would be involved in the restoration of the house or the yard. Even the idea was satisfying. She had already started bringing plants from her garden in Houston, and she was in back, watering some of them, when she heard the sound of a motor, and rounding the front corner of the cottage, she was surprised to see Beck's pickup coming up the drive, dust hanging in its wake like a shroud.

It wouldn't be good news that had brought him. That was her thought, and the somber look on his face when he got out of the truck seemed to confirm it.

3

Sandy would remember the terror in their silence as she and Emmett drove east to the hospital in Austin. She would remember Emmett reaching for her hand, the feel of the calluses on his palm rough against her knuckles. Even though he ran the company, Emmett would say he was a salesman, but he still did the hard physical work. It wasn't unusual for him to pitch in at a drilling site, doing whatever needed to be done, from operating a mud pump to working the rig floor. He'd come home at the end of the day as filthy as she'd ever seen him when he'd worked as a roughneck in high school. Back then he'd loved to grab her in a bear hug, making her squeal. Nowadays, she made him peel out of his clothes and wash up in the laundry-room sink.

But the sense of him beside her, his solid presence now in the driver's seat, the sure grip of his hand, grounded her, the way it always did. They didn't talk much. Words came, but they crumbled in her mouth before she could utter a sound.

Night was lifting as they hit the Austin city limits. How they found the hospital would always be a blur. Inside, the nurse at the first reception desk they came to was engrossed in something on her computer screen. A game of solitaire or Words with Friends, Sandy thought. She played those silly games, too, when she was bored or needed a distraction. She frittered her time away. That's what her mother would say. Translated, it meant: *Why can't you be more like your sister? Disciplined? Responsible?*

Emmett rapped the counter.

Unperturbed, the nurse glanced up.

"Jordan Cline. He was flown here from Wyatt via helicopter with his cousin, Travis Simmons."

She frowned slightly. "Ah. Those two. Both still in triage, I think. Hold on, and I'll get someone to take you there."

Moments later a different nurse appeared. Charlotte was a critical care nurse. "I've been working with both boys," she said.

"Are they all right?" Sandy asked.

"Still unconscious, but Jordan's vitals are good. We'll have a better idea of his prognosis once we get back the results on his latest blood work and CT scan. If you'll come with me, we need you to fill out some paperwork."

At the nurses' station, Charlotte fished a clipboard with forms attached out of a stack and handed it to Sandy. She clutched it to her chest, feeling her heart beat against it. "What about my nephew, Travis? How are his vitals?"

"As long as he's breathing, there's hope. That's what I believe," Charlotte added.

Well, you would have to, working in a place like this, wouldn't you? The thought passed through Sandy's mind.

"You can fill out the forms there while you're waiting." Charlotte gestured toward a large open area off the corridor that was furnished with rows of blue-padded, metal-framed chairs. "Either myself or the emergency-room doctor will keep you posted."

Sandy looked at Emmett, but what did she want him to do? Argue? Demand they be taken to see Jordy immediately? *I'm his mother!* She wanted to shout it, as if that fact alone afforded her certain inalienable rights. As if saying the very word *mother* would part the waters and move mountains. But that relationship carried little weight here. Other adults, experienced in ways she never would be, were in charge of Jordy and Travis. Their well-being, even their lives, depended on *them* now, not on her or Jenna. The revelation, its truth, was overwhelming. It made her light-headed.

Emmett looked after the nurse, who was walking briskly away. "I'm going to see if I can find some coffee," he said. "Want some?"

Sandy glanced at him. *Coffee?* How could he think of it, of wanting anything other than to see their son? But he needed to move, after the time in the truck. "No, thanks," she said.

The waiting room appeared empty, and although it was after seven now, the lights were dim as if it were night. A television mounted on one wall was tuned at low volume to an early-morning news program, a local show: *Austin at Daybreak.* It came on at five thirty. Sandy had watched it occasionally. Mornings were hectic, getting herself and her men out the door. She stood, leafing through the clipboarded paperwork, mind churning. Mercy Hospital. Was it in their insurance network or out?

She stared into the middle distance, feeling the sand of exhaustion burn her eyes. The voice in her brain pecked away, oblivious. If they were out of network . . . *God!* The air transport alone must have cost thousands. Were such extreme measures even covered? She remembered a childhood friend, diagnosed with the sudden onset of a particularly virulent cancer. When she'd died six months later, her parents had been devastated. And broke. They'd lost everything—their savings, their retirement, even their house. The panic, crouched in Sandy's belly, started to rise. She clamped her teeth against it. There was already more than enough to fear.

She stepped into the waiting area, and that's when she saw Jenna. Her sister was huddled in a chair in a back corner of the room, where the light was murkiest.

Sandy went to her, sitting down beside her. "Where is Troy? He shouldn't have left you alone."

"That should be the least of your worries."

Sandy kept Jenna's gaze.

"Jordy's in a lot of trouble. You know that, don't you?"

"I—we don't know anything for sure at this point. It could as easily have been Trav—"

"Huck was first on the scene, Sandy. He said Jordy was driving."

"Of course he would say that. We both know how he feels about you even if no one else does."

"Jordy said it, too, that when he came to, he was in the driver's seat."

"But he's never the designated driver."

"Because he drinks, and Travis is always the responsible one, the way I always was."

Sandy wanted to argue, to defend Jordy. How would he live with it if something happened to Michelle, or to Travis, who was like a brother? Closer, even. They were like twins. They'd been born in the early summer of the same year, nearly on the same day. She smoothed her hand down the clipboard, speaking to it in a low voice. "Right now all that matters is for Jordy and Travis and Michelle to be okay."

"Well, they aren't. And Travis—Trav may never be—" Jenna's voice broke.

Sandy put her arms around Jenna, and they were heedless when the clipboard slipped from Sandy's lap and clattered to the floor.

"I haven't been this scared since you had surgery," Sandy whispered.

"That was nothing," Jenna said. She pushed out of Sandy's embrace, dug a tissue from her purse, and blew her nose. "Losing a boob is nothing compared to losing your kid."

"You aren't going to lose him, Jenna. Don't talk like that."

"He's on life support," Jenna said with such venom that Sandy recoiled. "Machines are breathing for him, beating his heart. His brain is bleeding, and they can't stop it. Six of his ribs are broken. His lungs keep collapsing, and his leg is fractured so badly it nearly severed his femoral artery. Do you want to hear more?" Jenna shot to her feet.

Sandy stared at her. Had she been able to find the right words, she still couldn't have spoken.

"But Jordy apologized, so that makes it all right with you, I'm sure. He said he was sorry. Hot damn. I am so touched."

"This is not happening," Sandy muttered, retrieving the clipboard.

"Oh, that's so like you." Jenna wheeled a few steps away, hands thrust into the air. "Avoiding everything. Pretending it's wonderful when it's shit. But that's okay, you'll still have Jordy, your perfect prince, Mr. I Can Never Do Anything Wrong in My Mama's Eyes. Because according to what I've heard, Jordy's going to be just fine!"

"Hey! What is going on here?"

Sandy heard Emmett, and she stood up, feeling wobbly, feeling a jolt of relief.

"We could hear you clear down the corridor." Troy sat down.

"She's blaming me," Sandy said, and thought how childish she sounded.

"I just talked to your mom. She's been trying to call you."

Sandy said, "I couldn't talk to her."

"Me, either," Jenna said.

"Well, she caught me off guard. She said this morning when she woke up she knew something was wrong. I had to tell her. She and your dad are on their way."

"Did you tell them who was driving?"

"When they asked, yes."

"What did you want him to do, Sandy? Lie?"

It sounded like a dare. It sounded as if Jenna thought that's exactly what she would expect of Sandy.

"You don't know what happened any more than I do, Jenna," Sandy said.

"I know Jordy caused this. I know you'll lie, and so will Jordy, whenever the truth doesn't suit you."

"Call a truce, you two, okay?" Emmett said.

"Please." Troy underscored his request.

"Why are you accusing me?" Sandy barely registered their calls for peace. She was searching Jenna's eyes, hunting for a sign of something familiar, the bond they shared, an understanding that they were in this together. But Jenna's glance was shuttered and cold.

Emmett took Sandy's hand, pulling her down beside him. "We're all under stress," he said.

"What about your mom?" she asked, needing a moment, a space to steady herself.

"I'm not going to call her yet. I want to wait until we know more."

Something good, he meant. Irene was fragile, the result of a failing heart. Sandy thought Irene had been losing a bit of her heart every year since she'd lost her husband, Frank, the year Sandy and Emmett turned eleven. Their families had been neighbors; she and Emmett had grown up running in and out of each other's houses on Adams Avenue in an older section of Wyatt. Their parents were close, too, close enough that they had vacationed together. Irene and Sandy's mom, Penny, were best friends. Weekends when Emmett and the dads went camping, Sandy and Jenna would shop and do girl things with the moms. They'd been having one of those weekends—the girls at home, the guys off fishing—when Frank drowned.

They'd gone to the Guadalupe River to fish. There was nothing out of the ordinary, no prescient sense of disaster. It hadn't rained in weeks, and the water was placid. Like glass, Sandy's father, Harvey, would say over and over afterward. The only thing making a ripple was the dog. Sandy's father would say that, too. All three of them were strong swimmers, so when they saw the dog struggling in the current, losing strength, they didn't think twice about diving in after her. Frank went out the farthest, and when Sandy's dad saw he was in trouble, he swam toward him, but then Emmett foundered, caught in the same freak undertow. Sandy's dad got hold of Emmett and hauled him to safety, but by then Frank was gone, and the dog had clambered out of the water on her own. Emmett had blamed himself for needing to be rescued. Sandy's dad had mourned that he couldn't save them both.

The memory haunted them and yet it bound them. Sandy had been jealous of Emmett's and her dad's connection until she was old enough to realize their shared grief was forged with love, and that love was what had healed them. Irene had eventually moved north, to Norman, Oklahoma, where she shared a house with her sister, Leila. But she'd never been the same. After she lost Frank, she went into herself. She often gave Sandy the sense she was listening to some other conversation, one no one else could hear. Sandy had decided it was Frank she talked to. Emmett said to leave her alone.

"I hope this doesn't kill her," he said now.

Sandy was the only one who heard him. She bent her head to his shoulder.

An hour passed. The shift changed, and foot traffic increased. A man came into the ER waiting room cradling his arm; a mother brought in her small daughter. Fever spots burned on the child's cheeks, and her cough was so rough it made Sandy's chest hurt. Charlotte's replacement, a nurse named Rebecca, knelt before them and rattled off a speech that seemed rehearsed. "They're holding their own," she said. "Everything that can be done is being done," she said, adding, "Dr. Showalter is the best. He's the one I'd want treating my kid, if I had a kid."

She said the hospital had contacted Family Services and that someone would be by later to talk to them. She told them where they could find the hospital chapel and said the reverend, Terry Murphy, would be making rounds later. "Should you feel in need," she explained.

Of what? Sandy wondered. *Prayer? Blessing?*

A miracle?

"Travis is going to die," Jenna said when Rebecca had left them alone again.

"Please don't say that." Sandy found Jenna's hand and held it, and she was grateful when Jenna allowed this. But even pissed to the max at each other, they were there for each other. They had always been able to talk through everything, even the hard stuff.

"Trav's a survivor," Emmett said. "Just like his mama."

Jenna put her other hand on his knee. She was his big sister, too.

It was late morning when Rebecca returned to say that the boys were being moved to the ICU.

"That's good news, right?" Emmett asked. He and Sandy stood up.

Troy put his hand under Jenna's elbow, assisting her as if she were old, and holding her close, he said, "I told you Trav was going to make it."

The look in Rebecca's eyes seemed pitying, but she answered cheerfully enough, saying, "Dr. Showalter will be up in a few minutes to talk to you all, and then you can visit your kids. Just be aware, visiting hours are different in the ICU." She started to turn away, then turned back. "One other thing, and I'm not trying to scare you, but you should be prepared. Both of your guys are in critical condition. There's a lot of equipment, a lot of tubes. Travis especially—"

"I saw him," Jenna said, "before he left Wyatt."

"But the bleeding in his brain has stopped, right?" Troy asked.

"For now," Rebecca said. "His condition is critical, though." She repeated it as if she couldn't stress the fact enough.

"But there's hope," Jenna said. "As long as he's breathing, right?"

Rebecca frowned slightly, then she said, "Sure. Of course. As long as he's breathing."

.   .   .

Dr. Showalter was last to the meeting. He was tall and silver haired. Distinguished looking, was Sandy's thought. His eyes were blue, arctic blue, and as quiet as ice. He sat down across from them, and after the introductions, he began to address them, speaking in medical terms, the universal language of calamity, tossing out words like *hematoma, hemorrhage, subarachnoid,* and *intraventricular* as if they should know. Emmett stopped him finally and asked if he would tell them in plain English how their children were hurt.

Showalter looked vaguely impatient. "Basically, both kids have suffered a good deal of trauma, in particular to their heads."

"At Wyatt Regional, Dr. Dermott said the air bags only deployed partially." Emmett sounded angry, but Sandy knew it was fear that clipped his tone.

"I don't know the details," Dr. Showalter said in a tone that was equally truncated.

"We were told Jordy's brain is bruised?" Sandy watched Showalter, hunting for signs of denial.

There weren't any. He said a follow-up CT scan had confirmed the bruising, and then he dismissed Sandy's concern with the wave of his hand, repeating Dr. Dermott's opinion, that in most cases such bruises—he used the word *contusions*—healed on their own.

Emmett asked where the damage was located. "What part of the brain?"

"Right frontal lobe."

"What does that mean?" Sandy asked. "How will he be affected mentally?"

"Probably not at all in the long run. Right now and in the immediate future, there may be difficulty with memory. He might be confused. His motor skills, language, and emotional expression might be affected. But whatever symptoms there are shouldn't last. Neither should there be sustained damage to his vision."

"His vision?" Sandy asked faintly.

"You haven't seen him?"

"No," Emmett said. "By the time we were allowed into the ER at Wyatt Regional, they'd already put him on the helicopter."

"Well, Jordan sustained a number of severe lacerations to the right side of his face and scalp. Possibly from the air bag, but more than likely from the steering wheel and the windshield. His vision should be fine, as I said, but we did remove a large piece of glass from his right eye."

Emmett found Sandy's hand. "We were told his ribs are broken and his shoulder was dislocated. Is that right?"

"His shoulder is back in place now."

"It's been dislocated before," Sandy said.

"He played football in high school," Emmett explained.

"He and Travis were cocaptains their junior and senior year." Sandy felt more than saw the look Emmett gave her. She clamped her mouth shut.

Showalter cleared his throat. "It's good you're familiar with the injury. You know there could be subsequent fallout—what to watch for."

They did, Emmett said.

Dr. Showalter flattened his palms on his knees, looking almost cheerful. "All right, then. That's about it. There's no sign of internal bleeding; he's breathing on his own. He's responsive to stimuli, and he's wakened several times since his arrival here. It doesn't mean something can't happen down the road, but he looks good for now. He's a lucky young man—"

"Travis." Jenna leaned forward, and Showalter switched his glance to her. They all did. Her tremors were obvious. "Is Trav breathing on his own?" she asked.

"I'm afraid not." Dr. Showalter looked away, looked back, reluctance written all over his face. There might have been the slightest softening of his expression. "Your son's injuries are numerous and severe—"

"They said at Wyatt Regional that his leg might have to be amputated?"

"It's possible, but that's not the most concerning issue at this point."

"It's the head injury, right?" Troy spoke up.

"Yes," Showalter said. "It's one of the more serious types, I'm afraid. He has what's called a basilar skull fracture."

"Bas—what?" Jenna sat back.

Sandy capped her hand over Jenna's shaking knee.

"Basilar refers to the base of the skull." Showalter drew his hand across the back of his neck. "In Travis's case, the fracture is across multiple areas of the brain. There's pressure on the stem, which has created a number of intraventricular hemorrhages that are also adding pressure. The skull is a very small space—imagine a room with fixed walls. In its normal condition, it's already packed as tightly as an overfull closet. There's nowhere for the swelling to go. Do you understand?"

Jenna said yes, but she looked dazed. Her knee trembled.

Dr. Showalter continued nonetheless. Maybe he didn't notice Jenna's agitation, her bafflement, Sandy thought, or if he did, he couldn't take time to deal with it. Or perhaps he felt it was better to deliver horrible news as quickly as possible and have it over. Like ripping off a Band-Aid in one motion.

"While he was still at Wyatt Regional, Travis was started on medication to reduce the pressure and prevent seizures, but the CT scan we did when he arrived here indicated there's been—" Showalter paused before he said the word *little* to describe Travis's level of improvement. He might just as well have said there was *no* improvement.

"What are you doing for him?" Sandy asked, because Jenna didn't or more likely couldn't. Her jaw was so tightly clenched, the white knot of bone at the corner was visible.

"The medication he was given that we continued for a time after his arrival here was helpful, but ultimately we didn't get the result we were looking for." Showalter took another moment.

"So?" Troy prompted.

"So we performed a surgical procedure called a craniotomy. It's used to extract tumors, but it can also be very quickly effective at relieving pressure on the brain, much like opening the door on a too-full closet can give the contents somewhere to go."

"You cut into his brain?" Jenna's voice rose.

"It was our only option."

"Did it work?" Sandy asked.

"He's still not wakened, nor is he responsive to stimuli." Dr. Showalter stood up. "It's a waiting game for now."

"I want to see him." Jenna pushed herself from her chair. Troy was on his feet instantly to steady her.

Sandy and Emmett got up, too, and the four of them trooped after Dr. Showalter, ducklings in a row. Once they entered the ICU, Showalter handed them off to a nurse, an overtly cheerful young woman dressed in pink scrubs printed with green-and-yellow kites. She was Claire Overman, she said, smiling adamantly. Travis and Jordy were her patients. "This way." She led them along yet another nearly featureless corridor. "Since they're family, we've put them next to each other." She pushed open another door, holding it, allowing them to pass.

Sandy crossed the threshold, and her heart faltered. She found Emmett's hand. She had an impulse to pinch her nose against the harsh, astringent smell of disinfectant that overlay a darker odor of terrible harm to bodies too fragile to be thoroughly washed, the wasting stench of disease and death. The glass-fronted rooms loomed like giant fish aquariums and were crammed with every possible kind of machine, beeping and whooshing. Yards of tubing hung from silver poles like party garlands. Thick electrical cords snaked the floor. The sense of dread was pervasive. She felt ill with it. In here, she could no longer imagine that Jordy was less mortally wounded than Travis, or that either of them would survive.

Claire stopped midway down the hall. "This is Jordy"—she indicated the cubicle on her left—"and Travis is here." She nodded to her right.

Sandy looked at Jenna and saw her own panic reflected in her sister's eyes. There was her accusation, too, stronger now. Jordy had been driving. Jordy had done this. Brought them here to this nightmare place. What if it was true that Jordy had been driving and Travis or Michelle—or both of them—died as a result, and Jordy lived?

Sandy's head swam. She put her fingertips to her temple. *Don't. Don't go there,* warned the voice in her brain.

She felt Emmett's hand on the small of her back, gently prodding her. She managed to cross the threshold into Jordy's room, but then she stopped only steps inside to get her bearings, to stare at the body lying so still in the bed. A monitor on the opposite side dinged, and she glanced at it, for a moment spellbound by the numbers and lines that rose and fell across its face in life-measuring increments.

Behind her, in a low voice, Emmett asked, "Is he awake?"

"That's not him," Sandy said, because Jordy was never so still. He twitched even in sleep. And that face, that poor swollen face, could not be Jordy's face. There must be some mistake.

"What is the gauze on his eyes for?"

Sandy raised her glance to Emmett, who had gone around her and was now standing at the bedside, looking down. She walked to the other side of the bed and looked down, too, at the boy lying there. A sheet and thin blanket were tucked around his chest and under one arm. Only one hand was visible, with strong fingers and flat, square fingernails, bitten to the quick. She recognized that hand and slid her palm over it. Her gratitude, her relief on feeling Jordy's warmth, brought her to tears. She announced it to Emmett, a celebratory whisper. "He's warm."

His eyelids fluttered then as if he'd heard her. She spoke his name, softly. "Jordy?"

"Mom?"

"Yes, honey, I'm here." Bending over him, she tightened her hand around his.

"I'm sorry," he said, and the words were heartbroken and hopeless.

"No, no. You mustn't worry." She smoothed his hair from his brow, taking care not to disturb the gauze lying over his eyes.

"Trav is—he's hurt bad, Mom. I tried to help him."

"Of course, I know you did. Everything you could," Sandy added. "Dad's here." She glanced up at Emmett, her eyes intent on him; her message that he should speak was strong in her mind, and he did, but what he said appalled her.

"So, it's true. You were driving drunk. Is that right?"

"Not now." Sandy spoke over him.

"Wasn't—" Jordy answered.

"Wasn't what?" Emmett bent toward him. "Drinking and driving?" But Jordy didn't respond.

"Son?"

Sandy looked at Emmett. "He's fallen asleep."

"How could he? That quick?"

"Dr. Showalter said he would go in and out." Sandy straightened. "How could you accuse him like that?" She kept her voice low, but she was furious.

"Do you have a clue what could happen to him, Sandy? To us?" Emmett's whisper was equally heated. "If he was drinking and driving? Do you know the shit storm we're facing?"

"You heard him say he wasn't."

"I heard him say the word *wasn't*. What that was in reference to, I don't know. Anyway, according to everything I've heard so far, the evidence says otherwise. He admitted himself that when he came to, he was in the driver's seat, for fuck's sake. What other proof do you need?"

"We're not having this discussion here." Sandy pushed her hair behind her ears. Fatigue bowed her shoulders, throbbed dully behind her eyes. "There's only one thing that matters right now, and that's for Jordy to get better."

"And Trav? Michelle? If they don't—"

Sandy locked Emmett's gaze, and he had the good sense to stop and turn away.

"Aren't you always pointing out to me that it's ridiculous to speculate?" She spoke to his back.

He didn't answer.

She looked down at her son, at the gauze hiding his eyes. She remembered when he was born, the nightlong hours of hard labor that had ended in a protracted and hazardous breech delivery. *Don't take his diaper off,* the nurse who brought Jordy to her afterward had warned. *You'll cry,* she'd said.

Sandy lifted a corner of the gauze that hid Jordy's eyes now, the same as she had untaped his diaper then. He was her child. There was no possibility of blinding herself to the ways in which he was hurt. The damage was horrible. On seeing it, she lost her breath, and just as she had on the day of his birth, she fought a strong urge to avert her gaze. On the day of his birth, it had been his tiny lower torso that had been this severely bruised and battered. His scrotum had been the size of her fist, making it impossible to perform a circumcision until three days later. She still dreamed on occasion of his earsplitting screams, and her throat on waking would be packed with tears. She wanted to cry now at the hideousness of the injury confronting her—a radiant starburst of deep lacerations, centered at the outer corner of his right eye, gashed an arc across his brow and down to the bridge of his nose. Another network of cuts extended down across his right ear. A hunk of scalp at the hairline near his right temple was missing.

She could see the mangled edges of blood-crusted flesh had been sealed together, but it was impossible to detect how, whether with stitches or some type of glue. Both his eyes appeared swollen and were caked with blood and something yellowish. How could his vision be safe? Sandy couldn't believe it was. Wouldn't believe it until Jordy told her he could see.

Setting the gauze on a nearby cabinet, she carefully peeled back the sheet and blanket, exposing the shoulder sling. It was blue, a contraption composed of wide nylon bands and straps and Velcro. Jordy had worn a similar brace after his shoulder was dislocated during his sophomore football season, when he was broadsided by a monster lineman on the opposing team who had been built like a bull and looked thirty-five at the very least.

"It'll be hell if he's torn his rotator cuff again." Emmett came back to Jordy's bedside.

Sandy gently retucked the bed linen, not answering. A torn rotator cuff was nothing compared to the loss of one's eyesight.

She was aware of the monitor at her elbow, the rhythmic registry of Jordy's every breath and heartbeat. A call over the PA system summoned someone to the second-floor nurses' station, stat. Footsteps passed. Voices rose and fell. Sandy leaned on the bed rail, feeling her eyelids shutter, feeling her mind go numb.

"How are we doing in here?" Claire crossed the room to stand next to Sandy. She picked up Jordy's wrist, eyeing the monitor.

"Are you sure his vision is okay?" Sandy asked.

"Yes." Claire glanced at Sandy. "I know it looks scary, but trust me, his vision is fine. He might need a bit of reconstructive surgery to minimize scarring, but other than that, there won't be any bad effects. He was lucky."

How many times would she hear that? Sandy wondered. What was lucky about being in a horrendous accident, especially if you caused it? Had he? A sudden urge to slap Jordan awake leaped from the floor of her mind. She wanted to shake him, to demand the truth. To shout: *What were you thinking?* She asked Claire about Travis instead.

"There's no change, I'm afraid," the nurse said.

"I should check on him and my sister." Sandy glanced at Emmett, wanting him to come with her.

She didn't think she could face Jenna alone. The sense of this was new and terrible.

"Actually, she and her husband—" Claire began.

"She and Troy aren't married yet," Sandy said. "They will be; they plan on it."

"If Troy can ever get her to commit long enough to get her to plan the wedding." Emmett smiled.

They all did, the way anyone does when the word *wedding* is mentioned.

Claire said, "They've gone to the waiting room, I think."

Sandy looked down at Jordy. She smoothed his hair.

"Why don't you join them?" Claire pushed buttons on the monitor. "You can come back at the next regular ICU visiting hour."

"I want to stay," Sandy said.

"I'm sorry, but visitation is over." Claire was brisk. "You can come back at five for a half hour, and again at nine tonight. There's a schedule up on the bulletin board in the waiting room."

Emmett thanked her.

Claire, seeming to relent, said, "My guess? Your guy'll be out of here and into a regular room by this time tomorrow. He's doing really well. Barring something unforeseen," she added.

The fine print, Sandy thought. *The disclaimer. The thing that said, "I bear no responsibility for any promises."*

· · ·

Sandy and Jenna's parents arrived, white-faced and shaken, asking what had happened. Revisiting that awful question: *Who was driving?* Sandy wanted to scream. *What does it matter? We're all in this together. They're our boys, and this terrible thing happened to both of them.*

She was relieved when her folks offered to go to Wyatt and gather things from their homes, essentials like clean underwear and toothbrushes. After they left, Sandy and Emmett, and Jenna and Troy, followed a mostly silent routine, leaving the ICU waiting room at regular intervals to visit Jordy and Travis, then returning a half hour later to sit like strangers. The few times Emmett and Sandy found Jordy awake, he asked about Travis. Sandy was afraid to say much. Afraid of the effect it might have. She warned Emmett with her eyes. *Don't talk about the accident; don't ask him again about driving.* But once, Jordy himself brought it up. "I was in the driver's seat," he said, "but Travis was driving."

"How can that be, son?" Emmett was gentle.

"I don't know, Dad. It's hard—I got out somehow. I tried to help Trav." Jordy's eyes closed. Tears gathered at the corners. "He's hurt, hurt so bad." He spoke as if he were there, seeing it, Travis, the condition he was in. Suddenly his eyes opened wide, and he said, "I have to see him." He lifted his head, made as if to get up, groaned and fell back.

Sandy bent over him. "Rest, honey. Just rest. It's fine. Everything is fine." She smoothed the hair on the crown of his head, thinking she had probably never told a bigger lie.

. . .

Sandy sat beside Jenna in the waiting room. "You should eat something." She clasped Jenna's hand. It was cold. "We should all go to the cafeteria, even if we don't feel like eating."

Emmett braced his elbows on his knees.

Troy wiped his face, blew out his breath.

Jenna said, "I'm not leaving. Not when Trav could go at any moment."

"Go?"

"He isn't going to make it, Sandy."

"No! As long as he's breathing—"

"He's not. A machine is doing it for him. If you could see him—" Jenna stopped.

Sandy held on to her hand more tightly, but there was no response. It was as if Jenna were slipping away to a place Sandy couldn't follow. It came to her then how they would never be the same. It was as if the sisters they had been had ceased to exist, and the reality couldn't have struck Sandy more forcefully if Jenna had turned to her and slapped her across the face.

"He's having these little strokes now because of all the pressure. His Glasgow Scale is less than three."

"Glasgow—what is that? What does it mean?" Sandy wanted Jenna's glance.

But Jenna took back her hand and bent over her knees. "It means he's dying. There's almost no brain activity. They've asked me about organ donation."

"Holy Jesus Christ." Emmett got up and paced a short distance away.

Sandy said, "Remember when Travis and Jordy rode the four-wheeler and Trav fell off? He lost consciousness—"

Jenna's head came up. "How can you compare—" She paused. "Except—Jordy was driving then, too, wasn't he? And once again he was going like a fucking maniac! He'd probably been drinking then, too."

"He was only fourteen."

"What about last summer? When he borrowed my car and backed it into a light pole?"

"That was an accident—"

"He was drinking, Sandy. Believe it or not, it wasn't Santa Claus who left the empty pint of peppermint schnapps I found under the driver's seat."

"He swore to me it wasn't his, that he hadn't—"

"He lied to you. He lies all the time. You're the only one who doesn't see it, the world of hurt that kid is in." Jenna's voice pitched high. It bumped and slid. "You never stop him, discipline him, and now I'm going to lose my son, my only child, because you—"

"Jenna, Sandy." Emmett was warning them. He was telling them this wasn't the time or the place.

Troy crossed his arms and blinked at the ceiling.

"I want to see him." Sandy spoke into the god-awful silence. "Jordy has asked to see him."

Jenna sat up, ramrod straight. "I don't want Jordy anywhere near Trav."

"You don't mean that." Sandy was stunned. She waited, near breathless for several seconds, but Jenna didn't take it back. And then out of nowhere, a voice came over the PA, toneless, yet somehow urgent.

"Code blue, ICU," it announced. "Code blue, ICU."

4

Beck came through the gate, looking somber, as if the weight of the world burdened his back.

Libby's heart thumped. "What happened?"

"You won't believe it," he said, and he paused, then flashed her a grin full of mischief, and grabbing her, he whirled her in a circle. He was off the hook, he said. "We were dropped, severed, let go. No more lawsuit." He set her on her feet—both of them half-breathless—then returned to his truck and pulled out a couple of grocery sacks. "I shopped at Whole Foods in Austin."

In the kitchen he took items from the sacks, displaying for her inspection, her oohing and ahhing, a package of mahimahi, a box of wild rice, a rubber-banded bunch of fresh asparagus. Pulling out the final item, he grinned, pumping his brows suggestively as he held it up for her to see.

Peach ice cream. One pint. Some fancy brand.

She laughed. "Heaven knows what that cost."

"Only the best for my sweetheart," he said.

She snapped the towel at his leg, calling him an old fool.

"Watch out who you're calling old, woman." He stowed the ice cream in the freezer.

She loosened the asparagus from its tie and trimmed the ends. "What happened, exactly—with the suit, I mean?"

"The plaintiff's attorneys finally admitted the whole thing about it being a flaw in the design was bullshit."

"Thank God."

"You can say that again. Between the firm's legal fees and building the house, I was starting to get a bit worried."

Libby looked at him over her shoulder. "You never said anything. You called it an inconvenience."

"I didn't want you to worry, too." He unbuttoned the cuffs of his shirt, rolled his sleeves to the elbow.

"You must have told Mia. She bit my head off when she called me last week."

"You answered the phone?"

"Yes, it was ten o'clock in the morning. I didn't expect her to be drunk."

"Was she?"

"Probably. She accused me of pressuring you, making you move out here, forcing you to build a house you don't want. Is that how it is?"

"Why didn't you tell me?" He plowed his hands over his head, looking defeated, impatient. Defensive. Some combination. He didn't want to answer her question. He wanted to make it about his sister, his sister's drinking, her drama, rather than tell the truth about how he was feeling. Emotions were hard for him, the result of having been raised by neglectful parents. Sissy and Harold had loved their children, but only when they were sober, when they remembered Mia and Beck were around.

Libby had worked as a high school guidance counselor for most of their married life, and over the years she'd taken a lot of psychology courses. She'd worked with children like Beck and Mia, who'd grown up in troubled circumstances. He seldom spoke of the past, but he carried it. The boy he'd been—that frightened, brave, stalwart little boy, the one who had stood guard over baby Mia, who had harbored a fierce need to protect his little sister—still lived in the man he'd become.

But now Mia was a grown-up, and she drank. All the time. Beck didn't know what to do with that. He didn't know what to do with Mia's bitter envy of him, his sobriety, his success. Libby didn't know what to do with Mia, either. She couldn't change her upbringing, couldn't give Mia the moon or a million dollars to make it all right. She couldn't drink with her or talk to her, although at times she would still try, even though Beck's own advice was that Libby should ignore her. She'd been glad when Mia had moved with her boyfriend du jour to Las Vegas three years ago. Glad when after the boyfriend left, Mia had stayed out there.

Libby looked at Beck now, saying his name, prompting him, wanting his gaze, some reassurance that he hadn't gone to Mia with his stress, his concern over money.

"Can we just make dinner and eat? I'm starving." He handed her the package of fish. "I'll do the rice," he said.

"Okay," she said, but it hurt that he had trusted Mia over her. *How could you?* She clenched her jaw to keep from firing what would amount to an accusation at him. She refused to put him in the position of choosing. That was Mia's game.

He dumped the rice he had measured into the pan, and it sounded like rain. She rinsed the fish, scooting over a bit when he needed water from the tap. From the corner of her eye, she caught glimpses of him, adding the water to the rice, settling a lid over the pan, adjusting the flame under it. She seasoned the fish with salt, pepper, and paprika, adding snipped bits of fresh parsley and dill before drizzling it with olive oil.

The tension between them softened as they worked. She and Beck often shared meal preparation. It was a favorite pastime for them both, a way to unwind and be together. Beck poured each of them a glass of sparkling water, to which he added a twist of lime. Handing Libby her glass, he brushed a tendril of hair from her cheek and asked about her day.

She told him about being stopped for speeding, and he laughed, as she'd known he would.

"Here's to the ruination of your perfect driving record." He raised his glass.

"He only gave me a warning," she said.

"Yeah, but who knows what's next? I mean, here we thought I might be the one to get tossed in the slammer. I was dreading it, too. Orange is so not my color." He smirked.

Libby made a face. "Harris County inmates wear white, I think. And, anyway, the sergeant was just being diligent. There was an accident out that way earlier, a bad one."

"I heard about it when I stopped for gas in town." Beck leaned his backside against the counter. "Three kids lost control and hit a tree. Someone said they thought one of the boys died."

"Augie knows them."

"I guess as small as Wyatt is, everyone knows everyone."

"Can you imagine?" Libby set down her glass. "How you would feel if you were driving and you killed one of your friends?"

Beck's look was somber, probing.

She knew what he was thinking. "At least we never had that worry."

"No," he replied.

"There are some perks to not having children," she said, and she could tell from the slight rise of his eyebrows that by adding that bit, she'd surprised him. He'd probably thought he'd never live to see the day she'd find one positive thing to say about being childless. Not after the hell she'd put him—put them both through.

"You do realize we could lose our car insurance."

It took her a moment, but when Libby realized Beck was making a joke about her speeding, she laughed, letting the lightness of the moment carry her past the grief that would still come at the thought of the children they could never have.

After they finished dinner and did the dishes, Libby thought they would drive the four-wheeler to the house site. But Beck had other ideas. She was hanging the dish towel over the oven-door handle when he came up behind her, encircling her with his arms.

She leaned against him. "What are you doing?"

"Thinking about something better for dessert than that fancy peach ice cream." His breath stirred the fine hairs at her temple, raising a rash of warm, goosefleshed desire.

Libby turned in his embrace, and when he kissed her, she arched against him. It had been a while since they'd made love, long enough that the suspicion she'd believed she'd rid herself of years ago had returned, a demon that sat in a dark corner of her mind, and in unguarded moments, it would taunt her, asking: *What if history is repeating itself? What if he's cheating on you again?* She hated having that voice in her head, hated the paranoia that gave life to her doubt. A marriage couldn't work in an atmosphere of suspicion. Libby hadn't needed the counselor they'd seen at the time of Beck's betrayal to explain that to her. She hadn't even needed the benefit of her own expertise in the field to know that taking Beck back meant her forgiveness of him had to be bone deep—soul deep—or it wouldn't work.

That much was common sense.

She leaned back in his embrace, locking his gaze. "It'll be dark soon—too dark to see the work they did getting ready for the slab pour tomorrow."

"You said it was fine. That's good enough." He bent his head, kissing her again, sliding his hands up the bare lengths of her arms, making her shiver, making her ache with wanting him.

Together, they fumbled their way into the bedroom. They were like—not teenagers, but heated in the way of the much younger couple they'd once been, when their appetite for each other was fresh and . . . *insatiable*. The word darted through Libby's mind, and it was ridiculous, but she wished she could stop time, hold on to this moment. Once out of their clothes, they lay down, facing each other. Libby ran her hand down Beck's back and over the contour of his hip and buttock, warm and smooth beneath her palm.

She felt greedy with need, but he was in no mood to rush. His eyes were locked on hers as he trailed his fingertips along her hairline and cheek, tipping them from the edge of her jaw to the curve of her shoulder, the fullness of her breast, the dip of her waist. The rueful notion surfaced, as it often did now that she was in her fifties—soon to be sixty—that she'd gone soft. They both had, but she regretted more the changes in herself. It was useless. She knew that. And it wasn't that she wanted to go back, to be again that feckless and often-silly, albeit slim, lithe girl Beck had married.

The girl he had met by accident when he found her sitting white-faced and shaken that day at the hospital, the day Helen had died.

People said three was a crowd, but when Libby and Ruth had met Helen at an SMU freshman mixer, they clicked. Somehow within minutes they'd been bent over laughing, finishing one another's sentences. Within a short time, they were sharing a suite. Helen was the jokester, Ruth was her straight man, and Libby their audience. But the hilarity had ended on one awful day before Christmas break their junior year. Ruth, who to this day had never married, had been out with her current boyfriend, one in a long line, leaving Libby to play both roles, that of straight man and spectator. She'd been the one laughing when Helen, mugging for the camera—Libby was also filming—wound a string of twinkle lights loosely around her head, climbed onto a wobbly bar stool, and while holding a tape dispenser in one hand, reached across the top of the doorway with her other hand, lost her balance and fell, cracking her head on a desk corner. At first, she'd sworn she was fine, but when a fierce headache hours later was followed by nausea and rounds of vomiting, Libby overrode her objections and called an ambulance. Too late. Within hours of reaching the hospital, after suffering a massive stroke, Helen died.

Libby was leaning against the wall outside the triage room when Beck approached her. He'd come up from Houston to visit a client who'd had surgery, and passing Libby in the hallway, he'd thought she was the patient. When she said no and in a broken voice explained why she was there, he'd sat her down gently in the ER waiting room and brought her a paper cup filled with cool water. He found tissues, called Ruth, and stayed until she came. He'd supported them both then.

He was so steady and sure, so quietly brilliant and ordinarily happy, that she'd been astonished to hear, prior to meeting his parents in a Denny's restaurant in downtown Houston, that they were avid consumers of welfare and food stamps and mostly survived on liquor and lottery tickets and pie in the sky. They had died within eleven months of each other, Beck's father of cirrhosis and his mother of hepatitis, a few years after Libby and Beck married.

He touched her temple now. "Where are you?" he asked, and she smiled.

"Thinking how lucky I am," she whispered.

• • •

Libby was dreaming, and in her dream she heard a coyote howl. She recognized the monotonous two-note song of crickets, the chirr of frogs, the whishing of the night wind. But there was another sound, one that didn't seem to belong. It needled at her consciousness. But it was the light that woke her, that sent the dream scuttling behind a door in her mind. She rose on one elbow, blinking when the room was suddenly plunged into blackness again. She could barely make out the dresser's edge, and except for the even draw of Beck's breath to anchor her, she might have thought she was still asleep.

But now light flashed once more over the walls, dousing the room in an eerie glow. Heart tapping, she tossed aside the covers, getting up, but whatever the source was, it was gone by the time she reached the open window. Still, she could hear something in the distance. An engine? Libby glanced at Beck; he hadn't moved. She didn't want to wake him; he was exhausted. She thought of the recent vandalism that Sergeant Huckabee had mentioned and of Ricky Burrows, the guy on Augie's crew whose truck door had been badly keyed here on her property.

Ricky had been pissed. He'd said he didn't have any liability insurance on the truck and couldn't afford to get the damage repaired. He'd looked after the cop, leaving in his shiny near-new squad car that day, and he'd said, "Fucking kids, my ass," under his breath, but he'd meant her to hear, Libby thought. He'd kicked his truck tire. "I'll be driving this piece of shit like this till I die."

Libby had felt bad for him. He was a young guy, midtwenties to early thirties, maybe. Thin, with a wary, hurt look in his eyes, like a stray dog that had been abused. He'd come to Texas from Colorado, Augie had told her, looking to make a fresh start. He was a hard worker, down on his luck.

Likely going nowhere, Libby thought now. She bet the cop wouldn't have been so cavalier that day if it had been her Lexus that had gotten keyed. It made her squirm inside. It made her think of words like *entitlement* and *privilege*. Maybe if she were to go to the Greeley police department and ask them, they would investigate the matter, since the police in Wyatt didn't seem to care. Or maybe, if she asked him personally, Sergeant Huckabee would look into it.

When he'd stopped her, he'd given the impression that he was thorough and professional, that he *did* care. She thought of how he'd driven up behind her and lingered there after they'd both left the road's shoulder. She hadn't mentioned that to Beck because of how it had unnerved her. He'd gotten a radio call, obviously. That's what Beck would say.

The light had disappeared; the room lay in near utter darkness. Libby went back to bed, crawling into it carefully so as not to wake Beck, spooning against him. He pulled her close, murmuring something, and she smiled, drifting. It was only in the subliminal regions of her brain that she registered it, what sounded like a squeal, the same squeal the service gate made every time it was opened or shut.

Her last thought before sleep consumed her, though, was of those children, the ones who had been involved in that awful accident. She really was grateful to have been saved from that particular hell, at least. She couldn't imagine what it must be like as a parent, getting that call in the middle of the night. But neither would she ever resolve the question of what was worse: losing a child or never having one.

5

Sandy's parents returned to the ICU waiting area on the heels of the code-blue call, and they were there when the nurses burst through the ICU doors, three of them, racing alongside a gurney. One of the nurses rushed to where Sandy and her family were standing, rooted, terrified.

"Oh dear God," Sandy heard someone say. Her mother, she thought.

Travis. It was Travis on the gurney. Something had happened to him, something worse . . . That was Sandy's thought.

But no, the nurse stopped in front of her—KAREN, her name tag said—and her eyes were soft with pity, backed by the resignation that must go with her job. The delivery of bad news was inevitable in this place. Somebody had to do it. Sandy felt sorry for her.

"Jordan's blood pressure," Karen said. "It just suddenly nose-dived."

Nose-dived. Sandy would remember that word. She would remember thinking it was what planes did, or stocks. A stock could take a nosedive. You could lose everything. She would remember hurrying beside the gurney bearing her son into an elevator. She would remember looking at him, her eyes fastened in horror on the only part of him that was visible: his head, his face—his swollen, disfigured, unrecognizable, precious, and once-beautiful face. She would remember Showalter, the two minutes' worth of explanation he gave them in the surgical waiting area. She'd watched his mouth make the words, retaining only a few: *blood in the gut, organ rupture, laceration.* They would open Jordy, Showalter said.

Like a book, Sandy thought.

Emmett had been angry. "You said there was no sign of internal bleeding."

Showalter had shrugged. Win some, lose some. He might have said it, for all Sandy knew.

It was midmorning now. Saturday? Sandy wasn't sure. Hours had passed, or what felt like hours. "What is taking so long?" She spoke from where she stood, looking through the windowed door down the deserted corridor where they'd taken Jordy. "Why doesn't someone tell us something?"

"Come and sit down." Her mother patted the seat of the faux leather–upholstered chair beside her.

But Sandy couldn't abandon her vigil to sit next to her mom, whose anguish, despite her aura of calm, was as palpable as Sandy's own.

"Look, Emmett's back. He's brought coffee."

Sandy turned as Emmett crossed the waiting area, bearing a small cardboard tray that held three paper cups. Steam rose from the rims. She didn't want it, but she took the cup when he handed it to her, feeling the heat through its thin paper walls soak the cold palms of her hands. She met his gaze, but only for a moment. It was all she could stand; he looked so haggard, the fear she felt herself was so raw in his eyes. There was something else there, too, that she recognized—it was helplessness, and she knew how it felt, that they might lose their son, their child, and there was nothing they could do to stop it.

"I went by the ICU," he said.

"How is Travis?" Sandy's mom asked. "Any change?"

"No." Emmett sat next to her. "They're saying—Jenna says they keep telling her the same thing every hour: there's no response, no brain activity." He raised his cup, then lowered it without drinking.

Sandy resumed her post by the surgical-room doors. The image of her face, reflected in the glass, was as faint as that of a ghost's. Her ears rang. Panic held her heart in its unyielding fist. *Please please please.* The word echoed through her brain as if begging were her last and only resort.

Her mother asked about Michelle. "Jenna said that right as they got her to the hospital, she had a stroke."

"Yeah. Still in a coma, last we heard." Emmett went on, saying even more useless things that didn't matter, like the whole situation was *god-awful* and it shouldn't have *happened*. As if that wasn't already apparent, Sandy thought. She didn't really care, wasn't even really paying attention, not until he started in repeating the totally pointless what-ifs: "What if Michelle doesn't make it? What if Travis—"

"Stop it!" Sandy wheeled, heedless when hot coffee sloshed over the rim of her cup, burning her fingers. "Stop awfulizing. I'm sick of it! It's all bad enough."

"We've got to face facts, babe." Emmett's look was resigned, bleak. "I'm trying to think, do we even know a lawyer? Jordy's going to need representation, a good criminal attorney."

Sandy stared at Emmett. *If he lives.* The words rose in her mind, but she pushed them down. She couldn't say them, couldn't let herself think them—not about Jordy, Travis, or Michelle.

"The cops in Wyatt had it in for Jordy even before this happened. God only knows what kind of charges they'll lay on him now."

"What do you mean, Emmett?" Sandy's mother asked.

He looked contrite. He hadn't meant to raise the issue, to spark her curiosity, because of where it would lead. Sandy could see the regret on his face. Her mother thought the world of Len Huckabee. The whole family—the entire town did. He'd done the hardest thing a cop ever had to do when he'd gone to Jenna's door in San Antonio to tell her that her husband, his best friend and partner, had been shot and killed in the line of duty, trying to stop a couple of bank robbers—with Huck's own gun. Jenna had blamed the crooks, but Huck had blamed himself, and ever since, he'd devoted himself to Jenna and Trav.

He was part of the family. That was how they thought about him. That was why Huck's professional harassment of Jordy as a Wyatt police officer was so hard to understand. Jordy wouldn't talk about it, and when Sandy and Emmett had questioned Huck, he'd acted as if he didn't know what they were complaining about. *Jordy broke the law, simple as that,* Huck had said. *You could have worse problems with him, trust me,* he'd said.

"It's nothing, Mom," Sandy said now. "Huck's given Jordy a hard time lately, stopping him for the least little thing."

An elevator bell dinged faintly in the silence. The squeal of rubber soles approached and fell away. A voice over the PA system asked for a Dr. Van Zandt to come to the third-floor nurses' station.

Emmett said, "Harvey saw Trav."

Sandy set her coffee down untasted. "They let Daddy in?"

"Really?" Her mother's surprise echoed Sandy's own.

"Yeah, I guess because he's Travis's granddad. It was only for a minute. Harvey said it was hard. It shook him up."

Sandy thought seeing her dad shook-up had shaken Emmett.

He took out his cell phone and held it, staring at it. "I've got to call Grant, see if he can cover for me." Emmett looked up, blinking. "Man, I'm not sure I can talk about it."

Without breaking apart, he meant. Sandy hadn't even thought about work. She remembered she had two consultations, one today and one on Monday, that she'd have to cancel. And the koi-pond install. That was scheduled for Wednesday. She doubted this was going to be over by then. She didn't have anyone to cover for her, really, other than Hector and his crew. They helped her with the installation of the gardens she designed, but she met with the home owners and drew up the plans. At least it was summer; the hottest part of the year was her slow time. It was different for Emmett. There wasn't really a slow time in the oil industry.

"I guess Dad will have to put off retiring for a bit," her mom said. "Not that he was that serious about it."

Her mother wanted it more than her dad. She was ready to travel, do things other than work. Sandy didn't blame her. She'd helped them sell their home in Wyatt and move into their patio home in a community for older folks, where lawn-care and housekeeping services were provided if you wanted it. You could even have your meals brought in or walk to a centrally located restaurant if you didn't feel like cooking. But her dad still came to the office in Wyatt a couple of times a week; he and Emmett would drive around and talk to customers together. Emmett missed him, though. He'd been used to running with her dad almost every day. They'd go as much as five miles, sometimes more. They'd competed in marathons together.

It had started when Emmett was in high school. Her dad had coached him on the side when he joined the track team. Even then no one had questioned the notion that Emmett would go to work for her dad after he got his business degree from the U of H. It was the motivation for hiring on as a roughneck, so he could learn the business from the ground up. It was Emmett's nature to be thorough and methodical, to follow a plan. As long ago as their high school days, Emmett had talked about how important it was to do the grunt work. The shit work, he called it. He wasn't too proud to get dirty, to work hard. He'd work till he dropped, if that's what the job took. The guys he bossed now respected him; they looked up to him.

Jordy admired him, too, but he didn't share his dad's drive, his no-nonsense work ethic, or his sense of responsibility. They'd fought about it in May when the letter came from UT, advising Sandy and Emmett that Jordy was on scholastic probation. Jenna had gotten a letter, too, telling her Trav had made the dean's list. Sandy had barely been able to offer congratulations. Emmett had yelled about the money Jordy was pissing down the drain, not to mention his future. He'd accused Jordy of being a slacker. Sandy thought Emmett was too hard on Jordy.

Emmett had dismissed her concern. "We're throwing our hard-earned money down the drain while he wastes time," he'd said.

Neither one of them had talked about the way in which Jordy might be wasting time; they hadn't considered that his poor performance might be the result of excessive partying and drinking. Instead, Sandy had brought up the past.

"You wasted time. Remember?" she'd said. "When you took off and went to Berkeley in the middle of our junior year, when you decided you didn't want to be tied down? How many hours did you lose—that my dad helped you pay for?" Sandy had regretted bringing up all that old business, but she'd felt pushed to remind Emmett that even he wasn't perfect. "I thought I'd never see you again," she'd told him, loud voiced, offended.

They'd gone to bed angry, slept little, and woken up still fuming and feeling as if they were hungover. Sandy cringed now from the memory. Jordy had been in need of guidance, a firm hand; there had been all kinds of warning signs, but she and Emmett had left him to founder. Shame rose hot and thick in her throat. She had never wanted to be that sort of mother, the one who clings to her delusions, who can't face the facts.

"Grant sends prayers," Emmett said. "He wanted to know if there was anything he or Brenda could do."

"They're always so nice," Sandy said.

Grant Kennedy had worked for the company going on twenty years. He and his wife, Brenda, were close friends of her parents, and god-grandparents, an honorary title they'd laughingly created, to both Jordy and Travis.

"He offered to donate blood. Harvey and I talked about it, too."

Sandy turned to look at Emmett.

"In case Jordy needs more than the transfusion he's getting now."

"Aunt Frances had a transfusion once," Sandy's mother said. "When we were girls, she fell off a horse and fractured her shin so badly the bone broke through her skin. She lost a lot of blood before they got her to the hospital."

"I remember that story," Sandy said. "You almost fainted." Frances was gone now. She and her mother, Sandy's grandma Florence, had died of breast cancer within three years of each other a little over seven years ago now. It was Sandy's mom's insistence on regular mammograms that had saved Jenna's life. So far.

Emmett bent his elbows onto his knees. "If I'd done it before, Jordy could be getting my blood now instead of some stranger's."

Sandy went to him and sat beside him, and he pulled her against him, as if she were a rock he could hang onto, when he said, "I wish I could take this on for him. I wish it was me in there." His voice caught on the words.

Sandy bit her teeth together to stall the press of her tears. On the other side of Emmett, she heard her mother say, "You're a good man, Emmett, a good father," and she closed her eyes, feeling them burn from fatigue and sorrow and panic. *What about me, Mama? Am I a good mother? A good person?* The query fell, unbidden, a specter down from the attic of her mind, and it hung there, unvoiced.

• • •

"What's he doing here?" Emmett straightened.

Sandy looked at the lawman in uniform who was crossing the waiting-room floor toward them. He was from Wyatt. Not Huck. A different patrol officer. He was young, late twenties, maybe early thirties.

New on the job, Sandy thought. His mother might have pressed the crease into his uniform pants; she might have shined his badge with her hankie and told him how proud she was of him before he left the house to work his shift.

He wanted to know if they were Jordy's parents, and Emmett said they were, getting to his feet. "What's this about?" he asked.

Sandy stood up, too, and so did her mother, taking Sandy's hand. Her grasp was dry and cool.

"I'm Patrol Sergeant Ken Carter," the cop said. "I worked the accident scene with Sergeant Huckabee."

"You're the one who called us," Sandy said.

"Yes, ma'am. I'm real sorry for what you folks are going through."

"What do want, Sergeant?" Emmett wasn't buying the lawman's sympathy.

"I need to get your son's statement is all."

"Obviously that's not possible right now," Sandy's mother pointed out sharply.

Sandy had heard friends of her mother's call her feisty. *That Penny Galbraith,* they'd say, *you don't want to get on her bad side!* Growing up, Sandy had seen only rare flashes of her mother's temper. She was ordinarily calm and almost always up for fun. Jordy and Travis adored her. Everyone did.

The sergeant was wearing a sorrowful look. Maybe he'd been told to put it on like part of his uniform. "It's my job," he said.

"Huck told Jenna that Jordy was driving. Is that right?" Sandy felt Emmett's glance, but she kept her gaze on Carter.

He looked off in the direction of the corridor he'd come out of.

"Sergeant? Is that your conclusion, too? Was my son driving?"

"Yes, ma'am, I'm afraid so."

"I think you should wait somewhere else." Sandy's mother sat down, pulling Sandy down beside her.

Carter started to go.

Emmett stopped him. "How come it's you here to question Jordy? Where's Huck? Isn't he the officer in charge of the accident investigation, or is it you?"

Sandy knew what Emmett was thinking—hoping, really—that they wouldn't have to deal with Huck. But that hope was short-lived.

"He's on a call, but he'll stop by later," Carter said.

"Give him a message for me, will you? Tell him we're contacting a lawyer. My son—in fact, no one in this family is going to talk to you guys without an attorney present."

"I'll tell him." Carter paused, and after a moment, when no one spoke, he said, "Okay, then . . . good luck."

Good luck? Sandy and her mother exchanged a half smile, but her mother's eyes were troubled. Sandy could almost see her sorting through the turmoil in her brain, the painful awareness that her loyalty was about to be ripped in half. Would she believe Jordy if he told her to her face he wasn't driving? *Would anyone believe Jordy?* Sandy wondered.

• • •

It was almost noon before Dr. Showalter came to talk to them. "Jordy's doing well. He's in recovery now."

"Can we see him?" Sandy asked.

"They'll be taking him to the ICU soon. It's a precaution. We'll want to monitor him for the next twenty-four hours or so. You can see him there."

"But what happened?" Emmett wanted answers. "What caused the bleeding?"

"It was the tiniest laceration to his liver, so small it didn't show up on the initial scans. It happens."

"It happens," Showalter said, Sandy thought later, *instead of "shit happens."* That saying she hated. Probably because it was true. Otherwise she wouldn't be sitting here in the ICU waiting room on a Saturday.

She wouldn't be in this hellish place, waiting for her son to come fully back to her, a thing she both longed for and dreaded.

Because somewhere in the grim reaches of this hospital, Patrol Sergeant Ken Carter was waiting, too, for the same thing.

. . .

They were sitting in the row of padded chairs against the back wall of the ICU visitors' room—Sandy, her parents, Jenna, Troy, and Emmett. *Like sitting ducks,* Sandy thought. *Easy prey, fish in a barrel.* Her dad was on the end, bent over the pages of *Time* magazine, an old issue with Donald Trump's face on it. Beside him, Troy looked at his phone. Emmett was in the third chair; he stared into the corridor, gaze unfixed. Next to him, Sandy let her head fill with the noise around her, the squeal of rubber-treaded soles on tile flooring, the ding of the elevator, the faceless requests that came from the PA system. Anything to keep from thinking. She couldn't bear to look at her mother's and her sister's hands, twined together, a death grip. They were going to lose Travis. Everyone kept warning them to prepare for it. They kept saying nothing more could be done.

Make your peace. Say good-bye. Tell him all you want him to know.

That was the advice from the nurses, from Reverend Murphy, who had come to pray with them every couple of hours or so. Sandy did not pray. *What God?* she wanted to ask the reverend. *Don't speak to me of miracles or acceptance,* she wanted to tell him. *Don't mention God's will to me.* If it would not have horrified her parents, offended their sensibilities—they were faithful attendees of their Methodist church—Sandy would have said these things.

She was thinking of that, and of how much she would like to order the good reverend to leave them alone, when Emmett stood up, and while she did register what he was doing, a voice in her brain was still holding forth, telling the reverend to go: *Take your stupid God with you and don't come back,* so that when Emmett spoke, when he said, "I'm going to donate blood," while she did hear him, she didn't really register his intent.

She did note it when her dad looked up from his magazine and said he would come, too, and she was aware of the others looking at Emmett, but she had no thought of foreboding, no sense of dread, which would seem astonishing in hindsight, except, in her defense, she had already been exposed to so much dread in such a short period of time that perhaps in that moment, she was immune.

Emmett walked into the corridor, but then he came back. "What if no one had figured it out? Jordy could have bled to death internally, you know?" He looked around at them. "Because of Showalter's screwup, missing that his liver was damaged. What if he's missed something else? What if Jordy needs more blood?" He paused and cleared his throat, obviously agitated. "I'm his dad," he began again, and his voice caught in a way that pierced Sandy's heart.

"You aren't his dad," Jenna said.

Sandy looked at her.

"What?" Emmett was looking at Jenna, too.

"I said you aren't his dad."

6

"What is that stench?" Libby asked. It hit her as soon as she and Beck got out of his truck at the homesite. The air was saturated with it, something as sweet as it was acrid and sickening. She was thinking *blood* when Beck said it.

"A lot of it," he added. "Close by, I think."

Her heart stuttered.

They had parked off to one side of the construction site, keeping the road clear for the concrete trucks. Although it was still early, not quite seven, they were due at any time.

"Maybe someone hit a deer out on the highway." Libby joined Beck.

"Could be," Beck said, though he didn't sound certain, and his wariness raised the hair on Libby's arms. She walked with him, and as they drew nearer to the slab framework, the smell became overwhelming.

"Holy Christ." Beck saw it first. "I think that's a hog." He went closer. "It's a goddamn wild hog. Somebody has gutted a hog, sliced the damn thing open from head to ass end, and strung it up in our tree."

He was pissed, offended. It was the giant cedar, the ancient druid that at Libby's instruction, he had taken pains to protect.

"Was it hunters?" she asked.

Feral pigs were a plague all over Texas. They had been for years. She and her dad had shot their share of them along with their allotment of deer in season. If they couldn't use the meat, they'd donated it to a food kitchen. A lot of people did.

A breeze smartened, making the rope that bore the eviscerated hog's weight creak. It was a sound from a nightmare, a horror movie. Still, Libby was glad to have the air move, to have the stench of blood and entrails carried away.

"If it was hunters," Beck said, "they weren't after the meat."

Augie's truck came into view, and within minutes, he joined them. "Y'all been hunting hogs, have you?"

"Yeah," Beck answered. "We wanted your breakfast bacon to be extra fresh this morning."

"Hot damn. I like that. I take my eggs over easy, but not too easy." He grinned, then sobered. "Really, that is one big son of a bitch. Who brought it down?" Augie went closer, apparently impervious to the smell.

"That's what we'd like to know," Beck said. He pulled his cell phone from his pocket. "Let's ask the police." He called the office number rather than 911, and whoever answered said someone would come out.

It was after Beck ended the call, when they walked over to the building site, that they found the damage to the form for the slab. It looked as if someone had used a crowbar to wrench it apart. Random two-by-fours had been shattered, the plumbing pipe bent, and the electrical conduit and plastic moisture barrier slashed. Much of the wreckage was blood soaked and smeared with the hog's entrails. Its heart—Libby recognized the organ—was impaled on a piece of rebar that had been jerked upright near the front entryway. Had she not had the experience of hunting, had she not shot and dressed her first deer under her daddy's supervision just days before her tenth birthday, she might have fled. But the gore, as bad as it was, wasn't what bothered her the worst. No. It was the utter wantonness of the devastation.

Augie said it first, what they all knew. "I don't see how the concrete can be poured today."

Beck grabbed a mangled section of rebar and flung it as far as he could into the nearby cedar brake, where it landed with a ringing thud.

Augie took out his phone and said he'd try and head off the concrete trucks.

Libby looked back at the gutted hog carcass, twitching in the early-morning breeze, huge head lolled to the side, tongue protruding swollen and red, making its mouth appear more like a wound. Was it a prank? Was this how country kids joked around?

They were sitting on camp stools upwind of the butchered hog, drinking coffee from the thermos Libby had brought, when the patrol car from Wyatt pulled in beside Beck's truck. Libby recognized the sergeant as soon as he stepped outside.

"That's the cop who stopped me for speeding," she said quietly to Beck.

"Better watch your step, then." He grinned briefly.

Joining them, Sergeant Huckabee found her gaze. "Thought you said when we met again it'd be under better circumstances."

She smiled. She remembered saying that. "Well, at least nobody's speeding."

The sergeant shook hands with Beck and Augie. Nodding downwind, he said, "Looks like somebody's been doing some hunting."

"Yeah," Beck said, "and I'd appreciate it if they did it somewhere else."

"Especially if they're going to leave such a mess," Libby said.

"What do you make of it, Huck?" Augie asked. "Had to be somebody pretty big to string up that animal. It's got to be close to two hundred pounds. You see the tusks on that sucker?"

Libby said, "We called the police out here before, when one of the construction workers—Ricky Burrows is his name—his truck was keyed. The officer who came said it was kids, but this is more than that, don't you think?"

"I dunno." Huckabee walked around the animal. The flies had begun to find it now that the sun was up, and the carcass was crawling with them. "There's some good-size young guys around here who like nothing better than to chase these wild hogs all over this county. They're good with a knife, too."

"But to hang it like that—in our tree—and not even take the meat—" Libby couldn't accept that it was kids.

"They might not know this is your property now. They could have been drinking or high on something."

"I could believe that," Beck said, "if there was any evidence of it. But there's not. Not even a beer can."

"Did either of you hear anything last night?" Huckabee divided his glance between Beck and Libby.

She thought how she'd been wakened by some kind of noise. She remembered the light that swamped the bedroom walls, and she described all of this. She mentioned the squeal that might have been the service gate and said, "It could have been part of a dream."

"You never told me," Beck said.

"Honestly, until now, I'd forgotten."

"About what time was this?" Huckabee asked.

"Around four, I think."

Huckabee continued his inspection, examining the damaged slab framework, squatting to look more closely at the mess of tire tracks, footprints—all the signs of disturbance in the area that Libby, Beck, and Augie had already looked at before his arrival—and he came to the same conclusion. None of it was much use.

"There's no way to tell who did this, is there?" Augie said.

"Or catch them," Libby added.

"I'd like to shoot the bastards," Beck said.

"Now, don't go talking like that." Huckabee straightened.

"This is the second time in a month we've had you all out here," Libby reminded him.

"Yes, ma'am. We'll step up patrol of this area, and I'll talk to folks, too. Maybe somebody knows something."

A silence came and stayed through a handful of heartbeats.

Huckabee broke it. "Anybody you know with an ax to grind?"

"All my enemies live in Houston," Beck said. He told Huckabee about the lawsuit, and the various threats that had been made. "But the architects, me included, were severed from the suit as of yesterday. We're in no way considered liable."

"Maybe somebody didn't get the message," Huckabee said.

"Maybe," Beck said. "But it's a hell of a drive, coming all the way from Houston to butcher a hog. And what for? What's it supposed to do? Scare me?"

No one answered.

Beck spread his hands. "It makes no damn sense."

"No, but folks can get crazy." Huckabee widened his stance, eyes considering the long view. "Especially when they're angry and looking to blame someone."

"Yeah," Beck said, "but it's hard for me to imagine that the hog and the lawsuit are related." He shook his head. "It's crazy even for crazy."

"But didn't some of the people—the plaintiffs in the suit—weren't their cars keyed like Ricky's truck?"

"Cars get keyed all the time, Libby." Beck sounded impatient.

"Yeah, it happens," Huckabee agreed. The sergeant passed his glance from Beck to Libby. "I'd advise you to keep your doors locked, ma'am."

"I think you suggested that before," she said.

"Never hurts to repeat it." He smiled.

"An ounce of prevention," she said, but the joke wasn't well received. "I've got a shotgun. Belonged to my dad, and I know how to use it."

"Well, I've got a buddy on the force in Houston," Huckabee said. "I'll touch base with him, get him looking into the possibility of a connection on that end. Meanwhile, here's my card. You can call anytime, okay?"

Libby nodded, taking the card. She wondered if he meant it, about contacting his buddy. When it came to crime, on a scale of one to ten, she doubted a slaughtered hog and a few keyed cars flew very high on the radar.

Sergeant Huckabee said he had business in Austin.

Augie straightened. "You going to see Trav and Jordy? How are they? Do you know?"

"Not good." Huckabee looked at the ground, and Libby had the sense he was taking time to prepare them, or himself, perhaps, for the hard thing he had to say. And she was wondering which one of the boys had died when he said it, that Travis Simmons hadn't made it.

The passenger, she thought.

And over Augie's "Oh God" and Beck's "Jesus," Huckabee said, "Jordy's in pretty deep shit," and then he apologized, his eyes grazing Libby's. She waved him off.

"You're arresting him?" Augie asked.

"Don't have much choice," Huckabee said. "He was driving, and his blood alcohol was more than twice the legal limit. In the state of Texas, you drive drunk and kill somebody, it's manslaughter."

Libby wasn't sure, but she thought she detected an element of satisfaction in Huckabee's voice, some degree of smugness, as if he were happy about the circumstances. But she dismissed the notion. It wasn't plausible.

. . .

They dug a proper grave for the hog using Augie's backhoe, which had been left at the site. Libby considered it a fortuitous gift. "Imagine if all you had was a shovel," she said when they'd finished the job.

"I'd let the carcass rot," Beck said.

"Let the coyotes take it," Augie said.

It was hotter now; the breeze had mostly died. Both men were sweaty and red-faced. She ought to have brought water, Libby thought.

Beck's phone buzzed.

Augie gave a salute. "I'll call y'all," he said. "Let me know if you want to stand guard. I'll bring my twenty-two. We'll catch the bastards."

"Thanks, buddy." Beck grinned. He answered his phone.

Libby walked Augie to his truck and came back.

"That was Robert," Beck said. "You won't believe it." He held Libby's gaze.

"What?" She felt the faint stirring of fresh alarm.

"He found a dead coon gutted on the hood of his car this morning. Somebody had opened it up, taken out the organs, and scattered them around it—sound familiar?"

"You're joking," Libby said.

"I told him he got off easy."

"Beck, I don't believe this. Did he call the police? Should we let Sergeant Huckabee know?"

"Yeah, I guess. Can you call him?" He headed for the truck, Libby trailing him. "I need to get back to the cottage, get a shower, and get on the road. Robert wants to get the media involved, hold a press conference with the plaintiff's attorneys. He wants them to make it clear we're not the ones responsible for what happened to the folks who died when that balcony collapsed."

"Well, it makes sense, getting the word out. That should put a stop to this—this—whatever it is."

"If the whack job who's responsible is even tuned in, listening."

They got into Beck's truck. He keyed the ignition.

"It must be more than one whack job." Libby looked at Beck.

He was looking over his shoulder, backing up.

"There's no way the same person could have slaughtered two different animals in Houston and out here in one night, is there? The drive one way is almost five hours."

"I don't think you should stay out here alone." He pulled onto the service road. Dust rose on either side of the truck, making wings.

"But if I leave, too, Augie might move on to some other project."

"Maybe we should let him until we figure out what's going on. You're too isolated here."

"I have Dad's shotgun. I'll be fine." She'd brought it to the cottage their first trip out after they closed on the property. It was never a bad idea to have a gun handy when you lived in the boonies. "Anything moves, I'll shoot first, ask questions later." She smiled.

Beck sighed. "Who knew I was married to Annie Oakley."

Libby punched his arm. "I can take care of myself, and you know it."

"I don't like it."

"But once the word gets out through the media, I bet whoever is behind this will either stop or get caught."

"I'll come back as soon as I can."

"Yes," Libby said. "You have to, because we were supposed to go to that salvage place today, remember? The one that could very possibly have the big ceiling beams we're looking for."

She kissed him before he left, winding her arms around his neck, lingering, wishing he didn't have to go.

He held her gaze. "I don't know what it is," he said, "but out here with you, I feel like a new man—twenty years younger, at least."

She laughed.

He rocked his eyes up, looking at the sky, shouting out, "God!" And then, leveling his glance, said in a low, husky voice, "I want to stay, rip off your clothes, eat that peach ice cream in the freezer from your belly button."

"You never did that twenty years ago," she said.

He folded her in close. "If I didn't, I should have. When I get back here, I'm going to."

"Promises, promises," she murmured, and she was making light of it, but something in his voice, some note of tender regret, pulled at her heart. She searched his gaze. "You aren't sorry for our life together so far, are you? Because I'm not. I wouldn't trade any of it."

"No," he said. "Only the pain I caused you." He took a moment, his gaze resting on her. "You know, I've been thinking, we don't have to pursue—" He stopped, looked away, looked back. "What I'm trying to say is that just because we're finally here doesn't mean we have to go through with anything. You understand that, right?" He tipped up her chin. "I never want you to be hurt like that again."

Libby was surprised when her throat closed, when her eyes filled with tears.

He wiped them with his thumbs. "I should get on the road," he said, and he smiled. "The circus is waiting."

• • •

"What are you doing out there alone?" Ruth wanted to know when Libby called her that evening and caught her up on all that had happened. "Come into town now and stay with me till Beck gets back."

But Libby said no. She was happy where she was, tucked into the corner of an old chintz-covered settee. The night had cooled off, as it often did in the hill country, and she'd opened the windows. A breeze ruffled the wisp of embroidered linen she'd tacked up over the living-room window, sending moon-driven shadows trembling over the walls.

"Are you sure?" Ruth wanted to know.

She was, Libby said. "I'm not letting a bunch of kids run me off my property."

"Kids?"

"That's who Sergeant Huckabee thinks is behind it."

"Him." Ruth huffed the word.

"You don't like him?"

"It's not that." She heaved a little sigh. "He wants me to hire his wife, his little *chica*, Coleta."

"Augie mentioned her. He said if I were to ask you about her, I should stand back."

The sound Ruth made was half laugh, half snort of disgust.

"Augie said she's young." Libby said.

"Yeah, you could say that. Huck could be her dad. Wait till you see her. She's gorgeous, boobs out to here, tiny waist, and her skin—my God, I don't think she has a single pore."

"I hate her already." Libby was teasing.

"Me, too." They shared a beat of silence, then Ruth said, "She's trying to get green-card status."

"She's here illegally?"

"Not exactly. She let her visa run out. She would have been deported if Huck hadn't married her. But there's still a lot of rigmarole to go through, forms and stuff; it's a long process, and part of it requires that Coleta be able to speak and write in English. She's taking a class, but Huck thinks if she works in the office with me and the other agents, she'll learn faster, and I'd be fine with it, I guess—"

"But?" Libby prompted.

"Nothing in particular. Some folks in town think she only married Huck to get citizenship, that she'll leave him flat once she has it, and that's just wrong, doing that to him, especially now that they have a child together. Hold on, can you. Clemmie wants out."

Clemmie was Ruth's Aussie, and so sweet natured Libby had threatened to dognap her.

Ruth had never married, although she had always had a man in her life. Her current guy was the head of some hotshot Internet-based business in Santa Monica. They'd been together for eight years, seeing each other every couple of months or so. Like Libby, Ruth had no children.

The difference was that she'd never wanted them. She was a dog lover, she would say. They made the perfect companion.

She should get a dog, Libby thought. She thought of the peach ice cream in the freezer, what Beck had said about eating it from her navel—her fiftysomething navel. It was ridiculous; it made her groan inwardly even as it made her smile.

"Sorry." Ruth came back on the line. "What were we talking about?"

"Coleta."

"Oh yeah. Well, honestly, I am totally gossiping here—you know, baseball may be the national pastime, but here in Wyatt, it's gossiping. I was bound to get sucked into it sooner or later."

Libby laughed.

"Just wait," Ruth said. "You'll be doing it, too."

"Augie was telling me he gets all his information from Mandy, his wife."

"Oh," Ruth said, "she is the worst. Sweet as can be, but can she talk. That old saying comes to mind—telegram, telephone, tele-Mandy."

"You're terrible," Libby said. "But since we're talking, isn't it considered fraud when a marriage is arranged for the sole purpose of gaining citizenship? Wouldn't Coleta be deported if immigration were to find out? Lose custody of her—" Libby laughed again, interrupting herself. "God, you're right. I'm gossiping like a pro, and I'm only living here part-time so far."

Ruth snorted. "Told you. I think it's all a bunch of hooey, anyway. People around here don't have enough drama in their own lives. They always want to go around stirring it up in someone else's."

"I'm glad I live out here in the sticks."

"Yeah, except for finding the occasional gutted hog swinging from a tree, what's not to like? Are you sure you won't come stay with me?"

"I'm already in my pj's, thinking of raiding the fridge for peach ice cream and watching the ID channel."

"Oh, you and your crime shows. Have you ever considered you might have a problem?"

Libby laughed. It was true; she loved them all. *Dateline, 48 Hours,* and everything IDTV. Beck teased her, saying he was afraid to sleep nights for fear of all the ways she might be planning to do him in. "You think I should find a twelve-step program?"

"Ha! Listen here, tootsie, if you change your mind or get scared, just come over, hear me? I don't care if you wake me up."

Libby said, "Sure," and "Thank you," but she knew she'd be fine. After all, didn't she have her dad's shotgun?

· · ·

On Sunday morning, she called the number on the card Sergeant Huckabee had given her, and when he didn't answer, she left a message, telling him about Beck's partner, Robert, finding the raccoon's entrails smeared on his car in Houston. "I thought you should know," she said, "so you could pass it along to your friend on the force down there." She left the cottage after that and drove to Yesterday's News, the salvage warehouse near Fredericksburg, to look at the beams. Beck had called earlier and told her to go, that he had no idea when he'd make it back. The news conference wasn't going to happen until two o'clock that afternoon. Meanwhile, he was dealing with a client he called a pain in the ass. Beck had said it might be Wednesday before he saw her again. Unless she came home. To Houston, he meant. He was still worried about her being at the cottage alone. But she'd repeated she was fine.

"I know I'm being a pain in the ass, too," she'd said.

He'd laughed. "But what an ass it is."

Yesterday's News turned out to be a vintage lover's gold mine. In addition to a lean-to housing dozens of rough-hewn barn beams, there were three warehouses packed to the rafters with everything from doors and windows to porch columns, beadboard, and hardwood flooring.

There were oddities—a table made from a cypress knot, an iron lung, a rusted casket roller. Libby snapped a picture of that and texted it to Ruth with a note: See what ur missing?

Ruth texted back: I may need that later. Clients n la-la land! How much?

Libby grinned and texted: Stick with wine; it's way cheaper. I'll buy.

Ur on! Ruth responded.

Before Libby left she bought an old bee skep and talked to the owner, a gruff old man who told her he'd give her a 20 percent discount if she bought three or more of the beams.

"Can't beat that," Libby said, adding she'd have to wait until her husband got back. "He's the one with the truck."

"I was you, I'd bring a trailer to haul them things outta here," the old man advised.

Libby thanked him. She wouldn't have known, she said. "He's been saying we need a trailer," she told the old guy. "Now he's got an excuse to buy one."

· · ·

Somehow going home to the cottage, she ended up on CR 440, passing the accident scene again. There was only one vehicle parked there now, a pale-green vintage pickup truck with the name EJS Landscape Design painted on the door. The mementos that had been left behind only days ago—the sympathy cards and hand-printed messages, the flowers, candleholders and candles—had been blown about by the wind. They were caught in the tall clumps of grass; they scrimmed the broken fence line like so much fading party trash. Libby slowed as she neared the parked truck. A woman sat behind the steering wheel, staring into the field. Only the back of her head was visible, but Libby could see she was blonde and wore her hair in a messy ponytail. She turned as

Libby drew abreast of her, and her eyes locked with Libby's. She looked exhausted and sad.

Stricken.

The word surfaced in Libby's mind. She was related to one of the kids, Libby thought, possibly even one of the mothers. She looked the right age to be the parent of a twentysomething. Libby felt a commiserating pang of sorrow. Who by a certain time in life didn't suffer the heartrending loss of someone they loved? And sometimes death came so suddenly, taking a person who was way too young. Like this boy. Like Helen.

Libby's eyes smarted. She nodded at the woman and drove on, hurriedly, slowing only when she remembered having been stopped for speeding before on this road. She looked in the rearview, half expecting to see the flashing strobe of red and blue lights, but there was no one there.

• • •

Libby checked on the homesite before driving to the cottage, walking the ground around the shattered slab framework, but she found no further signs of damage. She paused on her future front porch, letting her gaze fly over the highway to the hills. Even in the glare of the sun's unforgiving eye, they were peaceful to look upon, a row of round-shouldered old men, caped in verdigrised shades of green and gold, inscrutable faced, eternal. She would sit here with Beck, evenings, she thought. At dusk the cardinals would come. Soon after there would be fireflies, hummingbird moths. They would come to the mountain laurel she would plant just there, off the porch's deepest corner. Imagining this, her heart flooded with joy. She couldn't wait to begin. A thought swam through her brain, that her vision was too perfect. But there had always been so much goodness in her life, enough that at times she felt compelled to apologize: *I'm sorry my childhood was so happy, stable, abundant.* It was only after she learned that the one blessing she longed for most—a child—would be denied her that she thought there was a price for having been given so much when she was young, that possibly there was such a thing as too much good, too much joy. The truth was that light required darkness.

At the cottage, she lifted the bee skep carefully out of the backseat and carried it onto the porch, setting it on the old table she'd found a few weeks ago while out junking with Ruth. Stepping back, she admired it. She wondered if she could learn to keep bees. Beck would probably laugh at her. He certainly wouldn't be able to tend them with her, though. He was allergic.

She was opening the front door, juggling her phone and purse, when some prescient sense of alarm tripped inside her brain. She didn't know what caused her sudden unease, but then it came to her that she hadn't had to unlock the door, the door she was certain she'd locked behind her this morning. After yesterday, the gutted pig, she was hyper-vigilant. Last night she'd checked and double-checked the windows and doors, making sure they were all locked up tight. She'd loaded her dad's shotgun and propped it against the wall by the night table.

She stood right inside the door of the cottage now, listening intently. The stillness enveloped her, feeling eerie, and yet at the same time familiar. Dust sifted idly along feathery air currents. Setting her purse down, she went through the arched doorway into the kitchen. It was a moment before she saw it and another moment before she recognized what it was—that dazzling, iridescent puff of color on the floor.

Hummingbird, said a voice in her mind, while another voice protested, *No.*

She bent over it, making herself take a closer look, but she knew. Knew it was one of the tiny black-chinned hummers that were prolific here, more prolific than the rubythroats she fed in Houston.

"Ooohh . . ." The syllable, a half-despairing groan, escaped her. How had it gotten in? She glanced around at the windows. Locked. She checked the rest of the windows. All locked. Every one. With screens intact.

It wasn't until she went back into the kitchen and crossed the floor to the kitchen-sink counter, intending to tear off a couple of sheets of paper towel to make a kind of shroud for the tiny fallen bird, that she saw the sheet of copy paper and on it the penciled scrawl—not one she recognized—that read:

I thought I told you to keep your doors locked.

7

Rather than three dimensions—past, present, and future—time could more accurately and simply be described as having two: before and after. There was the sweet ordinariness of life before the crash, and there was the nightmare that began after. And in the course of that nightmare's unfolding, there was the routine pause for breath before Jenna announced that Emmett wasn't Jordy's father, and there was the horrible, ringing shock of after.

Sandy would never forget it. Those moments when time slipped past in a vacuum without thought or movement. When even breath and heartbeats were suspended. When the very earth paused on its axis.

The silence lacked air; it lacked even a glimmer of comprehension. Everyone stared. Sandy's stare felt stupid on her face. Looking at Emmett, she found him looking at her, bewilderment lancing his eyes, a half smile wavering on his mouth.

Jenna's making a joke? he seemed to be asking her. *Here? Now? In these circumstances?*

"Jenna!" Sandy found her voice, and Jenna's name shot from her mouth, a warning, a protest, a plea. "What are you doing?" she asked.

Begged, actually, although, honestly, in some part of her brain, she knew it was too late. She thought of that old adage about closing the barn door after the horse gets out.

"Sandy?"

She looked up when Emmett prompted her, meeting his gaze and holding it even though it was hard. "Jordy is yours in every meaningful way a son can belong to his father."

She said what she had believed nearly from the moment Emmett came back to her from Berkeley at the start of her senior year at the U of H, when he'd said leaving her had been the worst mistake of his life and begged her forgiveness. Her joy and relief were overwhelming. She might have fallen right there in the doorway of their apartment, if Emmett hadn't caught her. If he hadn't held on to her.

When they'd made love that day, he had adored her with his mouth, worshipped her with his hands; he had entered her as if she were a priceless treasure. And she had returned his reverence, running her palms along the familiar and sorely missed planes of his shoulders. She had numbered the bones connecting his spine, outlined the smooth, muscled contours of his buttocks. He was her home and she was his.

And it would have been perfect, except she was pregnant, the result of a recent and unfortunate handful of encounters, exactly three, with a man who had mentored her over the summer. Who had been gentle and kind, and suffering from his own grief. And although the affair was over by mutual consent, she knew she had to tell Emmett about it. But every time she tried, panic closed her throat. On the day she finally managed to say it, to say, "I'm pregnant," Emmett misunderstood.

It was seven days after his return—ten days since she'd repeated the test three times that confirmed her nagging dread—and they were walking in Hermann Park. It was late in the afternoon. The light had gone silver, and an unseasonably chilly breeze skittered fallen leaves across their path. There was an urgency in the air; Sandy felt it pressing in on her. Soon it would be Christmas. They would be going home for the holidays. She would be showing by then. She had to tell. *Had to.* And so she did.

"I'm pregnant," she said, and the words came out blunt and hard, as hard as the knowing of their power to destroy her in Emmett's eyes.

She wasn't prepared when he wheeled, his face alight, when he practically shouted, "We're having a baby?" Without waiting for her answer, for the truth, he lifted her, spinning her around until they were dizzy.

His elation had been palpable, as agonizing to her as it was joyful to him. Her mind went blank. She couldn't say what should have been said: *The baby isn't yours.* She had only just gotten him back. She couldn't risk losing him again. And when the very next day she came home from morning classes to find a giant stuffed Tigger sitting on their sofa, with a copy of the Pooh stories and a set of Winnie-the-Pooh baby dishes carefully balanced in Tigger's stuffed lap, her heart stumbled. She thought the dishes were hers, from her childhood, until she read his note, saying he had found them at Macy's.

I remember how much you loved Pooh and Tigger when we were kids. And you will never know how much I love you. After that she thought telling him the truth would be cruel; it would be the same as ripping out his heart. That's when she'd gone to see Jenna, because she had to tell someone.

By then Jenna was married to John, and they were living in San Antonio. John was on the police force there. Sandy had been in fear of how Jenna might react. She was morally conservative, and she could be judgmental, but upon Sandy's arrival, she found that Jenna was bursting with the same news. She was pregnant, too, and in her ebullience—she and John had been trying for almost four years—it was almost as if she didn't register Sandy's troubled confession. They had hugged and laughed and cried, celebrating the prospect of raising their children together, and somehow Sandy's lie became the truth, the way lies do when they're repeated, and what everyone wants to hear anyway.

Once. She had spoken of her brief affair with Jordy's birth father only once, and only to Jenna. Sandy had put it out of her mind after that, deliberately and consistently, and Jenna's reminder now felt foreign, as if it bore no connection to her or her history. It had never crossed Sandy's mind that Jenna would betray her.

"Who is Jordy's dad?" Emmett's voice was hard, inflected with disbelief and offense. *How could she?* it seemed to ask. *How dare she?*

"You left me." Sandy's need to defend herself overwhelmed her. "I didn't think you were coming back."

"It's a guy she worked with," Jenna said.

"Does he know about Jordy?" Emmett asked.

"Yup." Jenna sounded exultant, as if she were pleased with herself.

That tone—Sandy couldn't stand it. She jumped up, flinging her arms. "Jenna! For God's sake, shut up. What is the matter with you? Why are you doing this?"

Jenna went on as if she were oblivious, disconnected from the fallout her bombshell had created. "Would you rather Emmett got the news from the nurse who took his blood?" she asked. "You know they'd tell him, right?"

Sandy had no idea what was right. She appealed to Emmett. "He—Jordy's birth father—I never saw him again after you came back. He understood that he was never to contact me, that he wasn't responsible for the baby."

Emmett looked on the verge of speaking, but Sandy would never know what he intended to say, because right then Dr. Showalter appeared, looking grim.

"Mrs. Simmons?"

Jenna stood. Very slowly, they all did.

"I'm sorry," the doctor said, and in response to his apology, Sandy, her mom and dad, Emmett, and Troy as a group pressed close to Jenna as if they might shield her. A moment came then, one that in Sandy's mind she could never characterize as before or after. It was an instant out of time, shot with love and the grief her family bore for the loss of one of their own: Travis, who had scarcely begun his life, a bird barely fledged, and now he was gone.

. . .

Later on that Saturday afternoon, a matter of hours after Travis slipped away, Sandy was parked alone on the shoulder of CR 440 at the spot where Jordy's Range Rover had left the road. She hadn't intended to come here. Home, where she'd been going, was in the opposite direction. She desperately wanted a hot shower, a change of clothes, a break from the hospital. It seemed somehow horrible of her to want any of these things when Jenna was at home now, so stunned at the loss of her son she couldn't even cry, according to their dad.

Because of what had happened here, in this place. What it had taken from her.

Sandy stared out at the twisted barbed wire, shattered fence posts, the churned and broken ground. The funeral display of condolences was windblown now, like so much trash along the highway's brush-choked verge. She had always hated the custom, marking an accident scene with gloomy memorabilia that after a matter of days resembled the aftermath of an ill-conceived and ghoulish revelry.

The sound of an approaching car brought her gaze around. She recognized the car, that it was a Lexus, but not the woman driving it. They were two strangers, and yet their gazes caught, and something universal passed between them, like commiseration, or perhaps it was pity, or Sandy's imagination. Who knew? But Sandy envied the woman, whoever she was, driving away. She could be congratulating herself that it wasn't her that was involved in this nightmare. No one had dropped a bomb on her family. But it was unkind, Sandy thought. She didn't even know the woman.

. . .

Travis was buried the following Tuesday, the same day Jordy was arrested.

Sandy was at the hospital, alone in Jordy's room—the other bed had remained unoccupied—waiting for him to be discharged when Huck and the other patrol sergeant, the one she'd met while Jordy was undergoing surgery, appeared.

Jordy was in the bathroom, changing into the suit she'd brought him to wear to the funeral, and she was standing at the window, looking out, when she heard them at the door.

She turned, and in the moment she registered the men in uniforms, she knew why they'd come, and her heart slammed into the wall of her chest. "No." Her protest came unbidden.

"Jordy here?" Huck asked.

She shook her head. "You can't do this now. Travis's funeral is today in Wyatt. We have just enough time to get there."

"I'm sorry, but as I told you on Sunday, I don't have a choice. I've given you a couple of days. That's all I can do."

"Trav was like Jordy's brother. They *were* brothers. You know that. You can't do this to him, take away his chance to pay his last respects to his brother."

"I understand—"

"I know you do, Huck. John was like your brother, wasn't he? And when he was shot and killed, you were there. You felt the same as Jordy does, that it was your fault John was dead, right? Could anything, anyone—*should* anyone have tried keeping you from paying your last respects? It's all Jordy has now, all he can do." Sandy's voice broke, and she took a moment, fighting for composure, steeling herself. "He blames himself, too, you know. He wishes he *had* been the one driving."

"He was, Sandy."

"My son isn't a liar, and he says he wasn't." Sandy fought her doubt.

"The evidence says otherwise, as I've already explained."

"No. You have it in for Jordy. You've got something against him. What is it? Why won't you tell me?"

"Is that what he's saying? How he wants to play it? That Madrone County law enforcement is out to get him? Because that's not how we operate, I can tell you."

"Jordy doesn't want to *play* it any way," she said. "Can we talk about how many times he's been stopped and ticketed for practically nothing? Something is going on between you two. There has got to be a reason why he's being targeted."

Huck kept her gaze and his silence.

"C'mon." Sandy almost stamped her foot, her frustration was that intense. "We've known each other for how long? You've sat at my table, Huck; you've spent time with Jordy. He looks up to you. He and Trav always did."

The other cop shifted his weight, and she shot him a glance. *Ken Carter.* His name surfaced in her mind. He looked so uncomfortable. *Too bad,* she thought. *You don't know the meaning of uncomfortable,* she thought.

"You break the law, there are consequences. He's a hard case, Sandy. He won't learn."

"I don't know what you mean. Why are you saying that? If that's what you think of him, why haven't I ever heard you say it before?"

"He drinks. You know that, right? That maybe he's got a problem, and it's not getting better?"

"But you've never ticketed him for that, have you? Minor in possession, isn't that what it's called? You've never called me, or Emmett, to say you thought Jordy was in trouble that way. Why is that, Huck?" She waited. "I thought we were friends."

Nothing. His stare, patient, long-suffering. Obdurate.

She wasn't getting anywhere, and she took a moment, and then very softly, she said, "Can't you please give him a few more hours? Let him attend Travis's funeral, then I'll drive him to the jail myself. This afternoon. We'll go through this ridiculous charade—" She broke off. Would she really drive Jordy there? She thought of the research she'd done.

On Sunday evening, after Huck's interrogation of Jordy, after Huck had agreed to wait until Jordy was discharged to arrest him, out of deference, he said, to Jenna and the other members of Sandy's family—not that she or Jordy were part of it anymore—Sandy had gone home and looked up countries that had no extradition agreement with the United States. It had turned out that Russia was the most likely place they could go and have a chance of surviving.

There were other countries—Somalia, Saudi Arabia, North Korea, and Syria—a handful of third-world countries, but even the thought of trying to go to any one of those mired her in fear. Overseas travel of any sort, though, would necessitate passports, immunizations, all kinds of arrangements . . . the idea was overwhelming, and it would all have to be done in secret, alone, without any assistance from anyone.

But giving her son up to the Texas criminal-justice system if—*when*—he was innocent was just as incomprehensible.

"You should know, if you don't already—" Huck paused.

Sandy looked at him.

"Folks around town aren't going to welcome Jordy at the church or the cemetery, if I was to let him go there. Even Jenna's not too keen on seeing him, or you, right now. I'm sorry to have to say it, but it's true."

"Jenna told you to do this, didn't she? She wanted Jordy arrested today to keep him from coming to Trav's funeral."

Huck didn't answer.

It was Ken Carter who spoke. "Your son committed a crime, Mrs. Cline. There's evidence to support the fact. We're here to arrest him because that's the law, not because anyone told us to."

"Ha." Sandy turned her back to the lawmen. "We're getting a lawyer—"

"Mom?" Jordy appeared in the open bathroom doorway, wearing the sweats and T-shirt she'd brought him, not the suit. That was folded over his arm. "I'll go with them," he said.

"But Travis's funeral—you have the right to say good-bye. You didn't do anything." Sandy was begging. Begging Jordy, of all people, when even he knew it was futile. He'd consigned himself to the outcome.

Sandy glanced at Huck, and the look of pitying commiseration he gave her was almost more than she could bear. He stepped over to Jordy. "Son," he began, "you have the right to remain silent . . ."

．　．　．

They were taking Jordy to the jail in Greeley, the Madrone County seat, twenty-five miles west of Wyatt. Visiting hours were posted online at the Madrone County website. Huck gave Sandy that information as he escorted her son out of the hospital's front entry doors and into the backseat of his waiting squad car. Jordy bent his face, his pale and exhausted face, to the window and mouthed something.

"What?" Sandy took a step toward him.

But now the car left the curb, and within moments it was out of sight.

She was still holding Jordy's hospital-discharge papers, the ones Showalter had signed, that in effect had released Jordy into police custody.

Showalter hadn't had the nerve, or the courtesy, or whatever it would have taken, to appear in Jordy's room himself. He'd sent a nurse, and when Sandy had asked her about Jordy's aftercare, she'd said doctor's orders included no driving for two weeks and no strenuous activity for six. Jordy, who had been handcuffed and Mirandized by then, had snorted so hard he'd almost choked. "Since the state took my license, driving's not an issue," he'd said. "Don't think strenuous activity is, either. Can't get too worked up in a jail cell, right, Sergeant Huckabee?"

Sergeant Huckabee, Jordy had called him. Not Huck or Len. Sandy didn't think she'd ever heard any member of her family call the man by his professional title. She had shot Huck a look and said to Jordy that he wouldn't be in a cell long enough to find out how arduous it might be, although she had no idea.

But the whole situation was impossible. She couldn't fathom how her life—her family's lives—had spiraled so far out of control.

Emmett had left her—again—on Saturday, as soon as he knew Jordy was out of danger. His aunt Leila had called him to say his mother had been taken by ambulance to the hospital, suffering from chest pain, and she'd been admitted for observation. Something was going on with her heart again; they weren't certain what. Emmett felt he had no choice. The sisters were old; they had no one but him. Even Sandy's father had encouraged him to go.

"Irene isn't strong," her dad had said. "You can't expect Emmett to tell her over the phone that Travis has died and Jordy might well be charged with manslaughter. Who knows what more damage that might cause to her heart."

"Why tell her at all?" Sandy had asked. "Why worry her?"

"You want me to pretend everything is fine?" Emmett had given her a disbelieving stare. *Am I starring in an episode of* Twilight Zone *here?* He'd asked that of Sandy, derision heavy in his voice.

Did he think it wasn't the same for her—hearing Jenna blurt out the secret she'd been entrusted to keep? Sandy thought she would never grasp the enormity of that betrayal any more than Emmett seemed able to grasp her betrayal of him.

How could you lie to me? He had repeated the question, for possibly the tenth time, moments before climbing into his truck to leave her.

"I didn't lie," Sandy said. "I just didn't tell you."

"You're splitting hairs," he said.

She guessed she was. At least in his mind, there wasn't a difference between a sin of omission versus one of commission. The result was the same.

But she didn't have a better answer. Had someone handed her a million dollars in trade for an explanation, she couldn't have provided one. The woman, the wife and mother she was today, wanted to go back and choke the girl who'd lied. At the time, all those years ago, she'd done the only thing that had seemed right.

"What am I supposed to tell Jordy?" she had asked Emmett.

"The truth," Emmett had answered, driving away.

She had returned to Jordy's room alone to wait for him to wake up, to be alert enough to take in the terrible news not only of Travis's death but of his father's departure. She had waited through Saturday night in an armchair beside his bed, jolted from snatches of disturbed sleep each time a nurse came to take Jordy's vitals, every time he asked for water. It had amazed her when near dawn on Sunday morning, she wakened to find him much improved. The damaged right half of his face was still a carnival of reds, blues, and a sickly shade of greenish yellow, but the swelling was down, and the color had returned to the healthy side of his face. The white of his left eye was clear. He looked more like himself, and for the first time since the accident, she felt her fear for his physical well-being subside. But not her dread. No. It was pervasive, suffocating.

Jordy knew; she had an immediate and visceral sense that he knew Travis was gone before she pushed herself up from the chair and went to his bedside to tell him. When she managed it, she stood for a moment, patting his arm. Delaying, she asked how he was feeling. "You look better," she said.

He rubbed his eyes, tried a smile. He needed a shave. It still startled her, the sight of dark stubble on his face.

"Do you want anything? Water?"

He shook his head.

"I have something to tell you," she said.

He lowered his chin, still shaking his head, even as she spoke, quickly and quietly of the severity of Travis's injuries and his failure to survive them. "I'm so sorry, honey."

"I thought I was having a nightmare." Jordy's voice was hoarse. "The drugs—I didn't believe it."

She smoothed his rumpled hair. She didn't question his meaning, although he would explain it to her later, all that he'd heard, more than she suspected. In the moment, though, what consumed her was his need for comfort.

He asked when it had happened; he asked if it was really true, and finally, when there was nothing to do but accept it, he buried his face in his hands, and the sob that came was ragged and hurt. It pierced her heart. Without thinking about it, she slipped off her shoes and climbed onto the bed beside him, careful not to jostle him or the tubing that snaked out of his arms, and she pulled him against her. He was big, as wide shouldered and broad chested as Emmett, but she cradled him as if he were still small, her own tears dampening the hair near his ear.

She had told Emmett later, while Jordy slept, how awful it was, but he hadn't come home. Sandy had a feeling he wasn't going to, either, not until she told Jordy the truth—all of it.

She glanced at Jordy's discharge papers now, and stowing them in her purse, she found her cell phone. He needed an attorney, a criminal attorney, someone to get him out of jail.

The only one she knew was Roger Yellott. He'd been a client a year ago, an unhappy one. He'd moved to Greeley from somewhere in Florida. Tampa, she thought, and he'd hired her to design a look straight out of the tropics, using plants like date palms, brugmansias, cannas, and birds of paradise. It wasn't a look she especially cared for, but that was beside the point. The fact was that none of those warm-weather, humidity-loving plants were really suitable for the often windy and dry, occasionally subfreezing, hill-country climate. He'd been annoyed when she'd explained she couldn't give him her standard one-year, onetime replacement guarantee for plants so unsuited to their location.

She scrolled through her directory, and finding his office number, she dialed it, and she was so relieved to have his assistant put her through to Roger, to have him actually take her call, and when he answered, she said so.

"I thought we might not be speaking," she said, and he laughed.

Laughed!

And for some reason, Sandy's throat closed.

"Water under the bridge," Roger said. "I've been hunting for six months for the nerve, or whatever it is I need, to call you." As if he sensed her discomposure, he hurried on in a warm voice. "You were right, you see. About the plants. After last winter the whole garden looks like shit. Especially the date palm. Jesus, there is nothing uglier than a date palm clinging to life by its frost-blackened fronds."

Now Sandy laughed and pinched the bridge of her nose. She found her truck and got in. "So, you're ready to take my advice, is that what you're saying?"

"Eating crow as we speak. And yes, if you're offering your services. Absolutely. What was it you recommended, other than the serving of bird, that is. Cactus and rocks, wasn't it?"

"I think we can be a little more creative." She thought how genuinely nice he was. Even when they'd had their disagreement, he'd kept his cool.

He sobered. "Somehow I don't think that's why you called, though, is it? I heard about that god-awful wreck your son was involved in. How is he?"

"He's why I'm calling, Roger. Jordy's been arrested." She paused, waiting for the breath—the actual nerve to put it into words, and then it came. "My nephew, Travis, died from his injuries on Saturday, and Jordy was arrested today when the hospital discharged him."

"For?"

"They say he was driving."

"Intoxication manslaughter, then. Is that the charge?" Roger asked, gently.

"Yes, and intoxication assault. Michelle Meade is still in a coma. But how did you know? The news? Has it been on the news already?"

"I don't know about the news; I heard it from Mandy, Augie Bright's wife. She told me when I was getting a haircut earlier. That gal is cute, but boy, can she talk."

"Jordy says he wasn't driving, that Travis was the designated driver. He says Sergeant Huckabee—that's who made the arrest—has got it wrong." Sandy waited. So did Roger. She went on. "I think Huck—do you know him? Len Huckabee? I think he's got something against Jordy. Jordy won't say what it is, but Huck has stopped him so many times in the past couple of years for nothing. He says Jordy has an attitude, a chip on his shoulder." *A drinking problem.*

Sandy let her stare drift. Jenna had said it, too. She'd accused Sandy of having her head in the sand about it. But all the kids drank. Even Travis. Perfect Travis.

Oh God, where had that come from?

Sandy had thought it before, plenty of times, but that was when Travis was alive, when Jenna was busy comparing him to Jordy, making it sound as if Jordy was inferior.

Roger said he knew Sergeant Huckabee but not well.

Sandy said, "Jordy needs an attorney, Roger. Can you represent him? Can you get him out of there? Arrange for bail?" She didn't know what she was asking. What did arranging bail mean? Emmett would know, but he wasn't here. Jordy had no one but her.

When Roger said he would go to the Madrone County jail in Greeley and find out what was happening, Sandy almost cried from relief and exhaustion, and the constant wearing fear that she was on the brink of losing everything and everyone she loved, if she hadn't already.

He said, "Let me warn you, though, they might not set bail today. They will likely wait for the arraignment."

Sandy said, "Okay," but how would she know whether it was? The word *arraignment*, the process involved—whatever understanding of it she had was from watching crime shows on television. How accurate could that be? "When would that happen?"

"Tomorrow or Thursday. We'll see. You want to meet me there, at the jail?"

Sandy looked through the windshield. She was torn. "Travis's funeral is today," she began and stopped. Jenna didn't want her there, Huck had said.

Folks around town aren't going to welcome you . . . His further warning stood up in her mind, and it hurt; it left her feeling bitter. But she didn't have emotional space to spare for those *folks* and what they thought.

"Yes," she told Roger. "It'll take me a couple of hours to get there, though. I'm still in Austin." She keyed the ignition. Her mom and dad had brought her truck to her at the hospital after Emmett took off, leaving her stranded. At least they were still speaking to her. They would be with her, too, if Jenna's need wasn't greater. Jenna—who had lost her son, her only child. It fell over Sandy anew—the reality that Travis was gone. "Will I be able to see Jordy?" she asked Roger.

"Depends. Let's just get into it. I'll call you."

Sandy got off the phone and sat clutching her elbows. The enormity of it—the incontrovertible fact of Travis's death, what his loss would do—was doing to her sister, whom, in spite of everything, Sandy loved with her whole heart and self, frightened and sickened her. It stalled her heartbeat and stopped her breath. Her head swam, and for several moments, she couldn't see. She should be with Jenna. Be there for her. Sandy needed to be with her sister, and her need was physical. She ached with it.

But Jenna blamed her and Jordy.

I will never forgive you or him.

Those hard, angry words were the last Jenna had spoken to Sandy before she'd left the hospital on Saturday on her way to the funeral home, Macintyre's, in Wyatt. Sandy hadn't needed her mom and dad to tell her that Travis would be buried outside town at Haven's Rest, next to his dad.

Sandy wiped her face and blew her nose now. She had heard of near-death experiences, where people who had faced death came back telling stories of having seen a beloved family member who had gone before. She prayed it was true, that John had been there when Travis passed from here to wherever. Sandy closed her eyes, and for a moment she imagined it, John holding his son. He'd been a big man, quiet and thoughtful. He'd been the love of Jenna's life, the center of Travis's world. Jenna had borne his loss with grace, the same way she'd borne the loss of her breast to cancer. But this? The loss of her only child? It was too much for her sister to bear, too much for any mother.

But she could not sit here grieving over what she couldn't change. Her son was still alive, and he needed her help.

• • •

Greeley, Texas, the Madrone county seat, was north of Wyatt. Sandy had been through it on her way to other places. She was familiar with the town square and found the courthouse there with no problem. An old man dozing on a bench out front told her the jail was around back.

"In an annex," he said, and harrumphed. "Cost the taxpayers a bundle puttin' up that building. Just so a bunch of criminals could sit around in air-conditioning."

Sandy thanked him, got back into her truck, and drove behind the courthouse. The annex was a squat one-story building faced in native limestone, nondescript in style. Walking through the entrance door, she was hit with a blast of the taxpayer-financed air-conditioning cold enough to preserve meat. A woman in street clothes sat at the desk. "Help you?" she asked, giving Sandy a short glance.

She held the woman's irritated gaze, the one that seemed to judge her for being stupid and somehow deficient, given that she was here, in a county jail.

"My son, Jordan Cline, was brought here. His attorney, Roger Yellott—"

"Oh yeah. He just got through booking. Lawyer's with him now."

"Could I join them?"

"Don't know as it's allowed."

"Could you find out? Please?" Sandy added, although the woman didn't look as if she was the sort who was moved by politeness.

She summoned a police officer, though, who escorted Sandy down a short corridor to a closed, windowless door. On the wall beside it, a sign read: **INTERVIEW ROOM**. She steeled herself, but nothing could have prepared her for the sight of her son dressed in an orange jumpsuit and wearing handcuffs. The pads of his fingertips were smudged black from being fingerprinted as part of the booking process. Jordy would tell her this later, washing the ink off at the kitchen sink at home. When he half rose from his chair, so did her gaze rise to his face.

"Mom?" he said, and his voice was that of a bewildered child.

Sandy didn't know how she managed to withhold the frightened gasp that scraped her ribs. His eyes locked with hers, filled with pleading, that unfathomable confusion. Her need to touch him, to reassure him, was a reflex so strong she was barely aware of moving toward him until the cop barked, "No contact!"

She looked over her shoulder at him, taking in his gray buzz cut, his lined and dour face.

"Sandy," Roger said, "why don't you take this chair."

She did what he suggested, sitting beside him, opposite Jordy.

The cop backed out of the room.

"There's a camera," Jordy said, looking up at the corner of the room where the instrument was mounted. Its glass eye peered down, probing, empty.

"They're watching us?" she asked.

"Maybe," Roger said. "Look, I was just telling Jordy we've caught a huge break. Ordinarily he'd spend at least one night in jail, maybe two before arraignment. But Judge Becker expedited the whole process. You can get Jordy out today, right now. You just have to put up his bail."

"It's seventy-five thousand," Jordy said.

"Seventy-five thousand?" Sandy felt almost weightless with astonishment. She had no idea where she could get that kind of money. Not from their savings. There was maybe eighty-five hundred in there, last she looked. Sell their mutual funds? But why had the judge granted them favor? Sandy looked at Roger. "I was afraid Jordy wouldn't get bail at all."

"Evidently your dad knows Judge Becker. This is his court. There was some conversation between him and your dad."

"Really?" Her dad did know a lot of people in the area; he'd employed many of them. He was known as the sort of man who'd give the shirt off his back to help someone. She didn't know what he might have done for Judge Becker.

Roger said, "Look, I know most folks don't have seventy-five K in cash lying around, so you can see a bail bondsman and secure Jordy's release for ten percent, if that works. There's a guy down the street. He's reputable. I've worked with him before. I'll go with you, if you want."

"Yes, I'd be grateful."

"The only downside is if Jordy were to miss his court date—"

"If I take off," Jordy said, looking at Sandy, "if I go on the run, you don't get the ten percent back."

She thought of her Internet search, the short list of marginal countries Jordy might escape to and be free. She was aware of his knee, bouncing erratically. She was aware of the camera, its blank eye pointing directly at them. Were there lawmen—Len Huckabee, for instance—listening in? Was that legal?

"I've spoken to the DA's office," Roger said, and when Sandy turned to him, he searched her gaze, and while his eyes were steady and kind, she thought he was also trying to gauge the level of her composure. How close to the edge was she? How much more could she take? She wondered herself. But she had to take it. What would Jordy do if she went down? Who else was here for him, for them?

Roger said, "I was just explaining to Jordy before you got here, word is they're going to pursue this to the max. In addition to intoxication manslaughter and the DUI, they intend to try him for intoxication assault and aggravated assault."

"Because of Michelle," Sandy said.

"Her parents have spoken to the DA, too. Her condition hasn't improved. It hasn't worsened, either, but—" Roger's expression, the lift of his hand, was commiserating. Michelle's parents wanted justice. Who could blame them?

"Yeah, it's assault now," Jordy said, "but if she dies, too, then it'll be like Trav—God—" His head fell forward. When he raised his gaze, his eyes were red and scoured with panic and grief, and something hectic and sharp that might have been rage. "I did drink. I was probably drunk, but I wasn't driving." He looked from Sandy to Roger and back at Sandy. "I wasn't, I swear, Mom. You have to believe me. Do you?"

Sandy thought back to the day last summer when he'd bruised Jenna's car and sworn it was a total accident, not the result of his having consumed the contents of the empty pint bottle of peppermint schnapps Jenna had found. There had been other incidents: Beers had gone missing from the refrigerator. Even the occasional fifth of rum or tequila that they kept in a cabinet for friends had disappeared. Jordy always feigned innocence. But Sandy had known in the nether regions of her mind he was lying. The practice of deception came as easily to him as it once had to her. Like her, he would lie to get out of trouble or to endear himself. He would lie to fit in. To entertain. There were so many ways to lie, so many reasons when it made sense—when the truth would hurt someone, for instance. Travis was dead. Wasn't it easier now to make him the scapegoat when he couldn't defend himself? Even Emmett had expressed doubt.

Roger said, "It's what the jury believes that matters." He set his elbows on the table. The sleeves of his suit coat rode up, and Sandy caught the wink of his cuff links, tiny diamonds and emeralds set in a horseshoe pattern. They were understated, tasteful. Sandy wondered how much they cost, what sort of money you had to earn to afford such elegant jewelry. Her heart was beating so hard she could feel the repercussions in her head. When Roger said he didn't want to scare her, she almost laughed.

"The DA is asking for the maximum in regard to punishment. If they win—not that it'll happen, I'm just saying if they do—Jordy's looking at a possible twenty to thirty years in prison. That's if the jury was to find him guilty on every charge, and if the judge was to stack the sentences. If Michelle were to die, then the situation—"

"What do we do?" Sandy cut him off.

"We pay his bail and get him out of here. We start building a defense. I've already put in a request for a copy of the accident report. I'll have a look at the accident scene, too, and interview any witnesses, other drivers who might have been on the road that night."

A pause lingered, taking on significance. *Money.* Lawyers required it, a retainer up front, and after they used that up, there would be an hourly rate. *Billable hours.* The phrase came from some recess of Sandy's memory, a holdover from her days of watching *LA Law*. She met Roger's glance. "What will it cost?"

"Ten thousand to start. That retainer should cover pretty much all the pretrial expenses. My hourly rate is two-fifty, which will be deducted from the retainer amount unless or until that's used up. If we go to trial, it's another thirty-five thousand. Steep, I know, but Jordy's case, the charges—it's pretty complex. There's a lot riding on the outcome."

Sandy felt he added the last part in deference to the shock and dismay that must be visible on her face. Lucky for him he couldn't also see the sick knot of her panic, the one that kept tightening its grip on her stomach. *Where?* Where would the money come from? She thought again of the mutual funds Emmett had invested in; she thought of Jordy's college fund. What was the use of that, though, if he was in prison? She was rewriting her version of O. Henry's short story "The Gift of the Magi." But instead of selling her hair, she would give away Jordy's college fund to buy his freedom, only to be unable to afford his education, assuming he was granted a reprieve. It would have been laughable if it weren't so alarming and sad. "I have enough to pay the bail, but your retainer—I'll have to move funds around."

"It's all right," Roger said. "You can drop a check by my office later."

She hazarded a glance at Jordy, the battered wreck of his face, the shamed, dejected slump of his shoulders. She didn't imagine he understood the scope of the financial pressure this would put on their family except in the most ephemeral way. Yet she knew he was sickened, too. As sickened by it as she was. She touched his hand. "All that matters is getting you out of here, okay?"

The look he gave her said it was so much more than that. She searched his eyes, trying to see past the bruised damage into the core of him, where she imagined the truth lay. She wanted so badly to believe him, for him not to have done this. She had heard parents say they would love their child no matter what. She had said it herself. Was it true? Would she love Jordy if his recklessness had killed Travis and so cruelly injured Michelle? If she died, too? Sandy didn't know if she would, and it shamed her. She found Jordy's glance. "You have to tell him about Huck. I'll leave—"

"No, Mom." Jordy straightened, lifting his chin, indicating the camera.

He was right. It wouldn't be smart talking about Len Huckabee here.

A cop took Jordy from the room, where he'd wait in a holding cell, while Sandy and Roger secured his bail. Sandy went to her truck first, and using her laptop, she transferred money from the savings to the checking account. She thought of calling Emmett, but Roger was waiting. The legal meter was running.

She brought up Len Huckabee's harassment of Jordy again as she and Roger walked to the bail bondsman's office, a block from the courthouse.

"When did it start? Can you remember?" Roger asked.

"The summer after his senior year is when Emmett and I talked to Huck about it, because Jordy had so many traffic tickets. He was working for me, but most of what I paid him went to the city of Wyatt." Sandy glanced at Roger. "I think he and Travis both helped out when I did the install on your project."

"They did. We drank a beer one day and talked football."

Sandy winced inwardly at the mention of Jordy drinking a beer. *He and Trav were underage then,* she wanted to say. But she knew Jordy and Travis had taken beers from the other guys on her crew after they were done with work for the day. She'd never mentioned it to anyone, not even Jenna. She'd wanted to believe it was harmless. Growing-up boy stuff. "They were football cocaptains their senior year. Huck always went to the games if he could. He worked out with the guys." Sandy paused. She had forgotten how much a part of their lives Huck had once been.

She said, "He hasn't been around as much lately, but I figured that was because Jordy and Travis were away at UT."

"Is the harassment still going on?"

"Five speeding tickets so far this summer. It's crazy. A few weeks ago when Huck stopped Jordy, he searched the car." Sandy hesitated, but then she said it. "He seems to think Jordy is a drinker, a party boy."

"Has he arrested Jordy for that?"

"He's never so much as mentioned it. You'd think he would have, as close to our family as he's been. I don't understand it."

"Do you think Jordy is a drinker? In a way that causes you concern, I mean?"

"No. No," she repeated. "But what if he tries to make the DA believe Jordy has a drinking problem?"

"He'd need proof. The prosecutor isn't going to be influenced by hearsay."

Sandy had her doubts, and she almost said so. Roger was from Florida. Maybe he didn't know about the Texas good ol' boy networking that went on, the deals that were made under the table. The media was full of such stories. As far as Sandy could tell, Texas was the living example of the old adage *You scratch my back, I'll scratch yours.*

"Huckabee is on thin ice anyway, conducting a search of Jordy's car. Unless he was given permission, or he had some reason to suspect Jordy of committing a crime, he had no right to do it, not without a warrant."

"That's what Emmett and I thought. We told Jordy to call us if it happened again. He cooperated because he wants to believe Huck is his friend, and he's got nothing to hide."

Roger stopped outside a narrow storefront. A sign hanging under the awning was lettered with the name FASTLANE BAIL BONDS, and in the window neon numbers announced they did business from 7:00 a.m. to 7:00 p.m. Inside, she filled out forms asking for basic information and handed over her debit card, and within an hour, after turning over the necessary paperwork at the courthouse annex, Sandy was able to take Jordy home.

He asked if they could go to the cemetery first, and she drove there, stopping on the way at the grocery store for a bouquet of flowers—a mix of carnations, alstroemeria, spider mums, and lilies in a range of hues. Jordy set them on Travis's grave, where they were immediately lost among much grander arrangements. In addition to flowers, someone had left a football helmet with the number twenty-three on it, Travis's number, and a miniature horse and rider dressed in green and yellow, the Wyatt High School Raider mascot. A banner lettered in glitter with Travis's name and team and attached to a pole fluttered in the breeze, catching the last of the day's light. Jordy touched the temporary sign that marked Travis's grave, and the sound that broke from his chest was somewhere between a sob and a cough. Sandy laid her hand on his back. She willed herself not to cry, and she didn't.

"I should have been here when he was buried," Jordy said.

Sandy agreed; they both should have been, but what she said was, "You couldn't help it."

"Yeah, Mom, I could. I could have died instead of him." He straightened.

"No, Jordy." She grabbed his arm, and her thought was of how impossible the situation was. No matter what outcome she wished for, it was wrong, devastating, for someone else—unless the whole thing could have been prevented. Keeping his gaze, she said, "If only you guys hadn't been drinking." Oh, it was useless, useless and too late. She knew the moment she said it how pointless it was to take even one step down that road.

"You think I don't know that?" Jordy jerked his arm free. "That I don't see how fucking stupid—" But now, abruptly, he wheeled and took off, walking.

He wanted to run. Sandy could see the urgency in him. She read his frustration in the rigid line of his shoulders. It was only the pain of his injuries, his recent surgery, that kept his pace in check.

"Jordy!" Sandy set off after him.

When they reached her truck, she was almost surprised when he got in.

"I heard Grandma and Granddad talking. That's how I knew about Travis." He was staring through the windshield.

Sandy looked at him, brows raised, waiting. She hadn't a clue of what was coming. She would think in the awful days ahead that maybe the way Jordy learned the rest of the truth was for the best; she might never have found the words to tell him.

"I heard them talking about Emmett, too," Jordy said. "I know he's not my real dad."

8

Jordy had come down with tonsillitis once when he was five and a half. He'd woken up in the night, making small noises of distress. She and Emmett had retired the baby monitor by then, but Sandy had heard him and had gone to him. His forehead and cheeks had been hot and dry. She'd given him baby aspirin and had wiped his face and arms with a cloth dipped in cool water. It seemed that hours had passed before the sun came up, before the pediatrician's office opened. By then Jordy's fever had risen, despite her ministrations, to 104.

Sandy had held him, limp and listless, on her lap, while Emmett had driven them, keeping his hand on Jordy's small knee the whole way. Emmett had carried Jordy into the doctor's office, and after the exam and diagnosis, he'd brought them home and had then gone back out to get the prescriptions filled.

Emmett's caretaking of them had been nothing new. He was good like that. He'd changed his share of Jordy's diapers and washed his clothes. When Jordy was little, Emmett had called him Choo Choo. Now he called him Ace or Chill, tough-guy names, out of affection.

But Emmett could land hard on Jordy, too, when he got out of line. The saying in the family was that Jordy could drive God to drink, but Emmett almost never lost his temper. He'd wait until the heat was gone, then act. He was their guiding light, their steady ground.

Sandy wasn't that good. She would yell and slam doors if her temper got the better of her.

She looked at him now. "Emmett? Really, Jordy? He's still Dad, *your* dad."

No answer. He was turned away from her so that all she could see was the back of his head, the stiff angle of his neck.

"Do you want to drive by Aunt Jenna's on the way home?" Even as she asked, Sandy wondered whether Jenna would bar them from her house.

"I doubt she'd let us in," Jordy said.

Sandy glanced his way again, pained to hear him echo her doubt. That Jenna would do this, close them out—but Sandy guessed Jenna was capable of anything now. She didn't feel she'd been wrong to reveal the secret she'd sworn to Sandy she would keep. Their mother had told Sandy that, and she hadn't disagreed. She hadn't offered Sandy reassurance of love or support or forgiveness. No. Instead she'd made excuses for Jenna, that she couldn't be held accountable. Basically Jenna was being given carte blanche to express her grief in whatever mean, vindictive way she chose. The sense of this was implicit in every exchange Sandy had with her parents. After all, Jordy was alive. What more could Sandy ask for, feel entitled to?

"Your aunt may not want us around right now," Sandy said, "but there's other family there. Even some of your friends could be there. It might help, seeing them. What do you think?"

No answer.

"I'm so sorry, honey. Finding out about your dad the way you did— it shouldn't have happened. I should have been the one to tell you." She stopped. Did her parents know he'd overheard them? But surely they would have told her. To believe anything else meant believing they were like Jenna, out to hurt her, out to make her pay.

She said, "I never wanted you or your dad to know, and maybe that was wrong, but Aunt Jenna was wrong, too, blurting it out the way she did. I was going to tell you—"

"When you had to, right? That's great, Mom."

"Do you remember the Christmas Dad got you the train, how thrilled you were?" she asked him.

Emmett had bought it the year Jordy turned four, after Sandy gave him *The Little Engine That Could* for his birthday that spring. By Christmas she'd lost count of the times they'd read it. Emmett came up with the idea that Santa's gift that year should be a model train, and he'd set to work constructing a table to run it on out in the barn. The train was still there, and sometimes Sandy turned on the locomotive, watching it pull the cars along what now amounted to several dozen feet of track. Over the years, while Jordy was growing up, he and Emmett had embellished the landscape, making mountains and trees, creating farmlands, and constructing a tunnel and a river. They'd even built a small town very like Wyatt, where miniature people walked on Main Street.

But the single moment that Sandy most loved to remember was Jordy's first sight of it on Christmas morning, the year he turned four. When Emmett had rolled the barn door open to reveal it, Jordy's eyes had widened as recognition dawned, and then a look of utter joy had suffused his face so completely, she'd been reminded of the halos of angels. When he'd hurled himself at Emmett hard enough to make him stagger, it had brought Sandy to tears. Emmett had laughed, scooping Jordy into his arms. *Can we run it now, Dad?* Jordy spoke in her mind. She could still see him, that little boy, hopefully studying his dad's face.

She asked him now if he could remember it, his happiness that day. "I'm only bringing it up because that's how your daddy felt when I told him I was pregnant with you." Sandy looked at Jordy, but he kept his face averted. "What if the train had been taken away?" she persisted. "How would you have felt?"

It was pathetic as an analogy—trains and babies weren't exactly equal—but she'd never been good at words. She always thought of the best ones to say hours after the need for them had passed. "I couldn't do that to your dad, couldn't take his joy in his anticipation of having you for a son from him any more than I could have taken that train away from you."

He looked at her. "Can we go home now?"

"Sure," she said, and she started the truck's engine, and shifting into reverse, backed out of the cemetery parking space.

•   •   •

The house was the same as when she and Emmett had left it five days ago. The weeds in the perennial garden that bordered the front porch were taller, and the wind had blown the cushions off the swing that hung in one corner, but other than that, nothing appeared out of the ordinary. Sandy realized she'd almost expected the house to be damaged, too, in some horrific way, the way their lives had been.

Jordy reached for his canvas tote in the backseat.

"Let me," she said. "You aren't supposed to lift anything, remember?"

He was uncomfortable with it, letting her carry his stuff, but whether that was out of regard for her smaller stature or out of disgust with her, or confusion, or anger, she didn't know.

Jordy's bedroom and a guest room were at the end of a small hallway off the kitchen. The master bedroom and a small study were on the other side of the house, separated by what Sandy thought of as the heart of the house, the kitchen–dining–great room area. They had taken down walls in the circa 1920s farmhouse to make one central living space so they could be together, accessible to one another. It felt huge and vacant to her now. Without Emmett. Without her family.

The one she and Jordy, for different reasons, had been cast out of.
"Are you hungry?" she asked him.

He shook his head and said he was going to get some sleep. But he didn't look at her. He didn't wait to see if that was okay with her.

She said, "We should talk, Jordy." But he was already gone. She lifted her voice. "We're going to have to sometime."

She heard his door close, and then nothing. The pull of her breath. The plodding gait of her heart. Getting her cell phone from her purse, she dialed Emmett, and when her call rolled to his voice mail, she said, "Dammit, Emmett, where are you? Please call me. Please," she repeated. Clicking off, she dialed his mother's landline, but there was no answer there, either, and she hung up without leaving a message.

She spoke to her parents at Jenna's. They didn't have to say Jenna needed them more.

"She hasn't had much more than a bite or two of food in days," her mother said.

"Make her a breakfast shake," Sandy said, "with strawberries and watermelon. It's her favorite. Make sure the melon is really sweet, okay? And add some yogurt. You know what a health nut she is."

Her mother said she'd try it. She asked how Jordy was. "You were able to bring him home, thank God. Judge Becker said he'd been released."

"Yes, but how does Dad know the judge?"

"Do you remember several years ago the girl who was driving drunk and crashed her mother's SUV here in town? It was in the news. Her boyfriend was with her. He was pretty seriously injured."

"That was Judge Becker's daughter? She went to jail, didn't she?"

"A juvenile facility, I think. Anyway, when she got out on probation, your dad hired her. He wrote several letters of recommendation when she applied to law school at UT in Austin, and she was accepted. Trust me, Sam Becker was glad to return the favor."

The good ol' boy system, Sandy thought. Love it or hate it, it had come through for Jordy. Maybe he had an ally in Judge Becker. Maybe the judge was a better-connected good ol' boy than Len Huckabee.

"You found an attorney."

"Roger Yellott," Sandy answered, although she felt as though her mom had already heard it from the judge.

"He's the client you had so much trouble with a while back, isn't he? I didn't know he was an attorney."

Of course her mother knew all about Roger. Sandy had always told her pretty much everything. With one exception. "I'm sorry," she said. She kept saying it as if those two words would undo the damage.

"You did what you felt was best at the time." It was the response her mother had given Sandy the first time they'd spoken after Jenna had so helpfully revealed the truth about Jordy's birth father, and the same one she'd given the handful of times she and her mom had discussed it since.

Sandy didn't know if they meant the things they said. She honestly wasn't sure she was sorry for having kept her parents in the dark. Look at them now—were they better off for having learned the truth? Were *any* of them? "Jordy knows. He told me on the way home just now that he overheard you and Dad talking."

"About Emmett? That he isn't—oh no. Oh dear, we never meant— is he all right? What did he say? It must have been such a shock."

"He didn't say anything, really." Sandy was almost grateful for her mother's distress. Until now, hearing it, she had been so afraid that, like Jenna, her parents hated her, too, for her lie, for Jordy having ever been born, only to grow up to become the means of Travis's needless and horrible death.

"Well, maybe, like Emmett, he needs some time to wrap his mind around it."

"Maybe." Sandy trailed a fingertip along the countertop. There were worse things, scarier things, confronting them, she thought. *Do you know how much the helicopter cost?* Sandy had asked Emmett that yesterday when they'd talked. But the helicopter was only the leading edge of the financial landslide coming down on them. Because they'd been forced to go out of network, insurance was almost no help. She'd told Emmett they'd have to sell the mutual funds. *What funds?* he'd asked. She'd forgotten—conveniently, Emmett said—that they'd sold the funds when the oil industry took a nosedive and business fell off. Now, on top of that, there were going to be astronomical legal fees. Emmett might have a stroke when he heard. Or maybe he would be the one to flee the country. Or maybe he would eschew obligation entirely by saying Jordy wasn't his son.

"How is Irene doing?" her mother asked.

"Better," Sandy said. "She's going home today or tomorrow, I think." The doctors had replaced a valve in her heart the day after Emmett's arrival. He had yet to tell her about the accident. He said her health was too precarious. Sandy had stopped asking when he was coming home.

"Jordy's birth father—" her mother began.

"I don't want to talk about him right now, Mom." Sandy sat at the table in the breakfast nook, and as if it had been waiting for an opportunity, she felt swamped by a wave of weariness. It pulled at her limbs, weighted her breath. Her mother said Jordy might very well want to know the man's identity, and it was as if her voice were coming at Sandy from over a hill.

"You won't be able to put him off, I don't imagine."

"I'll cross that bridge when I come to it," Sandy said, although she had no idea how.

"Honey? Do you think he might have a problem with alcohol? I don't want to pry, to interfere, but is it possible he's depressed or—"

"Has anyone in our family been a drinker? I mean to excess—like they were addicted?"

"No, not that I know of. But I don't think it's always genetic, is it, when someone abuses alcohol or drugs?"

Sandy didn't answer.

"A doctor could tell you. Maybe that would be a good place to start."

Did her mother mean a psychiatrist?

The silence grew heavy with her mother's consideration, the debate she was having with herself on what more to say, how far to push. Sandy imagined hanging up.

Her mother veered in a different direction. "Jenna didn't mean it," she said. "You realize that, don't you?"

"It's all right," Sandy said, even though it wasn't. She knew how it troubled her mother when she and Jenna fought. But this was no child-ish squabble between siblings. It fell far outside that realm.

"She needs time. Huck was saying when he was here earlier that he—"

"Huck?" Sandy straightened. "What was he doing there?" *Poisoning everyone's mind?* The question burned through Sandy's brain.

"He's been by every day. It helps her, I think. You know how protec-tive he's always been of her."

"Obsessed is more like it. He shouldn't be coming there now." Sandy stood up. "For God's sake, Mom, he arrested Jordy."

"It's all right," her mother soothed. "He doesn't talk about the accident."

Sandy didn't believe her mother, and she called and asked Roger about it later. "It isn't legal, is it? Even if Huck isn't discussing the case with Jenna, he's probably talking about Jordy, saying who knows what."

"I can understand why you're concerned," Roger said.

"But you aren't?" Sandy asked.

"I've had a chance to go over the accident report."

"And?"

"If everything is correct, Sandy, Jordy was driving. I'm sorry."

Sandy felt her head swim. She walked out the back door and sat on the end of the wicker chaise longue. "They were both thrown from the vehicle."

"No, remember? Jordy says when he came to, initially, he was in the driver's seat. He remembers getting out under his own power and going to help Travis, where he collapsed. There's a witness, too, mentioned in the report, a tow-truck driver from Greeley, Pete Hoskins, who was picking up a car out near the scene—he says the Range Rover passed him. He ID'd Jordy as the driver."

Sandy left the chair now, barely registering her actions, mindlessly walking the path that led between two perennial borders to her vegetable garden. Except for a row of poblano peppers, the summer-planted crops—tomatoes, squash, melon, and green beans—were mostly brown, their fruit rotting. She seldom had time to work her own gardens. She was like the cobbler whose children had no shoes.

"Try not to worry. There's still a lot of investigating to do. I'll be interviewing the witness myself and checking every other fact in this report. It's possible there were other witnesses, too, that the cops overlooked."

"This is so scary, Roger," she said.

"I know, but, hang in there, okay? I'll call you when I know more."

•　•　•

She started dinner—Jordy's favorite meal—baked pork chops and scalloped potatoes. She pulled what was left of the green beans, and she fixed those, too. When everything was ready, she went to his room and tapped on his door, and she was surprised when he answered, when he said he would join her.

She sat at the table, waiting. Outside, early-evening shadows crept from the woods, encroaching on the lawn, dulling its rich green color, softening the signs of neglect. Who would mow it if Jordy went to jail and Emmett didn't come home? Sandy bit her lips together. She couldn't think like that.

Jordy slid into the chair opposite her. He picked up his fork, set it down. "Does he know about me? Has he ever seen me?" His stare was hard.

Her mother had warned her Jordy would ask, that he would want to know. She saw his bewilderment, his hurt and vulnerability, and it wrenched her heart. It occurred to her how it must look to him, that he'd been born through a man who did not care about him, one who had contributed his DNA and walked on. "It's not like what you're thinking," Sandy said. "It isn't that he didn't want you, or want to know you. I never gave him a chance."

Jordy sat back. Like her, he had little appetite.

She tried to explain, but it was difficult finding the words to describe the unhappy place she'd been in, the events that had led her into having the affair, that wouldn't cause Jordy further pain. She couldn't say that she'd known the first time it was a mistake, and still there had been two other occasions. She couldn't say the affair was something both she and his birth father had regretted, or that was her understanding, anyway. She took her time, choosing her words carefully, and in the end there were few of them, and they were both true and not quite true. She had been thrilled, she said, when she found out she was pregnant with him. She didn't say she had also been frightened out of her mind and heartbroken that he was not Emmett's child.

She did not speak of her shame. Suppose he got that twisted in his mind and somehow associated her shame with his birth? "I loved you before you were born," she said. "So did your dad. Emmett. The guy who was there, watching you come into the world. The guy who has been here with you ever since. I know you're confused and angry at me, and you have every right. But, Jordy, it takes more than DNA to be a dad."

"You never told me who he is."

"I will, if you want me to." Could she? She felt as if she were free-falling through space, and there was nothing to stop her. Nothing to grab onto.

"I already know," Jordy said, and Sandy gaped at him, astonished.

"How?" she asked.

"Aunt Jenna told Troy, and he told me."

"You talked to them?"

"Not her. I called Troy. I didn't know if he'd talk to me, but he did. He said Aunt Jenna will come around, some crap about forgiveness." Jordy wadded his napkin and tossed it onto the table by his plate. "I said I didn't need forgiveness. Not for that, anyway. I didn't do anything better or worse than Trav. We were stupid. Michelle, too. She had as much to drink as we did."

"Roger's read the accident report. There's a witness who says he saw that you were the driver."

"He's lying." Jordy stood up. His gaze narrowed on hers. "You believe him, don't you? Over me, your own son, the one you loved before I was even born. What horseshit!"

"Jordy," she protested.

At the doorway that led out of the kitchen, he wheeled. "You know what?" He came back toward her. "You're like everyone else in this fucked-up family. You think I'm a liar. Well, what about you, huh? Doesn't seem as if you know how to tell the truth, either, does it?"

Her eyes were locked with his; her heart ticked in her chest.

"I'm going to get in touch with him, Mom, and there's not a damn thing you can do to stop me."

●　●　●

It was late when Emmett called. Sandy had made herself clear up the dinner they'd left uneaten, and she was sitting with her laptop in the kitchen when her phone rang. She saw his name in the ID, and for a moment, the turmoil of her emotions was so fierce, her mind went blank. They were careful with each other, guarded in their speech. He talked about his mom, his decision to find someone qualified to come in and help his aunt Leila take care of his mother. He was saying he didn't know how long it would take when she interrupted him.

"You have to come home, Emmett. I got Jordy out of jail on bail today. I had to transfer funds from savings. I hired a lawyer—Roger Yellott—"

"Wait, wait. Are you telling me that son of a bitch went through with it? Huck actually arrested Jordy?"

"Yes. Emmett. There's going to be a trial." Sandy paused. Her ears were ringing. She was trembling, and she crossed her free arm over her midsection. She found her voice again and explained about the charges; she mentioned the accident report, the witness statement. She said, "It could get worse—if Michelle were to die."

Emmett's muttered "Jesus Christ" was as much a prayer as it was a protest.

Sandy wanted to ask him if he thought Jordy had a drinking problem and whether he believed Jordy when he said he wasn't driving, but she was afraid of his answer, his doubt that would mirror her own.

He said, "This guy you hired to represent Jordy, he was a client of yours, wasn't he? An asshole, right?" There was no heat in Emmett's voice, only the recollection of her frustration and his commiseration at the time.

"I didn't know who else to call." *You weren't here.* That thought ran through her mind, too. "I think I misjudged him. I mean, he's gone out of his way to help. Jordy likes him. He says he can talk to Roger."

"Has he dealt with this before? Intoxication manslaughter, all the rest?"

"I don't know. I guess he has. He's a criminal, not a civil, attorney." She had looked at his website earlier to be sure. Using her mouse now, she opened the page again. A photograph of him in the upper left corner showed him looking very grave, but there was a glint of mischief in his eyes and in the curve of his mouth. Even though he'd been a pain to work with, she remembered he'd laughed a lot. He'd made her laugh. She guessed his temper could be as quick as his humor.

"It says he handles DUIs," she told Emmett, scrolling a list of Roger's specialties. "Manslaughter," she read. "Intoxication manslaughter is here, too. There's a whole page about it, what to do if you're charged, how he handles it."

Sandy took the noise Emmett made as his assent, and when he asked about Roger's fees and the next steps, she explained all that Roger had told her. She had done nothing to rid herself of the burden, but she felt lighter now that Emmett knew what she knew. "We can talk to him together when you come home." It didn't occur to her that he wouldn't. She went on. "Mom told me Huck is over at Jenna's every day. She claims he isn't talking about the accident, but you know he is. He wants Jordy to be guilty."

"Yeah," Emmett said. "Because that's what Jenna wants. God, this is so fucked up."

"Mom and Dad are trying to be fair, but they're not here for Jordy or me at all."

"What about his friends?" Emmett asked, and he named a few. "Cory and Evan, Georgie Fallon, all those guys?"

"Haven't seen them. Emmett, none of them are calling. It's as if they blame him—" Sandy stopped, not wanting to continue the litany, to say she felt she was being ostracized, too. None of her and Emmett's couple friends had called or come by, either, since she'd been home. No one had offered her their condolences on the death of her nephew, or brought her a casserole as a token of their regret. She hadn't received so much as a sympathy card.

The silence lingered, and it was awful for the way it lacked so much as a glimmer of hope. They couldn't even fake it, the sense that things would get better.

"You realize you're going to have to cash out Jordy's college fund," Emmett finally said, as if it was easier for him to deal with the financial rather than the emotional cost.

"No," she said. "I've thought about it, and we have to find a different way."

Emmett didn't answer. He was waiting for her to see it, the lack of other alternatives.

"We can't take that away from him, Emmett," Sandy insisted. "He's hurting so badly right now. He needs to know we believe in him and in his future even if no one else does. If we unload his college fund, how will it look?"

"I know about the hurting," Emmett said, and for a moment Sandy was lost as to his meaning, and then it came to her that he was referring to the pain her deception had caused him. His reminder, the way he'd tossed it out there, irked her, and it frightened her. He didn't know the half, she thought. The fact that Jordy had a different flesh-and-blood father was no abstract idea now. He was real, a physical entity, a man Jordy insisted he would know, a man who had, two years ago, written Sandy to say he would like nothing better than for her to grant his request to meet his son. Sandy had ignored his note. It had been easy enough to do when he was still a secret kept between sisters.

"You mentioned a witness." Emmett was back to the business at hand.

"Yeah, Pete Hoskins." Sandy matched his flat inflection. "He's a tow-truck driver from Greeley. He was picking up a car when he says the kids passed him, going fast, music blasting. He was under the billboard near that turn—the one for Lion's Creek Barbecue?"

Emmett knew the place. "That board is lit up like daylight at night."

"That's how he saw it so clearly—that Jordy was driving." Sandy walked to the back door and looked out. The yard was full of shadows. In the distance, the barn hovered in an eerie wash of moonlight. They'd had a horse once. Jordy and Trav had asked for one, a joint gift for their thirteenth birthdays that fell within days of each other, and thinking the care of a horse would be a good tool to teach responsibility, Sandy and Emmett had gone in halves with Jenna and bought a retired quarter horse, a gentle old mare named Girlie Sue. They had barely had her a year when one night, late, during a thunderstorm, she became so frightened she broke down her stall gate and left the barn at a full gallop. They'd found her the next morning, dead in a thicket of live oaks, about a quarter mile from the house. She'd run into one of the oaks head-on and fractured her skull. The same way Travis's head had been fractured when Jordy's car crashed into the same kind of tree. The similarity seemed freakish to her now; it seemed alien, but that was probably the product of too much emotion, too much wanting to find some kind of sign, sense, message. When there was none.

Who knew? Her thoughts weren't coherent, really. She couldn't rely on them.

"There might be other witnesses," she said now to Emmett, because clearly the fool that lived in her head was determined to cling to hope. "Other drivers might have seen something different. Roger's not finished . . ."

Her pause invited Emmett's answer, but he didn't supply one. Maybe he was like her when she'd been told the witness had positively ID'd Jordy. Maybe it had knocked the wind out of him, too.

"It looks bad for him, Emmett. Roger says if Jordy's found guilty, he could be sent to prison for as many as thirty years. Thirty years." She repeated it softly, more to herself. Jordy would be fifty when he got out. She and Emmett would be dead, or close. She was fighting tears when she told Emmett she couldn't handle it, that she needed him, wouldn't he please come home.

She was working so hard on not crying that when he answered, she only caught the gist of his response. It was something like *I don't know what to tell you* or *I don't know what you want from me.* Whatever it was, she felt he was blaming her or punishing her, and it made her furious.

"I can understand that you're angry at me," she told him, "but you're the only dad Jordy has ever known, and he needs you. I don't care what either of you thinks of me. You have meant the world—been the world—to each other, and you need to come home. For him, Emmett."

Silence. The sense of his breath heavy with the weight of her betrayal of his trust in her.

She tried again. "He's not to blame, Emmett. Can't you see that? Please come home for him. Please," she repeated, and she gently recradled the phone.

• • •

It was after midnight when she entered his name, Jordy's birth father's name, into a search engine. She hadn't kept a record of his contact information when he'd written to her before. She'd wanted nothing to do with him other than to continue pretending he didn't exist. She could never have foreseen the circumstances that would change her mind.

She was surprised by the number of entries that appeared on the page, the most recent involving media coverage of a balcony collapse in Houston that had killed nine people. Reading through the information, she learned that only days ago the architects had been severed from legal liability. Digging further, she came across the website for his firm, and that was where she found his e-mail address. She clicked the link, and when it opened a message window, she cupped her elbows, staring at it. It was a while before she could make herself put her fingertips on the keys, but then she did.

> Dear Beck, I don't know if you remember, but two years ago you e-mailed, saying you and your wife were thinking of moving to the area and asking if I would consider letting you both meet my son—

She stopped, looked at the words *my son*, typed *Jordan*, and stopped again.

> I didn't answer, which was probably wrong of
> me, but I was scared—

No, she thought, and erased all she'd written. There were more false starts. An hour passed, but finally she had composed a letter that she hoped would accomplish what she intended, which was, in part, to warn Beck of Jordy's intention to contact him, and to ask him to be gentle, to be kind. It was what she remembered most clearly about Beck Hennessey—his kindness.

It was a week before she found a response in her in-box.

> We are sorry to inform you, but Mr.
> Hennessey has passed away.

9

Beck had been dead four weeks and three days when the young man appeared at the cottage. It was early, not yet eight o'clock, and Libby, taking advantage of the still-cool morning air, was on her knees near the rose arbor, wielding a shovel. She looked up and was startled to catch sight of someone rounding the corner of the house. With the sun in her eyes, he wasn't more than a dark shape, tall and wide shouldered. Big. Much bigger than she was. Given all that had happened in recent weeks, she was wary and rose from her knees, slowly, keeping the shovel, a sharpshooter with a honed blade, in her grasp.

"Can I help you?" she asked.

He stopped several feet from her and said he wasn't sure. He seemed as leery of her as she was of him.

"Who are you looking for?"

He made a sound, like a laugh but not. "I'm Jordan Cline," he said, and Libby's breath dipped.

The reality of him—Beck's son—in the flesh, standing only feet away from her, was much different from the abstract idea. It shook her more than she'd thought it would when she'd imagined the encounter.

She'd known about him since before he was born. She'd been wrecked emotionally when Beck told her of this boy's existence. The memory of her pain was what had led Beck to say, before leaving for Houston, that simply because they were in the same vicinity as the son he'd never met, it didn't mean they had to pursue making contact. Now, she felt only sadness that Beck wasn't here. It didn't seem fair.

"Do you know who I am?" the young man asked.

"I do," Libby answered. She might have been less certain if not for Sandy's e-mail. Beck's assistant, Julie, had forwarded it during the week following his death with the comment that she'd advised Mrs. Cline that Mr. Hennessey had passed. Ever since Libby had wondered what Julie had made of it, if even now Beck was the talk of the office, of Houston, that for all its big-city swagger had a gossipy good ol' boy network that would rival the one in Wyatt any day. She had no way of knowing what was being said, having left Houston just days after Beck's funeral.

"I didn't plan to come," he said. "I mean, I did—"

"How did you find me?"

"I looked online. That's how I found out y'all had bought land, part of the Little B. I live on 1620, too," he added. "But I'm about fifteen miles out from the other side of town."

"Ah." Libby had thought maybe his mother had told him.

"I told my mom, but she already knew you were here."

"Yes," Libby said. Ruth had heard Sandy was asking questions around town about the Hennesseys. Sandy had even approached Ruth at the grocery store to ask if she was Libby's real estate agent. Ruth had thought it was nervy, but not near as nervy as Sandy's e-mail to Beck.

A cloud slipped over the sun; he took off his ball cap, and she saw it. His resemblance to Beck—the dark, curling hair and startling blue eyes, the strong jaw and chin with Beck's same cleft—all this young man's features, even his stance, the shape of his knees, the swell of his calves, was so strikingly reminiscent of her memory of her husband as the young man who had come upon her at the hospital on the day of Helen's death, that tears rose, a fist, seizing her throat. Here was the son she had prayed to give birth to, the boy she had nearly lost her mind over, trying to conceive. Grown up now, healthy and fit—the very image of his father. Beck's incarnation, or, at least, that's how she wanted to see him.

The sense of this thrilled and yet unnerved her. An urge came to drop the shovel and run. She stood her ground, keeping his gaze. He looked worn-out, somehow haunted. Older than the grainy images she'd seen of him in the newspaper, as if all that he was undergoing now—the criminal charges, the revelation about his birth—was aging him.

"You look like him," she said, and she could tell he wasn't sure how to take it.

"It's true, then." He wasn't asking, really. He seemed resigned.

"You didn't know."

"I overheard my grandparents talking when I was in the hospital."

"That's how you found out?"

"Yeah. They didn't know it, either. No one did except my aunt, and she kind of blurted it out when Emmett said he was going to donate blood in case I needed it. They would have figured out it wasn't a match, I guess."

Libby was appalled. She thought she wouldn't have kept such a secret in Sandy's place. But who knew? It was easy enough to predict what you would or wouldn't do from the sidelines. "I heard about your accident," she said. "I'm so sorry about—everything."

"Thanks." He bent quickly, and scooping a pebble out of the dirt, he pitched it, hard, into the woods.

Libby had the sense he wasn't dealing with his grief so much as he was fighting it, trying to hold himself together.

"Mom told me she wrote to your husband. That was before she—we knew he died."

"Yes." Libby passed the shovel to her other hand, feeling his eyes on her. She felt the pressure of his every unasked question taking shape in the lingering pause. Did Libby know about the e-mail? Had she read it? Was it a shock to her, finding out about him, or had she, like his aunt and his mother, known of his existence all along? But why should she feel compelled to explain, to become part of his dilemma? She didn't want it, not the aggravation or the worry. *Ask your mother,* she wanted to say. Let her tell you her sex with my husband was a mistake, and the resulting pregnancy was an accident. *You* were an accident, one your mother kept for herself and lied about, the one your birth father was sworn never to contact.

It was only now when all hell was breaking loose—and wasn't it, oh, Libby didn't know, convenient, ironic, something—that Sandy had changed her mind and relented. When Beck was no longer here to handle the situation, to assume any of the responsibility. *I have nowhere else to turn,* Sandy had written in her note to Beck. *Between the out-of-network medical fees and all the legal expenses, an attorney retainer, the cost of going to trial . . . you will surely agree that to use Jordy's college fund isn't . . . would never have approached you if the circumstances weren't . . . I know this is out of the blue . . .*

Out of the blue? Try outside the known universe, Libby had thought a month ago reading Sandy's message to Beck. *Try outside the realm of sanity. Try two years ago you couldn't be bothered to reply to my husband's very reasonable request to establish a connection. And now you want his involvement, his money and support?* The day she'd received the forwarded e-mail, her anger at Sandy's effrontery had driven her from the cottage. She'd walked for miles and come back red-faced and sweating from the heat, and her fury had persisted. She'd consoled herself with the thought that, given the fact of Beck's death, Sandy wouldn't contact him again.

And she hadn't. She'd sent her son instead.

"My mom doesn't know I'm here. She wouldn't like it."

Libby met Jordan's glance, not sure if she believed him. Desperation could drive a person to insane lengths.

"She says you have enough stress, you know, because of losing your husband."

"You came on your own? Why? I don't mean to sound—Beck is dead now."

He shrugged, looking away, seeming bewildered, almost stunned.

She remembered once in her days as a guidance counselor, working with a group of kids who'd lost whole chunks of their existence—homes, pets, loved ones—in a hurricane-spawned tornado. They'd had this same look, as if they were lost and searching for a landmark, solid ground, anywhere they might feel safe again. Jordan hadn't lost his home, but he had lost his identity—or half of it, anyway. He had lost his known and familiar world. He'd been lied to and betrayed. And all of that in addition to grappling with the enormous consequences of his own actions.

Her heart twisted with concern for him, for the outcome, the impact this was bound to have on his life. And as much as she did not want him here, as much as she did not want to deal with him or his mother, she couldn't get enough of looking at him, this boy, young man, Beck's son, who could have been—should have been—her son. She touched her temple. Thoughts like that—she would have to watch herself.

"Are you planting those?" He nodded at the collection of shrubbery in nursery pots behind her.

"Trying," she answered. "It's not easy digging here. There's so much rock."

"You have a rock bar? A posthole digger? I could help."

She wanted to say no, but the truth was she didn't want him to go. "I have both," she said. "They're so heavy, I can't use them."

He had experience, he said. "I've worked for my mom summers since—" He stopped to think. "Junior high? Maybe before. Me and

Travis—" He stopped again, looking away, but his pain and grief, like her own, were still raw and too fresh to hide.

She noticed now, where the sun picked at it, the fleshy, reddened scar that carved a cruel path from the corner of his right eye to his ear. There was a fair-size divot where the flesh had been gouged out, near the hairline above his temple. Libby had to quell the urge to touch his arm, to do something to show she did care.

He said, "My mom's a landscape architect."

"I know," Libby said. She wasn't sure exactly when she realized that the woman in the vintage pickup with the landscaping sign she'd seen parked alongside CR 440 back in July had to have been Sandy. Much of the time surrounding Beck's death was a blur. Jordan followed her to the shed, and they found the tools. "You're at UT, right? Are you thinking of going into the same line of work as your mom?"

"I don't know if I'm going back to school. Who knows where I'll be. Where do you want me to dig?"

She was disconcerted for a moment, her mind hanging on what Jordan had said. Did he think he would be in jail? But his trial was months away, scheduled for spring, she thought. She could have asked. Beck would have if he were here, but as Jordan's father he'd have a right to such information. Wouldn't he? Even if he hadn't raised him?

"Ma'am?" he said, prompting her.

"Yes," she said. "Where is a good question." She cast a glance around, explaining her plan was to renovate and restore the old garden that had once surrounded the cottage. Together, they lugged the pots, arranging and spacing the shrubs, a mix of mountain laurel, rough-leaf dogwood, and American beautyberry she'd bought locally and hauled to the cottage the day before in Beck's truck. She'd been thrilled to find such a great selection at a nearby native nursery. *Wait until Beck saw . . .* The thought had risen, a moment's elation, gone as suddenly as it came in the cold swoop of reality.

"You have to let me pay you," she said at one point. She was on her knees, settling dirt around the root ball of one of the mountain laurels.

He rammed the thick iron bar into the rocky earth hard enough that she felt the ground shudder. "To tell you the truth, it feels good, working like this."

"Yes." She went back to her task. Augie and Ruth had told her how close Jordan and his cousin had been. As close as brothers. She couldn't imagine what it must be like, what kind of hell it was, to be accused of killing your brother.

"We were going to build a house here," she said during a water break later. It was after twelve now, and although they were in the shade, working on the north side of the cottage, it was getting hotter, and she was worn-out and hungry, ready to stop. She asked if he'd like a sandwich. He demurred, not wanting to be any trouble, but when she said she would like having the company, that meals alone were kind of a drag, he followed her into the cottage.

He's a stranger, a voice warned, *a strange man. Kid,* corrected another voice. But who knew why he'd come, what he was after? For all she knew, he could be as twisted as the kid who'd strung up the slaughtered hog in the cedar tree, left a dead hummingbird on her kitchen floor, a threatening note on her countertop, or who'd most recently left a nest filled with butchered baby rats in her mailbox on the highway. She'd found that last week. She didn't know what to make of it. If Beck, as a consulting architect on the condo project where the balcony had collapsed, was the target, what was the point of threatening him now that he was dead?

She and Jordan moved around the small kitchen, taking awkward turns at the sink, washing their hands and drying them. She invited him to sit down at the table and felt better when he did.

"I have almost anything you'd like." Libby opened the refrigerator, contemplating the contents with dismay. She rattled off a list: there were casseroles—turkey, ham, or tuna—several pasta salads, a fruit salad, two cakes, and four kinds of pie. "I could open a restaurant. People from town have been so kind." *Kind or nosy,* she thought. News of Beck's death had spread like a virus in town. Ruth had said folks in Wyatt liked nothing better than to join a disaster brigade.

Their hearts are good, Ruth had said.

Yes, but not their pity, Libby replied.

She turned to Jordan. "Really. What would you like?"

"Whatever you're having is fine," he said.

She took out a plastic bowl filled with fresh spinach and the egg salad she'd made the day before when, perversely, her stomach had wanted something she'd made herself. She got a loaf of wheat bread from a cabinet.

He broke the silence. "You're building a house, you said."

"We were. Beck and I were until he died." She pushed the sentence out, stripping the emotion from it. Sometimes it was possible. Sometimes she could think of his loss, speak of it, and it did not take her breath, did not leave her wishing—oh, not so much for her own death, as for a way to be free of the constant, jarring reality of his. There was nothing she could do to fill the vacancy he'd left behind. She'd told Ruth if it ended up breaking her, oh well. Ruth thought Libby meant she would harm herself. Libby didn't know what she meant. So far, she and the grief were wary adversaries, walking around each other, taking each other's measure. So far, she still got up every morning and made the coffee and greeted the sun and proceeded with her plan to renovate the old perennial borders that framed the cottage. She talked to Beck in her mind and out loud. She thought sometimes he answered her.

Maybe that was why she'd felt compelled to let this boy—Beck's son—into her house. Beck wouldn't have closed the door on him, not even if he were the one behind the so-called pranks. Beck would have gotten to the bottom of it.

"At first when I said I wanted to move here from Houston to be close to my friend Ruth, Beck wasn't sure it was a good idea." Libby spooned egg salad onto the bread slices. "Do you know Ruth Crandall? She has a real estate agency in town."

"I know who she is. Mom designed their gardens."

"That's how we found out you and your family were here. Ruth told us."

Jordan frowned.

"We're close, Ruth and I. Best buddies since college, so when she moved here to look after her aunt, we were in touch." She turned to him. "I don't know how much you've been told."

"Just my mom and your husband—" He broke off, shifting his glance. A flush reddened his neck, fanned over his cheeks. "She said it was a mistake; it didn't last."

Libby was sorry for him. The fact that he knew of the affair, that it was a source of embarrassment, of shame on his mother's account, pained her, and she turned her back, giving them both privacy. She said, "It must be hard, dealing with this now—with all the other . . ."

"I want to know, though, as much as you want to tell me."

"Beck met your mom when she was in college, getting her degree in landscape architecture. She was interning for a landscaping company that was doing the grounds for one of Beck's big projects, a business park. It was a huge undertaking, lasted an entire summer. It was before your mom's senior year, I think." How easily Libby told it now, those details that had almost killed her soul to hear when Beck related them. But she had asked; she had pushed him to tell her. *Glutton for punishment,* Ruth had said when Libby confided in her.

"Did he know about me? I mean, before I was born."

"He knew about the pregnancy." Libby paused. How best to say it, the truth, without causing more harm? "You aren't a mistake. You understand that, right?" Libby found Jordan's gaze.

"I guess." His expression asked what she was getting at.

"It was a difficult time." She looked away, trying to find the words. "It's hard to explain."

"No, I get it. I mean, he was married to you, and having a kid with her—"

"He didn't necessarily want to be cut out of your life. He went along when your mom asked him to promise not to contact her or try and see you. It seemed best for everyone at the time."

"But he knew I lived in Wyatt, you said. When did he find out?"

"A couple of years ago, when Ruth hired your mom, they got to talking one day, and your mom mentioned her degree from U of H and the internship. She talked about you, too. You were the right age." Ruth had actually asked Sandy about children. She had wanted verification of what she had begun to suspect. *I was stunned,* Ruth had said, relating the details to Libby later over the phone. *But I didn't let on. I'm such an actress. I could win an Oscar for my performance. You should have been there.* Libby had hooted.

"So, Ms. Crandall knew who my real dad was, too, two years ago?"

"Yes, but it wouldn't have been her place to tell you."

"She didn't let on to my mom."

"No."

"But she told you."

"Yes." Until Ruth's discovery, Beck hadn't known the outcome of Sandy's pregnancy, whether the child was a girl or a boy, but Libby saw no reason to tell Jordan that.

"You moved here anyway."

"We'd started looking for land out here by then. We didn't see a reason to change our plans." Beck had been unsettled about it, but more on Libby's behalf. What would she do, he had asked, if she met Sandy face-to-face? *Say hello?* Libby had joked.

It wasn't that she hadn't struggled with it. Ruth's discovery had made the fact that Beck had a child in the world real for him. He'd conceived a kind of hunger, a need to know the son he'd fathered, if only from a distance. Mothers who gave up their children for whatever reason often felt that way. Family members who had fallen out, fallen apart, were always seeking one another, trying to find their way back to one another. Libby might have resented it; on some level she supposed she did. But she had loved Beck more than she had wanted to cling to old bitterness.

"So he really did want to meet me?"

"He did. He wrote to your mom about it."

"When?"

"Two years ago, when we started looking at land and knew for sure we were going to build out here." Libby glanced at Jordan over her shoulder.

"She never told me."

"I didn't think she had. He never heard from her."

"It pisses me off," Jordan said.

"I can understand why it would, but maybe give her a chance to explain."

"Oh, she did that already. She said Dad—Emmett—got it wrong when she told him she was having a kid, that he thought I was his, and she let him. She thought he'd leave her if he knew the truth, because he'd done it before." Jordan's disgust was shot through with impatience, notes of disbelief and self-righteousness. He would have handled it better.

Libby remembered when she thought she'd had all the answers, too. She waved the knife, making light of it. "Well, there. You see?"

"I was eighteen two years ago, old enough to make my own decision about it. And what about Emmett? I know he feels like the biggest chump. Anyway, he did leave her, right after he found out, when I was in the hospital. He's still not home."

Libby stowed the lunch makings back in the refrigerator. She'd heard the talk around town. That Emmett had left to take care of his mother, who was recovering from heart surgery. But some said it was no time for running home to Mama, sick or not. Others said, who could blame him? His kid had killed his nephew, and that was a hell of a thing. The one aspect they agreed on was justice for Travis. Jordan had to pay. You do the crime, you do the time—that was the consensus. Ruth said she'd never seen anything like how folks had turned on the Clines. They'd always been well liked.

Beck would hate it, Libby thought, all the gossiping.

"I'm sorry," Jordan said. "About your husband, I mean. I wish I could have known him."

"He would have liked that very much." Libby cut the sandwiches in half, put them on plates, and brought them to the table. She ladled fruit salad into two berry bowls and served that, too. She offered iced tea.

Jordan shook his head. "Water's fine." He wrapped his hand around the bottle she'd given him earlier. His fingers were strong, his nails flat and square, and bitten to the quick. They were nothing like Beck's. He'd had beautiful hands.

"You should probably pay attention to your heart." She sat opposite Jordan.

He was biting into his sandwich but paused to give her a questioning look.

"Beck—" She had almost said "Your dad" and wondered what Jordan's reaction would have been if she had. But the whole concept of *dad* seemed confounding to him. He referred to the dad he'd grown up with as Emmett, and his birth dad was "your husband." She said, "Beck had a heart attack, and it was completely unexpected. He never had heart trouble." She took a small bite of the sandwich and set it back on her plate. Preparing food was all right, but eating it was problematic. She had no appetite.

Jordan said he'd read online about what had happened. "He was driving back here from Houston, wasn't he?"

"Yes. He'd gone there for a news conference. You read about the lawsuit, too, I guess."

Jordan said he had. "It's pretty terrible, the way that balcony fell, but the architects had nothing to do with it."

"That was the reason for the news conference. They were hoping to get the word out, to somehow reach whoever is killing the animals down there and leaving them around."

"Some sicko," Jordan said.

Libby made a noise of assent, dismissing the urge that surfaced in her mind to tell Jordan about the slaughtered animals she'd found around the property here.

He wiped his mouth with his napkin.

She said, "It happened fast—Beck's heart attack. The coroner said he didn't suffer." She stopped. Technically, it hadn't been a heart attack but a sudden cardiac arrest that had caused Beck's death, and it had occurred with so little warning, the coroner had said, that there'd been almost no chance for survival. Libby glanced at Jordan. "I'm glad for that—that it was quick, I mean." The part that was hard to bear was that he'd been alone, and his death on a rural county road had gone undiscovered for more than a day. A farmer passing on his tractor had spied the truck poking out of the underbrush that verged on the asphalt; its tailgate and a bit of the bed had caught the light of a blazing afternoon sun, and he'd stopped to investigate. He'd nearly had a heart attack himself on finding Beck's lifeless body slumped over the wheel. "What makes no sense—to me, anyway," she continued, "is the location where he was found. Why was he so far south of here? He was almost to San Antonio." She toyed with her fork. "The coroner said Beck may have been confused, that he might have been trying to drive himself to a hospital."

"You don't think so?"

"I don't know." It was the simplest explanation, and she badly wanted to be satisfied with it. The alternative was to go along with Mia. Beck's sister had come from Las Vegas to stay with Libby over the week of Beck's funeral, dragging her usual black cloud, weeping and shouting to anyone who would listen that her brother had been murdered by the same maniac who was killing the animals. The killer had escalated, she said. Beck was only the first human victim; there would be others. Everyone associated with the collapsed balcony, even Libby, was at risk. Mia had worn everyone out with her harangues, slurring her words, gushing tears at random moments, making a fool of herself.

Libby thought—and she would likely go to hell for it—it had to be one of the more cruel tricks of life that Beck, who had sworn off drinking, who had been gentle and kind, who as an architect and genuinely good human being had contributed beauty to the world, was dead, while his sister, a drunken, unemployed drama queen, was alive, if drinking one's days away could be called living.

Still, Mia's theory continued to run a restless circuit around the walls of Libby's brain. The similarity of the incidents—in Houston and here at the cottage—was undeniable, and if you added in the timing of Beck's death, which Libby couldn't keep her mind from doing, it seemed suspicious. Suppose the person behind the animal killings *had* followed Beck from Houston and run him off the road? An autopsy would never show it—Beck's autopsy certainly hadn't—but his heart, giving up the way it had, that might have been brought on by panic all the same.

There had been other animal killings in Houston since Beck's partner, Robert, found the entrails of a dead raccoon spread over the hood of his car, and in a city like Houston, animal killings were newsworthy, a cause for alarm, but out here, gutted animals were business as usual. Kid hijinks, Sergeant Huckabee had insisted when Libby called to report the hummingbird. She was wary of him now. The note that was left on the counter at the time she'd found the tiny, fallen bird—*I thought I told you to keep your doors locked*—was nearly the same advice the sergeant had given her twice before, the day he stopped her for speeding and again when they'd discovered the hog hanging from the limb of the cedar tree. She'd never mentioned the note to Huckabee; she wasn't sure why. He had followed through and made contact with his cop friend in Houston, but it had come to nothing. He'd agreed with Huckabee that the slaughtered animals here were acts of small-town malicious mischief, unrelated to the balcony collapse or anything else going on down south in the big city.

Libby couldn't buy that it was simple vandalism. Someone had defiled her property; they had possibly run her husband off the road to his death.

They had been in her house.

She glanced at Jordan. What was she doing, letting this stranger in here? So he looked like Beck and said he was Beck's son. He could be anyone. The world was full of schemers, charming people who would ingratiate themselves, and once they had you in their thrall, they'd take everything you had, including your dignity. Widows with their senses dulled by grief made the best victims. Wasn't that what everyone said?

A knock at the door startled her; she was aware of Jordan bolting upright.

"I have no idea who that could be," she said, going to the door.

"I should go." Jordon got up, began gathering their dishes.

She peeped from the window and glimpsed Sergeant Huckabee, standing with his back to her, on her front porch, and even as she announced this to Jordan, even as she said with some dismay, "It's Sergeant Huckabee," she saw Jordan's glance darting around as if he were hunting an escape route. But she had no time to puzzle it out. She'd already opened the door.

The sergeant turned, smiling, and Libby saw he had brought what she assumed was his family with him. He urged a young woman and little girl forward, introducing them: "This is my wife, Coleta, and my daughter, Heidi." He beamed down at the child. "Say hello to Mrs. Hennessey, Heidi."

She ducked behind her mother.

"It's nice to meet you, Heidi," Libby said. "And you as well, Coleta. I've heard a lot about you."

Coleta dropped her gaze. Her thick lashes were dark against her skin, which was flawless. The rose blush blooming across her cheeks was in pretty contrast to the café au lait shade of her complexion. Libby thought of Ruth's description of her, that it hadn't captured how truly lovely Coleta was. She was like a china doll, fragile looking and vulnerable, self-effacing in a way that made you feel she had to be protected. Ruth had finally given in and hired Coleta against her better judgment. *She can scarcely speak English,* Ruth had said. *What am I thinking?* Ruth would never admit it, but she was a softy.

"Come in." Libby widened the door.

"Oh no, senora." Coleta lifted a casserole dish swaddled in a blue-checked dish towel, and in halting English, she said, "We come, bring you this. Tamale. I make."

"Best you will ever eat. I promise," the sergeant said.

Coleta said, "No. He is—" She broke off, looking for the word, frustrated when she couldn't find it. Blushing, she looked up at her husband, who towered over her, for help.

"She thinks I'm prejudiced," he said, and Libby knew it was true and that it made him happy. She thought how when he had stopped her for speeding, she had found him patronizing, a little menacing. Even on his subsequent visits out here, he'd been brusque, every inch the cop. It was disconcerting now, this soft glow of affection emanating from him, this glimmering pride. But she guessed he wouldn't last long on the job, showing this side of himself in the course of enforcing the law.

"Won't you all come in?" Libby repeated her invitation, and this time he shepherded his little family across the doorsill, asking if she would call him Len or Huck, whichever she preferred.

Libby took possession of the still-warm casserole dish, and said, "Okay, then, I'm Libby."

Heidi peeped from behind her mother's skirt.

"You are adorable," Libby told her. She found Coleta's gaze. *"Bonita."* She tried the word, thinking it was the right one. *"Muy bonita."*

Coleta's smile was pleased; she dipped her chin, shielding it. *"Gracias."* Her offering of thanks came on a murmur of air.

"How old are you, Heidi?" Libby asked, smiling down at her.

The little girl held up four fingers, spreading them wide like rays of the sun.

"Almost four," Huck corrected her gently. He glanced at Libby. "She'll be four in September."

"Ah," Libby said. "You're getting to be a big girl."

"We can only stay a moment," Huck said. "We're taking Heidi swimming at Lake Hershey in Ten-Mile Park. Just up the highway," he added, and Libby thought it was because she was a newcomer and might not know. But she did know it.

"Beck and I hiked there not long ago."

Huck's eyes went loose with apology. He hadn't meant to rake up a memory that caused her pain. As if she didn't remember every moment. "It's all right," she said, and then quickly, she said, "I've been thinking I might stay here in the cottage."

"I wondered if you would, in view of the vandalism—" But now he caught sight of Libby's first visitor, and his demeanor hardened. "Jordy Cline. What in the hell are you doing here, son? I hope you didn't drive out here."

His voice was hard; it was his cop voice, and Libby deplored it.

"No, Sergeant, I didn't drive. I hitched. "

Hitched? Libby thought. Had it really meant that much to him to come here?

"You know, I'd think you'd tone down the attitude given the circumstances, but, hell, that's just me. I'd like to know what you're doing here, what your business is with Mrs. Hennessey."

"I'm not required by law to explain that to you, am I? You can't revoke my bail if I don't, right?"

Huckabee, to his credit, Libby thought, didn't take the bait.

"He's doing some work for me," she said, in an attempt to defuse the situation. It wasn't a total lie. She realized, too, that she didn't want the true nature of Jordan's visit exposed any more than she wanted to see him create more trouble for himself. "That's all right, isn't it?" Libby addressed the sergeant. "He can work, can't he?"

"As long as he can get himself around without driving," Huckabee answered, and while he seemed less formidable now, Libby sensed he was alert, watchful in the way that's characteristic of lawmen, of bullies. In her mind there was a fine line between the two. She remembered how he'd followed her, closely, from the shoulder of the road for a short time after stopping her for speeding. She had felt threatened by him in those few moments. She felt wary of him now, although she realized he was only doing his job, that his advice was spot-on, and warranted, and very likely well meant. Still, the undercurrent of authority remained, as lethal and menacing as the duty weapon he strapped on his hip before beginning a shift.

He said, "Everybody's got eyes on you, Jordy. You mess up, some-body's bound to see. I'm telling you for your own good, okay?"

Libby looked at Jordan, at the storm fuming in his eyes. She sensed the effort he was making to keep a grip on the hot words she could only imagine were boiling on his tongue.

"Len?" Coleta edged Heidi toward the door, her gaze darting between Jordan and her husband and back to Jordan. She was clearly worried, as if she didn't understand what was happening, or perhaps, Libby thought, Coleta understood all too well that there were grounds for her apprehension.

Huckabee seemed not to hear her, though. His focus was on Jordan.

"I know you're hurting, son. Losing Travis, your best buddy, know-ing it's your fault—it's one hell of a hard thing. I've been where you are. I can tell you the pain never goes away entirely, but it'll get better. Tolerable, anyway. You'll get past the worst of it, and you'll make some kind of life. If you don't screw up more than you already have, you can learn from this."

Libby waited for Jordan to object, but he only looked at the sergeant with something like derision riding in his eyes. Libby sensed he wasn't buying Huckabee's speech, which had sounded to her almost fatherly, in a pointed way.

And yet she couldn't quite trust it, either. She didn't know what bothered her. Huckabee seemed to care. Augie and Ruth said he was a good guy, a good cop. Fair. Even tempered. What did she know, anyway? Everything the sergeant said matched the facts: Jordan had driven a car drunk and caused an accident that had killed his cousin and left a young woman in a coma.

Libby took a quick step to the kitchen table and set the casserole down, and turning, she found Coleta's glance. "Thank you for the tamales."

"*Sí, senora. De nada.* You are welcome," she added, her translated English halting and unsure.

"Yes, perfectly said." Libby couldn't resist encouraging her.

Coleta smiled, glancing at her husband.

He smiled, too, but the look he gave Libby held none of that warmth. She felt he was assessing her, putting her on notice, but then he and his family were quickly gone, and she thought it might as easily have been her imagination.

• • •

She drove Jordan home in Beck's truck, over his protests. When she stopped at the end of the road that led to the highway, he got out and opened the gate, waited for her to pass through, then locked it behind her.

She thanked him when he got back into the truck, and after they'd driven several miles in silence, she said, "I could really use some help at the cottage with the landscaping, but I don't want you hitchhiking—unless you already have a job." She hadn't thought of that.

But he said he didn't. "I could probably get somebody to bring me. Not my mom," he added quickly.

No, Libby thought.

"It might be hard to work out a regular schedule, though, since I'd have to rely on somebody to give me a ride."

Talking further, they decided he would call when he could arrange transportation, and when she offered him fifteen an hour, he said it would be great. "It's more than Mom pays me."

Now that it was settled, Libby questioned her sanity. Why was she doing this, involving him in her life? But she could already tell there was no use in arguing with herself. *This is Beck's son,* a voice in her head said, and it was as if Beck were there, riding beside her. She could reach out and touch him, and he would be warm and real. *If all things were truly possible.*

She glanced at Jordan. He didn't resemble Beck so much in profile. His nose was shorter and slightly upturned. Beck's nose had been long and straight, what people called a Roman nose. Libby had never seen Sandy close up. Jordan might have her nose, for all she knew. She said, "I'm surprised you aren't working for your mom this summer."

"It's better if we're not around each other right now."

Libby waited, knowing from her work as a guidance counselor that silence could be unnerving, that it would often get a person talking simply to fill the void. She didn't know what to say, in any case. She didn't know why she was thinking of tactics that might lead him to confide in her. To what end? What would she do with any information he gave her? She didn't know if she had ever in her life felt so uncertain, so unsure of her role. But she was drawn to him, that much was undeniable.

He said, "It's no secret, I'm in a lot of deep shit. Sorry."

"No, it's okay."

"Huck is a great guy, or he used to be. He was at my aunt Jenna's a lot when me and Trav were kids."

"I heard your uncle was killed in the line of duty," Libby said. "In San Antonio? He and Sergeant Huckabee were partners, right?" They'd reached town, and Libby stopped at a red light.

"Yeah, Huck was kind of like a dad to Travis. He did stuff with both of us. Once he even helped me and Travis build a soapbox-derby car. We raced it in Dallas and a few other places around Texas."

"Did you win?" Libby headed through the intersection and picked up speed.

"Nah. We didn't care. It was just for fun. You should slow down. My house—see that little road up there with the green mailbox? That's where you turn."

She followed his directions, cresting a short hill. The house, a low-slung ranch style with a rusty metal roof and a deep front porch, came into view. What if his mother was home? The possibility had needled Libby's mind the entire way here.

"My mom's on a job."

Libby darted a glance at Jordan, and it was in his eyes that he'd read her mind. She parked in front of the basketball goal. The net was missing, and the plastic, sand-filled base was faded. It looked well used. "Do you play?"

Jordan said, "For fun, yeah."

Libby said, "I grew up in a neighborhood full of basketball-playing boys, mostly older than me. Sometimes they let me hang out with them. They taught me the game." She remembered the slap of the ball on the concrete, the endless taunts and whoops of laughter, summer nights playing endless games of H-O-R-S-E. They'd never liked it when she won.

"Trav and I played football in high school. We were cocaptains. I don't really know why I got picked for the job, but Trav—he was a natural-born leader. He never let anyone quit, never let them get down. No matter how bad you screwed up, he'd be there for you. You know the rule 'No pass, no play'?"

Libby nodded.

"The center on our team, Brad Strong—he couldn't get algebra, not the simplest equation, and he was flunking big-time. He was all, like, ready to quit to avoid getting booted him off the team, but Trav wouldn't let him. He tutored Brad—nights, weekends, before school, whatever—and he never asked for a dime. He knew Brad didn't have it. Trav helped other kids with their grades, too, not just football players. He never took a fee unless they could afford it."

"Brad passed?"

"He made a B."

"Pretty impressive," Libby said. It was. She remembered what Augie had told her about Travis, that he'd worked with special-needs kids when he had extra time. It made her heart ache to think of his loss, of what he might have become, the contribution to the lives of others he might have made had his life not been extinguished so soon. Such a waste.

"Trav was the best," Jordan said, and then, after a heartbeat, he added, "I wasn't driving."

Libby looked at him; he was staring straight ahead.

"We were on the lake all day. Michelle's folks have a real nice place. They've got boats, a couple of Jet Skis. Her mom and dad are pretty cool, too. They're not all uptight if we have a beer or something."

Libby didn't say anything.

"We're almost twenty-one, anyway." He waited, and when Libby didn't fill the silence, he said, "I know you shouldn't drink and drive. I mean, I know it when I'm sober. Everybody does, I guess."

"But that night you weren't sober."

"No. We'd been drinking pretty much all day. We slept some in the afternoon when it got really hot, but you know . . . we kind of started in again when we got up. Michelle's folks cooked hamburgers, and we ate. I wanted to just chill there, watch a movie or something, but Trav was wired, like, he ate dinner, drank a couple more beers, and got his second wind or something. He wanted to shoot off firecrackers."

Jordan wiped his face and made a noise deep in his throat. It sounded to Libby like a protest of sorts. It sounded like a wish to not tell the rest, or to change it somehow.

He said, "We'd already shot off everything we had over the Fourth, but the stands stay open around here for a few extra days till they sell out, or sell as much as they can. I didn't know how bad off Trav was, or I would never have given him my keys, but he's usually all right to drive. He doesn't get wasted."

"Were you doing something more than drinking?"

Jordan didn't answer. He wiped his face again. "X," he said. "We took some Ecstasy, but I don't think they found it when they did the tox screen at the hospital, or they would have said something, so maybe it wore off."

"I don't know," Libby said. "Alcohol and drugs in combination—" She stopped, not wanting to come off as if she were preaching. She sensed it was important to let him talk.

"We were going to go to this stand outside Greeley, but we couldn't find it, and somehow we got off on 440, and Trav's flying down the road like he's Mario Andretti. Michelle was in back, and she's screaming at him to slow down, but he said no, he was going to see how fast the old mothereffer could go—it was crazy. I never saw him like that."

"You weren't wearing seat belts." Libby had heard this from Augie or Ruth.

Jordan shook his head, pinched the bridge of his nose. "I looked at the speedometer right before he lost control; he was pushing a hundred miles an hour. I was freaking, too—440 is bad enough when you're sober." His voice caught. He cleared his throat.

They shared a silence, Libby looking in the rearview. She kept expecting to see Jordan's mother pulling up onto the driveway.

Jordan scrubbed his hands down his thighs. "Airbags only partially inflated. Travis went out the driver's-side window. He landed about twenty feet away in some grass. I remember my head slamming into the passenger-side window, but when I came to, I was in the driver's seat. I don't know how I got there, or how long it was before I woke up, but I was real confused. I thought I was at home and had fallen out of bed. It was weird."

He stopped and took a breath, steadying himself. His throat worked with the effort. A pulse throbbed at his temple. She wanted to tell him he didn't have to go on, but he lifted a hand, as if he'd read her mind again.

"Michelle was, like, whimpering, but she said she was okay when I asked her." Jordan took a moment, scouring his legs with his palms again. "Then I looked around for Trav, and I saw him in the grass, all twisted up, not moving—I don't know—it's like something took over, and somehow I got out of the car and over to him. I said his name, I tried to get him to wake up, but I kept passing out. 'C'mon, man. I love you, man.' I kept saying it. I kept saying his name and that I loved him and then I'd pass out—"

Libby put her hand on his arm; she couldn't stop herself. He sounded so broken.

"If people find out Trav was driving, they're going to hate him like they hate me. I don't want that to happen. He's dead now. All that's left is his memory, and I'm not screwing that up. If I have to go to prison—so I will."

"I can understand why you feel that way, but would Travis want you taking the blame?"

"Well, I'm not. I keep telling everyone I wasn't driving."

"But you have to do more, say more than that, right? What about your attorney? Have you told him the whole story?"

"Yeah, but the evidence—plus, everybody—I mean, I've got kind of a reputation for drinking a lot, you know?"

"Do you? Drink too much?"

"I don't know. Maybe. Probably. Anyway, there's a witness who says he saw me driving that night. I remember there was this pickup truck coming from the opposite direction. We were in his lane, going right for him. I don't know how we kept from hitting him head-on."

"The driver of the truck that was coming at you? He's the witness?"

"I don't think so. That guy says we passed him, and he saw me in the driver's seat. The truck I remember was coming from the other way, but my brain was messed up, I might not be remembering right. Anyway, I was yelling at Trav the whole time. I was so scared."

"I can only imagine," Libby said, and it was true. She'd never been in a car accident, not even a fender bender.

"My attorney seems pretty sure we can make a deal. I could get off with probation, community service, since it's my first offense. The only problem is Huck. He's not going to let me off. He knows the judges around here. He's got all the cops on his side. They'll make sure I go to prison. It's what Huck wants."

"Why?" Libby asked. "Why is he after you?"

Jordan looked at her, looked away, and then back. And then he told her.

• • •

Ricky Burrows was sitting on the front porch steps at the cottage when Libby got back from Jordan's.

He stood up when she got out of the car. "I hope you don't mind that I waited."

"No. It's fine." She'd stopped in town at the grocery store and bought a few things, a fully cooked rotisserie chicken, the makings for a salad. It was ridiculous when she had a refrigerator full of food. Coleta Huckabee's tamales, for one. But after talking to Jordan, she wasn't in the mood for tamales, or much of anything else associated with the Huckabees. She shifted the sack to her other arm, letting herself through the gate.

"I was wondering about your plans for the house," Ricky said. "I talked to Augie, but he wasn't sure."

"That's because I'm not sure." Libby paused at the foot of the steps. "It's awfully big for one person. I really don't know what I want to do." Part of her wanted to build the house anyway, because Beck had designed it. She had the money. The attorney who was handling Beck's estate had said she would be fine, that Beck had been overly cautious in his concern about their finances, which was typical of him.

"You could make it smaller." Ricky looked intently at her.

"I suppose I could."

"So, are you going back to Houston, then? Maybe you want to renovate this." He waved an arm, indicating the cottage.

"Are you looking for work? Is that why you came?" She scrambled, trying to come up with any odd jobs she might hire him to do. She asked about his truck, whether he'd ever heard anything from the police regarding the damage, who was responsible, and it only made her feel worse when he said no. She thought how she'd meant to go to the Greeley police about the incident and hadn't. So much had happened.

"I'm so sorry," she said.

"Not your fault," he said.

"No, but it happened on my property." It didn't make much sense that she felt responsible, but there it was—her brain, taking on the sins of the world. "You know it's possible that Beck was the intended target, not you, and whoever did it keyed the wrong truck. They would have come from Houston," she said when Ricky looked perplexed. "It's a business thing, a grudge, I guess you'd call it." She didn't want to get into the whole issue with the lawsuit and the hostility that had ensued as a result.

Ricky's grin was one-sided, commiserating. He said he knew about grudges.

"If you get me an estimate for a repair on your truck, I'm happy to pay for it. I should have offered before now." Why hadn't she?

"Nah. How would it look? A shiny door on my old beater?" He went to the gate.

"I'll make a decision about the house soon," she said.

"I talked to Sergeant Huckabee." Ricky went through the gate, and as he closed it he looked back at her.

"Was he any help?"

"Everything these days is for a price. You ever notice that? Cops are no different."

"I'm not sure what you mean."

"Nothing. Cops just piss me off in general, you know?" He smiled another crooked smile and got into his truck, and when he waved as he drove away, she waved back, thinking it must be so frustrating, coming all the way here from Colorado, looking for a break, a fresh start, only to have every door slam in your face.

10

Sandy saw the woman loitering by the cart-return area nearest her truck when she came out of the grocery store, and as she passed her, she had a sense of the woman's stare drilling her back like the hot August glare. She stowed her bags of groceries, searching her mind for a reference, and found none. She was pretty sure she'd never seen the woman before. But when she turned, there the woman was, so close Sandy took an involuntary backward step.

"You're Jordy Cline's mother." The woman wasn't asking so much as she was making an accusation. Her arms were crossed over her chest, and she was shaking as if she were cold, which was ridiculous given that the temperature was still hovering near one hundred degrees. She was sweating, so much that her short, dark hair was plastered to her cheeks and temples. She looked worn-out, used up, battered by fatigue, maybe, or grief, or insanity.

Something about her was off. Sandy could feel it. She realized the woman had no purse, no car keys in hand. How had she gotten here? Common sense warned she should get into her truck and go, but a less cautious impulse ruled, keeping her in place, trying to sort out the woman's identity, her problem, whether she needed help.

"I'm Patsy Meade," the woman said, watching Sandy as if waiting for a sign of recognition.

But Sandy was clueless and shook her head.

"Michelle Meade's mother?" The woman—Patsy—bit off the words. "I'm the mother of the beautiful girl your son put into a coma. The one who had her whole life ahead of her until your son got her into his car and drove her around drunk. I understand he's fine now, out of the hospital, walking around free, while his cousin is buried in a graveyard and my daughter might never wake up again. How does it feel? To be the mother of a monster?"

"Jordy isn't a monster." Sandy dug in her purse for her keys. "He wasn't driving."

"Oh, for God's sake. Do you think denial serves you now? My understanding is your kid drinks—a lot more than he should—but you and your husband are blind to it."

"Jordan doesn't drink more or less than—you don't know anything about him."

"My daughter knows him quite well. She was concerned about him. Concerned! Both she and Travis were. As if it ever does any good to care about a drunk. They talked to me about him the weekend they were at the lake, and that's what I told them. Cut him loose, stay away from him. I knew your son was bad news. I knew this was bound to happen. I just didn't think—didn't believe my daughter would be in the car—" Patsy broke off, looking away. She was shaking harder now.

Sandy wanted to leave, but she didn't feel able to lift her foot onto the truck's running board. It was beyond her. She apologized, saying, "I'm sorry," and it was difficult to hear her voice over the thudding of her heart, the ringing in her ears. She wasn't sure about the apology. Something warned her that Roger wouldn't be happy to hear she'd offered it. It might be construed as an admission of guilt. But that wasn't it. She was sorry the way any human being, any mother, would be for what Patsy was going through—the fear and the worry, the constant dread for her child. She was sorry for Michelle, lying in a hospital bed, her outcome uncertain when she should be getting ready to return to classes at UT.

She was sorry for Travis and Jenna and her parents. Emmett, Jordy, herself. Her sorrow pushed into her throat, as hard as a brick. It gripped her heart. She didn't cry. She thought if she were ever to start, she'd never stop. She couldn't see the end of it—all this grief.

"I came to warn you."

Sandy looked at Patsy.

"My husband and I hired an attorney. We're suing you, and your insurance company, to recover medical costs, of course, but also to make sure Jordy is punished. If the criminal-justice system lets him off with nothing more severe than a slap on the wrist, then we'll get justice for Travis and Michelle through the civil system—along with the settlement money."

Go fuck yourself. The retort was there, branding Sandy's tongue with its bitter heat. She didn't know what kept her from shouting it out, and to hell with what anyone thought of her—the wild woman, yelling her head off in the grocery-store parking lot.

She got into her truck, heaving herself into the seat. She was sick of defending herself, and Jordy, to her family, to folks all over town—and now to Patsy, whom she didn't even know. She thought how uncertain she was of Jordy's story, his conviction that Huck was setting him up. It had once seemed plausible, when she'd believed in Jordy's claim that Huck had a motive. *What motive?* She'd asked Jordy repeatedly. So had Roger. Nothing. It was bogus, that was all. A way to buy time, maybe. Not smart. Not even close to smart. Now Roger was talking about Jordy taking a plea.

Patsy stepped around the open door. "You did hear me?"

"Yes," Sandy said. "My attorney—or I should say, Jordy's attorney, told me to expect this." Roger had said not only was it likely the Meades would sue but that Jenna might as well. He had said in cases like this when the loss was uncountable, when emotions were raw and the nightmare never ending, blood did not run thicker than water.

Sandy looked at Patsy. "I'm sorry it's come to this."

"Not as sorry as you're going to be."

"Patsy?"

A man called her name. Sandy saw him standing several feet away, a grocery sack dangling from his hand. Mr. Meade, she assumed. She wondered what they were doing here in Wyatt. Their daughter was hospitalized in San Antonio, two hours away.

Patsy backed up.

"I really hope Michelle will be all right," Sandy said, because it was the truth, the truest thing she knew in the moment.

Patsy's snort was derisive. "We'll see you in court," she said.

. . .

She and Jordy had done the yard work together on Sunday, and she was cooking hamburger for taco salad when he came into the kitchen and opened the refrigerator, staring inside it.

"Shut the door. You're letting all the cold air out." The admonition was mechanical, automatic.

He swigged milk out of the carton before returning it to the refrigerator shelf, making a face when she said, "Jordy, honestly."

In the old normal days, he would have said, "Yep, I was raised in a barn," answering the question that was implied, a family joke. But they didn't share many of those lately, or any, in fact, and what he said was, "I got a job yesterday." He set forks and napkins on the countertop.

She turned the browned meat into a colander. "Really? Where?"

"On 1620." He named their rural route. "But on the other side of town."

"Don't classes at UT start next week?" Sandy glanced at him.

"Yeah, but I already said I'm not going back. What's the point? We both know I'm going to jail. It's where I belong, anyway."

Sandy set the colander in the sink hard enough that bits of meat flew out of it. "I hate that attitude. It's as if you've given up. I don't understand you, in any case. You say you weren't the driver, that Travis was, and Huck's out to get you, and yet you're willing to take the blame. Why?"

"I've driven wasted plenty of other times, Mom. Maybe if I go to jail, I won't do it again."

"What do you mean?" It shook her, hearing him talk this way. "You don't have a problem. You don't drink more than the rest of the kids."

He seemed not to hear her. "If I go to jail, maybe you and Dad'll get back together, and Aunt Jenna will get that closure everyone is always talking about." His disdain for the concept was evident in his voice. "It'll be better for the whole family if I'm gone. Might even be better for me."

"You were just a passenger, Jordy. You had no control over how Travis was driving. It wasn't even your idea to go out that night. You said Trav initiated—"

"I wasn't *just* a passenger, Mom." Jordan brought his hands down hard on the counter, making the silverware jump and clatter. "I participated. I didn't do or say one damn thing to stop him, and I could have. I could have stopped him. I could have coldcocked him. Something—" His voice broke.

"You don't know that, honey." Sandy extended her hand toward him. He backed out of her reach. "Okay," she said. "I'll assume you're right, but that still doesn't make what happened your fault."

"I'm working for Mrs. Hennessey."

"What? You went there? When I expressly asked you not to?" Sandy couldn't have been more astonished if Jordy had punched her. "She just lost her husband. What are you thinking?"

"I don't know, Mom, but since I never had a chance to know the guy before he died, maybe she can tell me about him."

He was accusing her. Sandy knew that, but she sensed his bewilderment, too, and his uncertainty. *He needs Travis,* Sandy thought. Travis would help him. He would make Jordy laugh about all this somehow. He'd make it easier for Jordy to live with it, the bombshell discovery that his father of record wasn't his father of birth. If all else failed, Trav would drag Jordy out to the driveway to shoot hoops till they both dropped, then they would grab a pizza.

How had it helped, what Jenna had done, blurting out Sandy's secret? In the wake of so much other loss, what had she accomplished dropping that bomb? The questions cut through Sandy's mind. She thought if Jenna were here, she might kill her.

"We should eat dinner," she said. At least she could do that; she could feed him.

He shrugged. *Whatever.*

She turned to the sink. He took the napkins and forks to the table in the breakfast nook, muttering something about prison, that if he was old enough to get tossed into a cell for murder, he should damn sure be able to go to work wherever he wanted to.

"Manslaughter, not murder," she said, uselessly.

"So what?" He raised his voice. "I'm screwed either way."

She turned to him. "I know you're scared, honey—"

"Look"—he interrupted her, throwing up his palms—"don't take this the wrong way, okay? But you don't know jack shit." And wheeling, he grabbed the keys to her truck from the hook by the back door, pushed through the screen, and went out, letting it slam behind him.

"Jordy, come back here!" She followed him through the door, several steps down the drive. She had slipped off her sandals, and the pavement burned the soles of her bare feet, but she was heedless of that. "You aren't supposed to drive," she shouted.

"I need to clear my head," he yelled over his shoulder.

There was nothing she could do but watch him get into her truck. He keyed the ignition and then he was gone.

Sandy didn't know how long she stayed outside, looking at the empty space where her truck had been, where Jordy had been. Where now the only thing to see was the heat shimmering off the pavement. She felt it firing the bottoms of her bare feet, needling her calves, and when she turned and walked back to the house, she wanted her mother. Or Emmett.

But when she picked up her phone, she called Roger. It wasn't that she couldn't have a conversation with either her mother or her husband. Or her dad, for that matter. Or even Troy. They were still on speaking terms, unlike a lot of folks who flat-out refused to talk to her, who crossed the street in town to avoid her. But the only one of those she cared about was Jenna.

Go figure.

Sandy wanted to kill her sister, and she missed Jenna like crazy. If Jenna died the way Travis had, she wouldn't know how to cope. But if she thought in that vein for too long, she would cry for Jordy's grief, for worry over how he was coping. For herself.

She thought how as sisters, she and Jenna had squabbled endlessly over silly things like whose turn it was to vacuum or take out the trash. But they'd seldom gone a day without speaking. And if one of them was facing something horrible, like Jenna's breast cancer, the other one was there to enfold her, to carry her, however figuratively.

In the past weeks since Jordy's arrest, Sandy had parked in front of Jenna's house in town several times and stared at the windows. She didn't know what she expected. That Jenna might come to the door and beckon her in? That she would have the courage to take herself up the front steps, knock on the door, and ask to come in? Nothing like that ever happened. She only felt worse. She felt Jenna's absence, her censure, in her core. It cut her from the inside in places she couldn't see or touch.

There was one thing about it, though—Jenna's shunning of her—it was honest. Sandy had no doubt in her mind where she stood with Jenna, and on that level, it was preferable to the false sense of concern she was treated to by some people, including her parents. It pissed her mother off when Sandy wondered out loud whether her parents cared about her, or that Jordy might lose his freedom.

After all, that was nothing by comparison. Travis had lost his life. Death trumped every other circumstance life could foist on you. That was how her family saw it. How everyone did. How could they not?

And where was her mom most of the time nowadays? Where was her dad if not at Jenna's, or on their way to or from Jenna's? Her mother had said they were going home to Georgetown more often now, that they needed to sleep in their own bed. And she assumed her dad was minding the business while Emmett holed up with his mother.

Sandy suspected Emmett talked to her dad on a regular basis, confiding in him while he had almost nothing to say to her. But there again, no one felt they owed her anything. She was the liar, the keeper of the secret that had shattered their lives.

Roger came on the line.

"Jordy's taken my truck," she said.

"Uh-oh. That's not good. What happened?"

"I can't say anything anymore that doesn't set him off. He's so angry with me. This whole thing about his dad—"

"It's a lot to take in." Roger was cautious.

Or wary of her. Sandy couldn't decide. She had burdened him with her confidences, her confessions, telling her son's lawyer of her affair with Beck, how it had resulted in Jordy's birth and that Emmett hadn't known, not until Jenna opened her mouth. She'd talked and talked, as if her tongue were hinged in the middle and flapped at both ends. But she was as isolated as Jordy, and she understood more than he knew about how you reach in your mind for your people, the ones you have loved and trusted and relied on. But they're gone. And they aren't coming back. And now there was no one. Only the cold, hollow place they left behind in your heart. That Jordy, at twenty, was experiencing this, too, made her ache. She would take on his pain, if she could.

"He's gone to see Libby Hennessey."

"Beck's wife?"

"The very same. He's working for her. Beck's widow, of all people."

"Is that where he is now, do you think?"

"I don't know. I feel like I should call the police before something terrible happens. He's upset. Who knows what he'll do?" A new worry came. "What if he buys beer and gets caught?" She thought of all the stories she'd heard about kids who were rootless, how they fell in with bad company, drifting into a life of crime, drug abuse, homelessness. She saw, vividly now, how it could happen, and it terrified her.

"Let's back up." Roger said this forcefully.

Sandy bit her lip.

"First, let's not involve the cops just yet, okay? I really think Jordy's just out to clear his head, like he told you. He's under a lot of pressure, you know? What he's facing—it's a lot to handle for a kid, and he *is* still pretty much a kid. But I keep telling you, he's doing it, he's handling it pretty well, from what I see. He's holding up."

"You really think so?" Maybe Jordy was talking to Roger more than she thought. She didn't ask. Roger would only say it was privileged.

"Why don't I take you to dinner? I bet he'll be home by the time we get back."

Sandy started to say no, but then overriding her better judgment, she invited him over. "I've got makings for taco salad, if you're hungry. If Jordy comes home, I want to be here," she added, and when Roger said he'd bring the beer if it was all right, Sandy said she had some, opening the refrigerator to make sure. She'd bought it for Emmett. She wondered if she should let Roger drink Emmett's beer.

Ending the call, she wondered if it was smart, having Roger over.

Looking down the length of herself, she thought of changing out of her jean shorts and T-shirt into linen capris and a peasant blouse. She realized she was nervous, and it only made it worse. It struck her that if Emmett were here and she'd invited Roger to the house, it would be entirely different, and somehow it seemed unfair. Why should asking a man to dinner suggest one thing when it was a woman alone and something else entirely if her husband was present?

When Roger arrived an hour later, she had tidied the kitchen, but she hadn't changed, and she was still nervous.

And he had brought a six-pack of beer anyway. "Hostess gift," he said, following her into the house.

"You didn't have to bring anything." She took it from him, handing him a bottle before stowing the rest in the refrigerator.

"You aren't having one?" He twisted off the cap.

"I'm not much of a drinker," she said. "I don't like the taste unless it's something sweet like a frozen grasshopper."

He made a face.

"I know." She smiled. Emmett made the same face, but he would get out the blender and whip one up for her if he thought she had a yen.

"Nothing from Jordy yet?" Roger leaned against the granite-topped island. He was good-looking for a fiftysomething man who was going gray at the temples and maybe a little soft in the middle. There was about him—that element of mischief she'd noticed before, something boyish and lighthearted in his demeanor. She wondered if he seemed less burdened because he had never married, never had the worry of children.

Answering Roger, she said she hadn't heard anything. "I called his cell phone, and it rang in his bedroom." She'd gone there and looked in, and then, defeated by the mess, she'd left, closing the door behind her. She used to nag him about the dirty clothes and the endless, mostly nacho cheese–flecked paper plates thrown everywhere. But at some point, she realized she had to pick her battles. A messy room, even a filthy, food-encrusted room, wasn't as life threatening, say, as AIDS. Or driving drunk. At summer's end, when he'd returned to college, she'd wade into the garbage pit, feeling as if she needed a hazmat suit. If history was any indicator, it would take her four days to restore the area.

Roger said, "He's not going back to UT. Did he tell you?"

"Yep, and he knows I'm not happy about it. His dad will be furious." But maybe Emmett would be relieved, Sandy thought. He could argue then that there was no need to hang on to Jordy's college fund. She found Roger's glance. "Won't it look bad if he doesn't go back?"

"It would certainly be better for him to be occupied. The trial's months away. It's a lot of time to fill. He needs something to do."

Sandy thought of his new job, working for Libby Hennessey. Why had the woman hired him? Did she know the circumstances?

"He can't drive," Roger said. "I think that's a huge roadblock, not to mention a blow to his pride. He'd have to hoof it around campus, and never mind the dent it would put in his social life. I told him he could get a bike, a good one, pretend he's training for the Tour de France." Roger laughed. Sandy didn't.

She invited him to sit down on the small overstuffed sofa in the breakfast nook. She rarely had time to curl up there herself, although that was how she'd envisioned using the space when she'd furnished it.

"I really like your house," Roger said. He unfolded his arm along the sofa's back, propped his ankle on his knee, looking around admiringly. "It's comfortable, pretty, like a garden, but without being—" He paused.

She eyed him, brows raised. "Without being?"

"Froufrou. You know, a lot of that lace-doily stuff like my granny had." A flush bladed his cheekbones, and the look in his eyes was abashed and yet delighted. He'd cut himself shaving beneath his left ear, and a bit of tissue clung to the spot. It was somehow endearing. Sandy looked away. But it took effort. She had wanted to keep holding on to his gaze.

She got tomatoes, a head of lettuce, and an onion out of the refrigerator.

Roger asked if he could help, and it startled her to find he was right beside her, near enough that she caught the scent of his aftershave, something lemony.

"I'm a pretty good prep chef."

"I think I've got it," she said. "But you could get the meat for me. It's in a saucepan in the fridge."

He found it and set it on the counter. He got a second knife from the rack and diced the onion while she chopped the head of lettuce. She looked at him, at his hands, the sure way he handled the knife. The muscles of his forearms knotted and unknotted smoothly below the rolled cuffs of his oxford shirt.

As if he felt the weight of her attention, he turned to her, their eyes locked, and she felt the jolt of his desire. The slightest twitch, and he would close the distance between them, lower his head, and fuse his mouth to hers. She would be lost. Sandy doubted they would make it farther than the little sofa, and a part of her desperately wanted that, wanted to abandon herself to him. It had been weeks since Emmett left, weeks of fighting to keep her panic at bay, keep her head level, keep working and earning, keep food on the table. Pay the bills, see to the household chores. She was tired, so tired of the fear, of carrying it alone.

She lowered her glance and kept still, almost afraid to move.

"I'll get the salad bowl, if you tell me where it is." His voice, so close she felt the warmth of his breath, was pitched low. It seemed intimate, like an invitation.

Heat flooded her face, the back of her neck. "The cabinet to your right," she said. "It's white with green stripes."

He stepped away from her.

Had she imagined his interest, then? Flattered herself? She felt deflated and relieved. And horrified. Some combination. What was she thinking? Suppose Jordy came home and found her—she swallowed, and finding her breath, told Roger about Patsy accosting her in the parking lot. "You said I should expect it." She brought plates, silverware, and napkins to the table.

"It's unfortunate." He followed her with the salad. "I'm surprised Michelle's parents have waited this long to file."

"But you haven't heard from their attorney?" She sat down.

"Not yet."

"If Michelle doesn't recover—"

"Don't take that on, Sandy. Not now." Roger sat across from her, his gaze intent, purposeful. He was trying to keep her whole, keep her functioning. She thought without him she might spin straight off the planet.

"I didn't tell Jordy about it—the run-in with Patsy."

"Good. Don't, okay? It won't help him. I wish to hell the woman had left you alone."

"Better me than him." Sandy drew her napkin across her lap and picked up her fork.

Roger took a bite of salad and sighed, eyes closed, savoring the flavors of spicy meat, freshly diced vegetables, grated cheese, her special cilantro-and-lime dressing. "Delicious," he said, and tucked another bite into his mouth. He ate the way he did everything else, with eagerness and gusto. It was refreshing.

Sandy thought how she missed it, the pleasure of having someone here who enjoyed the meals she prepared. Jordy ate in his room these days, or in front of the television. In ordinary time, TV during meals was banned. But these weren't ordinary times.

Roger finished his beer, and she brought him another.

He picked at the label on the bottle, watching her for a moment. "What?"

"You're not eating."

As if to defy him, she picked up her fork and tucked a bite into her mouth, keeping his gaze, hoping for—what? Something to happen between them? These feelings she kept having—they were disgraceful, warped, even, and yet somehow they enticed and beguiled her. She didn't know what to do about them.

"I've got some news," he said, and when he looked away, her stomach tightened.

She set down her fork, waiting.

"You won't believe it, but it turns out there's a second witness. The cops have known from day one, but they only let me know a couple of days ago. They said his statement got separated from the accident report somehow. I'm not sure I buy that excuse—"

"Why didn't you tell me?"

"I wanted to hear what the guy had to say first." Roger's glance dropped from hers and came back.

The knot in Sandy's stomach tightened. "What?"

"Well, first thing after I got the word, I texted the guy photos of Travis and Jordy, and he ID'd Travis as the driver. That was a couple of days ago."

"But that's good. That's the best news—"

"He's got a record. I just found out."

"What kind of record?"

"He's a trucker, Nat Blevins, out of Detroit. I asked a friend of mine up there to check him out. According to what he faxed over, it's mostly domestic stuff. He and his wife evidently like to drink and knock each other around on a regular basis. There have been multiple calls to the Detroit cops, a whole avalanche of restraining orders."

"Please don't tell me he was drinking the night of the accident."

"Says he was as sober as a judge, but that's not really the issue. God, I hate having to tell you this." Roger looked at the ceiling, brought his gaze back. "When I called to ask him about his trouble with the law up there this afternoon, he told me he wasn't a good witness anyway. He's not sure anymore who was behind the wheel."

"He changed his story?"

"Looks that way."

Sandy fiddled with her napkin.

"It's possible he was pressured."

"By who? Huck?"

Roger shrugged. "It would help a lot if I knew the motivation for his harassment of Jordy."

"I don't understand it, why Jordy won't say. On the one hand, it's as if he wants to end up in prison, but I know he's scared, too. Really scared of going there."

"Yeah. I'm getting the same impression. Look, try not to worry, okay? We've got weeks to go before the trial. Anything could happen." Roger went on, saying all the right things in an attempt to comfort her, to reassure her.

The dishwasher was on the fritz, and he helped her do the dishes by hand, drying what she washed. When they were finished, he had a look at the machine. It was a simple fix, he said. He'd get the part tomorrow when he went to Georgetown, and if she would be home, he'd stop by after work and do the repair.

"I don't want you to go to all that trouble," she said, but it wasn't only that. It was the intimacy they'd shared earlier, coupled with the further intimacy that allowing him to do a home repair—a job that was essentially a husband's duty—suggested. Or else she was imagining all of it. She didn't know, and it disconcerted her that her world, the one she'd been accustomed to, was so chaotic now, so altered by events beyond her making or choosing, that she couldn't tell anymore what was real or where the boundaries were, or how to feel about any of it.

"It's no trouble." Roger pulled his keys from his pocket. "But I should go now. I've got court first thing in the morning." He headed for the door, and she followed him. She didn't want him to go, to leave her to wait for Jordy alone. She thought of his embrace, of how it might feel to be held by him, to lean against him, to lie down next to him, even to make love with him.

They stepped onto the front porch, and he turned to her. Her hands hung at her sides, and he circled her left little finger with his own fingers, and his look was heated, regretful. "If things were different," he began, and she gave her head a brief shake.

"I know, don't worry," he said. "But don't think for one moment you're alone in this, okay? I'm right here. You can count on me. Just call. Okay?"

She nodded, and he left her there.

"Thanks for dinner," he said, walking backward, finally turning from her. He got into his car, something black and sporty and built low to the ground. Jordy had told her what it was, a Porsche, she thought. He had said it could really go. She thought of the trucks she and Emmett drove. She had a truck kind of life, not a sporty kind of life.

She wondered what that might feel like—a sporty life.

Back in the house, she found her cell phone and called Emmett. It didn't ring once before rolling to his voice mail. He was avoiding her. It wasn't the first time she'd had the thought. "I need you," she said, and stopped when her voice broke, when tears salted her eyelids. And when she found her composure again, she said, "The dishwasher's broken, and a witness Roger found out about who would have testified for Jordy changed his story." After that, she carried her phone into the kitchen and curled into a corner of the little sofa to wait—for Emmett to call, for Jordy to come home.

• • •

She hadn't meant to fall asleep, and at first she wasn't certain what woke her up, or where she was. She lifted her head inches from the sofa arm, smacking her mouth, mopping at the drool that crusted one corner. Her back and neck—everything—ached.

"Mom."

"Jordy?" She got up, fumbled with the wall switch.

"No," he said. "Don't turn it on."

Her attention caught on the urgency in his voice. "Why? What's wrong?"

He walked past her, going from the kitchen through the great room and into the living room to the pair of windows that overlooked the front yard. "I think someone followed me home. They're parked out there, at the end of the drive."

"What time is it?" Sandy came up behind him.

He had his knee in the seat of an armchair, finger parting the drape behind it, peeping out. "Look," he said. "Isn't that a car? See it? To the right of the oak tree."

She bent over his shoulder. It was a moment before her eye found it, several inches of car hood, a chunk of bumper, the only parts of the car that were visible in the wind-scattered moonlight. *Midsize sedan,* she thought. *Light colored.*

"Why would anybody follow you?" But even as Sandy asked, she was thinking of Patsy Meade, that if Michelle Meade's mother would accost her in a parking lot, then she was probably capable of almost anything. "Should we call the police?"

Jordy straightened. "What if it is the police?"

"You keep coming back to this idea that Huck has got it in for you, that he's framing you. Why would he do that? Something so terrible? Why would he risk his job that way, Jordy?"

"Because he's an asshole?" Jordy headed for the kitchen.

Sandy followed. "If you can't tell me, then you've got to tell Roger. He's your attorney. Anything you say to him is privileged."

"You think he wouldn't use it at the trial, that it wouldn't come out then?" He opened the refrigerator, got out a bottle of water. "If it was anything, I mean."

Sandy saw the time: 2:06. The numbers glowed red on the microwave. "Where have you been all this time? I hope you weren't drinking." She thought she smelled it, beer. But maybe that was a memory left over from when Roger was here. And maybe she was deluding herself, the proverbial ostrich.

"I'm whipped; I'm going to bed." Jordy drained the water bottle and tossed it in the recycle can. He was in the doorway to the hall when he stopped. "I'm sorry," he said, keeping his back to her. "For taking your truck, for being pissed off and making you worry. I'm sorry that Aunt Jenna lost her only kid, and that my best friend is dead, and that Michelle still hasn't woken up, and for the whole damn mess, but I can't fix it, Mom."

His voice was gruff. He turned to her, and she took a step toward him, but just as he had earlier, he warded her off, showing her the flat of his palm. "I think it would really be best for me to plead guilty, you know? Get it over with, take whatever's coming. It won't make up for Trav—"

"But if you weren't driving—"

"There's times I wish I was gone with him."

"No, Jordy—" She started toward him again.

"Stay," he said, and the syllable was blunt edged, hurt.

"You don't have to go through this alone, honey." Sandy repeated the comfort Roger had offered her. "I'm here. I'm in this with you, and I support you no matter what."

"But you don't believe me."

"I never said—"

"No, Mom, we both know where everyone in this family stands. No one believes me. Not you or Aunt Jenna or Dad or the grands. No one. Roger only believes me because it's his job. That's what happens when you get a reputation for being a liar—when you *are* a liar."

A silence came. She didn't know how to break it. She thought he would go, but he seemed not to know how, or maybe he had more to say.

She touched her brow and said, "I don't know how we got here," and she realized she didn't even know where *here* was.

"Does it really matter, Mom?"

11

Libby was anxious to talk to Ruth about what Jordy had confessed to her, the alarming predicament he was in, but Ruth didn't have time for a serious talk until Monday. They agreed to meet at her office before the other real estate agents and the office staff arrived. Libby drove into town, early, stopping for danish on the way.

"What is going on?" Ruth asked, greeting Libby at the door.

"You won't believe it," Libby answered. As she explained it all to Ruth, heard it all again out loud, she thought how crazy it sounded. She thought of the jeopardy Jordy was in.

"I don't know what to do now," Libby said when she finished. "I don't think I've slept for longer than two minutes since Jordy told me all of this."

"What if he's lying?" Ruth asked over her shoulder. They were in the tiny office kitchen, and she was making coffee.

"I know. People lie so much nowadays, it's practically an art form." Libby opened the paper sack containing the cheese danish she'd brought. It was their shared favorite, and now that they were older, an illicit treat.

"But?" Ruth brought napkins from the coffee service bar, setting one in front of Libby and keeping the other for herself. She poured coffee into mugs and brought those to the table, too.

"I think Jordan's too scared to lie," Libby said, glancing at Ruth.

"But isn't that what people usually do when they're scared? They lie because they're guilty and afraid of the consequences, right? You ought to know. You're the big crime-show nut. How many times have you seen a husband murder his wife and then cry about it?" Ruth asked. "Big, lying tears streaming down their big, lying face, dripping off their lying jaw? Not from grief, or even out of remorse, but because they got caught."

"I keep wondering, why did Jordan tell me? Why did he come to see me? It's not as if we're related."

"He wants to know about his birth father. Some adopted kids do."

"I always forget you were adopted." Ruth had found her birth mother while she and Libby were still students at SMU in Dallas. She'd been living in Wichita Falls twenty miles south of the Texas–Oklahoma border. Libby had gone with Ruth to see her. She'd told Ruth she was fifteen when she got pregnant, and when it was her time, her parents sent her to the Edna Gladney Home in Fort Worth. They had stood over her, too, after Ruth's delivery, while she signed away her right to mother her child.

"It's ironic, in a sad way," Ruth said now, "how Jordy found out, and the timing couldn't be worse."

"If only he'd known a bit earlier, he and Beck might have met."

"I've always wondered why he didn't try and find Jordy sooner."

"He promised his mother he wouldn't."

"I know, but it doesn't seem as if some promise he made in the heat of the moment to a woman he cared nothing about would have stopped him. It wasn't as if you were making a fuss about it. You forgave him."

"That was later, long after he confessed. In the beginning, I made a lot worse than a fuss. You must remember. You took the brunt of it. I was a wreck."

"But once you worked through all that—"

Libby folded her napkin and folded it again. "Well, not to be too crude about it, but do you have any idea how many times he was in some fertility specialist's office masturbating over a stack of porno magazines because I couldn't let go of the idea of having our child?" Before they'd gone that route, on her doctor's advice, Libby had kept a record, taking her temperature religiously, calling Beck home when the chart indicated she was at her most fertile. Something broke inside her brain when the cause was shown to be her cervical mucus, that it was killing off Beck's sperm, murdering every dream of the child she so desperately wanted to make with him, before it could even become a possibility. There were cures for her condition, but none of them worked. She moved on to artificial insemination, attempting round after round, and finally as a last resort they suffered through five failed attempts at in vitro fertilization. Her obsession had lasted seven years, during which she had nearly bankrupted them financially and emotionally.

She poked her napkin into the bakery sack. "He never once blamed me. He never said it was my fault he had an affair. He blamed himself. He always said it was his stupid mistake, and I blamed him, too. I made his life hell."

"He broke your heart."

"Yes, and he knew it. After that the last thing he was going to do was start a search for the child that was the result, the very symbol, of everything I could never give him." Libby paused to consider. "Had I been a mother and given away my baby, I would have wanted to find her or him. I mean, when we're in the heat of some horrible time in our lives, when we aren't thinking clearly, we make mistakes and later regret having made them. Like Beck regretted his affair. Like your birth mom. She was so glad when you found her."

"She cried," Ruth said.

"Beck must have wanted to reach out to his son for years." Libby was caught up with the idea of Beck's longing. "But he didn't do anything about it because of me, because of how he thought it might affect me. It was a relief when we could finally talk about it."

"It might not have happened at all if I hadn't moved here, if Aunt Tildy lived in some other town," Ruth said.

"It's strange how it came together, as if it was meant to. Even though it scared me when you said Sandy was here. But looking back now, who's to say it wasn't the universe's way of getting everything into the open and resolved, once and for all?" Libby pressed her fingertips to her eyes.

"Libby, honey, what is it?"

"I'm fine. I just miss him, and yet, if he had to go, then I'm so happy we were at peace with all of that." Libby sniffed, pinching her nose. "I think I'm even happy about Jordan seeking me out. He looks so much like Beck."

"I think so every time I see him, which isn't often."

Libby picked up her mug. The coffee had gone cold; she set it down.

"I've heard he drinks—Jordy. I know they all drink at his age, but I've heard he's a bit more deeply into it than that."

"He told me he thinks he has a problem."

"Really?"

"It made me think of Mia. Even Beck in the early days, and their parents. I've heard it can be genetic."

"I've heard that, too. I've also heard Sandy is good at ignoring it."

"I ran into that a lot from parents in my guidance-counselor days. If you pretend your kid is okay, then yea and amen, he is."

"If only."

Libby smiled.

"So, do you think you'll talk to Sandy about this—what he told you?"

"I don't know." Libby picked at her thumbnail. "It's easy to *say* I'm good with it, that when I see her I won't claw her eyes out, but when I think about that e-mail, the fact that she waited until all hell was breaking loose—"

"Uh, yeah, maybe you're not that good." Ruth made a face.

"What if I talk to her and she doesn't believe me? And what about the promise I made to Jordan not to tell anyone, especially his mom?"

"Well, you blew that when you told me. Why does it have to be a secret, anyway? I mean, the kid's freedom is at stake—"

"Senora Ruth?"

Ruth's glance darted over Libby's shoulder.

She twisted around.

"Perdón." Coleta spoke from the doorway. "Sorry." She repeated her apology in English.

Libby looked at Ruth.

She stood up. "Coleta? Uh, *buenos días.* Good morning. I didn't think you were coming in till ten?"

"Good morning." Coleta repeated the words, smiling, uncertain.

Ruth pointed to her watch. "Ten o'clock? Um, *diez—las diez?* That's when you were supposed to come? Uh—*venir aquí?*"

"Ah, *las diez. Sí.* Len bring, um, *vengo ahora?*" She shrugged.

"She doesn't drive." Ruth addressed Libby. "Huck has to take her everywhere. Let me get her settled, and I'll be back."

Libby rinsed their coffee mugs and wiped the table, and when Ruth reappeared, she said, "You found work for her to do?"

"Folding brochures and stickering on addresses. She seems to understand, but she's so quiet, like a little mouse. I said to Huck the other day if she doesn't talk more, engage with us, I don't see how working here is going to help her gain enough fluency in English to pass the test to get her green card."

"What if she heard us earlier and tells her cop husband what Jordan told me about him?"

"Oh, don't worry about that. She understands even less English than she can speak." Ruth crossed her arms and leaned against the coffee bar. "Besides, you can see how shy she is."

"Well, I know if I wanted citizenship as badly as you say she does, I wouldn't be taking such stupid chances. Suppose she were to get deported? They wouldn't let her take her little girl back to Honduras with her, would they?"

"I don't think so. She'd be staying here with her daddy."

"So she'd lose her opportunity to become a US citizen and her little girl."

"And she is totally devoted to that little girl, let me tell you."

Libby hung the hand towel she'd used on a hook next to the sink. "But she's very young and very pretty." Libby looked at Ruth. "*Muy bonita* and what? *Muy* younger? *Mucho* less years-o than Huck-o?"

Ruth laughed. "How have we lived in this state all our lives and not learned to speak decent Spanish? It's a crime."

"I don't know about you, but I took French in high school and dreamed of romance in Paris."

Ruth sobered. "Well, if it felt odd having her here before I knew all of this, it feels downright weird and uncomfortable now."

"I probably should have kept my mouth shut. For all I know, you're right and Jordan is lying."

"What I hear, he has kind of a reputation for it. It's for sure there's no love lost for him in town now. Or Sandy, either, for that matter. I can't think of anyone who believes he wasn't driving that night, and he's not doing himself any favors, accusing Travis."

"I want to help him, though. I know it's crazy."

Ruth eyes flooded with compassion. "It keeps Beck alive."

Libby's throat tightened. Of course Ruth of all people would get it. But Libby might have added that she herself felt more alive. Jordan's appearance on her doorstep, and the Gordian knot his actual and real physical self presented, even the tangle of old emotions and memories that his flesh-and-bone substance enlivened, was better than staring bleakly into the dark tunnel of her future without Beck. Being the one of them left behind was something she'd seldom contemplated.

"Will you talk to Sandy, then?" Ruth asked. "Want me to come with you?"

"Not right now. I'm going to try a different way first, go straight for the horse's mouth, if you know what I mean."

"If by horse's mouth you mean Huck, I think that's a bad idea."

"Why? It's not as if I'm going to accuse him of anything. I have a good reason to talk to him anyway. I don't think he, or anyone at the Wyatt police department, cares one thing about finding the person responsible for killing those animals on my property. But I am serious, and he'd better know it. Plus, there's what happened to Ricky Burrows's truck. It was damaged on my property, too, but there again, local law enforcement has dropped the ball. It's a disgrace."

"Who is Ricky Burrows, anyway? I can't place him."

"I only know him through Augie. Ricky works for him. Augie told me he's from Colorado, that he came here because he couldn't get work there."

"Or he's on the run from something or someone."

"Ha! I thought I was the one who watched too much IDTV. He's just a young guy who's had a run of bad luck, and now he's out of work altogether since I stopped construction on the house. I feel bad for him."

"There must be other jobs. Your house isn't the only one Augie's building."

"No, probably not," Libby allowed. "Maybe Augie fired Ricky."

"You need to find out, Libby. The guy could be in trouble. Maybe his truck was keyed by accident, or maybe it was a random bunch of hooligan kids who did it. But if it was random like that, why stop with his old beater truck? Why not scar up your shiny new Lexus or Beck's practically new Ford F-150? They were both there, parked nearby, right?" Ruth paused.

Libby didn't answer.

"Okay, let's say it *was* someone up from Houston, out to get revenge—a bizarro plan if I ever heard one—"

"I didn't say that."

"You didn't have to. I know how your mind works. Let's say that's the case. Would they have made that mistake? What's the point of gouging the paint off a vehicle where most of the paint is off already? And don't even get me started on the mutilated-animal routine, or the significance behind finding a note on your kitchen counter advising you to lock your doors. *Bizarre* is too mild a word for all this stuff. It's past that now. It's dangerous. You shouldn't even be staying out there."

"Why do you think I'm going to have a chat with Sergeant Huckabee?"

"To talk about Jordy, another terrible, if not downright dangerous, idea."

"I already said I'll be discreet."

"Suppose Huck *is* the one leaving the dead animals around at the cottage?"

Libby hooted.

"Come on, Libby. Even you've said it's concerning the way that note is an almost exact verbatim quote of the advice Huck gave you about keeping your doors locked."

"Yes, but aren't you the one who told me it was a coincidence? Otherwise I would have taken it to the captain, or to Greeley. I still could."

Ruth crossed her arms.

"It isn't as if I want to be involved in any of this."

"Then let it go."

Libby made a face.

Ruth flung her hands. "Why am I wasting my breath when you're so hardheaded?"

Libby grinned. "Don't you think maybe you're being just a tish paranoid? *Un poco?*" She held her index finger and thumb a little apart, expecting Ruth to laugh. She didn't. Instead she hammered away, saying Libby didn't know whom she was dealing with, which didn't sit well, and Ruth knew it, but she went on anyway.

"You don't get it—how this town works," she said. "It's not Houston."

"You're starting to sound like Mia." Annoyance sharpened Libby's voice.

"I'm offering you a perspective, not conspiracy theories and soap-opera dramatics." Ruth wasn't less annoyed.

"Beck would get this mess sorted out," Libby insisted. "You know he would. Especially where it concerns Jordan. How can I do less?"

"Beck wouldn't want you to put yourself at risk, Libby. That's what I know."

She picked up her purse. "I'll call you later."

"I'll look forward to that," Ruth said. "And if I don't hear from you, I'll call the law—in another town—to come check on you!"

Libby lifted her hand, waving without turning, a *whatever* gesture, and then she caught sight of Coleta. She was sitting at a desk in a cubicle near the entry doors. There was a stack of brochures in front of her, but she wasn't doing anything with them. She was watching Libby, and while she was smiling, there was something other than humor working in her eyes. Libby couldn't decide what it was. Frustration, maybe, over the language barrier. But while Coleta might not be so fluent in English, Libby thought she knew her way around another language quite well.

She had no plan, driving over to police headquarters. No ideas about how to get to the bottom of it, as she'd told Ruth that Beck would do. If only Beck were here. Why was the truth never simple? But no, the truth *was* simple. It was people who complicated it. Why couldn't they tell the straight facts, own up, say they did a thing, and then do their best to make it right? Why was it easier to lie? She could take that question back to Sandy Cline, Libby guessed, if she ended up having to talk to her. If she couldn't find another way.

Sergeant Huckabee, dressed in his uniform, was on the sidewalk outside the building that housed local law enforcement. Libby saw him as soon as she pulled up. He was talking to another man, dressed in civilian clothes, jeans and a T-shirt. Ricky Burrows.

She got out of the truck, smiling and waving when Ricky caught sight of her. She didn't know what to make of it when he suddenly wheeled and walked quickly away in the opposite direction.

She and the sergeant exchanged greetings. He was warm, almost effusive, asking how she was, whether or not she'd enjoyed the tamales. He went so far as to extend his hand, but she pretended not to see it, not wanting to make physical contact. His demeanor changed after that, becoming professional. It was hot, standing on the sidewalk, but she swore the air between them cooled.

She said, "I keep meaning to return your dish."

He nodded curtly and asked how he could help her.

"That was Ricky Burrows you were talking to, wasn't it? Did he come about his truck?"

"No," Huckabee said. He didn't elaborate.

"What do you know about him?"

Although the sergeant appeared to be looking at her, he had on mirror-lensed sunglasses. She couldn't see anything of his expression, only her own reflection. It annoyed her. She wanted to ask him to take them off. She said, "He's working on my property, part of the construction crew that's building my house. That's why I'm interested. I'd want to know if he's in any kind of trouble."

"Not the sort you need to worry about." Huckabee looked off in the direction Ricky had disappeared. "He's got a fondness for Coors beer, but he doesn't start until quitting time—beer thirty."

"He's not local, from around here, is he?"

"Nah. Came from up north somewhere. Colorado, I think."

It was the same story Libby had heard from Augie, verification of a sort, she guessed. "Is he in any legal trouble that you know of?"

"Not as of today. The boy has finally got his story straight. Look, I'm real sorry to cut this short, but I have an appointment."

"If you could spare another few minutes, I'd like you to go inside with me and talk to the captain." What she really wanted was to see Huckabee's eyes without the mirror lenses.

"About?"

That car accident, she thought. "What's being done to find the person responsible for leaving dead animals on my property." Libby studied her twin images captured in the lenses of his sunglasses, wondering what he'd do if she pulled them off his face. It aggravated her; he aggravated her. But she couldn't really picture Huckabee committing wanton acts of vandalism, even though she was aware that cops could be as mentally twisted as the next guy. The drawback with the sergeant, though, was the lack of any motive. Why would he do it? Not for any reason she could see.

There was nothing new, he said, with obvious impatience.

"Is it possible I'm being targeted?" Libby raised Ruth's suspicion. "I know no connection has been found to the animal killings in Houston, but that just makes what's happening on my property more worrisome. Whoever is behind this—they were inside the cottage. It's unnerving. I don't know what their reason is, or what direction they might come from next."

"You might want to make other living arrangements," the sergeant said. "You might consider going back to Houston for the time being. I've advised your neighbors to do the same."

"What neighbors? I wasn't aware anyone else had bought property at the Little B."

"Ruth didn't tell you? A couple with three kids, teenagers. Grayson is their name. They bought the fifteen-acre parcel next door to you, on the east side where the old farmhouse is."

"Did something happen there?"

"They found a gutted hog, too, hanging in one of their trees the day before you found the one at your place. I didn't know about it until I saw the report a day or two ago."

"Do you still think it's kids?" She couldn't keep the disgust from her voice.

"I've told you before, Ms. Hennessey—"

"Libby."

"Libby. We've stepped up patrols out that way, and if we get any leads, we'll run them down, but right now we've got nothing to go on. Now if you'll excuse—"

"I'd really like to see your captain." She was thinking of the note. If Huckabee didn't consider the vandalism on her property a threat, maybe his captain would. Or the cops in Greeley. She could take the note there.

"He isn't going to tell you anything different, Miz—Libby. Captain Perry isn't the one you would speak to about this matter, though. He's head of the patrol division. You would need to speak to Captain Mackie with the criminal division. But they're neither one here, in any case. They're in Dallas, attending a police conference."

Libby searched her mind, but she could come up with no response, no reasonable way to detain him.

"Is there anything else I can help you with?"

"Jordan Cline?" She said his name, and it was completely off topic, but she was out of options. "I wanted to mention again that he's working for me now."

Huckabee's eyes narrowed. "I'd be careful having him around your place, if I was you."

"I'm curious, why are you so sure he was driving that night?"

"It's what the evidence suggests."

"Isn't it possible his cousin was the driver? Weren't they both out of the car by the time you arrived? How could you tell who was at the wheel?"

"Well, as much as I might like to, I really don't have time to discuss the ins and outs of an accident investigation. I'm on duty, and as I said, I'm late for an appointment."

"Is Officer Carter here? Ken Carter? He was the other officer on the scene the night of the accident, right? Maybe I could talk to him."

"What is your interest here, Ms. Hennessey?" He stared hard at her.

She retreated a step. She needed more facts before she could answer his question.

"All right, then," Huckabee said, "if we're done?"

She nodded, and he left her, walking toward the back of the building. Libby could see several cars parked there, a mix of civilian cars and a handful of squad cars. She waited until Huckabee got into one of the patrol cars before going inside to the duty desk.

But according to the dispatcher, Ken Carter wasn't available. It was his day off, the woman said; he wouldn't be in until the following day.

Libby was there when Ken arrived the next morning, waiting for him on the same section of sidewalk where she and Huckabee had talked the day before. And she got the same vague response from Ken, with the added caveat that he wasn't at liberty to discuss an ongoing police investigation with her unless she had information that pertained to it.

The difference between Huckabee and Carter was that Ken Carter wasn't wearing sunglasses. Libby could see his eyes, and they were full of some jittering anxiety. He seemed nervous in a way that Huckabee hadn't, but Carter was young. He hadn't been on the job long enough to perfect his cop face, that casual-appearing air of authority that could turn lethal in the space of a heartbeat. Ken Carter had something on his mind, Libby felt sure of it; he was bearing some burden he'd like to be free of, one he probably resented. One that belonged to Sergeant

Huckabee. There was a code among cops, wasn't there? Didn't they talk about something called the blue line?

Cops were like doctors or attorneys; they protected one another.

She went back to her car and got in, watching Carter get into his squad car. Passing her on his way out to the highway, he touched his forehead in salute and smiled. What if she was wrong about him? It was only conjecture, intuition, coupled with a boy's story—a boy whom she didn't know, who had a lot to lose, who was a known liar. A self-admitted drinker. Beck's son. And she—she was a woman with no experience of children other than as a high school guidance counselor. She had always fancied herself a person with a mother's brain and heart who lamentably had nothing to mother. Was she still so desperate for the experience that she would take this on? Interfere with someone else's kid as if he were hers and she knew best? How was this any of her business? What if she was letting emotion rule, letting her heart get the better of her? But then again, how would she feel if she did nothing and Jordan went to prison?

Her cell phone rang and she pulled it from her purse. Ruth's name was in the ID window. "I don't know what to do," she said instead of hello.

"Ricky Burrows, the guy who got his car keyed on your property, the one you feel all kinds of sorry for?"

"Uh-huh?" Libby drew out her assent, making it a question.

"I don't think he's who he says he is."

12

Jordy didn't come home at all on Wednesday night, but Sandy wasn't alarmed until Thursday morning, when he still didn't answer his cell phone. He'd stayed out several nights in recent weeks, but all those other times he'd answered his phone when she'd called and told her he was with friends. She didn't know what friends. Not the old gang he and Trav had hung out with. *New friends,* he said. He was evasive about their identity, furtive in a way that worried her.

Leaving her cell phone on the kitchen counter, she went to his bedroom and looked inside. She didn't know what she expected to see—a clue, a sign, something to explain where he was? She doubted the FBI could have found anything useful in all the mess. The bed was buried under an assortment of litter. Who knew if he'd slept there? Except she did know, in the way a mother knows things about her kid. She leaned against the door frame, feeling anxious, frustrated, a heavier weight of disappointment.

She'd made the mistake over the last few days of letting herself believe things were improving, however slightly. Because Jordy had stayed home and hung out with her—sort of. They'd caught up on yard work over the weekend. Done stuff like that. When Hector hadn't been able to help her with the annual cleaning of a client's koi pond on Tuesday, she'd called Jordy, and he came right away.

Ponds were his thing.

It was big, close to two thousand gallons, and cleaning it took longer with only two of them to do the work. By the time they refilled it and put the last fish back into the water, the sun was almost down, and they were both worn-out. Still, Sandy's heart lifted, as it never failed to do, when they left Wyatt behind, picking up speed. The highway opened to the view, a wide-ranging panorama of hills, dipping in and out of lengthening shadows, even as they were crowned in a late-day fizz of light the color of pink champagne. Above that, a band of soft lilac held aloft ribbons of silver clouds as transparent as vapor. She turned to Jordy, to remark on the beauty, but he'd reclined his seat and pulled his old Dolphins ball cap low over his eyes. It was when she was turning her glance back to the road again that she saw the car in the rearview mirror, the one that had followed them out of the subdivision.

The sedan was midsize and light in color. Gold? Green, maybe? Sandy couldn't tell. She couldn't see the driver clearly, either. It could have been a man or a woman. It gave her a bad feeling, though. Worried her in the same way the car parked in front of her house last Sunday night had worried her. But it wasn't as if she had actually identified that car, other than it had been light colored, too. Still, there must be hundreds of cars that fit the description. And while FM 1620 wasn't a major highway, it was well traveled. She thought of waking Jordy but then didn't. It seemed ridiculous to assume they were being followed. Who would do such a thing? Patsy Meade? A cop out of Wyatt, or a Madrone County sheriff's deputy in an unmarked car? One of Jordy's new friends?

Sandy checked the rearview again. A vehicle was back there, but so far away she couldn't tell if it was even a car, much less the same one. It was the stress, she thought. It was causing her mind to run away with itself.

She hadn't mentioned it to Jordy, not after they got home, nor yesterday morning, the last time she'd seen him, when wonder of wonders, he'd gotten up before her and made bacon-and-scrambled-egg breakfast sandwiches. That was when she'd let herself become foolishly optimistic. When she'd entertained the possibility that he'd forgiven her, or set aside his hard feelings, or somehow come to terms. What an idiot she was to think it would be—that it *could* be—so simple.

Picking her way across his bedroom floor now, she sat gingerly on the edge of his bed, pulling his pillow onto her lap. It smelled faintly of soap and whatever shampoo he was using now. After breakfast yesterday, when she'd asked if he wanted to give her a hand with the work she'd scheduled, he'd said no. *I've got stuff to do,* he'd said. She'd felt let down, anxious.

She hadn't seen or heard from him since then. Every one of her numerous calls had gone to his voice mail. She'd finally given up on hearing from him at midnight last night and gone to bed, where she'd lain awake imagining every worst-case scenario: he was too drunk to call. He was with Libby Hennessey, unable to tear himself away long enough to extend his mother the courtesy of a phone call. Sandy had entertained the idea of calling Libby, and she might have followed through if she'd had the woman's phone number. She'd thought of calling Emmett, too, but what could he do from Oklahoma other than worry?

Of course she hadn't slept, not really. She'd gone from berating Jordy in her mind to arguing with herself. Why couldn't she let go? He was nearly twenty-one, a grown man. Gone were the days when she had any legal right to know where he was every minute. She left his bedroom now. She wasn't angry anymore. She just wanted him home. She wanted to know he was safe, and the sense that he was not was cold inside her, like chips of ice darting through her veins.

She could tell she'd wakened Roger when he answered her call, and she apologized. She said, "I should have waited."

"What's wrong?" he asked.

She heard rustling as if sheets were being tossed aside, and the sound was oddly intimate. She was flustered by thoughts of what he was wearing: Did he sleep in boxers like Emmett, or in long joggers the way Jordy sometimes did, or briefs? She knew even as she thrust the thoughts away, she was drawn to him. "Jordy didn't come home last night, Roger. I thought he was with friends, or maybe at Libby Hennessey's, but he would have come home, or called by now."

"Have you called around?"

"I don't know any of the guys he's hanging out with now." Sandy hated admitting this, hated that she didn't know. "He doesn't bring them here. He hasn't even told me their names."

"Yeah. Okay. You haven't called the police?"

"No."

"Good. Don't. Not yet, anyway."

"I don't trust them." Sandy paused. "Is it possible you could check with Libby Hennessey and find out if she's seen him? Do you know her at all? I'd do it myself, but I don't think she'll talk to me."

"Do you have a number for her?"

Sandy said she didn't.·

"No worries," Roger said. "I'll find it." He paused, then said her name—"Sandy?"—making a question of it, and his tone caused her teeth to clench. "Has it occurred to you that Jordy might take off? He was pretty stressed last time we talked."

"When was that?"

"Yesterday, around noon."

"He didn't tell you where he was calling from?"

"No, but he talked about how everyone might be better off if he was gone."

He had said virtually the same thing to Sandy on Sunday night.

"I want to believe he was just blowing off steam. I kind of let him go on, and by the time we hung up he seemed to have settled down, so I didn't really think it was worth telling you and adding to your worry."

Yes, she thought, there was that, Roger's reluctance to upset her. But there was also this awkwardness between them now. She'd felt it since they'd shared dinner, and again on Monday evening when he'd come by to repair the dishwasher. Jordy had been home then; Roger hadn't stayed, but still there was this undercurrent of awareness between them, that he wasn't simply Jordy's attorney anymore. He'd become more than that. But Sandy didn't know if it was real—at least when it came to her part, she didn't. It could as easily be a feeling born of her isolation, the lack of anyone else to turn to. She said, "You aren't suggesting he would harm himself, are you? Because I can't—" She broke off. Her heart was beating so heavily, she felt the throbbing in her skull. She put her fingertips to her temple.

Roger protested that he hadn't meant to alarm her. "He's conflicted, you know? He wants to clear his name, but at the same time he knows if he does, the accident will become Travis's legacy, the thing Travis is remembered for. That's his perception anyway, that no matter what he does, it's a lose-lose. Do you see what I mean?"

She did, and the sense of it, Jordy's burden, his fear and confusion, made her feel weak. She sat on the edge of the love seat. "Maybe that's why he won't say what it is Huck has against him, because it will somehow implicate Travis in a negative way." Sandy frowned. *Could that be right?*

"Maybe."

"But I just don't think he'd hurt himself, Roger." She couldn't allow the idea; she would break into a million pieces if she did. "He wouldn't run off, either. I think, ultimately, what he wants is for the truth to come out." She cradled her elbow in the cup of her hand, praying she was right, vowing to herself she would do all she could to help him.

"But if you think about it, what better way is there to avoid the whole damn mess than leave? Find somewhere to hide out? The law considers him a man, but he's just a kid, really, and he may not be thinking straight. I'm not saying he'd actually go through with it, but he could be considering it as an option. I'm not sure I wouldn't if I were in his shoes."

Sandy thought of the countries she'd looked up on the Internet, the ones that didn't allow the United States to extradite. Jordy could have done his own research; he could be on a plane right now, bound for Russia, or Syria, or some other godforsaken place in the world that refused to do legal business with the United States. She bent over her knees.

"Sandy? Let's not go off the deep end here." Roger was rational; his voice was a soothing hum in her ear. "He'll turn up. I'll get hold of him, and once I do, I'll make sure he calls you. I promise. Okay? Don't worry."

"Thank you." Her gratitude to Roger made her throat tighten.

"Listen, before we hang up, I want to let you know I've hired a private detective, a guy I've worked with in the past. I don't have much confidence in what I'm hearing from the Wyatt police or the DA. I think we should undertake our own investigation."

"What makes you say that?"

"Just a hunch. That business with Nat Blevins backing off his witness statement. Something's—off, and I want to know what it is."

Sandy thought she detected an element of optimism in his voice, but she wasn't buying into it, not this time.

• • •

She was on her knees in the vegetable garden behind the barn late that afternoon, jerking weeds from the row of poblano peppers when his shadow fell over the ground and her gloved hands. At first glance, sitting back on her heels with the sun in her eyes, Sandy thought it was Jordy and started to her feet, feeling the thrust of her fury at him pierce the swell of her relief. But when he stepped down the row toward her, she saw it was Emmett and sat back on her heels.

"Be careful where you're walking," she said, and marveled at herself, at her brain that would deliver an order like that to the husband she hadn't laid eyes on in a month.

He stopped, eyeing her warily.

She kept still, too, her gaze locked on his.

They were actors on a stage awaiting direction, a prompt to remind them of the lines they were to speak.

"I don't want you to get pissed, okay?"

"I don't think I'd characterize that as a future event, since I'm already pissed, not to mention scared out of my mind. Jordy's gone."

"No," Emmett said. "No, he's been with me."

There was the moment of heady lightness when her dread lifted, and she uttered, "Thank God," but then confusion took over. "With you where? In Oklahoma?"

"No. Here. I'm back here now." He looked uncomfortable, twitchy.

"When did you get back?" Sandy felt an inkling of alarm, as if she'd stepped off a ledge and was uncertain of how or even where she might land.

"A month ago. Since you called and told me Jordy'd been arrested."

"My God! And you didn't tell me?"

He apologized. He said, "I can't be with you right now. Too much has happened, but I want to be here for Jordy. He's in a lot of deep shit, and I'm not just talking about the legal stuff."

Sandy bolted to her feet. "You think I don't know that? That I haven't been here, living it with him every damn minute?" The heat of her sudden fury seared the backs of her eyes; it licked at her temples.

"He doesn't trust you, Sandy. He's having a hard time trusting anyone. Have you thought about it? How it's affected him, finding out his dad—me—that I'm not—" Emmett looked away, looked back. "Have you thought how he must have felt when he looked his birth dad up on the Internet only to discover the guy had died a few weeks before and not a hundred miles from here? He told me Beck Hennessey had property on 1620, on the other side of Wyatt. Jordy said that he and his wife are building a house there. That's scarcely fifteen miles from here. I couldn't believe it, that they were going to be so close. Did you know?"

"Yes," she said, and she could have bitten off her tongue. But it was time for the truth, wasn't it? To let the chips fall where they might? She was too tired to dodge it any longer, anyway, too weary to try and force the issue, to make Emmett come back or stay. Not unless he chose it, once he knew everything.

"I thought so," he said. "When? When did you find out?"

"He e-mailed me—Beck did, a couple of years ago."

"Two years ago? Are you kidding? Jesus Christ, this is all such a fucking mess—"

"Because of me. Go ahead, say it. We both know who you're blaming."

A breeze kicked up as it was wont to do late on summer afternoons, but it was hot, restless. There was no relief in it. Sandy pulled off her gloves. She unstuck her hair from her cheek, the corner of her mouth, lifted it off her neck.

"Jordy told me you e-mailed the guy, asking for his help—money, basically. Jordy is pretty blown away that you did that—out of the blue, you contact your ex-lover? But maybe you've been in touch all this time."

"No, absolutely not, Emmett. I lied about the affair, it's true, but not now, not about that. I was never in contact with the man until now. Even when he wrote to me two years ago, I didn't respond." Sandy couldn't read Emmett's expression; the bill of his cap shaded his face, and it irked her somehow. She was frightened, too. She slapped her gloves across her open palm. "You weren't here, Emmett, and your advice to me was to liquidate Jordy's college fund. Your mind was on your mother. You barely listened to my concerns. There was no discussion. Just clean out the college fund, and to hell with whether or not Jordy would ever be able to go back to school."

"That life is over, Sandy. Face it. The family we had, the life we shared—the one where Jordy and Trav were students at UT, and you, me, Jenna, and your folks were here, their home base—that routine is not coming back. And Jordy may well get his degree, but it'll be through some prison program, if he can even survive in one of those hellholes."

"Jordy is not going to prison. Not as long as I'm breathing." Sandy stepped toward Emmett. "I will take money from the devil himself to keep that from happening."

"But you won't cash in his college fund? You're not making sense."

"Do you believe him, then? Because when you left here, you acted like you weren't sure."

"You don't believe him, either, according to Jordy, and it's killing him. You could at least fake it."

"Is that what you're doing? Faking it?"

"You know what scares the shit out of me? That he's got Huck and the rest of the cops in Wyatt on his ass, doing everything they can to see to it he's convicted."

"Roger hired a private detective. He's hoping to find another witness since Nat Blevins changed his story."

"Yeah. I heard. Roger's right; Huck probably did put pressure on him. I just wish I knew why—"

"You've talked to Roger?" She felt faintly dizzy.

Emmett disregarded her question. "I don't know how we're going to pay a lawyer, much less a detective."

"I've thought of asking Mom and Dad for help."

"They're in deep with Jenna. If our medical bills for Jordy are through the roof, hers for Trav are astronomical. Plus, there were all the funeral expenses."

Sandy hadn't even considered that Jenna would be saddled with Travis's medical bills. She wondered how they even existed. "He died," she said, and she knew her protest was unreasoning. Still she questioned it. "How can they charge her when Trav died?"

"That's how the system works. Showalter tried. It cost a bundle. Your dad thinks Jenna may have to declare bankruptcy."

The fist of her tears slammed the wall behind Sandy's eyes. "It's so wrong. All of this!" She shook her gloves. "I should be with her—"

"It needs time." Emmett's voice was rough with emotion.

She looked at him, searching his eyes for a sign that if she were to walk toward him, he would meet her, with open arms, but she found no certainty of that within him or herself. "You're in touch with Jenna, my folks?"

"Your dad, mostly. The business—between us we've been handling the operation. And it's a good thing, because we for damn sure need the income."

Sandy picked up her trowel and shoved its blade into the ground.

"I'm staying with Grant and Brenda, in their garage apartment. It's not leased right now, and they're letting me camp out there."

Sandy straightened. "I saw Brenda last week at the grocery store. She never said a word about you. She barely spoke."

"I asked her not to. She was probably afraid she might if she stopped to talk. I've put her and Grant in a bad spot. That's why I came today."

"All this time, I've wondered why they didn't call or come around. I thought it was because they didn't support Jordy. Are you telling me they do?"

"Honestly, I think they're waiting for the trial. They think he's a good kid, but they know like we do that he lies."

Sandy looked off, hating it that Jordy was being judged and labeled—and as his mother, so was she, by inference—in unflattering ways. She didn't care how many times the so-called experts said parents weren't responsible for a child's bad behavior—she felt guilty and ashamed all the same. She felt accused. She felt the stab of fingers pointing at her.

"How is your mom?" She brought her gaze back to Emmett.

"Doing much better. I found someone, a retired nurse, who comes by every day and stays a few hours with her and Aunt Leila."

"So, what does it mean, Emmett, that you've been back nearly a month, living in the Kennedys' garage apartment, without telling me? Are we separated? Do you want a divorce?"

"Jordy's got to be the focus right now, don't you agree?"

Of course she did. Sandy plucked her trowel from the dirt, turning it in her hands. The metal was hot enough to burn her fingers. "All this time, the nights he was gone—he knew how worried I was. You must have known it, too. But the two of you just let me go on thinking the worst?" She couldn't keep the hurt from showing.

"That's on me, and I'm sorry. I should have come here right away when I got back."

She could have asked him why not, but she didn't need to. She didn't want to hear more about his reluctance to be anywhere near her.

He said he had to go. "I'm picking Jordy up. He's working at Libby Hennessey's. You knew that, right? I've been driving him to and from."

The look she gave him was sour; she could nearly taste it—the bitterness. She wasn't proud of it.

Emmett lifted his cap and shoved his hand over his head before resetting it. "I know you don't like the idea, but it's his right, and only natural he'd want to know who his real dad was. She's the only way he can do that now."

"Blood doesn't make a dad real, Emmett. Being there, loving your kid, caring for him, guiding him, teaching him—all the things you've done Jordy's whole life—that's what makes a real dad."

"Spare me the bullshit speech, okay? Maybe blood doesn't count, but the truth damn sure does."

"I didn't answer the e-mail from Beck two years ago because nowhere in my mind did he have any place in our lives."

"How could you make that decision, though? How could you— how can you think it was only yours to make?"

Sandy didn't answer. She couldn't say her secrecy then had made sense to her, that it was only now, today, standing here under the hot glare of a late-summer sun, caught up in Emmett's even hotter and more offended glare, that she saw the scope of her miscalculation. She couldn't say to him if the accident had never happened, if you had never been called to give blood . . . *if if if* . . .

So much more than her honor was lost.

"You realize you're going to have to tell Jordy, don't you? That you turned down the opportunity for him to know his birth father? If Libby Hennessey hasn't already."

"He'll hate me." Her voice broke, tears came, and she blinked them away.

"You owe him the truth. All of it. I've told you that. You're going to have to do the hard thing, Sandy."

He was right, Sandy knew he was, but the prospect only made her heart pound more heavily in her chest.

"You know what gets me?"

Sandy met Emmett's gaze.

"Before this I would have said I knew you better than I know myself. I would have said I knew your heart and your secrets. Out of everyone I've ever known, I have trusted you without question. But you're a minefield, you know it? One wrong step and boom, I get set down on my ass by some new revelation. I don't know even know if I've heard the whole story."

"I'm sorry, Emmett." It was everything Sandy could do to work the words by the knot in her throat.

"Yeah, that's the hell of it," he said, "because I know that, too."

His gaze on hers seemed to soften, and for a moment, she thought he might relent. He might embrace her. She would feel the strength of his arms around her; his breath at her temple would stir the fine hairs there. She thought if only she could bring him that close, she wouldn't let go of him. She would make it right; they would work it out between them and save Jordy, too. It wouldn't ever be the way it was, but it would be something better and more. If only he would take that step.

And he did—backward, saying he'd let her know if he would be bringing Jordy home. It depended, Emmett said, on what Jordy wanted to do. "I'm sorry you were worried," he said. "I won't let it happen again." And then he turned, taking more steps, and every one took him, and Jordan, too, farther down a path away from her.

• • •

"I've located Jordy," she said to Roger when he answered his cell phone.

"You've spoken to your husband."

"So, you did know he was here—all this time."

"I've encouraged him to talk to you."

She went to the kitchen window and stared out.

"You're pissed, and I don't blame you. I'm really sorry for how this went down, my part in it." Roger's apology sounded heartfelt.

"I don't understand why—"

"Look, Jordy is my client. What's between his parents is beside the point. I can't get sidetracked by it, can't be involved in it."

Really? The smart-ass who lived in her head goaded her to ask. "Okay, but this morning, you knew I was worried sick about where Jordy was—"

"When you called, I had no better idea than you, and that's the truth. I don't keep tabs on him. He could have been anywhere."

• • •

Sandy believed Roger. Later as she showered and washed her hair, she thought it was because he didn't try and make her believe he was telling the truth. He simply stated the facts; she could take them or leave them.

She was sorting the laundry that had piled up when she heard the sound of an engine. *Jordy,* she thought, and went to look. Instead it was Roger, carrying a brown, handled shopping bag. Foolishly, despite her aggravation, she was glad to see him. At least when he looked at her there was no scrim of disgust in his eyes. At least he didn't think of armed-and-dangerous minefields when he thought of her—if he thought of her. More foolishness.

"What have you got there?" she asked once they were inside.

He set the sack on the counter and began removing the contents, enumerating them as he did so. "One bottle of crème de menthe, one bottle of crème de cacao, and a quart of whipping cream. And I'm hoping you have a little nutmeg—that is, if you like nutmeg sprinkled on top of your grasshopper."

"You brought this for me?"

"Yes, as a peace offering. But maybe you'd rather take a punch at me?" He stuck out his jaw, and she laughed.

"C'mon. Take your best shot."

"No. Maybe before I would have, but I'm past it now."

His eyes held hers, and she was almost undone by his smile, the tender concern in his glance. "I've got to tell you, now this is out in the open, when I heard from you this morning, I was worried. I thought Jordy and his dad might have gotten on a plane."

Sandy hadn't considered the possibility before, that Emmett might be the one to spirit Jordy out of the country. Would they go and not tell her?

Seeing the look on her face, Roger said, "They would have taken off by now if that was their plan."

"Yeah, probably." She realized Roger wanted to reassure her. She had the sense he would like to touch her, that it was costing him not to.

"So it must be a good thing, right, that Jordy's been hanging out with his dad? It's what you wanted, isn't it? For the two of them to see they have a relationship in all the ways that count?"

"Yes. But I'm not sure Emmett does see it. He's so angry at me. It's as if he can't get past it. Maybe he never will."

"Well, I've probably got no right to say this, but it pisses me off the way this has been handled." Roger folded the paper sack as he spoke, keeping his eye on it. "Not by Jordy. He's at the mercy of—aw, hell—" He tossed the sack aside. "I don't like seeing you hurt, that's all."

She shifted her glance, fighting with the complicated mix of her emotions—gratitude at having Roger's defense of her, and pain at the way in which she was being closed out of her own family. "I'm afraid Jordy hates me." She whispered the fear that was uppermost in her mind.

Roger lifted her chin, bringing her face around. "I was pretty horrible to my mom, too, at his age. I put her through hell. She felt the same as you. We laugh about it now."

She wiped her face, pinched her nose, gathering herself, the scattered fragments of her composure. "Were you ever arrested? Is that why you became a lawyer?"

"My brother was. Where's your blender?"

Sandy opened the cubby where it was stored and found a shot glass.

Roger uncapped bottles and measured ingredients. "I was a freshman at Florida State and partying hard when he was wrongfully accused and convicted of raping and assaulting a woman. After he got sent to prison, I transferred to Stanford and started working on my law degree. He did eight years in prison before I could pass the bar and get to work on the petition for a retrial. My whole focus was on getting the guilty verdict overturned. I wanted him to be exonerated, totally."

Sandy kept Roger's gaze. "He didn't do it?"

"Nope. It was a setup. The sex was consensual, but the woman's husband found out and took exception. He was a batterer, and there was an afternoon when he came home and somehow knew what was going on."

"Your brother was there?"

"He'd just left, but the guy hammered his wife until she confessed. When she did, he hit her a few more times, then he took her to the emergency room, where they did the rape kit, the whole nine yards. When the cops came, the husband did most of the talking. The woman was terrified and went along. Given that they had my brother's DNA, he didn't have a chance."

"How awful. How did you ever get him out?"

Roger's smile was one cornered, an odd mix of chagrin and rue. "The husband eventually recanted after he was diagnosed with prostate cancer, end stage. He had some kind of come-to-Jesus moment." Roger flipped on the blender.

Sandy took two cocktail glasses from the cabinet but put one back when Roger declined to join her.

"Grasshoppers are a little froufrou for me," he said. "I'll stick with beer." He poured her drink and handed it to her, watching as she took a sip.

She closed her eyes, savoring the minty, sweet flavor, cool on her tongue. "Delicious," she said. "Thank you. It's just what I needed." It was. She felt the effect of the alcohol uncurl, warming the blood in her veins, loosening the tension coiled in her muscles.

"Sure." Roger stowed the blender jar in the refrigerator and got out a beer. "I might have killed the guy if he hadn't already been dying. But it was pretty crazy, the way it ended. Ironic, really. That whole shit storm, for lack of a better way to describe it, changed my life, and in the end, nothing I did made the difference."

Sandy didn't believe that. "You kept your brother going, I bet. Just knowing you were out there, an advocate—it had to mean a lot to him."

"Yeah, you're right. It did."

"You're close."

"Yeah. Both of us and our mom."

"What about your dad?"

"He took off when we were young. Haven't seen much of him since."

Sandy peered into her drink. "I miss my family."

"I know," Roger said. "I'm sorry."

She was grateful when he didn't say it would get better.

They took their drinks outside on the deck that overlooked the backyard and sat in adjacent chaise longues, and Sandy knew it was dangerous, sitting here, drinking on an empty stomach. Even worse, drinking with Roger, and imagining there might be something between them that was based on more than her loneliness, her overwhelming sense of isolation, her feeling that for all intents and purposes, she was on her own. She shouldn't allow such ideas into her mind. Shouldn't encourage them. But the idea of being alone with her fear and uncertainty frightened her.

"Nice night," he said.

"Yes."

They took care not to turn to each other, studiously looking into the yard instead, at the day that was steadily losing its shape to the oncoming twilight of evening. The air seemed alive with a kind of nervous anticipation. A breeze fretted. Crickets chittered madly among themselves. A roadrunner dashed a few steps through the long grass in the meadow beyond the fence line and paused to look around. Sandy followed its progress when it took off again, dashing a longer path, neck forward, full of itself. She was aware of Roger watching the roadrunner, too, and then she was aware of his hand, reaching across the space that separated them. After only a moment's hesitation, she extended her hand, meeting his. His grasp was warm; his thumb slid over her knuckles. Heat flared low in her abdomen.

He said, "I have feelings for you, Sandy. I can't lie."

She started to object, which was ridiculous, given that she'd allowed him to take her hand. He overrode her anyway.

"I'm not going to put the moves on you as much as I might want to—as badly as I want to be with you, because I know you're vulnerable now." He stopped, and setting his beer down, he swung his feet to the deck floor and turned to her, keeping her hand, finding her gaze. In the fading light, his eyes were dark with emotion, his longing.

Sandy felt her breath go.

He said, "I won't overstep, but I won't pretend, either, that I'll be glad if your husband comes home to you. He should. How he could leave you to handle this—but no, you fool." Roger was talking now to himself. "Shut up before she kicks you out of here." He didn't drop her hand so much as give it back to her. His smile was chagrined, asking her indulgence.

It didn't please her, being relieved of his touch.

"Forget I said anything."

She thought of saying she was flattered, but she didn't like the sound of it even in her own mind. She thought of saying she might not want to forget, but that would take them beyond the point of return. Her mother had always said to be careful with your words, that it wasn't as if once you said them, you could get them back.

"Do you want me to leave?" he asked.

"No," she said, and she didn't.

He sighed. "Then if you don't mind, I'll get myself another beer." He stood up. "Freshen your drink?"

"Yes, please." She acquiesced, handing him her glass even though her head was already swimmy. Why should it matter what she did or with whom? No one needed her to be sober. No one cared what or how she was doing. Jordy was off, happily, with Emmett, at the apartment of their good friends, eating pizza and watching the Astros game. Maybe he would spend the night there, as Emmett had said he had done all the other nights when he'd made up stories about nonexistent new friends.

It came over her then—and she thought of Roger's earlier reference to irony—that Emmett and Jordy were fine together in spite of how disturbed they claimed to be over learning they weren't blood relations. They'd been shocked, but that hadn't interfered with their relationship, which was how it should be, what she'd tried pointing out to them both. And just look at them now; they'd moved on, without her. When she'd said those words—*separation* and *divorce*—Emmett hadn't so much as flinched. What would he think if he could see her, sitting in the gathering dusk with Roger, sipping grasshoppers, thinking of how it might feel to have him kiss her, to have his hands on her?

The patio door slid on its track. She half turned, thinking when Roger gave her drink to her she would take his hand, pull him down beside her. What was there to lose, other than herself for an hour or two?

He was looking at his phone, though, when he came back, or who knew what might have happened?

That was her first thought the following morning when she woke on the sofa, where he'd evidently put her. She had the vaguest memory of it—his arms supporting her, half carrying her into the great room and laying her gently down on the sectional. He'd covered her with the cotton throw she kept folded over the back.

Sandy thrust it aside now and sat up, moaning softly, touching her fingertips gingerly to her temples. She imagined a pair of little monkeys, one on either side of her skull, wielding tiny but lethal sledgehammers. The inside of her mouth was as furry as moss, and it tasted faintly of mint and something darker, like dirt. She looked at her bare feet, then sidelong at her sandals nearby. At least she was still wearing the shirt and capris she'd been dressed in when Roger arrived last night. She was almost positive he hadn't taken advantage of her. And she had one other near certainty: she would never drink another grasshopper again, not as long as she lived.

He'd made another batch, teasing her, telling her how much she'd regret it. She remembered that. And she remembered that he'd shown her what he found so interesting on his phone. The text from the private detective he'd hired to help with Jordy's case had read:

```
Third witness confirmed. Travis not Jordan
was driving. Talk tomorrow.
```

13

Libby never knew what to do with herself at dinnertime, and Sunday evenings were the worst. Beck had always made something special for them on Sundays. He'd been the executive chef, and she the sous chef. They would have shopped together, bought the makings for an elaborate meal. There would have been music, conversation, laughter, and afterward, when the dinner dishes were done . . .

But what was the point in remembering that sweet ritual? Libby was grateful when her phone rang. She left off making what passed for her Sunday dinner nowadays, a ham and Swiss on rye, and answered it.

"Libby, how are you?"

She recognized the voice of Robert, Beck's partner, and said she was doing well, hoping he would let it go at that.

He apologized. "I don't want to interrupt your dinner."

She eyed her sandwich, the single glass she'd gotten from the cabinet for iced tea, and said it was fine.

"Well, I've got some news," Robert said. "I thought you might like to know that law enforcement arrested the guy who's responsible for the animal killings down here in Houston. They caught him about two weeks ago. I meant to let you know earlier, but things have been hectic at the office. It's been really difficult since—"

"Who was it?" Libby interrupted. It was selfish, but she wasn't in the mood to commiserate with Robert over the loss of his business partner.

"It's as we suspected: he's the father of one of the victims who was killed when the balcony fell. The poor guy just went insane with grief, wanting someone to pay. He's a single dad, and it was his only child, only son. You can imagine."

"How awful for him," Libby said.

"I don't think he'll do any jail time. The DA is recommending probation and community service. Something like that."

"Oh, good. He's already been punished enough." Libby was surprised when her throat tightened. It was the sense of the man's loss, what he was enduring now, that touched her.

She and Robert talked for a few more minutes about his wife and people they knew in common and then ended the call, promising to stay in touch. But Libby knew they wouldn't. That life, the one she and Beck had built and led together, the one she'd loved with her whole heart, was over. She lived here now, and it might as well be a different country, a different planet, even. The trick would be learning to navigate the terrain, and she couldn't do that living in the past.

• • •

The next morning, Monday, Libby took her coffee outside and, wandering though the garden, decided she wanted boxwoods. She pictured them in the beds that flanked the cottage's wide front porch steps, trimmed into globes and interspersed with a mix of spring blooming bulbs and, later, blooming perennials. That was the only reason she drove to Inman's Native Garden World outside Wyatt that morning—to buy boxwoods. And it was crazy, planting anything in the August heat. Still, she had a vision, and she was hot on the trail to see it come together. Jordan had spent most of last Wednesday pulling off the old, crumbling lattice that screened the foundation. She'd bought new lattice at the Home Depot on her way into town, and she was up in the bed of the truck, shifting it around to make room for the wagonload of boxwoods when she caught sight of Sandy Cline's distinctive vintage truck nosed in on the opposite side of the parking lot, down several spaces. Her heart paused, and after a moment when it resumed beating again, she settled the sheet of lattice she'd been holding onto the stack and lowered herself from the tailgate to the pavement, thinking: *Now?*

Would she—did she have—? Was it nerve she was looking for? The nerve to tell Sandy what Jordan had told her? He didn't want his mom to know. He'd been red-faced, confiding in her, embarrassed, half-defensive. Sex wasn't something boys felt comfortable discussing except among their peers. Libby didn't want to talk to Sandy at all, really. About anything, much less sex. Could there be a topic more awkward to discuss with your husband's ex-lover of twenty-plus years ago? But here she was, confronted with the perfect opportunity, as if the universe had set it up. She could choose not to take advantage of it, load up her boxwoods, and drive away.

Stay out of it, Ruth had advised. But how could she? How would she feel if Jordan was convicted and sent to prison when she might have the very piece of information that could save him from that? If he was telling the truth. Because she still lacked that total certainty. What if she only wanted to believe him for Beck's sake? What if her impulse to engage with Jordan, and now to involve herself with his mother—what if it was all tied up with some sentimental hogwash about keeping Beck's memory alive, clinging to him through a connection to a boy they had never known? She was a fool if she thought she knew him now. *People lie; they lie all the time.* The thought floated to the surface of Libby's mind.

But who else was there to tell this to who would do the right thing about it?

Jordan's dad? The aunt who wasn't speaking to any of them, so far as Libby knew? Or maybe Jordan's grandparents?

Sandy was at her truck now, unloading her own wagon, filled with what from where Libby stood looked like red autumn sage and Mexican feather grass, and something purple-flowered that she didn't recognize. Still, she hesitated, wanting to leave, knowing she couldn't. Regardless of the circumstances that had created Jordan, or who his father was, he was a human being, a young man in jeopardy. If there was any possibility she could set this right, then she had to try, or never sleep again for the rest of her life. She hesitated a moment more, steeling herself, then she approached Sandy, her stride purposeful, full-out and obvious. Still, Sandy, who by now had finished loading her plants and was at the driver's side door, didn't look up until Libby rounded the bed of the truck, and she was startled. Libby could see that by the way her eyes widened.

"I'm Libby Hennessey." She gave her name straight off, wanting her identity out in the open. Wanting there to be no doubt in Sandy's mind about it. Libby didn't know what reaction she expected, and at first Sandy only frowned slightly.

But after a moment, comprehension came, and Libby watched the color drain from Sandy's face. "You're Beck's wife." Something in Sandy's voice seemed to underscore the inevitability of their meeting, or that was how it felt to Libby.

She said, "We need to talk," and it came out a bit more forcefully than she'd meant it to, but she was nervous. So was Sandy. It was pretty clear they both shared a wish that the earth would open and swallow them whole.

"All right." Sandy briefly met Libby's eyes.

"We can sit out back. They have picnic tables, don't they? And a drinks machine?"

"I think so. Just let me get my purse." Sandy reached into the cab of her truck.

They went behind the garden nursery's gift shop, and after getting bottles of water from the machine, they sat on either side of a picnic table that stood in the shade of a live oak, taking longer than was necessary to settle in, both of them squirming, fussing with their purses and water bottles, shifting their sandaled feet in the weedy scruff under the table. Finally they looked at each other, gazes tentative, uneasy.

"I think you know Jordan has been to see me," Libby said.

"I didn't want him to bother you."

"He said as much." Libby put her hands around her water bottle, feeling the wet soak her palms. *It's all right.* The words were perched on her tongue, but she hesitated before saying them, thinking how Sandy might interpret them as absolution of some kind. *It's all right that you seduced my husband and had his child. It's all right that you cut him from his son's life. It's all right that now that the going has gotten rough, you need his money and his support.*

Libby said it anyway. "It's all right." Because the bottom line was she had no control over Sandy's interpretation, and maybe she *was* offering absolution. And maybe later she'd be angry at herself for it. "He's doing some work for me. I think you know that, too."

Sandy nodded, and Libby could tell she was perplexed, wondering where Libby was going with this. Where was the fight, the show of claws, the hissed accusations? Sandy wouldn't ask, though. Libby could see that, too. It wasn't that she was intimidated, exactly, but there was sorrow haunting her eyes, and she wore an air of regret that felt true to Libby. She said, "This is very weird."

"Yes." Sandy nodded with fervency and near-palpable relief. Thank God one of them had at last named the elephant sitting on its haunches on the table between them.

"I'm not here to rake over the past, okay? I was angry about what happened between you and Beck, but that's been over a long time, and now he's dead—" Libby broke off. It was harder than she'd anticipated.

"It was such a mistake," Sandy murmured. "It didn't mean anything."

Libby might have objected. *It meant something to me.* Instead she shot Sandy a look, one that warned she didn't want to hear Sandy's defense of herself, or her excuses. Sandy must have gotten the message, because she clamped her mouth shut and shifted her glance.

Libby said, "I haven't really known what to do about this, but Saturday, a week ago, when I was driving Jordan home, he told me something in confidence that could have ramifications for him legally. I think his lawyer might be able to use it to Jordan's advantage." It occurred to Libby then that she could have gone to Jordan's lawyer herself; it would have been much easier, and she wouldn't have broken the promise she'd made Jordan not to tell his mother, but it was too late now.

The silence seemed to fill with Sandy's perplexity, her wariness and hope-inflected dread. Clearly, she had no idea what to expect. The understanding rose in Libby's mind, and against her will, she felt the faint unfolding of some newborn compassion—for this woman, of all people. But there was no accounting for the heart's propensities. It had a mind of its own.

"You know Sergeant Huckabee—Jordan said you're aware the sergeant has a grudge against him."

"He told you?"

"Is it true?"

"Yes, but why is he talking to you about it?"

Libby heard more than annoyance in Sandy's voice; she was hurt that her son had talked on a personal level about a private matter to a virtual stranger rather than his mother. Libby said, "According to Jordan, you don't know the reason behind it—the harassment, I mean."

"No, he would never tell his—Emmett and me, or his lawyer. What are you getting at?"

Libby looked away. Jordan *had* told the truth. Sergeant Huckabee had targeted him. Every time Jordan was pulled over, the sergeant had meant to needle him, to bait and provoke him, and Sandy was clueless. She had no idea. All of which meant Libby was going to have to find the words to tell her. But even assuming she found the right ones, how would she manage to say them?

"Until I retired a few years ago," Libby began, and she guessed she was going to come at the issue sideways, "I was a high school guidance counselor. I don't mean to make a thing out of it, but I'm trained to get kids to open up. Some have said I showed a real knack for it. A lot of kids over the years trusted me. It's easier sometimes, confiding in a stranger."

"What is your point? Why are you talking to me?"

"You're asking because if our roles were reversed, you wouldn't?"

"I'm not sure. I guess it would depend on what was at stake."

"Beck would be here instead of me, if he were still alive."

"Oh, I'm sorry, so sorry." Sandy spoke in a rush, sitting forward, giving Libby the sense that she'd been waiting for the right moment—a second chance—to offer her regret. She sounded sincere; she sounded as if her apology was meant to cover far more than Beck's loss.

It came as a surprise, but Libby felt lighter somehow, as if Sandy's contrition had loosened a last bit of sore anger and heartbreak she'd been carrying unaware, and she was grateful. "Beck wanted to know him."

"Yes."

"Would you have let it happen? I know when he e-mailed you two years ago, you didn't respond, but once it was definite that we were moving here—"

"I don't know, to be honest." Sandy turned her water bottle side to side, studying it.

Libby watched her. It was as if they were both enthralled.

When Sandy looked up, she said, "I want you to know that if I could go back, I'd do things differently."

Libby nodded once. *Wouldn't we all.* A heartbeat of silence passed, and then two, and then Libby said it, the hard thing she'd come back here behind the garden nursery to say. "Jordan was—for lack of a better way to put it—seduced by Sergeant Huckabee's wife."

"Coleta?" Astonishment lifted Sandy's voice, rinsed the color from her face. "She can't even speak English. That's what he told you?"

"Until last summer, he said, he had a lawn service, that the Huckabees were customers? That's how he got to know Coleta."

"He and his cousin, Travis, were partners. I helped them start their business when they were still in junior high. When did it happen? When did they—"

"Sleep together?" Libby came up with the only palatable euphemism she could think of. "The first time was during the summer after his senior year."

"There was more than one time?" Sandy's voice was faint with surprise, notes of distress, outright alarm. She looked as if she'd been hit upside the head, as folks in these parts might put it.

Libby answered: there had been a number of occasions. "They saw each other steadily, whenever he was home on vacation until last summer when he was caught."

"I don't believe it. How could I not know? I mean, I know he was sexually—" Sandy couldn't continue.

"Coleta initiated it," Libby said. "She invited him in for lemonade one day when he was mowing the lawn, and things progressed from there."

"Well, I guess she didn't need English to make that happen, did she." Sandy cut short a dark laugh. "Where was Travis? They always worked the jobs together."

"Jordan didn't mention him, and I think he would have—" As Libby spoke, she searched her mind, making sure. "I'm almost positive he would have told me. He's pretty shook up, really scared."

"Too scared to lie, you mean." Sandy's smile was brief, rueful.

"Yes," Libby said. "He's not the only young guy she's been intimate with. Evidently she's been the hot topic of a lot of so-called locker room talk around town. I suppose she still could be."

"Jesus." Sandy put her head in her hands.

"I know. The times I've met her, she seemed very shy and quiet."

"Still waters." Sandy smoothed her hair behind her temples. "When I think of the times Emmett and I asked Huck . . . and the attitude we got back, that blank stare as if he didn't know what we were talking about, and the only thing Jordy kept saying was that it would blow over. How did Huck find out? Did he walk in on them?"

"Not exactly. He found Jordan's wallet under the bed—his and Coleta's bed."

"Oh my God! Really? Something so—"

Stupid, Libby finished in her mind.

"I remember when it went missing. It was a nightmare, getting everything replaced, his driver's license, student ID, the credit cards. When I said I was concerned he'd get his identity stolen, he told me not to worry, that it had come out of his pocket when he was swimming at the lake. 'No one'll ever find it, Mom—'" Sandy waved her hand breezily. "It doesn't make sense, though," she said after a moment.

"I'm not following," Libby said.

"Huck isn't with Coleta because he loves her. I know that's what everyone in town believes, but it's an act. They're really just using each other."

Ruth had said this, Libby remembered. She remembered, too, the day the sergeant and Coleta had come to the cottage with Heidi, bearing the tamales Coleta had made from scratch. *Best you will ever eat.*

I promise, Huck had said fondly, and Coleta had blushed. They had certainly fooled Libby.

"He's in love with my sister, obsessed with her, actually." Sandy set her elbows on the table. "He only married Coleta to help her get citizenship, and the fact is he only agreed to do that after her family agreed to pay him. He even told Jenna he was doing it for the money."

"Won't they get into trouble if INS finds out?" It was the question Libby had posed to Ruth.

"Yeah, well, Huck is like a lot of cops who believe they're above the law, but then, I've lost most of my respect for him lately." Her smile was more grimace. "Honestly, I don't think he realized it would take this long, or be this complicated, and I don't think he planned at all on there being a child, although I've got to wonder now if Heidi is even his."

Before she could finish speaking, Sandy's gaze locked with Libby's. She was doing the math, Libby thought, trying to determine if there was a way Jordan was Heidi's father.

"I think that little girl is too old," Libby said. She remembered asking Heidi her age the day she'd come with her family to the cottage. The little girl had held up four fingers, and Huck had corrected her, saying almost four. *Four in September,* he'd said.

"I hope you're right," Sandy said. She toyed with her water bottle. "I remember several months ago, Jenna asked me if I knew anything about how an annulment worked. She said Huck was looking into it, that he thought there was some way to get out of a marriage through the Catholic Church even after there are kids. I told her I didn't know, that I couldn't imagine it."

"Are they serious? Your sister and Huck?"

"He's been serious about her since they were in first grade."

"But she was married to his partner, John, right, who was killed? Forgive me if I'm prying. I don't mean to. Augie Bright told me the story."

Sandy said it was okay. "Everyone in town knows everyone else's business, including mine." She made a face. "I used to think it was charming, you know, in a *Mayberry RFD*, Aunt Bee kind of way, if you can believe that. But that was back when everything was—"

Ordinary. The word shimmered, unspoken, in the air.

Ordinary was a sham, Libby thought, an illusion. People, most of them, didn't have a clue that what passed for ordinary could be over in a breath, in a step from here to there. She thought of her boxwoods, broiling in the bed of Beck's pickup. She thought of leaving. She'd done what she'd intended to do, said all there was to say, and yet, still, she remained as if glued to her seat.

Sandy said, "John and Huck were like brothers, and that's how Jordy and Trav were. It was a real source of comfort for Jenna after John died that Travis had Jordy, but she's always thought Trav was better, smarter, more mature than Jordy. Nothing was ever Trav's fault."

When Sandy paused, Libby sensed she was fishing for composure, a way to go on. She said, "It must be very difficult for you and your sister now."

"You have no idea," Sandy said, and her voice was thick with emotion; her jaw trembled. "The thing is, Travis *was* special. It was more than the fact that he made good grades and did the right thing. He was steady, and he had a good heart. He shouldn't have died in such a stupid, senseless way; he shouldn't have died at all. I don't know how Jenna or Jordy are going to get through it, but at least Jenna has our parents. Jordy's got no one. I mean, he has me, but he's not talking, so—" Sandy shrugged. Tears gathered in the corners of her eyes, and she pinched the bridge of her nose.

Libby thought of the things she might say, that it would take time, that the human spirit could be remarkably resilient. In the end she said nothing.

"Jenna can't stand the idea that Travis was doing anything as stupid as driving drunk, and I don't blame her, but I can't let Jordy go to jail if he isn't responsible."

"No."

"Do you think he's lying?"

"I want to believe him," Libby said.

"I do, too."

But Sandy wasn't sure. Libby could see her doubt and how it unsettled her. "Is there any word about the girl who was injured? Is she expected to recover?"

"Michelle?" A look crossed Sandy's expression, some odd mix of disdain and worry. Libby didn't really know. Sandy said there was no change. "She's still in a coma."

If Michelle were to waken, she would settle the question of who was driving, Libby thought. Jordan must be desperate for that to happen. Libby would be if she were innocent, as he claimed to be, but he had never mentioned Michelle. Libby couldn't decide if that was significant.

Sandy said, "Huck is like family to Jenna and my parents. They love him. I felt that way about him, too, until he started his harassment campaign."

"But they must not like it, that he's targeted Jordan."

"They don't believe that's what he's doing. They think he's providing Jordy with the guidance and discipline he's lacking at home. According to them, Jordy has a drinking problem, and I'm in la-la land, letting him get away with it. While we were in the hospital, before Travis died, Jenna even said that to me—words to that effect."

It hurt; Libby could see the evidence of Sandy's pain at her sister's judgment lodged in her eyes, and like a deeply embedded splinter, it festered. "So, I'm guessing Travis was never part of this, he was never pulled over?"

Hell no. Sandy didn't say it, but she might as well have. "Huck is like everyone else. He thinks Travis hung the moon. But Huck's feelings went deeper than most, you know, because Trav was John's son. Not only was he never pulled over, he was never in the car when Jordy was. To me it's proof that Huck's intention all along has been to single Jordy out, to make his life miserable. But he's always made sure there weren't any witnesses."

After a moment, Sandy met Libby's eyes. "I can't even imagine what you must be thinking, that I—that Jordy and I both have made the same mistake—it's—"

"At least you know you aren't imagining it." Libby cut Sandy off. "The harassment, I mean."

"Huck's motive makes sense now, I guess, but I don't understand why, with so much on the line, Jordy wouldn't tell me or, at the very least, his lawyer, what was going on. Or Emmett."

"The sergeant warned him not to shoot off his mouth about it, or he'd find a way to get Jordan for something a lot worse than a traffic violation."

"Are you serious? He threatened Jordy?"

Libby nodded. "Not recently, but back right after he found out."

"That bastard."

"It shook Jordan. He's always thought of the sergeant as a friend, like family, as you said."

"It just doesn't make any sense. Huck doesn't care about Coleta— unless that isn't behind it. Or maybe it was originally about her, but now—" Sandy's expression seemed to lighten, as if she'd been struck by some newfound comprehension.

Before Libby could prompt her, though, Sandy gathered her things and said she had to go; she was late. Libby followed her to the parking lot, and when they reached Libby's truck, Sandy turned to her, saying, "I'll never be able to thank you enough. I know it can't have been easy for you to talk to me."

"What will you do now?" Libby asked.

"Well, one thing's for sure, I won't be asking for help from the cops in this town."

"It seems to me the sergeant is risking his job. His whole career could be destroyed."

"He may have lost sight of that."

"You're suggesting he isn't rational," Libby said.

"I don't know. It's all so crazy." Sandy looked into the middle distance. "There was a witness, a trucker from Detroit, who was on 440 and saw what happened that night. At first he identified Travis as the driver, but then he changed his story. Roger hired a private detective when that happened, and while he was digging around, he found another witness, a local guy, Ricky Burrows—"

"Ricky Burrows?"

"Yes. Do you know him?"

"I do, but—"

"When the detective showed Ricky photographs of Jordy and Travis and asked which one of them was driving, Ricky swore it was Trav, the same as the trucker."

"Really?"

"Yeah. He not only witnessed the accident, but told the detective he was almost involved in it. We need Ricky to tell the police, to be a witness at the trial, if it comes to that, but the detective can't find him. Do you know where he is, how to get in touch with him?"

"I wish I did—" Libby loosened her gaze. *I don't think he's who he says he is.* Ruth's warning from a week ago came to Libby's mind. Ruth had heard it from the Graysons, who'd bought the parcel of land with the old farmhouse on it next door. Ruth had thought she'd already told Libby about the sale, her new neighbors. They weren't moved in there yet full-time, Ruth had said, but already Mr. Grayson had called the local law enforcement about a man the family had found sleeping in one of the bedrooms. They'd caught the same man cooking on the old woodstove. *As if he owns the place,* Mr. Grayson had said. And in fact that's what the man told them. He had insisted to the Graysons that they, and not he, were the trespassers. Mr. Grayson had told Ruth that the deputy who'd responded to their report of an intruder had identified the man as Ricky Burrows. Mr. Grayson had also told Ruth that around a month or so ago, they'd found a gutted hog on their property. *Exactly like the slaughtered hog you found on your property,* Ruth had said to Libby. She'd added that the Graysons believed Ricky was responsible, but when Libby asked why—why would Ricky do something so awful?—Ruth couldn't answer.

"What is it, Libby?" Sandy prompted. "What do you know about him?"

"I'm not sure my information is accurate," Libby began. *It doesn't matter what his motive is. He's not rational.* Ruth's voice rose again in Libby's brain. But Ruth was basing her opinion on what the Graysons had told her. It wasn't much better, really, than the gossip they both deplored. She hadn't repeated it to Robert, either, for the same reason. It was hearsay.

"Please tell me what you know. It could make the difference for Jordy."

It was the way Sandy put it, in terms of what was at stake for Jordan, that pushed Libby to relate the details of the Graysons' encounters with Ricky, but when she finished, she added a caveat. "Who knows if he's still around there?"

"You said he's worked for Augie Bright. I could call him and see if I could find Ricky on a job site."

"Yes, but, Sandy, I think you should go to the police—"

"In Wyatt? No way. Huck has threatened Jordy and pressured at least one witness. If he finds out about Ricky, he'll pressure him, too. I've got to get to him first."

"I think it might have already happened," Libby said, and she went on, telling Sandy about finding Huckabee and Ricky together at the police department in town on Monday. She repeated the bit Huckabee had said, that Ricky had finally gotten his story straight. "I don't know what he meant," Libby said.

"Huck got to Ricky," Sandy said, her shoulders falling. "He's threatened him, too, somehow; I'd bet money on it."

"Can you go over his head?"

"I don't think it would do any good, not with the good ol' boy network we've got in this town."

"You could go to another town. Greeley, maybe."

"Maybe," Sandy said, and she smiled, briefly. "I've got to run; I've left a client waiting. But thank you for this, talking to me. I'll never be able to make up for what I did, the trouble and pain I caused you, but that was my mistake. No one should blame Jordy."

"No, of course not. I don't—"

"It doesn't matter to me, you know? I mean if he was driving that night or not. Either way, he's my son, and I love him. I would give my life for his, do anything to keep him safe. Huck should know that. Everyone should. It's just that simple."

And just that complicated, Libby thought, watching Sandy go. She didn't have a good feeling about any of this. In fact, her stomach ached with apprehension, the sense of foreboding, of some ill wind brewing. But from what direction it might come, she didn't know.

Libby got into Beck's truck, tracking Sandy's progress across the parking lot. Debating whether it was wise, letting Sandy go. Watching as her truck backed out and another car, a light-colored sedan, fell in behind it. Libby kept her eye on both vehicles as they turned left out of the lot. Ruth had wanted to talk to Captain Perry in Wyatt about Ricky. But like Sandy, Libby was wary of that.

She pulled her cell phone from her pocket and called Ruth.

"I've been trying to get hold of you," Ruth said when she answered. "Was your phone off?"

"What's the matter?" Libby asked.

"After we talked earlier, I called Aunt Tildy about Ricky Burrows. You know how she is. She knows everything about everyone in this town."

"But he isn't from here."

"Oh, but he is. He's a descendant of the Scroggins family. He was born here. Fran's sister, Jewel, is his mother."

"No, that can't be right. Ricky's what? Late twenties, early thirties, maybe? Fran's in her seventies—"

"Jewel was a lot younger. Aunt Tildy called her a change-of-life baby. She said Jewel's mama was way over forty and didn't handle the news of the pregnancy well." Ruth sniffed. "Maybe that explains why Jewel was such a nutcase. She sure did a number on Ricky."

"What did she do?" Libby asked.

"There are various stories, that she locked him in a closet or chained him up outside with the dog if he misbehaved, but the worst thing was the day she went to Ricky's school—he was in fifth grade at the time—and started shouting about aliens and a massive invasion, screaming they had to leave the building immediately or they'd all be killed."

"Oh my God, that's horrible."

"I know; the kids were scared to death, Tildy said. Ricky was so scared and humiliated he wet himself. He was sobbing, a complete mess. It was awful for him. You know, the cops came, medical people. The way Tildy described it, it was total chaos."

"I can't imagine the effect it must have had on Ricky. But how does Tildy know all this?"

"She worked in the office. She brought him home with her that day. She let him take a shower, found him some clean clothes, and fed him. They played checkers until his dad could come for him. She told me he came to see her."

"What? You mean like recently?"

"A few days ago. I almost fainted. It's so scary, thinking of the hours he was in her house alone with her. Tildy said she thought he came by because he remembered her kindness to him when he went through all of that."

Tildy was kind. Libby loved her, too, but she was also old and garrulous. When it came to this or any other story, no way did she even begin to approach the status of a reliable source. Libby was on the verge of pointing this out when Ruth said she knew what Libby was thinking.

"I didn't entirely trust Tildy's story, either, so I called Fran."

"She confirmed it?"

"Yeah, that and worse. Fran was contacted not long ago by someone at a Colorado mental hospital who told her that her nephew, who'd been locked up there for the past five years, had escaped. Fran had no idea he was there. But evidently this person found her name in one of Ricky's files and wanted her to know he might be headed to Texas, specifically to Wyatt and home, and he was dangerous."

"But how did he get out?"

"He got hold of a knife and managed to incapacitate a male nurse. He didn't kill him, but after he took his uniform, he sliced the guy up badly enough that he passed out. Ricky left him in a closet, then he walked out pretty as you please. It was hours before they discovered he was gone."

"This is unreal."

"Ha! Wait till you hear this part. Fran said Ricky had a fascination with knives even when he was young, and he liked carving things up, including the occasional animal. Fran said Jewel thought he might have a future in forensic or mortuary science." Ruth's laugh was dark, truncated. "Fran also said they tried to help both Jewel and Ricky. There were psychiatrists involved, antidepressants, yada yada, but the situation didn't improve."

"It must have been heartbreaking," Libby said.

"I'm sure, but you see what this means, don't you? That it has to be Ricky who gutted the hog at your place and the Graysons'. He's the one who left the dead rats in your mailbox, the hummingbird on your kitchen floor, the note—"

Libby's pulse tapped lightly in her veins. "But why?" She asked the same question she had asked earlier. "What's his motive? What does he want?"

"I don't know. He called the Graysons trespassers. Maybe he wants the ranch—the Little B?"

"But that's crazy."

"Yeah, well, we are talking about a mental-hospital escapee, a known lunatic. Fran told me the police in Colorado issued a BOLO when Ricky escaped, but that's two months ago now."

"And he was here, right under my nose—"

"All our noses, Libby. Don't go blaming yourself."

"But I should have warned Sandy." Libby felt awful. "Suppose she finds him and he goes off on her? What if he uses a knife on her?"

"Sandy? Sandy Cline? What are you talking about?"

Libby gave Ruth the gist of her meeting with Sandy, scooting by Ruth's exclamatory *Oh my God*s and *You must be kidding*s, getting to the heart of it—that of all people, Ricky had apparently witnessed Jordan's accident, and Sandy was trying to track him down. "She's afraid Huckabee has already pressured one witness. She's worried about him getting to Ricky first, but I think he may have already." Libby paused and let out a little groan. "But what am I doing, Ruth? As you have so often pointed out, it's really none of my business, is it?"

"No, but now that we know all of this, how is either one of us going to feel if this all goes wrong and Jordy lands in prison for something he didn't do? Or Sandy gets hurt trying to convince Ricky he has to testify for Jordy, assuming she can find him?"

"You haven't spoken to anyone at the police department in Wyatt, have you?"

"No," Ruth said. "I wanted to talk to you first."

"Good. I'm coming to pick you up. We'll go to the police in Greeley," Libby said.

Ruth said she'd be waiting, and Libby clicked off her phone.

She wasn't a mile from Inman's when it rang again. She pulled over to check the ID, and when she saw who it was, she answered quickly. "Jordan? Is everything all right?"

She didn't know what prompted her to ask. Some weird intuition, she'd guess, and when he answered, "No," and said, "Can you come and get me?" her heart fell against the wall of her chest.

"What's wrong? Where are you?" She was already keying the ignition, pulling cautiously back onto the road. She didn't like driving and talking on her cell phone, but it seemed imperative.

"I'm at my dad's apartment," Jordy said. "I'm really sorry to bother you, but I've called my dad like a hundred times, and he's not answering his phone. I didn't know who else—"

"It's fine, Jordan. I don't mind that you called me." In fact, she was pleased that he thought of her in terms of someone who would help, and she found that disconcerting. "But what's going on?"

"It's my mom. She's at my aunt Jenna's, and I think she's in some kind of trouble."

14

It happened in a flash.

Sandy saw the light-colored sedan in her rearview as she left Inman's, and her temper flared. She slowed, letting the car come close enough to her tailgate that she could tell the driver was a woman. *Patsy Meade. Surprise, surprise.* The snarky voice in Sandy's brain was a cover for the jolt of her alarm. She would never know what demon took possession of her, making her veer off the crumbling edge of the country road into the tall grass that verged on the pavement. Patsy did the same, stopping behind Sandy, their bumpers only inches apart. Sandy looked at Patsy in the rearview for a moment, then, heart hammering, she jumped out of her truck, thinking, *Fine.* Thinking, *Bring it on.* Thinking, *Lady, you picked the wrong day.*

It was irrational, totally not a smart move, but Sandy headed toward Patsy's car anyway, mind racing, primed for battle as soon as Patsy got out. Before she could open her mouth, blasting her indictment, shouting her accusations, Sandy would set her straight. But Patsy didn't get out. She just stared at Sandy through the windshield, flat mouthed, empty eyed. Motionless. Sandy's step faltered. She thought of all the whacked-out people in the world, the crazy things that could happen. Suppose Patsy had a gun? Suppose she was only waiting for Sandy to get close enough that a single shot wouldn't miss? Had Michelle died, then? And Patsy had gone over the edge? *Oh God—*

The certainty came down on Sandy hard enough that her knees buckled. She flailed her arms to keep her balance. Backed up, stopped. Stupidly, she had left her cell phone in the truck. Turning away from Patsy's eerie gaze, Sandy looked into the field at her right. The wind blew, hot, dry, noising in her ears, whipping stray tendrils of hair across her face. A cow moseyed over to the barbed-wire fence, and she thought how beautiful its eyes were, liquid and brown, somehow ancient and wise. She wondered if she would take the vision of the cow's eyes with her into the next world. If there even was a next world. Her dad didn't believe in an afterlife. This was it, he said. You get this one shot, then nothing.

Nothing. When she was growing up, the idea of nothing had scared her more than the idea of eternity.

How long did she stand there, waiting, for what, she would never be sure. Fate to show its hand? Another driver to come along, a hero who, magically, divining the situation, would stop and peacefully resolve it? It was probably only moments, but it felt like the fearful eternity of her childhood. The sound of a car engine cranking to life—Patsy's car engine—jerked her gaze around. Her awareness now was of her vulnerability, the vast open space around her and how easily Patsy might run her down. Sandy retreated, taking backward steps, breath coming in shallow dips, feet tangling in the grass. But when Patsy dropped the car into gear, she reversed, giving herself room to clear Sandy's tailgate, and then without a glance at Sandy, she drove away, leaving Sandy to stare after her, immobile, for long, disbelieving seconds.

After a while, feeling chilled despite the heat, she hugged herself. The fear that Patsy might come back or that she was parked off the road up ahead, lying in wait, kept her motionless. It was the thought of

Jordy, that she needed to be with him, that got her moving. And after all that she'd learned from Libby Hennessey, she had to get hold of Roger, too, she thought, heading to her truck. And Jenna. She had to talk to Jenna. Sandy didn't care what it took. She got into the truck and shut the door. She was trembling; she didn't feel safe. But there was no place safe right now, and there wouldn't be until she got Jordy clear of this, whatever *this* was. She was shaking so badly she had trouble keying the ignition. Then she gave the engine too much gas, and it nearly died. She glanced at herself in the rearview and almost didn't recognize the half-panicked woman looking back at her. *Settle down,* she told herself. *Breathe breathe. Just breathe.*

After a minute, feeling calmer, she drove onto the road, checking her watch, fumbling for her phone, thinking of the client waiting for her. More than an hour now. She looked in the rearview at the plants she'd bought at Inman's, wilted over, unhappy in the heat. Sandy drove, hunting the roadsides for any sign of the light-colored sedan, brain churning. She managed to key in Roger's number, and when he didn't answer, she left a message that she had a hunch that involved Jenna, and she was going there. She tried Jordy, too, but when his voice mail picked up, she only asked him to call her, saying it was important. She didn't want him to worry.

Clicking off, she thought of calling Emmett, and instead dialed her client Martha Langston, making her apologies, pleading a family emergency. Martha was gracious; she didn't ask for details. Given the Cline-family notoriety, Martha probably didn't want to know unless she was a fan of reality TV. Sandy dialed her mother's cell phone after that, but clicked off before the call could go through. She didn't want her mother to alert Jenna she was coming.

She was jittery, gripping the wheel, hunched over it like an old woman. Every time she crossed paths with a light-colored sedan, her heart stopped. She had no idea what might happen when she got to Jenna's. She would bull her way into the house if she had to; she would put her sister down and sit on her if that's what it took to make her listen. Sandy snorted. *Dream on,* she thought. She could scarcely breathe, she was so on edge.

Jenna's neighborhood, her street, her bungalow, in an older subdivision of Wyatt, looked the same as it had in the days when Sandy had come here routinely. But it felt alien now. It felt scary. She pulled to the curb and stared at the front yard. She and Jenna had put in the flower beds, planting them with a mix of mostly native perennials that were drought tolerant and deer resistant. Jenna never minded the deer, though. She had bottle-fed more than one motherless fawn. She'd nursed injured rabbits and raccoons, too, and once rescued a fox that had caught its leg in a tangle of rusty barbed wire. Travis and Jordy had grown up tramping through the woods with Sandy and Jenna, learning its lore, its dark, loamy secrets. It killed Sandy, remembering those days, the boys with their heads together, comparing the bounty scored on their treks—a feather, a nest, chunks of quartz that glittered in the sun like diamonds, pink-veined granite, the odd arrowhead, a fossil, and once the completely intact skeleton of a whiptail lizard. Thinking of those days made Sandy want to cry, and she tightened her teeth to keep from it.

Suddenly it made her so goddamned angry—that fucking accident, the blind fucking stupid idiocy of it, and the horrible consequences, twin horrors of unfathomable loss and endless grief. And what for? What was the fucking point? What was the use of life when it was this fragile and over so soon? Sandy knew without Jenna even telling her that she wished the cancer had killed her. Then she would have been spared this cruelty, the worst one of all, outliving your own child, the one you carried beneath your heart. *Ah God,* Sandy thought. She could just howl with the pain of it.

Instead she bailed from the truck, wiping her eyes, sniffing back a nose full of crud. She knew Jenna was home; she'd left her garage door up and her SUV was inside. Walking up the long, sinewy driveway to the back door—they never used each other's front doors—Sandy wondered if Jenna was watching her, if even now she was running through the house to bolt the back door, barring Sandy's entrance.

It caught her off guard to find Jenna standing in the doorway behind the closed screen, and even though the shadows under the covered porch were deep, Sandy knew her eyes were hard and her mouth set in a forbidding line. But she was there; the door was open. It must mean something.

"Hey," Sandy said, and the syllable came out croaky and tentative on what was little more than a puff of air.

"Mom and Dad aren't here," Jenna said. "I told them to pack up and go home."

"They were hovering," Sandy said, because she knew.

"I was suffocating." Jenna held the door open, but even as Sandy's relief and the leap of her jubilation lifted her heart, Jenna was sidestepping her hug, and the look on her face was dark and forbidding.

Sandy followed Jenna though the mudroom into the kitchen. Sandy paused at the marble-topped island. Jenna walked around it, going to the opposite end as if she needed not only distance but also a physical barrier between them.

"I've packed up Jordy's stuff. I want you to take it when you go."

Sandy had the sense that Jenna would welcome a fight, that she would grab at the chance to distract herself from her agony. How did she do it—pass by Travis's empty bedroom? Open a kitchen cabinet to see the mug he had decorated for her when he was five? If she ever gave in to it, Sandy thought, if she were to slip over the black edge of her grief, she'd be gone forever. She looked so exhausted; she'd lost so much weight, ten or fifteen pounds, Sandy guessed. "Why won't you let me help you?" she asked.

"You? I don't even want you in my house."

"You don't mean that." It took every ounce of Sandy's self-control to keep her voice level.

"Yes, I do," Jenna insisted, even as Sandy raised her voice, talking over her.

"Jordy wasn't driving. I've got proof."

"You've got nothing but a head full of delusions about Jordy, a head full of the lies you tell yourself about him so you can sleep nights."

"That's almost funny, Jenna. Jordy says he'd rather take the blame for the accident—anything to save *your* delusions about Travis. Jordy can't stand for Trav to be remembered as having been responsible for something so horrific."

"So he's falling on his sword, is that it? That's a great way to play it."

"He's not playing, Jenna. There are witnesses."

"Every one of whom has identified Jordy."

"I don't know about all of them, but I do know Huck pressured Nat Blevins somehow into changing his story."

"Why would he do that?"

"To protect you. Because he loves you. He can't stand that this has happened. It was awful enough for you, losing John. And now Travis, too? It's unthinkable. All you have is your memory. It's the last thing, the only thing now, Huck can save for you."

"You're wrong." Jenna traced her eyebrows, shoved her hair behind her ears.

It needed washing. And it was seeing that—and how broken Jenna was, how fragile and vulnerable—that kept Sandy from launching herself at Jenna, as she'd done a few times in their childhood, with the intention of bringing Jenna down and causing her bodily harm. Their mother was right. Jenna was incapable of sorting out her emotions, much less controlling how they were expressed. *I mean, my God,* said the voice in Sandy's brain, *she can't even wash her hair.*

Jenna went to the kitchen sink and stared out the window. Sandy went through the house to Jenna's bathroom and found her shampoo. Bringing it and a towel back into the kitchen, she stood next to Jenna, bumping her gently aside with her hip. She turned on the tap.

Once the water was the right temperature, Jenna wordlessly lowered her head under it, and Sandy moved the sprayer around, gathering and releasing Jenna's shoulder-length hair to thoroughly wet it. Then, working in the shampoo, she gently massaged Jenna's scalp, her temples, the back of her neck, giving herself to the ritual, letting herself be soothed by the sound of the running water and the citrusy scent of the shampoo rising on the steam. She closed her eyes, blindly mapping with her fingers the shape of Jenna's skull, the mystery of its uneven knotty surface. It was when she was rinsing the soap from Jenna's hair that she became fully aware of Jenna's distress, the heave of her shoulders, her grating, uncontrollable sobs, and without a second thought, she pulled Jenna up and brought her around, wrapping her in a tight embrace.

Heedless of the wet soaking their shirts and puddling the floor, they sank to the floor, backs to the cabinet, clinging to each other, rocking together. Sandy made the little humming noises their mother had always made when she held them, crying and inconsolable, as children. She had made these noises, holding Jordy, and even Travis, when the boys were small.

Minutes passed; gradually, Jenna grew quiet.

There was only the rough hiccup of her breath when Sandy at last reached up, groping for the towel. Pulling it down, she blotted Jenna's face, wiped the soft, nubby terry cloth over her hair. "Mom said you haven't cried very much."

"Couldn't," Jenna said.

"It's good, then. You needed to."

Jenna smiled ruefully. "I need a tissue."

"Use the towel; it'll wash."

Jenna did, and they settled back against the cabinet, shoulders touching.

"Have you heard anything about Michelle?" Sandy asked after a moment, and it seemed odd, but they had to start somewhere. They had to find the way to say all the hard stuff, to try and fix what they could, and now was the time, when Jenna's defenses were down.

"She's still in a coma. Why?"

Sandy told Jenna about her two confrontations with Patsy. "Earlier, when I stopped, I don't know what I was thinking. It was totally possible she had a gun, that if her daughter died she might want to kill me. Or Jordy."

"Wouldn't you, if Jordy had died and Michelle had been driving?"

"Probably. But, Jenna, Jordy wasn't driving."

She started to get up, but Sandy went up on her knees, putting her hand on Jenna's arm, stopping her. "Please listen to me. You remember when I told you how I thought Huck was dogging Jordy, ticketing him for no reason."

"Oh God, Sandy, not that again." Jenna got to her feet. "It's such a load of horseshit."

"No, it isn't." Sandy stood up, too.

"You need to get Jordy's stuff and go, okay?" Jenna sounded as if she were running out of the patience it took to be nice. She left the kitchen, finger-combing her still-damp hair back from her face. In the bathroom, she made a ponytail and fastened it with an elastic band.

"I met Libby Hennessey, Beck's wife." Sandy spoke from the doorway. "We talked out at Inman's for an hour this morning."

Jenna turned to look at her.

"Jordy told Libby he slept with Coleta. He thinks that's why Huck is after him."

"Jordy and Coleta?" Jenna's voice registered some note between stupefaction and disgust.

"She seduced him, and you'd better watch what you say, because according to Libby, Jordy isn't the only young guy in town she was entertaining."

"Travis would never—" Jenna stopped, breaking Sandy's glance. Even she knew better than to include the word *never* in some comment you were making about your kid. Turning back to Sandy, Jenna asked how it was she and Libby had come to meet and talk. Sandy had counted on it, Jenna's curiosity, and as quickly as she could, she filled Jenna in, telling her that Jordy had taken the matter into his own hands and gone there, that he was now working for Libby. "Emmett said the only way he can ever know his birth dad now is through Libby."

"But why confide in her? She's a total stranger."

"Maybe precisely for that reason. Or maybe he thought we wouldn't believe him, that no one would." Sandy wiped her face. "I think it's reached a point where he had to tell someone. He's pretty scared with Huck breathing down his neck—"

"I don't see why Huck cares who Coleta slept with. All he can talk about is finding a way to get out of his marriage to her. He's requested an annulment, and if that doesn't work, he's going to call her family in Honduras and ask if he can give the money back. Give Coleta back."

"When he first went after Jordy, Huck threatened him. He said if he ever heard Jordy talking about having sex with Coleta, he'd find a way to put him in jail. I think, then, Huck meant to put the fear of God into him."

"Why? It doesn't make any sense."

"It does if you figure the money Huck was getting paid by Coleta's family depended on her getting citizenship, and for that to happen, she and Huck had to look convincingly married. If INS found out their marriage was a sham, Coleta would get deported, and who knows— Huck might lose his badge. He had a lot riding on that little venture, but it's turned into something else now, since the accident. Now it's about you."

"He's not in love with me, Sandy." Jenna left the bathroom.

Sandy followed her into the kitchen. "Yeah, I agree. Obsession is not love. It's a mental, an emotional, disease."

"Oh, give me a break. Obsession? Really? I hardly think the guy's obsessed. Like I'm what? Irresistible? Like he can't get enough of me?

Days go by and I don't see the man. Besides, look at me. I'm a wreck. Is this something to get obsessed over? Even Troy doesn't come around much anymore."

"Think about it, Jenna. Who quit the force in San Antonio, uprooting what was a pretty successful career to come back here—basically the ass end of nowhere, for a cop, anyway—to look after you and Trav? He's been like a husband, like a dad ever since John was killed. Who fixes the toilet when it runs? Who takes the car in for its checkup? Who did you call in the middle of the night when Trav ran a fever and you needed someone to make a drugstore run?"

"Well, yeah, okay. But not—I haven't really called on him since Troy and I got serious." Jenna sat at the table in the breakfast nook.

Sandy came up to the chair adjacent to Jenna's and paused, balancing her hands on the back of it, thinking, working it through. "That's it," she said. "That's what happened, what pushed him over the edge."

"What are you talking about?"

Sandy came around the chair and sat down, leaning forward on her elbows, her eyes on Jenna's intent, searching. "All this time, Huck was fine as long as he had you to himself, as long as he could care for you and Trav, you know? The way a husband would—"

"He wasn't—there are no fringe benefits. We're just friends."

"In your mind. I think Huck was okay with it, too. A friendship was better than nothing. But then Troy came along, and he realized that in addition to fixing the toilet and running the car in, Troy was getting benefits."

"That's crazy," Jenna said, but Sandy could tell she was considering it.

"He's wanted you for years, since you were in high school. But you chose John, and he loved John, too." Reaching across the table, Sandy took Jenna's hand in her own, and it was cold in her warmer grasp. "You remember how horrible Huck felt when John was killed."

"He blamed himself. I wanted to blame him, too."

"But you always knew the risk, knew it could happen. You said you were prepared—"

"I lied." Jenna smiled ruefully. She wiped her face, sniffed.

Sandy leaned back. "Huck wanted to be your savior. I think he figured, eventually, if he hung around long enough, you'd let him in—all the way in. He'd take John's place, get the bennies—the bed and board, so to speak."

Jenna was looking at Sandy and shaking her head. "I've never felt that way about him and never will."

"I know."

"I love him the way John loved him." She got up, turning away from Sandy, groaning softly.

"He's setting Jordy up, Jenna. For you, so you don't have to look at what really happened—"

Jenna held up her hand, and the gesture was a warning, but it was also a plea. Sandy could see from Jenna's expression that something hard and resistant was giving way inside her. It was all coming together, the truth she didn't want to know, that she couldn't deny.

"A detective we hired has found a witness, Ricky Burrows. The night of the accident, Ricky was driving on CR 440 when the Range Rover came out of nowhere around a curve right at him. Ricky told the detective he saw Travis. They were eyeball to eyeball. You know how they say your mind will crystallize an image when you're in danger like that? Everything slows down; your brain registers every minute detail, and it remembers them; it prints them like photographs. That's what happened to Ricky. The image of Travis in the driver's seat is printed on his brain as clearly as a photograph."

Jenna went to the sink, leaned against it.

Outside a car door slammed, and they both jumped at the sound. Footsteps approached. "Jenna?" A man shouted. "You in there?"

She wheeled, glance colliding with Sandy's. "It's Huck."

Sandy stood up, blood pounding. She was afraid, and she saw that Jenna was, too, and it went through her mind that if she was wrong about Huck, it would be awful, and if she was right, it might be even worse.

He came through the back door without knocking, as if he were more than a visitor, which Sandy supposed he was now, after all these years. His focus, his look, and his tender smile were all for Jenna. His one-armed hug, the kiss he dropped on her temple, were rote, part of his usual routine when he visited.

But Jenna's slight recoil was not, and Sandy saw how he tensed.

Huck found her gaze now. "What're you doing here?"

"Telling the truth, the way you should be," Sandy answered.

"What truth would that be?" He leaned against the countertop, crossing his arms, affecting a casual air.

But Sandy's attention was riveted to the butt of his gun, jutting from his holster, and there was nothing casual about it. She made herself raise her gaze to his face. "I was telling Jenna about Ricky Burrows, the witness to the accident who says you threatened him into changing his statement." It was a shot in the dark, really. She had no proof Huck knew about Ricky's existence as a witness, much less that Huck had pressured him, but he must have. How else to explain Huck's cryptic remark to Libby that Ricky had finally gotten his story straight?

"That guy," Huck began, and the characterization was a sneer, a curse. "I guess if you can believe a whack job like him, you can believe anything."

"You know him, then." Sandy had expected that he did. Still, it shook her. There seemed to be no end to the ways Huck was prepared to get Jordy.

"What do you mean, whack job?" Jenna's voice was strident, accusing. "Sandy says he was on 440 that night, that he saw Travis driving the Range Rover. It ran him off the road."

"That's total bullshit." Huck addressed Jenna. "You know Fran Keller. Her folks owned the Little B."

"What does Fran have to do with it?"

Jenna asked before Sandy could.

"Burrows is Fran's sister Jewel's kid, and if you remember, when we were growing up, that whole Scroggins family out there at the B were just a bunch of nut jobs, with the exception of possibly Fran. Jewel got hauled off the place in a straitjacket more than once, though. Her kid Ricky is just as bad off."

"He's crazy, so he can't possibly know what he saw the night of the accident." Sandy stepped into Huck's field of vision. "Is that what you're saying?"

"I heard it's not only your boy who's been talking to Libby Hennessey, that you and her are getting pretty chummy, too."

"So? Is that your business?" He knew she'd met Libby? How?

"Well, you might want to ask her about Burrows. Ask her about the dead hog she found swinging in a cedar tree out at her place not long ago, blood and entrails smeared everywhere. He got in her house, too, left her a dead hummingbird on her kitchen floor, put rats in her mailbox. You think that guy's not psychotic?"

"Why?" Jenna asked. "Why did he do all that?"

"He thinks the Little B belongs to him, that Fran is selling it out from under him. His mama filled his head with all this bullshit about it when she was dying. She told him Fran forced the old folks, Fran and Jewel's parents, to give her power of attorney."

"He should take it up with Fran, shouldn't he?" Sandy asked.

"Well, I guess he would if he had a brain that worked, but, trust me, he's crazy as a shithouse rat. He keyed his own truck, for chrissake. Although that does indicate some of the cells up there are working. It kept the suspicion off him when the other stuff started happening. Slaughtering that hog, the other animals—he thought it would scare folks off."

"If he's doing all of this and you know it, why isn't he in jail?" Sandy looked intently at Huck. Something was off; she could see the swim of it, oily and deep, in his eyes. He didn't want her here. He didn't want her anywhere near Jenna. Sandy thought of leaving; she could drive to the police department . . . and say what? That Huck was obsessed with her sister, and to protect Jenna from the further trauma of facing that her son had foolishly caused his own senseless death, Huck was out to frame Jordy? Who would believe her?

Huck said something about Colorado, that folks in that state were hunting Ricky. "They have a BOLO out on him."

"Why?" Jenna wanted to know.

Sandy talked over them both. "You made a deal with Ricky, didn't you, the same as you did with the trucker from Detroit, Nat Blevins. What did you promise Ricky? Did you say if he changed his story about who he saw driving the Range Rover, you wouldn't arrest him for vandalism and trespassing? Or maybe you told him to get out of town, get clear out of Texas." She was baiting Huck, and she knew it might be dangerous, but what other option did she have to get the truth, or what she hoped and prayed for Jordy's sake was the truth? But she was shaking now, and scared. Scared enough that she felt her blood pounding the walls of her brain, hammering the space behind her eyes. She thought of her phone, feet away in her purse on the breakfast-room table, where she'd left it.

Huck took a step in her direction. "What are you trying to say, Sandy?"

She stood her ground. "I'm not *trying* to say anything. It's a fair question. You're in love with Jenna. You don't want her to have to face it, that Trav was the driver. You don't want to believe it yourself. You want it to be Jordy. At first you went after him because he's the punk kid who slept with your immigrant wife, and even if you don't give a shit about her, macho guy that you are, you weren't about to let Jordy get by with it. But now—now you want him put away for Jenna's sake."

"Sandy." Jenna's sharp protest was a warning.

"Hasn't that accident taken enough from us, Jenna?" Sandy kept her eye on Huck.

"Is it true?" Jenna came around Huck, distracting him.

It wasn't a thought process that prompted her when Sandy seized the opportunity and grabbed her phone and began pressing buttons, a ridiculous attempt to hit the right ones for Roger, or Emmett, or even 911.

"Do you think I'm that weak?" Jenna wanted to know. "That I can't handle knowing my son wasn't perfect? That he could be capable of being foolish, of making a horrible mistake?"

"No, hell no, Jenna. You're the strongest, bravest woman I know. It's just, you've been through so much shit, and so much of it is on me—I mean, John died because some asshole gets my gun? Jesus." Huck's head rocked back. Blinking, voice torn, he said, "I keep seeing it, the look on your face when I told you. It's like, etched into my brain, you know? I'd do anything—"

"Stop, Huck, please." Jenna touched his arm.

He looked down at her, and his face was a suffusion of love and despair. Even Jenna saw it, the way he was eaten up with his adoration of her, and she stepped back as if burned by its heat.

"Are you lying about Jordy?" she asked him. "Because I don't need that. I didn't ask you to do that."

Huck turned away, wiping his face, his upper lip.

"I don't know what I'm going to do if you've lied about this, Huck." Jenna's voice hitched. "If you've threatened Jordy, pressured witnesses. Did you? Tell me the truth."

"For you, Jenna, to save you—"

"Oh my God, Huck." Jenna sounded sick. She locked her gaze with his. "You realize I have to tell your captain. You must know that."

He wheeled, and Sandy saw it as if in slow motion, his hand whipping his service revolver from its holster, in one slick, practiced movement. He swung the weapon first in Jenna's direction, and then he pointed it at Sandy.

Her heart paused.

Jenna asked, "What are you doing?" and took a faltering sidestep, and that's what caused Huck to look at her and take aim at her again.

The moment would be seared into Sandy's brain—Huck's expression, his look of dumb devotion, underscored by the darker, welling shadow of his rage and his grief when he pulled the trigger.

15

Libby, you aren't going to take Jordy to his aunt's house. Call 911. Let them handle it, whatever the trouble is." Ruth's voice was anxious, almost shrill.

"What would I say, Ruth? That I'm picking up a boy who's worried about his mom? You know there are laws about calling 911 for no good reason."

"For all you know, this is some kind of a trap, and Jordy Cline is part of it. I've been thinking about it, you know, all of this business with Ricky Burrows being a witness to that car accident—why was he of all people out there on 440 that night of all nights? The fact is, the man is dangerous. I don't like it, Libby, not one bit. Come to the office. Let's talk about it."

"It'll be fine, Ruth. You worry too much." Libby turned right on Mystic Oaks Circle, where Jordan had said his dad's garage apartment was located. Behind a blue two-story with yellow trim, he'd said, on the right about midway around the circle. She caught sight of it, and of Jordan, standing in the driveway. "I'm here," she told Ruth, "and believe it or not, there's no maniac running around with a knife."

"This isn't a joke, Libby. For God's sake, will you please be careful? I'm going over to Greeley now to the police department there, since we can't really trust anyone here. Somebody has got to find Ricky and stop him. I mean, so far animals are his only murder victims. But who knows what the man is capable of?" Ruth paused. "I'll be scared for you and the Graysons till they get him."

"They will," Libby said, although how would she know? Ricky could be anywhere, carving up God knew what. He could be long gone, or hiding out somewhere at the Little B. But Jordan was right here, waiting for her, looking anxious, and she couldn't turn her back on him. Telling Ruth she'd stay in touch, Libby clicked off and pulled to the curb.

Jordan got into the cab of the truck, overriding her greeting with his apology. "I'm really sorry. I shouldn't have called you." His glance at her was rueful, anxious.

"It's fine. I'm glad if I can help. Did you get hold of your dad, or hear back from your mom?"

"No. It's like her phone is totally off now. It doesn't even go to voice mail. My dad must be somewhere on an appointment, maybe at a drilling site. He probably left his phone in the truck, or he can't hear it for all the equipment noise."

"We can't go to the police in Wyatt, I guess." Libby wanted to make sure.

"Oh hell no," he said, and then he apologized again. His hands shook when he ran them over his head.

"You're right. *Hell no* is the way to put it."

"I can't figure out what Mom is doing at Aunt Jenna's."

"But you're sure she's there?"

"I heard Aunt Jenna talking in the background when Mom's phone called me." He sat a moment, thinking. "She left me a message earlier to call her. She said it was important. She left my lawyer a message, too, telling him she was going to Aunt Jenna's. He's in Austin, but he's coming back, he said, as quick as he can. I didn't want to call my grandparents and scare them." Jordy turned his face to the side window and said, softly, "They've been scared enough. Everyone has."

His voice hitched, and Libby patted his arm. "You couldn't understand what your mom or your aunt were saying?"

"No. Has it happened to you—someone's phone calling you by accident? You can hear them, like if they're driving and the radio's on, you can hear music and stuff but nothing real specific. I know it was my mom and Aunt Jenna talking, and there was a man's voice, too. I couldn't place it. I don't know. I just have a bad feeling."

"Well, we'll go by and see if your mom's truck is there. But if it looks like there's any trouble, I'm driving away. We'll call 911 and wait for the police. Okay?"

"Okay," Jordan said, but Libby knew he wasn't listening to her, that he only wanted to go, to get there.

She followed his directions, and in an effort to distract him, to distract them both, she told him she'd spoken to his mom. "Right before you called," she said, and she could feel his astonishment and, on its heels, his dismay. "I was at Inman's earlier, getting the boxwoods you and I talked about putting in the front beds at the cottage."

"I saw them." He jerked his head, indicating the bed of the truck.

"Your mom was there, too, buying plants for a client, I think."

"Mrs. Langston. I talked to her. She said Mom canceled on her, that she said she had a family emergency."

"I guess Mrs. Langston didn't ask what it was?"

"No. But that's when I totally figured out something was up. Mom hardly ever cancels a job, and she always takes my calls. Always. And if she can't, she always calls me back."

He was so confident, so convinced of his importance to his mother. Libby wondered if she had ever inspired so much trust. Probably not, she decided. Such faith was likely limited to the mother-child relationship.

"I told your mom about Coleta." Libby glanced at Jordan and encountered his unhappy stare.

He shifted his gaze, and in profile he reminded her so much of Beck when he was pissed but determined not to let it show. She had seen the same muscle work the corner of Beck's clenched jaw.

Looking back at the road, she said she was sorry for breaking her promise. "I didn't want to, but the situation you're in is so serious. Your parents and your attorney need all the facts if they're going to help you."

He said it was okay, but Libby couldn't be certain whether he meant it. "Your mom mentioned there's another witness."

"Yeah. My attorney told me. Guy's name is Ricky Burrows. The detective found him, but now he's dropped out of sight. I don't stand much of a chance without him. Unless Michelle makes it. She knows Trav was driving. She tried to stop him." He fell silent; then after a bit, he said, "I hope so much she'll wake up, you know? Not for me, but for her family and for her. She didn't do anything."

Except ride with a driver who was drunk, Libby thought.

They rode in silence for several miles, and it seemed to Libby that their shared anxiety rode with them, a third wheel, an unwanted companion. It started to rain; huge fat drops struck the windshield, and then, as abruptly, it stopped.

Libby said, "You know the animals I've found dead at the cottage? I think Ricky is the one who killed them."

Jordan looked at her, startled. "Are you kidding?"

Libby said she wasn't, repeating what she'd heard from Ruth about Ricky's apparently groundless and twisted conviction that the Little B belonged to him.

"It figures, the one guy in the world who knows the truth is a total head case. Who's going to believe him, if they can even find him?"

Before Libby could answer, he was directing her to turn.

"It's the redbrick house with green shutters, there on the right."

"I see it," Libby said. "Your mom's truck is there."

"With a cop car behind it—from Wyatt." Jordan sat forward; he wanted out.

Libby sensed he'd be gone like a shot as soon as she pulled to the curb, and she slowed but didn't stop. Something was wrong; she felt it, a kind of panic. It crawled on spider legs up her spine. "I don't think you should go in there," she said. "I think we should call 911."

"The cops are already here." He was impatient. "Can you just stop, please, and let me out?"

"Okay, but I'm going in with you." Libby parked against the curb.

Jordan was halfway across the front yard before Libby could cut the truck engine. She followed quickly in his wake, heart pounding. She had no idea why she was so afraid, and then she heard Jordan's shout: "Mom? Oh my God, Mom!" and she ran up onto the porch and through the front door.

16

She stared uncomprehending at the body on the floor. How was it not her? She had stepped in front of Jenna. She should have been the one who took the bullet. Sandy turned to Jenna and encountered the reflection of her own uncomprehending shock. They groped their way toward each other, meeting in a clumsy embrace. Jenna was talking. Sandy felt the vibration of her voice, the urgency of her speech, but she couldn't hear the actual words. The blast from Huck's gun had deafened her. Her head felt hollow and as light as a helium party balloon, rising from her neck.

She was startled when Jenna grasped her by her upper arms, shaking her, not hard, but not so gently, either. "What were you thinking?" Sandy read Jenna's lips. "Going in front of me like that? He could have killed you."

I didn't want you to die. Did she say it out loud? Sandy didn't know.

She felt herself being pulled back into Jenna's embrace, and then as quickly, Jenna set her aside, going around Sandy, dropping to her knees beside Huck, heedless of the blood spreading beneath his shattered skull. She pressed her fingers to the space near the hinge of his jaw. Anyone who watched crime shows on television knew that space, where the carotid artery was located, where the pulse of life was the strongest. But it was stilled now for Huck. Sandy knew it even before Jenna turned to her and said, "He's gone." She sat on her heels, looking down at him, and then at Sandy, blank faced in her bewilderment. How had it happened? Huck here and alive one minute, dead and gone the next? The stench of his blood, his spent ammunition, an underscore of anguish and fear, perverted the air. Sandy didn't want to breathe; black dots encroached on her peripheral vision. She ground her teeth, biting back the scream she could feel gathering strength from some primal and dark corner of her mind.

Breathe. You have to breathe, said the voice in her brain, and she managed it.

She had her phone in her hand, and she was in the midst of dialing 911 when she heard Jordy shout for her, making her heart veer out of control again. She dropped her phone. Reaching to pick it up, she shouted back at him, "Stay there, Jordy."

But he didn't listen to her. Of course he didn't. She blocked the kitchen doorway, thinking she could keep him from entering the room, save him from having to see it: Huck's corpse on the floor to her left, lying in front of the kitchen sink. The hole in his right temple was so small and neat, almost surgically precise, and yet there was so much blood. It haloed his head, a thickening pool; it glazed the knuckles of his right hand, his shooting hand, and stippled the gun, Huck's service revolver, which lay nearby. Above him, the cabinet, sink basin, and adjacent marble countertop were flecked with bloody bits of tissue and fragments of bone, the brain matter Huck's bullet had reamed from his skull while on its deadly path. Sandy guessed the bullet was lodged in the wall somewhere. Her stomach lurched. She jerked her gaze away.

When Jordy appeared in the doorway, she slammed her flattened hand into his chest, growling, "Don't come in here," even as she bit down on a sob and the rush of her emotions, some complex mix of overwhelming love and relief at the living sight of him, combined with an urgent need to spare him seeing the carnage. There was her lingering horror, too, her shell-shocked numb amazement, the disbelief: Was it a dream? Please, God, would she, could she waken now?

"Are you all right? What happened?" Jordy searched her eyes, then looked past her at Jenna. "Aunt Jenna?" The way he addressed her, it was almost a plea.

But she didn't respond, didn't so much as look his way. She was staring fixedly at the wall, gripping the edge of the kitchen countertop, as if it alone kept her upright. Except for a white line around her mouth, her face was gray, the color of ash.

It was inevitable that Jordy would see it: the body on the floor. Sandy marked the moment. His breath went out in a whoosh, a kind of groan. She braced him with her arm, wrapping his waist. Not that she could hold him, or even that he was close to falling. It was the need to touch him, the need in the moment for physical contact between them. A way to say, *I'm here.*

"It's Huck? He's dead?"

"Yes." Sandy tried to steer Jordy back into the hallway, toward the front door. "C'mon," she said. "We'll go outside."

But he said, "No! Mom, for God's sake, what the hell happened?"

"Jordan? Sandy? I hope it's all right, my coming in. I—"

"Libby?" Sandy said. "Libby, wait. Something's happened here. You should stop right there." But Libby was no better than Jordy at heeding Sandy's warning. She came past him and around Sandy, and she gasped when she saw it, the body of a man on the floor. "Is that Sergeant Huckabee?" She looked at Sandy.

Did you do it? Did you shoot the man you suspect of framing your son?

The questions blazed in Libby's eyes, as vocal and stark as if she had asked them out loud, and Sandy realized how Libby could make the assumption. Even Jordy, or the police when they came, which they surely would, might assume she had killed Huck. God knew she had a motive. "He did it," she said. "He shot himself."

"Did you call the police?" Libby asked.

"I was trying to, but I don't think my phone is working."

"It's not," Jordy said. "It called me. That's what got me worried. I could hear you and Aunt Jenna, and a man—Huck, I guess—talking, so I hung up and tried calling you back to see if you'd answer, but it didn't even ring."

"Maybe I did something to it." Sandy looked at the phone. She remembered getting it from her purse before Huck drew his gun, and randomly, frantically, hitting the numbers. Maybe she'd speed-dialed Jordy.

Libby said, "He called me when he couldn't get hold of anyone else."

"She gave me a ride here," Jordy said.

Sandy looked unhappily at Libby, and it wasn't reasonable, blaming her that Jordy was here, a witness to this horror, but Sandy did.

"I tried to talk him out of coming," Libby said, and Sandy knew her feelings must show on her face.

Jenna came up behind Sandy. "We have to call for help." Her voice was cold and flat, too flat, and Sandy wondered if she was in shock, physical shock, the kind she would need treatment for. She wondered how much more Jenna could stand.

Libby had her phone out, tapping numbers, saying she would do it, and when the dispatcher answered, she said, "I need to report a shooting."

Sandy led the way outside, and it wasn't long before they heard the wail of the first siren. Soon after, there were multiple emergency vehicles clogging Jenna's street. A 911 call in Madrone County never failed to generate a full-scale production, starring a cast of what seemed like thousands of first responders, from firemen to paramedics to police officers to sheriff's deputies. Neighbors came out of their houses, looking alarmed, and yet they seemed avid, too, for the story, the details. *What happened?* As bystanders they would have the luxury of knowing the answers without having to suffer the consequences of actual involvement. Whatever the nightmare was, thank you, Jesus, it wasn't theirs.

Go home, Sandy wanted to shout at them. *It's none of your damn business,* she wanted to say.

The yard was cordoned off with yellow crime-scene tape. A few of the officers began questioning the neighborhood folks about what they might have heard or seen, and at what time. Sandy would read in the local newspaper that the sound of the gunshot had wakened Lyndsey Abrams's newborn baby and caused Marva Duerksen to spill iced coffee down her shirtfront. Dawson Pate, who was resting on his back deck after mowing the lawn, thought a car had backfired. It was the sort of newsy detail folks expected to read in the *Wyatt Times and Record,* the local biweekly newspaper.

A group of officers entered Jenna's house.

While Jordy and Libby were questioned where they stood on the front walkway, Sandy and Jenna were led several feet away by a detective from Greeley. He began by asking their names. He wanted to know who owned the house, who made the 911 call, how Sandy and Jenna were related, how they knew Huck. What Sandy was doing at Jenna's, why Huck had come there. He didn't question it when Sandy called it a suicide. He didn't even look at her.

He closed his notebook and, pocketing it, thanked her and Jenna.

She asked if they could go into the house. She felt under scrutiny from the growing crowd of onlookers.

"We need to get my sister's things," Sandy said to the detective. "I'm taking her home with me."

"Yeah. Okay," he said. "Just wait until the coroner removes the body. Shouldn't be much longer." He looked at Jenna. "There's a biohazard and crime-scene cleaning service out of Austin that handles this sort of thing. I can give you the information, if you want—unless you wanted to tackle it yourself."

"Oh no, no, no," Sandy said, emphatically.

Jenna shook her head, hugging herself.

The detective pulled out his notebook again and wrote down a company name and phone number. Tearing out the sheet, he handed it to Jenna. "Ask for Pat," he said.

Jenna thanked him, and when he was gone, she said, "We should call Mom and Dad before they hear about it somewhere else."

"Let's get out of here first." Sandy walked with Jenna over to where Jordy and Libby waited on the sidewalk.

Sandy put her arm around Jordy. "Are you okay?"

"Yeah," he said. "Are you?" He looked intently at her, and she knew he must feel as conflicted as she did about Huck's death. He was gone now, and so was his grudge against Jordy and his campaign to make Jordy the guilty one. Who knew if it would make a difference, but Sandy had hope now where she had not before. But at what cost? Hope in exchange for Huck's life? Wasn't there some better way?

Jordy said, "We overheard a couple of the cops talking. They were saying somebody found a letter Huck wrote back at the police station in Wyatt."

"A letter?" Sandy said. She was thinking suicide note. She was thinking if he had left such a thing, it meant he had planned to come here and do this on purpose—in front of Jenna. The idea horrified her.

Libby said, "We may have misunderstood."

"It's so messed up, you know?" Jordy sounded angry. "Why would he kill himself? I don't get it."

Sandy gave her head a slight shake. This wasn't a good time to talk about Huck's reason, not when emotions were so raw. She was unsure how Jenna might react, what she was feeling. It wasn't regret. Sandy wasn't feeling that from her.

"Do you realize none of these squad cars are from Wyatt?" Libby made a small arc with her arm.

It seemed as if she posed the question deliberately, as a distraction, and Sandy was grateful for it. She turned to Jordy. "Did the detective who talked to you just now say anything about the accident?"

"Yeah, he told me Ken Carter, Huck's buddy, would be in touch, but it's like, who cares? Carter's the same as Huck. In his mind I was driving."

Sandy glanced at Jenna; Jordy did, too, but she kept her face averted, and it seemed willful. It seemed to suggest she wasn't giving up on the idea that Jordy was responsible for Travis's death. It didn't matter to her that Huck had admitted to having pressured witnesses. Maybe it wouldn't matter to local law enforcement, either.

A police force was a brotherhood. They protected their own. They were even more likely to protect Huck now after his death. They would want everyone to think well of him, to honor and respect his memory— the way Jenna, and Huck, before he shot himself, wanted Travis to be remembered. *And to hell with the truth,* Sandy thought.

To hell with my son, and his reputation, his future.

Anger warred in her chest, backed its heat into her throat, but anger wouldn't help, and she bit down on it. If she could find Ricky Burrows, if she could talk to the Detroit-based long-haul trucker, Nat Blevins, herself, and tell them Huck no longer posed any threat to either of them, maybe they'd tell the truth. Thinking of this steadied her.

The fire trucks were the first of the emergency vehicles to leave. Someone came and drove Huck's squad car away, then several of the Greeley squad cars left, and finally two attendants from the coroner's office wheeled the gurney bearing Huck's bagged remains to the hearse parked at the curb.

Sandy went with Jenna into the house and helped her pack an overnight bag. When they came back outside, Jordy said he would ride with Libby.

"Her house is on the way," he said. "We can stop there and I'll unload the boxwoods. She can bring me on home after that."

Sandy said it was all right; she wouldn't argue. But she looked at Jenna, unsure of what she wanted from her. A sign that she was aware of how far they had fallen apart as a family, a family that couldn't even ride together in the same vehicle. There was nothing of the sort in Jenna's eyes, though. They were as vacant as the windows in an abandoned building. She looked shell-shocked, as if the slightest nudge would send her cartwheeling into some distant pocket of space from which she might never return. Sandy felt her earlier fury dissolve. She opened Jenna's door and, stowing her tote, told Jordy to come home as quickly as he could.

She thanked Libby. "I am so in your debt," she said. "For everything today."

Libby looked at her truck. "It feels like a lifetime ago that we were at Inman's."

"I know." Sandy's laugh was rueful. Someone else's lifetime, she thought, one she didn't recognize anymore as her own.

17

Thanks," Jordan said, getting into the cab of Libby's truck. "I couldn't ride with my aunt. I don't know what it's going to take for her to believe me."

"Maybe in time," Libby said. *Hard evidence,* was what she thought.

Jordan's phone rang. "It's my dad," he said, looking at her, and his eyes were worried.

"You need to let him know you're okay," she said.

From Jordan's side of the conversation, Libby gathered his dad had spoken to his mom and was aware of Sergeant Huckabee's suicide. Libby felt bad for Emmett, for his shock that would be profound, and his concern for Jordan that would be sharper still. Suppose she and Jordan had walked into Jenna's house minutes earlier? Suppose Huckabee had shot either Sandy or Jenna as he'd threatened to do? He might have taken Libby and Jordan hostage; he might have barricaded them all in the house. These days, perfectly normal-appearing people went over the lip of sanity in an eye blink, spraying bullets with abandon, mowing down whoever was in their path. For little to no reason.

Libby thought of the last time she'd seen the sergeant, wearing his sunglasses with lenses like mirrors, and his cocksure attitude. *The boy has finally got his story straight.* He spoke in Libby's brain.

Jordy ended the call. "Dad says he's going to the house, that Roger wants to meet us there."

"Your attorney?"

"Yeah."

"I'll turn around, then."

"No, we're so close to your place now. I told him I was going to help you, then I'd be home. It won't take that long."

Libby was hesitant. He needed to be with his family. But she guessed he could also use breathing space. She didn't turn around.

"I called my friend Ruth before we left your aunt's house," she said, breaking a short silence. "She was in Greeley, at the police station, when the call came in about the shooting."

"Did she find out anything? About Ricky Burrows, I mean."

"She seemed to think the cops there were giving her the runaround." *I have a bad feeling,* she'd said. It was nothing she could put her finger on. *I'd be willing to bet a year's worth of my commissions that Ricky's still in the area, though.*

Libby felt he was nearby, too. A person seized by an obsession didn't ordinarily give up easily. Sergeant Huckabee being a case in point. And Ricky Burrows was supposedly not only obsessed but insane. How could she have been so duped by him? She had felt his anger, but she had assumed it was rooted in despair. He'd seemed a sad case to her, a guy who'd not been dealt a particularly promising hand in life. She'd felt responsible, in a way, that his truck got keyed on her property. Now that she knew he'd done the damage himself, she felt like a fool.

"I think we need to keep an eye out for Ricky," she said, but pulling up to the cottage, she didn't feel any particular fear.

Jordy hopped out, and rounding the rear of the truck, he lowered the tailgate.

Knowing she'd be taking him home shortly, Libby left her purse in the cab. "You want a sandwich, something to drink? You must be starving."

His head popped up. "Do you have any more of that lemonade you made the other day?"

She laughed, going into the house, and said, "Coming right up."

She didn't see Ricky at first.

He was standing behind the front door. Then he was there, square in front of her the moment she closed it. Inches from her. Close enough that she could smell peanut butter on his breath. Fear clamped her heart. Her eyes darted past him, and she saw the open peanut-butter jar on the kitchen table, alongside a torn wax sleeve of Ritz crackers. The sweating jug of homemade lemonade was there, too, mostly gone now. It irked her, that Ricky had helped himself to the last of it, and it was ridiculous, but she was thinking of Jordan's disappointment.

"I hope you don't mind," Ricky said. "I been waiting awhile, and I got kind of hungry."

"It's fine, Ricky." She struggled to breathe normally, to appear as if finding him in her house were normal, a daily occurrence.

"I thought maybe you could help me."

"Help you?" Libby looked past him toward the bedroom, where her dad's loaded shotgun was propped in the corner beside the old chest of drawers. If she could somehow get across the living room, and into the bedroom—

"I don't think you knew when you bought this property that it was mine, right?"

Libby met his gaze. "Yours?"

"Yeah." He gestured toward the kitchen, inviting her to come and sit with him as if he were the host. "I want to finish my crackers."

She held his gaze for a moment, disbelieving she had heard him correctly, afraid she might laugh in his face at the utter outrageousness of the situation. "Okay." She managed to get the word out and waited, hoping he would go first. But no. The look on his face, the tight way he held himself, put every atom, particle, and cell of her body on alert. *Crazy like a fox.* The phrase jumped into her mind.

He fell in behind her.

She went to the table and, pausing, let her glance run quickly over him, hunting for a sign that he had a knife, but if he did, he could have it concealed anywhere on his person. He could grab one out of a kitchen drawer. It occurred to her he could have found the shotgun. She looked out the kitchen window, but she couldn't see Jordan or the truck. She was listening so hard for his step on the porch, the sound of the front door. Did Ricky not know Jordan was here?

"Sit," he said.

She sat, gingerly, on the edge of the straight-backed chair.

"I know that once you know the truth—" He sat opposite her, and picking up the knife, he slathered a cracker with peanut butter, wiping it clean, licking his thumb, smiling at her.

He had a nice smile. He'd never smiled at her before that she could remember. He'd always seemed sad, pissed at the world. *One of those down-on-his-luck young guys . . .* That's how she'd thought of him. How badly she'd misjudged him.

He topped the buttered cracker with another and popped the tiny sandwich into his mouth, working his tongue around, washing the sticky mess down with the lemonade. "So, here's the thing," he said, making another cracker sandwich. "I've got the deed and my grandparents' will that shows how they wanted the Little B left to Aunt Fran and my mom. Not just Fran."

"Your grandparents who lived in the farmhouse next door, right? They haven't died—"

"I know." He was annoyed. "Aunt Frannie stuck 'em in an old-folks' home. If my mom was here, she would've never done that."

"Your mom is Jewel, right? Fran and Jewel were sisters?"

"Yeah. After my mom had her breakdown, Fran sent her and me away to her uncle's house in Colorado. They said she would get better there, but she didn't. She got worse. She was doing real crazy shit, crazy even for her. One day men came and took her away. Her uncle said they were taking her to a hospital, where she'd get help. The bastard never checked on her, never took me to see her. They treated her like shit there, locked her up like an animal. It was no hospital. It was a nuthouse, the worst kind, and she died in there because of that asshole. He kicked me out. I ended up in foster care. You know what that's like living where nobody wants you? Nobody cares? Where they beat you down just for shits and giggles?"

Ricky's eyes on Libby's were intent, hard walls of anger, riven with defiance. Libby had seen the expression before on the faces of high school kids, the harder cases she'd worked with. The ones who'd been abused, damaged by their families or the system. Their rage was a defense, a tool of survival. Ricky was older than her students by a few years, but he wasn't different. Down underneath that brittle glare was the history of a little boy's bewilderment and his fear, along with an overwhelming sense of abandonment.

She said, "I'm sorry, Ricky, but I don't see—"

"This. Is. My. Land." He pounded the heel of his fist on the table with each enunciated word.

She kept his gaze but could think of nothing to say that wouldn't incite him further. Her dad's shotgun might as well be in another country. She thought how easily Ricky could grab a knife, overcome her, the same way he had evidently overcome the nurse in the mental ward where he had been locked up like his mother. She wondered by whose authority he had been committed there. Foster parents? Child Protective Services? The justice system? She thought of Jordan, outside, oblivious, that he would walk into this at any moment.

"It's okay," Ricky said. "I'm not mad at you. You didn't know. Anyway, you tried to help me, you and your husband did, with my truck and all. You felt bad, I could tell."

"Yes," she said.

"I didn't want to do it, but you kind of forced me."

"I don't understand," Libby said, even though she did.

"I did it. I keyed my damn truck; I slaughtered the hog, too, the bird, the rats."

"What about the note? Did you write that, too?"

"Yeah. I figured you'd think it was Huckabee who left it. You told me he warned you about keeping your doors locked."

"I did?"

"Yeah. You said we should keep our vehicles locked up, too."

Had she? Libby guessed it was possible.

"I figured you'd think it was him, that it'd scare you. I figured if I did what that wacko in Houston was doing, you and the cops'd think it was him, that he was after you all, and you'd leave. Get the hell off my land."

"Ricky, did you follow Beck from here? Did you run him off the road?"

He looked at her, brows knit, drawing a blank. There was not a trace of the canniness that had marked his expression a moment ago. He didn't know what she was talking about.

"Here's the deal," he said after a moment. "You get Ruth Crandall to take the Little B off the market, okay? Then you and the folks that bought the parcel of land with my grandparents' house—you guys can just sign papers, giving the ranch back. Simple." Ricky leaned back, smiling.

Libby smiled, too, as if it were the perfect plan.

He extended his leg the way men do when they're going to pull something from the pocket of their pants. Ricky was wearing worn but sturdy work jeans, and boots with thick soles. It was the uniform of a construction worker, regardless of weather or time of year. She wasn't surprised when he brought the knife into her view. Unfolding it, he began to clean his fingernails with the tip of the blade. He was still smiling.

Libby watched him, somehow fascinated, absorbed. "I'll call Ruth," she said, "but I'll need to get my phone. It's in the truck." She started to get up.

"No." He jumped to his feet. "I'll get it."

"All right," Libby said, and her voice seemed to come from a distance. It came from some part of her that was unaffected by the blunt force of her alarm. Thoughts surfaced, that if Ricky left, she would grab the shotgun. *Jordan—Jordan is outside.* That was her specific thought when he came in the front door, and her heart stuttered. She looked from Jordan to Ricky, expecting him to make some move on Jordan, to somehow threaten him with the knife.

But it was slack in his hand hanging at his side, and he was staring at Jordan as if transfixed at the sight of him. The color drained from his face. His neck worked when he swallowed. He looked scared. More than that. He looked terrified.

Libby's eyes met Jordan's. His shrug was almost imperceptible, an indication of his confusion that bordered on something more.

"You're dead, man, right?" Ricky closed his knife and shoved it back into his pocket. He took a step toward Jordan, stopped, cocked his head to the side. "C'mon now. I don't believe in this shit, you know? The walking dead? Shit like that? Hell no." Ricky glanced at Libby, smirked. "You seeing this?" He held out his hands toward Jordan.

"I don't know what you mean," Libby said.

Ricky rounded on her, punching the air. "Do you see that guy there? Because if you don't, I am fucking nuts like everyone says."

"I see him."

Ricky heaved a breath. "Okay, then. Okay. He was dead, but now he's not."

Libby glanced at Jordan and understanding came, leaping between them.

Jordan said, "You think I died in the car crash."

Libby was amazed at his equanimity, the quiet authority in his voice.

"I know you did." Ricky was half turned from Jordan and spit the words over his shoulder. He was shaky, suspicious, and still scared.

Vulnerable, Libby thought. Like you would be if you were worried about your sanity, worried about whether what you were seeing before your eyes was real or a specter up from the grave. He didn't trust her when she said she saw Jordan, too, and maybe she could make that work in their favor. She shifted her weight, taking what she hoped was an inconspicuous step toward the archway separating the kitchen from the living room. She didn't have a plan in mind other than if she could, she would get to her phone or the shotgun. She wasn't going to simply stand here and let herself or Jordan be carved up like this year's Thanksgiving turkey.

Jordan said, "You saw the wreck happen, right, man? I mean, you were almost in it, I heard."

"Car came right at me. Right fucking at me. I see it every time I close my eyes." Ricky shut his eyes now and shivered.

"Am I the driver?" Jordan asked.

"Nah. Passenger. It was like that close with you guys." Ricky held his thumb and forefinger apart, showing a sliver of space. "Then you went airborne. I never saw anything—heard anything like it. There was like a high whistling sound, then it was like some big giant was ripping apart metal, breaking glass. Goddamn driver popped up out of there like a cork out of a champagne bottle on New Year's Eve, you know what I'm saying? He went up like somebody tossing a rag doll, then came down—bam!" Ricky slammed his fist into his palm.

"You came over to us. I remember you were there. I heard you call 911."

"Yeah. I felt your pulse, bro. It was gone. I figured you had enough life left in you to get out of the car and over to your buddy, but then you, like, collapsed on top of him and died. You were dead," Ricky said. "I know. I checked." He was getting more distraught now.

"It's all right," Libby said. She took another slow step, darting a glance at Jordan, who nodded. His self-control was astonishing; she was grateful for it.

"Those ambulance guys," Jordan said, and Libby took another step, "the paramedics, they got me back. You'd left by then, by the time they came."

"Yeah. I had to. Cops were on my ass that night. I'd been doing some stuff—I mean, I was on my own fucking land, up at my grand-parents' house, but there's a warrant out—I couldn't stick around, you know."

"Well, I'd probably be dead if it weren't for you, so, it's like I owe you. Owe you big-time."

Libby had come even with Jordy and slipped behind him so that she was between him and the front door. She looked at Ricky, but he didn't seem aware of her anymore.

His focus was on Jordan. "You sure you aren't dead? I'm really see-ing you?"

"Yeah. I mean, it was bad for a while, but I got better."

"What about your buddy?"

"He died, man. Not there, but later in Austin, at the hospital."

"Christ. I'm real sorry."

Libby stepped from behind Jordan, going for the bedroom and the shotgun. She was afraid to leave Jordan in the cottage alone even for the minute or two it might take to get her phone. Ricky might appear oblivious, but she couldn't count on that or anything. He was too unstable. Like an armed grenade. The slightest vibration, one wrong word, might set him off.

"I guess you don't want to tell the cops what you saw that night." Jordan was making conversation.

As a cover for her, Libby thought.

Jordan said, "You know, the cops think I was driving, right? They're getting me for manslaughter. I could get thirty years. You could tell them what you saw; they'd let me off."

Ricky said he'd like to help. "But there's that warrant—"

"Ricky?"

He looked at Libby in the doorway, and when he realized she was holding a shotgun, he put up his hands and smiled, a rueful, one-cornered smile. "Now I know I'm dreaming."

The way he said it was so charming, Libby almost laughed; she was that fooled. She wasn't prepared when he put his head down and charged at Jordan, knocking him down.

Stumbling, Ricky yanked at the front door, kicking out at Jordan when he got to his knees. Jordan grabbed his foot, bringing Ricky down beside him. The men tumbled, a grunting mass of gyrating limbs.

Libby watched breathless, light-headed. She couldn't shoot for fear of injuring Jordan; she couldn't get through the door to her phone. She passed precious seconds in a kind of jerky, slow-motion haze of panic and uncertainty, and then the disturbance was over.

Ricky got free. Jordan had him, and then he didn't, and seizing the moment, Ricky was gone through the door. Jordan went out, too, Libby on his heels. She was in time to see Ricky vault the picket fence and head east into the cedar thicket. He was soon lost to view.

"Going to his grandparents' house, I bet." Libby set down the shotgun.

Jordan stood looking into Ricky's wake, hands on his hips, panting. "I had him, and then he went limp, like he was all out of fight."

"We need to call the police. They'll get him."

Jordan took out his phone; he talked to the 911 dispatcher, and when he hung up, he said, "We're keeping those people hopping today."

Libby sat down in a porch chair and dropped her head into her hands, taking a moment.

She felt Jordan's hand on her shoulder and looked up at him. "You were very coolheaded in there," she said.

"It was you," he said. "I was just following what you did." He sat in the chair beside her.

"It's not going to do him any good."

Jordan looked at her.

"Running," she said.

"I thought about it." He scooped something off the porch floor and tossed it.

"You're still here."

"Got no wheels. No way really to get anywhere. I could hitch, but where to?"

They looked out, over the porch rail. Libby waited to hear a siren, but maybe since Jordan had told them no one was hurt, the police officer who came wouldn't use it.

"Besides," Jordan said, "you can't run from yourself, you know? It's like my grandma says: 'Everywhere you go, there you are.'"

18

I'm so afraid I'll forget things about him. The sound of his voice, the way he laughed . . ."

"You won't," Sandy said. She reached over, cupping her palm over the knot of Jenna's hands in her lap. They were parked in the driveway outside Sandy's house, still sitting in the truck. "Trav's memory, his essence, will always be with you. Even if his physical characteristics, those tangible things, dissolve, still, you'll have your love for him." She looked at Jenna, the sharp outline of her profile, and she thought how stupidly inadequate her words were, any words in the face of such loss—they were like vapor. Even the breath used to utter them was worthless.

"I can't cry," Jenna said. "Earlier, that was really the first time."

"It's all right," Sandy said. "There's no rule book."

"Don't say I'll get through it, because I might not." Jenna turned to Sandy now, locking her gaze.

"You only have to be here this minute, okay?"

Jenna shifted her glance, looking out the windshield. "Thank God Jordy made it."

Sandy went still.

"I mean it," Jenna said. "I didn't want to believe Trav would do something so stupid as to drive a car drunk."

What mother would want to believe it? Sandy couldn't be sure that in Jenna's shoes she wouldn't have put herself into the same state of denial.

"I'm sorry." Jenna squeezed Sandy's hand, and she looked over at her, seeing her through a prism of tears, the tiny faultlines of their shared love and sorrow.

• • •

Emmett came to the house. Sandy had called him before leaving Jenna's—she'd called Emmett, not Roger, but Jordy's dad. She had needed Emmett, and the fact that Roger didn't even come into her mind until later wasn't lost on her. She was taken aback by it when Emmett knocked on his own back door. She opened the screen, and she was so grateful for his hug. The comfort of his presence, his smell, the familiar and sorely missed shelter of his arms. He hugged Jenna, too, and watching them, Sandy felt the smallest flicker of hope that there might be a way to mend all the damage, to begin again, to make something new.

Her phone rang, and her heart bumped when she saw Roger's name on the ID screen. She walked into the mudroom. "Roger?" she said, greeting him, and she was cautious, tentative. "I guess you've heard about Huck?"

He said he had and asked if she and Jordy were all right. "What a hell of a thing," he said.

She said yes, that it was, and then in a rush, she said, "About the other night. I'm so sorry for how I behaved—"

"No," he said. "It's all right. You were entitled, given all you've been through."

"Thank you for that, but I don't want you to think—I never meant to lead you on—"

Roger said, "No," again. He said, "I think you're the only one who might be confused about where your heart belongs."

Her throat tightened. "You are a lovely man," she said.

He laughed and as quickly sobered. He said he and Patrol Sergeant Ken Carter needed to meet with Jordy. "There have been some developments," he said, and he told her that Ricky Burrows had been apprehended, and how.

• • •

Libby brought Jordy home. Sandy and Emmett waited for him in the driveway. She threw her arms around him first, hugging him fiercely, and when she stepped away, Emmett did the same.

"You've had a hell of a day, kid," he said, holding Jordy at arm's length, checking him over.

"Not a dull moment," Jordy said, and Sandy smiled. His humor was balm.

She leaned into the truck cab. "You're really all right?"

"Yes, thanks," Libby said. "You heard Ricky was caught?"

Sandy said she had. "Up at the old farmhouse."

"One of the officers who was there when they arrested Ricky came by the cottage after and said Ricky was still pretty shaken up. He kept talking about seeing a ghost."

Sandy laughed; it was funny in a gruesome way, Ricky's mistaken belief that Jordy had risen from the grave. But as Jordy had said, it might well have saved their lives. Sandy asked if Libby wanted to come in, but she said no.

"I'm on my way into town to stay the night with Ruth Crandall," she said.

"I'm glad," Sandy said, and she was. She didn't want to think of Libby out on her place alone. Not after everything that had happened.

"I'm so grateful to you," she said, and it was hard, working the words past the knot in her throat.

Libby's gesture was dismissive, but Sandy sensed she felt it, too, that an odd sort of bond had formed between them, one that stretched across old bitterness and haunting regret, one that would exist somehow, perhaps stubbornly, in spite of their history. "Jordan told me there was news regarding his case. He didn't know what it was."

"None of us do, yet," Sandy said.

"Well, I hope it's good."

"Me, too," Sandy said. "We'll let you know."

"I'd like that," Libby said.

. . .

Sandy was following Emmett and Jordy into the house, where Jenna waited in the great room, when Roger pulled into the driveway. Ken Carter was behind him in his patrol car. Sandy felt panicked at the sight of them. She exchanged a worried glance with Emmett and then looked at Jordy. The color had drained from his face, and the scars that lanced the right side of his brow stood out, vivid and red, brutal reminders of how tenuous life can be. She looped her arm around his waist.

They sat in the great room—Roger and Jordy on the sofa, Jenna and Emmett in the armchairs on either side of the fireplace, and Sandy on the matching ottoman. Only Sergeant Carter remained standing.

He said, "You've heard we've got Ricky Burrows in custody—"

"Look"—Jordy sat forward, interrupting—"I know the guy is whacked, but he saw the Range Rover right before the accident happened. He knows—"

"You don't need Burrows anymore." Roger put a hand on Jordy's arm.

"What do you mean?" Jordy and Sandy asked together.

She was aware of Jenna and Emmett behind her; she would have sworn that, like her, neither of them was breathing.

"The night of the accident, like Sergeant Huckabee, I was on patrol in the vicinity of CR 440 and FM 1620," Carter said. "I was actually looking for Burrows. I'd followed him from the Little B. I knew he was up to no good—but that's another story. Anyway, I was right behind Huck, maybe five minutes later to the scene. I know why he got the idea you were driving, son." Carter looked at Jordy. "But I had a feeling about it, that he wasn't right."

"He wanted it to be me—see, because I—" Jordy looked at Sandy, eyes pleading with her. He knew that she knew about Coleta. Libby must have confessed to telling her, Sandy thought.

She said, "I think everyone here knows about Coleta now, Jordy. Well, maybe not Sergeant Carter."

"You told—?"

"It had to come out, Jordy," Emmett answered, and Sandy was grateful.

"It was in the letter Huck wrote." Sergeant Carter shoved his hand over his head, uncomfortable.

"We heard he'd left a note," Sandy said. "It's true?"

"It wasn't a suicide note, exactly. It was a letter of resignation," Sergeant Carter answered. "He said he was leaving town, but he didn't say how. Although he did say he was tired, that he felt like he wasn't up for the job anymore. He talked about John, about missing him. He blamed himself for how John was killed. That sort of thing. It kind of rambled."

"I didn't realize he was still carrying so much guilt," Jenna said quietly. "I didn't know about his feelings—he never said—"

Sandy patted her knee. "He took John's death hard. Probably harder than he let on."

"I know how that feels," Jordy said.

"What will happen to Coleta and Heidi?" Jenna asked, addressing the sergeant. "Do you know?"

"Preliminary word is she'll get her green card. Something about the death of a sponsor. It speeds up the process?" He shook his head. "Weird as that sounds, and I could be wrong."

The silence felt tense and confused, tangled with an assortment of emotions no one could really name.

The sergeant socked his fist into the palm of his other hand.

Emmett said, "You were saying Huck's idea about the accident wasn't right, in your opinion."

Carter looked relieved. "Yeah, so, without getting too technical, when a car spins, the people in it tend to go in the opposite direction of the spin. The Range Rover rotated in a clockwise direction, which is why Travis went out the driver's-side window and why you landed in the driver's seat."

"Yeah, and somehow, I got out. I had to help Trav."

"Adrenaline," Emmett muttered.

"Yeah. But here's the other thing about a crash—when the car collides with an immovable object like a tree, the folks inside tend to recoil, especially their heads. Those cuts you sustained on the right side of your face? That happened when your head collided with the passenger-side window hard enough to shatter the glass."

Sandy felt the hair rise on her neck, her arms. She cupped her elbows.

"When I examined the car, I collected tissue I found on that window. I just had a feeling, and I sent it to the lab to find out who it belonged to, you know, to determine whose DNA it was, because I knew that would tell us for sure who was riding in that passenger seat. We got the results this morning."

"It was mine?"

"Yep, son, it was."

"Oh my God." Sandy felt light-headed.

Jordy's fingers went to the divot at his hairline. He stood up.

Roger did, too. He laid his arm across Jordy's shoulders. "You're one lucky guy, you know that? I'm not trying to diminish what you've been through. But that was one hell of a hit you took. You're damn lucky you survived."

Jordy looked at Jenna. They all did. Sandy's breath paused, seeming to wait.

Jenna left her armchair and crossed the floor to Jordy, and when she was right in front of him, she reached up and cupped his cheek. Tears filmed her eyes.

Sandy brought her tented fingertips to her mouth.

Jordy covered Jenna's hand with his own. "I'm so sorry," he said, and his voice was rough. "It should have been me."

"No, Jordy." Jenna's tears slid down her cheeks, and she swiped at them almost angrily, then laughed, a small, broken sound. "He would have said the same, you know? If you had died, he would have wished it was him." She looked at Jordy. "You two," she said. "You were like the other half of each other, you know?"

A noise broke from Jordy, as if what Jenna had said, coupled with all they had lost, was too heavy to bear. Sandy and Emmett went to him, and together with Jenna, they held him, their boy who was left.

19

This is where you were the first time I came here."

Libby sat back, squinting up at Jordan. "Weeding," she said. "It never ends." She got to her feet. "You look good. Happy. Free."

"Yeah. I can't believe it's over."

"I'm happy for you," Libby said.

"You want to get those boxwoods in the ground? I heard a rumor we may get some rain tomorrow. Real rain. Not those little showers we had a few days ago." He was referring to the day Libby had picked him up outside his dad's apartment when they'd gone to Jenna's and everything had unraveled. It seemed like a lifetime ago.

"Let's do it," she said.

They worked in near silence for the better part of the morning, cutting the lattice, then nailing it to the front porch edge in a diagonal design. They stopped at one point and drank the fresh lemonade Libby had made the evening before. "I wasn't sure you'd be back," she said when they sat on the front steps to drink it.

He looked at her. "I said I'd plant those boxwoods."

Libby nodded. People said a lot of things.

"I was kind of hoping we could be friends. I don't have a ton of those right now."

"Well, I'm here anytime," she said.

When the boxwoods were settled in the ground and watered, she made lunch. Chicken-salad sandwiches on croissants, fresh fruit and chips.

"I'm going to build the house." Libby sat across from Jordan. She was so pleased he was here, ridiculously pleased. But she wouldn't let on. She might scare him.

"Really?" He grinned. "It means you're staying, right?"

"Yes, I think so. I think Beck would want me to follow through with our plans. Besides, it's the last house Beck designed. It should be built."

"I could help with the landscape," Jordan said, taking a bite of his sandwich, wolfing it down, really.

Libby thought she'd never seen anyone eat with such gusto. "I'd like that."

"Mom would help, too. She's great at design." He speared a grape with his fork, then paused it halfway to his mouth. "We could do a pond."

Libby smiled. It was his use of the word *we* that delighted her. She wasn't Jordan's mother; she couldn't hope to be part of his family, but she could see that she mattered to him.

"How is your aunt doing? Your mom told me she's living with your grandparents."

"Yeah. She has her house up for sale. She's thinking of building on my mom and dad's property."

"That's good. I was so glad to hear from your mom. It seemed as if maybe your family was beginning to put itself back together."

"Yeah. Except for Dad, I guess. He still hasn't come back home."

Sandy hadn't mentioned Emmett when she and Libby had spoken on the phone the other day. She dabbed at her mouth with her napkin. "I hope they can work it out."

"Me, too," Jordan said. "I told my dad he shouldn't hold it against her, something she did twenty years ago." Jordan met Libby's gaze. "I told him he's my dad, you know?"

"Yes," Libby said. "He certainly is. What did he say?"

"He knows it. He's just stubborn."

They ate for several moments in silence.

Libby broke it. "So, now that you're a free man again, will you go back to school?"

"Yeah. I wanted to tell you. I'm leaving tomorrow. I can still do late enrollment. It'll be tough at first, catching up." He stopped, bent his weight on his elbows, traced a pattern with his fingertip, not looking at her. "I drink too much," he finally said. "I don't know if I have a problem, you know, like whether I'm an actual alcoholic—" He looked at Libby and made a face.

"Beck, your birth dad—there's a history of drinking in his family." Libby set her fork down. She'd been waiting for the opportunity to tell him this. "His sister, Mia, still drinks a lot, but Beck quit, a long time ago. He never really knew why he started or why he stopped."

"Did he go to AA?"

"No. Are you thinking of taking that route?"

"I'm thinking if Trav had lived, he'd find a way to make something good come out of all the bad that's happened. That's the kind of guy he was."

"Do you have something in mind?" Libby asked.

"There are a lot of kids on campus who drink, and a lot of bad stuff goes down because of it. Not just car accidents, but fights and sexual assaults. You don't know half of what you're doing when you're drunk. You make bad decisions. It seems like there ought to be a way to put the brakes on it, to look out for each other better." Jordan leaned back. "I don't know. Maybe it's stupid, thinking I can use my experience to make a difference. It's just—I know it's what Trav would have done, and I don't want him to have died for nothing. I want to honor his memory, to make it stand for something. I don't want him to be another statistic. Another stupidhead who drove drunk and killed himself."

Libby reached out, cupping his elbow in her palm.

"If only something—one good thing—could come out of this. You know what I mean?" he asked. His voice was rough with emotion, and it tore at Libby's heart. She understood, she said. She surely did.

20

On a Wednesday morning in late September, Sandy was at the kitchen sink tossing the last of her coffee out and rinsing her mug when she spotted the car, a light-colored sedan, coming up the drive. *No.* The word appeared in her brain, a protest. She recognized that car. It belonged to Patsy Meade. What was she doing here? Sandy still had no proof that the woman wasn't as much of a lunatic as Ricky Burrows, who was thankfully back in the custody of the Colorado state mental hospital he had escaped from. It was unlikely, though, that he would be prosecuted for stabbing the nurse there. His mental state was too precarious.

Libby had told her that when she'd joined Emmett, Jenna, and Troy for a farewell dinner with Jordy before he'd gone back to UT a few weeks ago. They'd grilled hamburgers. Libby had brought a pot of cooked fresh green beans from her garden. They planned to get together again the next time Jordy was home for a weekend.

A knock came on the back door. There was a moment when Sandy considered pretending she wasn't home, but it passed.

"I was hoping you would see me," Patsy said when Sandy opened the door.

"Do you want to come in?"

Patsy said, "Yes," but she didn't sound at all sure.

"Can I get you anything? I have iced tea. I could make coffee?"

"No, thanks. I only came to say that I'm sorry to have caused you distress. I was wrong about Jordy, wrong to accuse him."

"I appreciate that," Sandy said.

"Is he here? I'd like to apologize to him."

Sandy explained he was back at school.

Tears came into Patsy's eyes. She wiped at them with the back of her hand and then pressed it to her mouth, obviously fighting for control. "Michelle's doctors don't think she's going to wake up."

"Oh, Patsy. Oh, I'm so sorry." Sandy's own eyes welled up. The wave of her compassion closed her throat. It was strong enough that she would have embraced Patsy, if there had been anything in her demeanor that suggested she would welcome such comfort. But there wasn't a shred of warmth. They were adversaries in a way, players in a mutual catastrophe. But Sandy had left the field with her child intact, while Patsy had not. She envied Sandy for that and resented her. At times, Sandy felt the same chill of antagonism from Jenna, and it was hard. It made Sandy feel as if she should apologize for her son's life. She never would, though. She would never say it, those words: *I'm sorry Jordy lived*, as if Jordy were a gift she didn't deserve.

Patsy found a tissue in her purse and blew her nose. "Her father and I have separated," she said.

"Are you sure you wouldn't like something to drink? A glass of water?"

Patsy seemed not to hear. "He wants to take Michelle off life support. He's talked with the doctors about harvesting her organs. He says she would give life to others. But how do you do it? Kill your own child? He says he can't stand seeing her this way. But it's not about him." She thrust the tissue back into her purse. "If there's one good thing, though, that has come from this, it's that I see my husband very clearly. I see the kind of father he is, one who can give up on his daughter. I see the sort of husband he is, that it's always about him. Well, not this time. I've hired an attorney, and I'm getting a court order. Michelle is not going to be offered up like a field of corn, ripe for the harvest. People come out of comas; they wake up. Miracles do happen. Don't you agree?"

Sandy said yes, that of course she believed in miracles. But looking at Patsy, her adamant, wide-eyed glare, Sandy thought not even Patsy believed there would be one for Michelle. It was simply that she couldn't face it yet, the heartbreaking reality that her daughter was already gone.

Sandy walked Patsy to her car, and she started to get inside, but then straightened, and turning to Sandy, she said, "You don't know how lucky you are."

Sandy started to protest. It was not all jolly times. Emmett was still living at the apartment. She and Jenna were still estranged to some degree, and their parents—well, their parents were doing the best they could to distribute their love and support evenly between their daughters. And Jordy was still groping in the dark. He had nightmares and questioned why he'd been spared and how his life mattered. Why hadn't it been taken. No, it wasn't all jolly around here.

Patsy put her hand on Sandy's arm. "I don't mean to dismiss what you've been through." She dropped her hand, looked away, looked back, and her breath came out in an irritated gust. "But your son is alive; he has a future. Everything else—*anything* else that's wrong in your life, or that you might have lost, or think you need and don't have—it's nothing by comparison. Trust me."

She turned away, opened her car door, then turned back. "You know, losing a child is the one thing I have always said I wouldn't survive. I guess I'll find out, won't I? If my husband wins. If the court says the doctors can stop the machines. You should thank God you don't have to learn this about yourself. That's all I'm saying."

Patsy settled in the driver's seat. "Treasure every moment. I mean, you must know, right? Since you got the same god-awful call in the night that I did—just how quickly it can all be gone."

In one second.

One breath.

Less, even.

After Patsy left, Sandy couldn't get it out of her mind, the sense of how fragile life was.

She had a busy day, back-to-back appointments, and by the end of it, she was tired, but instead of going home, she drove to the Kennedys' and parked at the curb behind Emmett's truck. Getting out of her truck, she hoped he was in the apartment and not the house. She hoped Grant and Brenda wouldn't see her and try to waylay her. She walked alongside the house with her head down. Emmett appeared at the top of the apartment stairs and stood watching her from the landing.

"I wondered if we could talk," she said, looking up at him.

"About?"

"Us. What we're doing."

"I'll come down," he said.

They walked to a nearby park. It was nearing dinnertime now on a school night. The park was mostly deserted. They sat in the swings.

Sandy said, "I don't know how to start."

"Why did you come?"

"Because I want there to be a way to fix this—fix us. But maybe there is no fix. We can't be like we were." She paused, hoping Emmett would say something, give some clue to what he felt, but he didn't. He only moved the swing idly and stared into the middle distance, where shadows made long brushstrokes across the rough ground.

"We aren't the same people," Sandy said.

"No," Emmett agreed.

"I'm not that girl anymore, the one who led you to believe Jordy was yours."

She felt Emmett look at her.

"I'll be sorry for that until I die; I can apologize until I die, but it won't change what I did." She met his gaze.

"It's my call, is that what you're saying? Whether we have a marriage, a relationship, depends on whether or not I can get past it. Deal with it."

"You have to forgive me, Emmett. If you can't, then we have no reason to go on together. I can't live with it—your resentment of me, the constant reminder of how badly I screwed up. I know it. I was wrong. I've admitted it, and I've apologized. I can't be sorrier. I can't take it back." Her voice shook. She wanted to touch him. If only there were a way to physically impress on him the depth of her remorse. She lifted her hand, and it hovered between them for what seemed like an eternity to her.

He didn't look at her. He didn't even seem aware of her presence.

It was in the moment that she, giving up, lowered her hand that he took it and, pulling her and her swing to him, kissed the tips of her fingers, her palm, the inside of her wrist. He gathered her into his embrace, and she breathed him in—his smells, the starch in his shirt, the pine scent of his aftershave, a fainter underscore of oil and earth. It was the way he always smelled after spending the day at a drilling site. The familiarity of it, the feel of him in her arms, made her ache. Tears of relief, happiness, a peculiar rush of anxiety, scarred the undersides of her eyelids. She thought of Roger, her brief attraction to him. She might have given in to it, especially the night when she'd foolishly had so much to drink, and she was so thankful she had not, and grateful to Roger that he'd been such a gentleman. Her old self, that long-ago girl she'd been, had once taken advantage of just such a distraction. She had used Beck Hennessey as a temporary remedy for her grief over Emmett's absence. Maybe she had learned something from that in spite of herself. If she were to have to face that again, Emmett's leaving her, then she would deal with it alone. She would find her own strength, her own way along the dark road, using the light she had.

"I don't want to lose our family," she said, and her face was pressed into Emmett's chest, her voice muffled. "I don't want to lose you. Please tell me you can forgive me, that you feel you can trust me again." She lifted her head, finding his gaze.

He kissed the damp trails on her cheeks. "I'm not sure of it now," he said, and she stiffened, but he held her firmly. "I'm not closing the door. I'm not saying I can't forgive you. I'm saying I think we should take it slow. We should spend time together and talk more. We should face a few things, like how Jordy could be drinking so much for so long and both of us not know it, or ignore it, or whatever in the hell we were doing." Emmett released her and left the swing. It danced on its chains. Sunlight barred the short path he paced.

He stopped in front of her, his shadow falling over her. "He could have been the one who died, Sandy. I can't stop thinking about how we could have lost him, and I—I—it would have been my fault, because I was blind to how he was growing up, the shit he was doing. Jesus Christ, it gives me chills, nightmares. How? How did it happen? One minute he's just a crazy little kid running around, riding hell-bent on a three-wheeler, and the next thing you know, you're in some hospital—"

"I feel the same, Emmett. Mistakes were made. I know that." Sandy went to him. "But we can't live in the past. We can't say *if only* this and *if only* that. We can only be here, where we are now. Hopefully smarter. Grateful. Counting our blessings. Talking more, like you said." She laced Emmett's fingers with her own. "We can be more aware, help each other."

He looked down at her, holding her with his gaze, and it seemed to her that whatever anguish he was feeling, whatever blame and sorrow was between them, it had eased. He touched her cheek, lifted her chin, and kissed her.

He didn't come home with her that night, nor did he come the next week, or even the one after that, but she knew he would come home one day, and that was enough.

•   •   •

Sandy waited in the audience with the rest of her family—Emmett, Jenna, and their parents, and Troy and Libby—for Jordy to be called on to speak. Her stomach was knotted with anticipation; her nerves jangled. He had healed a lot in the three months since the accident. His physical scars were less noticeable. He wasn't having nightmares as often. But neither was he the same. There was a reflective quality about him, a kind of stillness, that he'd lacked before. She would catch him staring, unaware, and even though he would say there was nothing on his mind, she knew his memory of the accident, and Travis's loss, continued to haunt him.

He needed more than Sandy's or Emmett's word that his life had value and meaning and purpose. That was why tonight had to work. Sandy felt his entire future might depend on how well the public-service campaign he and a handful of other marketing students had designed was received. It had been Jordy's idea, and Sandy, better than anyone, knew the germ of it had come from the darkest corner of his grief, the need to do something not only to honor Travis but in defense of him. Jordy had told her late one night when they sat talking that whatever idea he came up with had to reflect how Travis had lived, not how he died.

Stayin' Alive was the culmination, an endeavor weeks in the planning. Named for the old 1970s Bee Gees anthem, the student-operated, campus-based cab service he'd conceived would provide safe transportation for students who'd had too much to drink. The weekend he came home and laid out the bones of his plan, he'd been on fire. He'd talked about how he'd gotten the name first, telling Sandy the song had come into his head and wouldn't leave. It didn't really surprise her. Somewhere there was a video her dad had shot of her and Emmett dancing a routine to the music à la *Saturday Night Fever*. It had won them a high school dance-contest trophy their junior year in high school. Jordy had grown up listening to everything Bee Gees. It was kismet, he'd said. Couldn't Sandy see it? The song was all about survival.

She looked at him now, where he sat onstage with two other students and a small number of campus officials who'd agreed to Jordy's request to speak this evening. He was bent slightly forward, eyes fixed on the podium; his cheeks were flushed. She'd never seen him so filled with determination, and while it was gratifying that he had found a positive direction to go in, his intensity made her anxious. He seemed stronger to her than he had been before the accident; he seemed more grounded, but what if this project failed—what if he failed? He could so easily go back to his old ways. If anything, since the accident he had even more reason to drink, to let everything slide. The worry of it hovered, and not only in her mind, either. Jenna and Emmett, too, shared her apprehension. Sandy had seen it in their eyes; she sensed it now in their posture, their careful composure.

She glanced around the auditorium. It was almost two-thirds full, a larger crowd than Jordy had expected. When they'd met him earlier for dinner, he'd said he'd be happy if twenty people showed up, and elated if the number hit fifty. There were probably three times that many people assembled, and more still coming in, finding seats.

Sandy brought her gaze back to Jordy. She couldn't tell if he was nervous. Behind him, a banner that spanned the stage area asked: **DRUNK? DON'T DRIVE. STAY ALIVE. CALL CAMPUS CABBIES. IT'S FREE!** and listed a telephone number. Below that was a line of smaller print. Sandy couldn't read it from where she sat between Jenna and Emmett, but she knew what it said: **IN MEMORY OF TRAVIS SIMMONS, SON, NEPHEW, BROTHER, AND BEST FRIEND, 1995–2015.**

Sandy and Jenna had designed the banner, their first sister project since the accident. Sandy had been so grateful for Jenna's help. The ground between them was still fragile, their bond so recently reestablished, she'd been afraid Jordy's idea might tear it all over again. Instead, Jenna had cried when Jordy explained how he wanted to honor Trav. She'd loved the concept of Stayin' Alive and had even volunteered to become a parent liaison. Emmett and Sandy had joined her, and they'd formed a parent committee that was now seven members strong. Oddly enough, they continued to run into opposition from other parents. *We drank in college,* they'd say. *Nothing worse than a hangover ever happened.*

"Something worse happened to my son," Jenna would say. "He's dead."

Now the lights went down, the crowd hushed, and the opening bars of "Stayin' Alive" played as Jordy approached the podium. A round of applause broke out, small and polite.

Sandy briefly closed her eyes. *Please . . .* The word rose from the floor of her mind, a prayer, as the music swelled to the chorus. She could feel the bass notes vibrate through the back of her jaw, the soles of her shoes. The audience members came to their feet, clapping loudly now to the beat. Sandy stood, too, with her family—her family that had expanded to include Libby—all of them looking up and down the row at one another, grinning, hardly daring to believe it, thrilled for the response and for Jordy, who, though he did look slightly overwhelmed, was standing tall and confident nonetheless.

The song faded; the audience sat.

Jordy gripped the podium on either side. He looked around, and Sandy smiled when he found her gaze.

Bending to the microphone, he said his name and thanked everyone for coming. Then he paused and straightened, and for a moment Sandy was scared he might walk away from it, the chance to believe in himself. She held her breath, and she sensed Jenna doing the same beside her. Sandy found her hand, and on her other side she found

Emmett's, and she felt the warmth of their reassurance and love, and it was so strong that she willed Jordan to feel it, too. And maybe he did, because he bent to the microphone again.

"Last summer," he began, looking around at the audience, "my cousin and best buddy, Travis Simmons, and I drove drunk and crashed. I made it. Trav didn't."

Jenna's grasp on Sandy's hand tightened, but Sandy was afraid to look at her, afraid to take her eyes off Jordy.

"The thing is, it didn't have to happen like that," he said. "He'd be the first person to agree, too, if he was here. He'd be the one who'd want to try and prevent anything like it from happening again. So, I guess in a way, that's why I'm up here, to talk about how we can maybe save somebody else, maybe even you, or your best friend . . ."

Now Sandy did turn to Jenna, her heart so filled with a confused mix of emotions, she thought it might burst. She touched the tears that tracked Jenna's cheek and then took her into an embrace that was fierce with grief but also shot with joy. She felt the comfort of Emmett's hand on her back.

"I can never see him and not think of Trav," Jenna said in a broken whisper.

"Me, either," Sandy whispered back.

"He's terrific up there, though, isn't he?" Jenna asked. She sat back, wiping her face.

Sandy nodded, swallowing, fighting for composure.

Their mother passed tissues.

Jenna dabbed her nose. "I'm really proud of him," she said. "Maybe I could borrow him sometimes," she added.

"He'd like that, I think," Sandy said.

Jenna squeezed Sandy's hand. "My borrowed son," she said, and when Sandy looked, she was smiling.

ACKNOWLEDGMENTS

While it's true that writing is done mostly in isolation, the business of polishing the book that is the result is not accomplished without an entire village full of wonderful people. I'm so thankful for all of the people in my village. First, thank you to the imaginary ones, the characters who keep me company in the solitary hours, who give up their secrets to me, sometimes easily and sometimes not. Thank you to all the authors who have gone before me, who have written remarkable books about their remarkable characters that have kept me enthralled and instilled in me the fire to do the same.

Always, always, a huge and heartfelt thanks to Barbara Poelle, who is not only a fantastic agent but also an advocate, mentor, and guide. As the queen of fairy godmothers, it is her faith and encouragement, and her reminder—when I need it—of whose journey this is, that keep my focus where it should be, on writing the best book possible. B2, you are the unicorn in my closet!

A heartfelt thank-you as well to Tara Parsons. It's hard to put into words how grateful I am for her expert guidance as an editor, and for her faith in, and support of, me and my work. Her creative suggestions at the beginning of this project helped launch it in the right direction.

I met my lovely and brilliant current editor, Kelli Martin, through a phone call, in which I felt we talked like old friends. It only got better from there. Throughout our time working together, collaborating on *Faultlines*, it was as if we shared a mental wavelength, our similar vision for the story was so strong. I feel so lucky to have the benefit of her keen editor's eye.

My research for the book led me to talk at length with Horseshoe Bay Police night-shift commander John "Chip" Leake, who in a stroke of pure luck also happens to be a great neighbor. I am deeply appreciative of the time he spent sharing his experiences of the many rural highway car accidents he has encountered during his thirty-four-year (so far) career as a Texas law-enforcement officer. Huge thanks as well to my longtime critique partner, Colleen Thompson, who on my behalf has so often enlisted the help of her husband, Mike Thompson, a retired Houston firefighter. I so appreciate them both for their patience and assistance on more levels for more years and books than I can name! Thank you, too, to Dr. Elizabeth Neal for her patience in answering my questions about head trauma. With regard to law enforcement and/or medical issues covered in the novel, any inaccuracies in the story are mine and mine alone.

Thank you more than they can know to my Amazon/Lake Union team—Gabe, Michael, and Elise—who have answered my endless questions, sometimes more than once. You guys are great! And thanks very much, too, to copy editors Sara, Robin, and Jill. As the idiom goes, "The devil is in the details," and that is so true with a manuscript. There are any number of tiny errors and mistakes, all of them crucial, which escape me, and I'm beyond grateful for these professionals and their sharp eagle eyes.

I want to thank my family: my sister, Susan; brother, John; sons, Michael and David; cousin, Kate, who came with her husband, Joe, on a surprise visit as I was nearing the end of writing *Faultlines*; and dear friends, Jo and Jink and others who, knowingly or not, in sharing their stories with me, have gifted me with bits and pieces to weave into my books. Please don't ever stop talking to me! And finally, additional and special thanks to David for always being willing to listen and then give me a man's perspective. I don't think even he is aware of how much help his insight is!

Last, but never least, always and forever, thank you to the readers of this book and every other book in the world. Whenever I hear from you, I'm reminded all over again why I do this—for the love of sharing a story and the desire to have it touch others' hearts, perhaps enough that they will pass it on. Sending joy to all of you is such small payment for all the joy I've received on my writing journey. Thank you.

READING GROUP GUIDE

1. The story is told from the perspectives of two women, Sandy and Libby, who appear to have nothing in common. How do you think they are different? How do you think they are similar?

2. As sisters, Sandy and Jenna are close, but when one of their sons causes the death of the other, their relationship is shattered. How do you think you would react in a similar situation? Would you have difficulty separating your sibling from the actions of your nephew or niece if he or she were to cause your own child to be harmed?

3. Jenna has sworn to keep Sandy's secret, but then years later without warning, she breaks her promise and shares it with the rest of their family. What do you think made her betray Sandy in this way? What do you think she gained or lost from breaking the trust with her sister? Do you think Jenna had any conception of the pain she would cause?

4. When Emmett learns Sandy's secret, he leaves town, excusing himself to tend to his mother, who is ill. Given the nature of the secret,

do you think his reaction was reasonable or expected or wrong? Was there anything Sandy could have said or done at that point that might have changed his mind?

5. Imagine that as parents, involved in a similar calamity with two of your kids in an accident, you're put in the position of choosing which one's need for you is greater. Do you think you could make such a decision? How would you go about it?

6. Do you think Emmett and Sandy have had a good marriage? What are the chances their marriage will survive all they have endured?

7. Do you think Libby's marriage to Beck was a strong one, a good marriage?

8. Early in their marriage, how did Libby's desperate attempts to conceive a child impact the relationship between her and Beck?

9. What are some of the challenges that arise in marriages? How do challenges strengthen or destroy a good marriage?

10. Libby chooses Wyatt, Texas, as the place she wants to retire to with Beck, in part because her near-lifelong friend Ruth lives there. Do you think Libby used good judgment, basing a decision about where to live on the strength of a friendship? What factors have you used to decide where you would live?

11. Libby's background is in psychology, but when Beck is unfaithful, she doesn't need the benefit of her expertise in the field to know that taking him back means her forgiveness of him has to be bone deep or it won't work. Could you forgive a cheating spouse? Under

what conditions? Do you think certain situations involving infidelity would be unforgivable?

12. Libby desperately wanted a child of her own, but it wasn't meant to be. Ultimately, when she's asked, she chooses to involve herself with one who isn't hers. Do you think she makes the right decision? What are your thoughts when it comes to forgiveness in her situation?

13. What are your feelings about underage drinking and binge drinking among young adults? How do you think colleges and high schools should address this issue? How can parents help?

ABOUT THE AUTHOR

Barbara Taylor Sissel writes issue-driven women's fiction that is threaded with elements of suspense and defined by its particular emphasis on how crime affects families. She is the author of six previous novels: *The Last Innocent Hour, The Ninth Step, The Volunteer, Evidence of Life, Safekeeping,* and *Crooked Little Lies.*

Born in Honolulu, Hawaii, Barbara was raised in various locations across the Midwest and once lived on the grounds of a first-offender prison facility, where she interacted with the inmates, their families, and the people who worked with them. The experience made a profound impression on her and provided her with a unique insight into the circumstances of the crimes that were committed, and the often-surprising ways the justice system moved to deal with them.

An avid gardener, Barbara has two sons and lives on a farm in the Texas Hill Country, outside Austin.